Print Version Published by
PASSION & PLEASURE BOOKS
P.O. BOX 470403
Los Angeles, CA 90045

Cover Design and Interior Format

NECESSARY
LIES

MEN OF PHANTOM

THE
SERIES

Jacki Renée

I dedicate this to my moon and my sun, my daughters Jai'Lauren and Jos'Lynne. You have to crawl before you walk; walk before you run; then run so you can leap over the hurdles and cross the finish line.

To my heroine, a strong Black woman, my mom, Jacqueline, for whom I got my love for reading.

And to my dear friend, Joan Goldman, who encouraged me to share my love for writing with others.

Acknowledgments

I'm so grateful to my family, extended family, and friends for their love, support, and encouragement as I labored for two years to get the story just right. Thank you for keeping me uplifted. Some of you may see a few characteristics of yourself in this book. This was done out of love and appreciation. It would take a chapter to list everyone, but I must list some of the individuals and their contributions. Jonathan, thank you for traveling to Boulder, Colorado with me to take pictures of the locations described in my book. That drive up to a ski resort 10,000 feet above sea level was scary, but what an experience! Joelle, the amateur photographer, thank you for the shots at the beach, sorry about the tar that got stuck to the bottom of your foot. Paula, thank you for inviting me to a book club meeting to talk about my book. And my friend LaTara, thank you for offering to "windmill" on those who tried to steal my joy.

IAMJACKIRENÉE.COM website is the product of the vision and talents of Kenward Romero. Thank you for your generosity.

A big thank you to critique partners: Michal Scott, LJ Kendall, and the talented members of KOD's Lethal Ladies. And an overly curious co-worker who just couldn't wait until the book was edited and published, Cynthia Guerrero.

A special thank you to the enterprising team of The Killion Group, Inc. Their experience and support kept me from going into full panic mode.

My deepest gratitude to Mr. Patrick Hansen (Hansen's Cakes), General Motors, and University of Colorado Boulder (CU).

Prologue

30 June 2013

*B*uzz.
Buzz.
Buzz.

Untangling myself from the naked woman wrapped around me, I roll out of bed, grab my briefcase and walk out of the room. The bedroom door closes behind me. I can't ignore the vibrations of the cell phone.

"VRS identification." Riley doesn't wait for a greeting.

I clear my throat, and walk down the dark hallway toward the living room. "Kilo. Zero. Two. Alpha. One. One. Zero. Six. Hotel."

Voice Recognition Software verifies my identity.

"FRS identification," Riley requests.

I hold the phone out in front of me. The camera focuses. Facial Recognition Software confirms my identity.

"Good morning, Colonel Hawk. At zero two hundred hours, a United States Army soldier crossed the Syrian border onto Israeli soil without proper authorization. Request permission to transmit video footage."

Streetlamps provide enough light in the semi-dark room. I sit on the sofa, push the half-full wine glasses to the side and set the briefcase on the coffee table. Placing my right hand on the security panel of the laptop, I allow a scanner to verify my prints, and the military laptop turns on.

"Permission granted." I yawn.

A hawk glides onto the home screen, its wings spread wide, talons ready to strike. The image of a man dressed in a tattered U.S. Army combat uniform fills the screen. I'm wide awake now.

The American soldier sits on a metal chair in a dingy, windowless, closet-sized room. Two armed Israeli soldiers stand nearby. There's no audio, and from this camera angle I can't read their lips. Military training tells me they're questioning him.

To the untrained eye, it looks as if the American is handcuffed to the chair. One Israeli soldier approaches. Gun raised. The American lets him get within range, grabs the soldier, flipping back in the chair, and takes the man over, snapping his neck. He grabs the gun, then fires two shots into the head of the other Israeli soldier before the chair hits the floor.

Pushing the dead man off, the American jumps to his feet and changes uniforms.

He takes their guns, then leaves the room. The video stops.

I already know the answer, but I ask anyway. "Identity of U.S. Army soldier?"

"Sergeant James Andrew Edwards."

"How was his identity confirmed?"

"DNA-fingerprints in the room."

"What's his current location?"

"Location unknown. He successfully escaped."

"Contact the pilot. I'm going to Arizona from here." I reach for the overnight bag I left sitting in the chair when I got here. "Have Sweepers ready to clean up and alert Watchers. I want eyes on Edwards." I pull clean clothes out of the bag and start dressing.

"Roger that, sir." The line goes dead.

When I finish the laces on my boots, I close the briefcase, then grab the cell phone and overnight bag. I don't bother with goodbyes; the sleeping woman is conditioned to me coming and going.

While speed dialing my superior, I walk out the apartment door.

"Sir, I'm moving Danielle and Kourtney to Boulder."

I don't believe in ghosts. James Edwards should be dead. I know this because I'm the one who put a bullet in his head and another in his chest eight years ago.

Chapter One

Boulder, Colorado September 16, 2013

"GOOD EVENING. WELCOME TO BACK to School Night. My name is Malinda Williamson. I'm your child's second grade teacher."

"Good evening. I'm Danielle Edwards, Kourtney's mom." I shake hands with Ms. Williamson standing at the door to the classroom.

"It's nice to finally meet you, Dr. Edwards," she says, then greets the people behind us.

"Show me around, Kourtney." I hold my hand out to my daughter and we walk into the spacious classroom.

"I sit here. Emma sits next to me and Penelope sits up there." She points to the seat in front of hers.

"I'm happy you're making friends, sweetie." I give her hand a gentle squeeze.

"The other kids aren't very nice," she whispers. "The boy who sits next to Penelope sticks his tongue out at me all the time."

"Do you want me to speak to his parents?" I whisper back.

She shakes her head then leads me to the language and writing center where we spend a few seconds admiring her graded English work posted on one wall. In the math area, she points out the perfect score she got on today's math test. In the humanities center, she reads the social topic for the week. And in the art center, amongst the gallery of various art pieces, she briefly brags about Emma's drawing of the three best friends. The little girl has talent.

In the science center, Kourtney takes her time to explain the process of photosynthesis and the experiment she's working on for the science fair. Two of the four plants we purchased at a nursery are flourishing. She shows me her daily journal and the equipment she's using to prove her hypothesis. Big words for a seven-year-old, but she's a math and science buff, and I encourage it. The rest of the classroom is not important. This is where Kourtney wants to show me around, and this is where I want to be.

"Parents, if you would please find a seat. It's exactly five o'clock and we can begin our classroom meeting," Ms. Williamson calls out.

A migration of parents and students move toward empty chairs. My attention is drawn to the man leading a pretty little brunette to the desk next to my daughter's.

My heart pounds. Stomach jumps. An impression of him flashes in my mind. Immediately my eyes drop to his thick, muscular thighs encased in jeans. My mouth goes dry.

I'm oblivious to what's happening around me. I watch him like a thirsty woman covets a tall drink of cold water. Let's face it. I'm thirsty and could use a drink of him.

Nodding is his form of communication with the few parents who greet him. He's protective and paternal holding hands with his daughter.

He pulls out his child's chair and waits for her to sit before pushing the chair closer to the desk. I'll give him brownie points for being a gentleman.

Across the room, I watch in fascination as two moms gravitate toward him. They're childless and determined to get his attention. *Good luck, ladies.*

"Hi, Emma," my daughter greets the little brunette. "This is my mom."

Emma gives me a small wave and a timid smile. Out of instinct, I want to wrap my arms around her, but I settle for a return smile while studying her features.

Her father's smile shines in his eyes, as he stands up to greet us. "Hello, Kourtney, I've heard a lot about you." His tone takes on a more personal note. He winks at me and I become entranced by the longest eyelashes I've ever seen on a man.

A disgruntled whisper floats behind us, and two men approaching the desk in front of us distract me from speaking.

"Hi, I'm Max. This is my husband, Tom, and our daughter, Penelope." The stylishly dressed man grasps my hand in both of his. Their raven-haired daughter stands in between them.

I shake hands with both men as I introduce myself.

"It's good to see you, Bryan. Where have you been hiding?" Max asks.

"Work," he says, but keeps his eyes on me.

Hiding, huh? Interesting choice of words.

"Once again, I'd like to welcome you to Back to School Night," the teacher announces, and we take our seats. "I'm excited about my first year here. I'm originally from Dallas, Texas, where I taught second grade for six years. Tonight I will review the curriculum, classroom rules, school events, and parental expectations."

My mind wanders back to Bryan. I shift in the seat as I run my fingers through my hair. I try to stop the fantasies from clouding my reaction to seeing him, but for a minute or more, I allow myself to bask in the visions.

Bryan looks down at his cell phone, chuckles, and glances my way. I turn in pretense of paying attention to Ms. Williamson. I refuse to dip my head in shame. Men aren't as discreet when they're eyeing a woman.

"Many of you have completed your required monthly volunteer hours and I thank you for your time. A couple of you are a few hours short and I have a solution that'll put you ahead for the rest of the school year. This brings me to the next topic. The school's annual Halloween celebration." She walks over to her desk and picks up two file folders. "This year the teaching staff decided to have a classroom-decorating contest judged by our principal and board advisors. I am appointing the parents with the lowest volunteer hours to come up with the theme and decorations for our classroom." She looks directly at Bryan. "Mr. Hawk, you will do us the honor of heading up the parent committee."

"Thank you for asking, Ms. Williamson. This isn't the best time, but I'll sponsor the event."

"I appreciate your offer for sponsorship, Mr. Hawk, but I didn't ask. I'm letting you know I've selected you to head up the parent committee," she rebuts. "The decorations are to be made using recycled materials, and you must stick to a small monetary budget. Your time is required for this event, not your money. I'm sure you'll receive lots of support from the parent I've appointed to aid you."

His mouth turns down and shoulders stiffen the more she talks. Everyone in the room grows quiet as we witness the tug-of-war between busy, hiding parent and demanding teacher. I hope the other parent is more agreeable.

"Bryan, I'll be *more* than happy to offer my ass…" The woman fake sneezes. "Excuse me. I'm happy to accommodate you in any position you put me in."

All heads turn to the woman seated behind me. Looking over my shoulder, I am greeted with a fake smile from the bottled redhead, whose eyelash extensions show off green contact lenses, fake beauty mark beside collagen lips, and fake boobs falling out of a low-cut blouse.

"Thanks, Mrs. Brooks, but Dr. Edwards will be happy to take on the task. She's trailing in volunteer hours, too."

My head snaps to the front of the classroom.

Wait. What? Me work with him? On a project? Not in this lifetime.

"Aren't you, Dr. Edwards?" Ms. Williamson asks, sugar dripping from her tone.

Kourtney bounces in her seat, pleading with her eyes for me to accept.

"Um. Yes. I can assist Mr. Hawk."

"Great! I know you two can come up with something prize-winning. Here's the information you'll need." She walks over and hands each of us a folder. "Your idea has to be approved before you start. The proposal is due on Thursday, and as you can see, Mr. Hawk, your budget is one hundred dollars. Now, I'd like to bring to your attention, the school's zero tolerance rules on bullying…"

Ms. Williamson continues, but my attention is diverted. I'm ducking and dodging the eye daggers I feel being thrown in my back by Fake-Boobs.

I'm not shy, but I prefer to remain in the background—only now I've been thrown smack dab in the middle of the ring with Bryan Hawk. Inwardly, I cringe.

Chapter Two

ONCE BACK TO SCHOOL NIGHT is over, Bryan and I walk toward the parking lot with our children.

"We're going to the Play 'n' Fun Center tonight for pizza and video games. Come with us. We can plan while they play," Bryan suggests.

"Is your home number listed in the classroom directory? I can call you tomorrow and we can come up with a proposal over the phone," I counter.

"Please, Mom. Can we go with them?" Her hope-filled eyes punch me in the stomach.

"Don't you have homework?" Can I deny her pizza and video games with her— mentally I correct myself —best friend?

"We didn't get any because of the meeting."

I curse the day you left Texas, Malinda Williamson.

"The Play 'n' Fun Center?" I look up at him.

There's that heated smile again, making my thighs squeeze together.

"It's across the street from the mall," he says.

"We moved to Boulder two months ago. Other than my apartment, the school, work, and the grocery store, I don't really know my way around."

"I'll follow you to your apartment to drop off your car. You guys can ride with us."

I want to be in control of when Kourtney and I leave. "No, thank you. I'll follow you there."

The girls hold hands, whispering and giggling between us as we navigate the parking lot full of parents, children, and cars.

He gestures to a black Suburban blocking in my Range Rover.

As we get closer to our trucks, I push the button on the key fob to unlock the doors. Like a gentleman, Bryan opens the back door for Kourtney.

"Thank you, Mr. Hawk," she says.

"Call me Bryan, Kourt." He closes the door after she secures her seat belt. "Here." He pulls out his wallet and hands me a business card. "In case we get separated."

In the rearview mirror, I watch Bryan walk to his truck and hold the door open for Emma. Once he closes the door and climbs into the driver's seat, I back out of the stall and follow him.

Did he mean separated as in forced apart or wanting to be apart?

I push aside that voice in my head telling me to go home.

"Emma's dad is nice huh, Mom?"

"I guess so, honey." Those words tickle my throat causing me to cough.

"Do you think he's cute?"

"Tell me more about the experiment you're working on for the science fair."

Kourtney's project revolves around ideas on how she can save our planet once she becomes President of the United States. She uses the scientific names for the plants and explains why she chose them. Recycled materials for Halloween decorations is something she'll get into.

Now and then she throws in a question about the man we're following and I reply with a question about materials we can use for the project.

When we cross an intersection, I realize the main street runs near our apartment.

"Do you think the class will like making decorations?" I ask, turning into the parking lot of the Play 'n' Fun Center.

"Emma will. She's really good in art."

I park in the stall next to Mr. Hawk. He's helping Emma out of the backseat, then rushes to open our doors.

"Are you ready for pizza and fun?" he asks.

"Yes!"

My daughter sounds too excited.

"Come on, let's go." He takes the girls' hands and leads the way.

"What kind of pizza do you like, Kourt?" he asks.

"Pepperoni. Lots and lots of pepperoni." She skips along beside him.

"I like pepperoni too. And sausage. And olives," Emma adds.

"We'll get one with lots of pepperoni all over and sausage and olives on one side," he says, swinging their hands.

Kourtney is acting like she's known Bryan all her life. She normally shies away from men. Her reaction to him tugs at my heart. Tears blur my vision and I blink to keep them from spilling over. I thought I was all dried up after crying a whole year after her father was gone.

To keep my thoughts on the here and now, I let my gaze drop to the designer jeans hugging Bryan's butt. An image of a bare body flashes through my mind's eye.

"Are we walking too fast for you, Dr. Edwards?" He looks over his shoulder at me.

I haven't moved a step, but… damn, if his butt doesn't look good in those jeans. I catch up to them.

He opens the door for us to enter, a knowing look on his face. "What kind of pizza can I get you?"

Bells and whistles and automated voices are barely heard over the screams of children and tweens running around or playing video games. The smell of pizza and fries is in the air.

Kourtney raises her voice over the noise. "It doesn't matter. She picks off the stuff she doesn't like."

"I'm not picky," I protest.

Kourtney huffs. "Yes, she is."

I playfully poke out my tongue at her, and she returns the gesture. Emma laughs at us.

Bryan's eyebrows scrunch. "You're a vegetarian?"

"My mom doesn't eat red meat. Just get her a chicken and cheese pizza."

Ah, hello. I'm standing right here.

"Okay, find us a booth." He clasps his hands together, palms rubbing like he's warming them up. "I'll order the pizzas and get tokens."

We hold a casual conversation as we eat. Kourtney and Emma abandon us the minute they finish their pizza. With the buffers gone, Bryan and I have a lively discussion that ends in an impasse. We're able to agree on the list of ideas for Halloween decorations and nothing else.

"I didn't think it would be this much work." He rolls his shoulders and twists his head side to side, cracking his neck. My fingers ache to help him work out the kinks.

"You don't help your wife plan Emma's parties?"

In all actuality, I can't picture him tied down. Nonetheless, I should have asked before accepting his dinner invitation.

"I'm not married and I hire someone to do this stuff." He leans back in the booth and rests his arms along the top of the bench. A glimpse of his tattoo is visible on the inside of his muscular bicep. "Can we count on your husband to help?" His fingers tap the top of the bench seat. A gold ring circles the ring finger of his right hand.

I squint my eyes. "My husband died eight years ago."

"Your boyfriend doesn't mind you wearing that wedding ring?"

I twist the band around my finger. "I don't date," my tone warns him. He's trespassing on dangerous territory.

"Why not, Dr. Edwards?"

We stare at one another.

"What brings you to Boulder?" he asks.

"I was hired as a therapist at the hospital. How long have you lived here?"

"A friend of mine works there, too. Dr. Ignacio Acosta Jr. Have you met him?"

He still hasn't answered my question.

"If your friend doesn't work in the Behavioral Science Department then I haven't met him."

"Why did you take the job?"

Is there a problem with us being here? I shout in my head.

"They offered me the same flexibility in my work schedule that I had at the hospital and clinic in Arizona."

"How did you hear about the school?"

"I researched innovative schools in the Boulder area. What attracted me is the interactive approach to teaching. The board of directors recognizes that children no longer learn by sitting at a desk all day. The selling point is the school's test scores are way above the median."

"Why don't you date, Dani?"

My fingers curl into a tight fist. Teeth clench, I respond. "Please. Don't. Call. Me. Dani."

The girls come running to the table, prize tickets overflowing the buckets in their arms.

"We're out of tokens. Can we go turn in our tickets?" Kourtney asks.

"I'll help you," I say, scooting out of the booth. "Plus, it's getting late, and the girls have school tomorrow."

I walk them over and help load long streams of tickets into the counting machines, relieved the girls interrupted our conversation. I don't allow people to call me that nickname. It holds too many memories. Some good. Some not so good.

Ticket counting helps me compose myself and get my emotions in check. By the time we move over to the prize counter where the girls pick out matching trinkets and costume jewelry, Mr. Nosey-And-Needs-To-Mind-His-Own-Business joins us.

We stand without speaking while the girls shop until they are out of points. He takes their hands, leading the way to the exit.

"Thank you for dinner. I'll send a copy of my notes. Is that your *current* email address on the business card you gave me?" We walk through the parking lot to our trucks. I push the button on the key fob.

"It's one of them." He opens the back doors of both trucks and waits for Kourtney and Emma to climb in.

"See you tomorrow, Emmy. Don't forget to wear your orange ring."

"I won't, Kourty."

"Goodnight, Kourt. Sleep well." Bryan closes both doors.

"Are you okay to get home from here?" he asks, opening my door.

"Yes." I climb in behind the wheel.

He lingers. A big smile on his face. "Sweet dreams. Dani."

His croon makes my stomach jump.

Steamy thoughts of Mr. Hawk battle with years of celibacy as I pull out of the parking lot and head home.

At a red light, a sheriff's patrol car pulls up in the lane to my right. The light turns green and we travel down the three-lane boulevard. For several miles, the cruiser's headlights shine in my side-view mirror. We part ways when I make a left turn onto the street leading home.

Once I get Kourtney settled into bed, I take a shower hoping to wash away the effects of Bryan Hawk.

I fall asleep thinking of my late husband, James. He's warning me to be cautious and to trust no one. But another man walks through the door to invade my dreams. His arms comfort me in a time of sorrow. His long fingers softly touch me. His gentle lips follow an invisible trail down my stomach. Those hazel eyes framed in long eyelashes are the last things I see before his face disappears between my thighs. I give him my body and my soul.

By midmorning I come up with a more proper name for the man bringing me pleasure in a dream. Mr. Tall-And-Sexy.

Since I have a short break between patients, I email him a copy of the notes I took, along with a few creative suggestions inspired by Kourtney on the drive to school this morning.

Less than a second after clicking send, an automatic reply message pops up in my inbox. Bryan's out of the office until Thursday. I send a text message to his phone and greet the new patient walking through the door.

"Hello, Mr. Brumfield."

At the end of my shift, I leave work feeling disappointed. Bryan hasn't replied to my message.

I pull out the classroom directory after dinner and call the number listed for Emma Hawk.

"I'm sorry, Bryan is out of the country on business until Thursday," the housekeeper informs me.

How are we supposed to turn in the proposal on time if he's out of the country?

"I can give him a message when he checks in, if you'd like," she offers.

"No. There's no message. Thank you."

Kourtney helps me research creative ways to make the items on our list.

I go to bed frustrated but wake up sweaty and flushed. Mr. Tall-And-Sexy played a recurring role in my dream.

By Thursday afternoon he hasn't contacted me. I eat lunch at my desk and use the notes to come up with a proposal for the Halloween project. I email it to the Principal Dr. Barrett, and Ms. Williamson, and Mr. Hawk.

I refuse to dream about him, but my subconscious mind rules against me. We're doing things I've read about in romance books. James stands in the background frowning. The Danielle in my dream smirks back at him. She's loving her sexual expeditions.

Friday morning I'm at my desk typing notes in patients' records when a knock on my office door interrupts me. "Come in." I look up, expecting to see the new Psych intern, Vanessa.

Mr. Tall-And-Sexy walks through the door. I thought he looked like a tall drink of water in jeans and a T-shirt; he looks downright edible in a tailored-to-perfection gray business suit. My stomach twitches and so does that place between my thighs.

"Good morning, Mr. Hawk. What brings you to my office?"

He approaches the desk. My comfortably decorated office becomes too small with him in it.

His body language emanates sex and something else. His face is calm and composed.

"If memory serves me correctly, Dr. Edwards, and I have a damn good memory. I'm the head of this committee and you are *my* assistant. *You. Assist. Me.*"

I inhale, then slowly exhale. I count to ten. Fighting will get us nowhere.

We have to work together, but an alpha male will not bully me.

"As your assistant, Mr. Hawk, I covered for you and submitted the proposal on time. You're more than welcome to make revisions, but may I suggest you follow *my* lead. I have more experience in this area."

"I don't make a habit of neglecting my responsibilities. My business trip took longer than it should've. And for the record, Dr. Edwards"—he leans forward, towering over me—"I'm not a follower. I lead."

Most people think I can be coerced or intimidated. They take my standing-in-the-background persona for weakness until I unleash the fighter within.

I rise from my chair and lean toward him resting my hands on the desk. He overshadows me even though I'm wearing heels; however, intimidation tactics will not work.

"Mr. Hawk, a good leader knows when to follow the expert."

He steps around to the side of the desk. I stand up straight.

"You are familiar with that saying, seen but not heard?"

"You're familiar with that saying, behind every great man stands an even greater woman?" I tweak it in my favor, then roll my eyes for dramatic effect. Men think a woman rolling her eyes is a sign of typical feminine childishness. *Come on— take the bait.*

"Can't say that I have." He smiles. "But I've heard, behind every great man is a woman rolling her eyes."

I take the few steps around the desk to close in on him. *Thanks for the nibble. I'm about to end* this *conversation.*

"I don't recall hearing that one, Mr. Hawk. But I know, in *front* of this man"—my finger taps his chest—"stands a strong, wise and hardworking woman who eats alpha males for dinner."

I swear I didn't see him move. His hands capture my head while his body backs me up against the wall. Our tongues battle for dominance. He nibbles, then sucks my bottom lip and I surrender.

He tilts my head to gain better access to my mouth. Bryan deepens the kiss. His tongue tastes of cinnamon and hunger.

Intimate images circle in my head. No longer is this kiss about power. It's remembrance. Intimate. Longing.

My hands slide up his chest, resting on his strong shoulders.

He groans, then all too soon pulls away.

Familiarity overwhelms me and the knot in my stomach twists as I watch him walk out the door.

Dani's office door closes behind me. *What the hell was that, Hawk?* I yell at myself. *I had to. Her strong mind and quick wit are a mental turn-on.*

I do my best to walk normal, keeping my eyes focused on the elevator doors.

Passing the reception desk, I don't acknowledge Sergeant Larson. She's assigned to watch over Dani here at the hospital. One phone call and a sizeable donation, and Vanessa Larson's the new Psych intern. She's one of the top female ghosts in Phantom, and the only female on Delta Team.

Until we have eyes on that walking corpse, I can't ease up on Dani and Kourt's protection. Edwards was spotted in Germany a few days ago. By the time we got there, he'd disappeared. The trip wasn't a waste of time though. I learned a few interesting things about James Edwards. For one, he and Dani weren't legally married. That's a relief.

The elevator doors open, two men step into the cab, then turn and face me, leaving room in the middle. I nod, step in and turn around. Sergeant Larson and I make eye contact before the elevator doors close.

The atmosphere in here is like standing at a urinal and trying not to look at the man pissing next to you.

Porter hands me a folded newspaper. Even if I adjust the suit jacket, it'll barely hide my hard-on. Mitchells looks everywhere but at the reflection in the doors.

Willpower made me walk away. I have to stay focused in order to keep Edwards from finding Dani and Kourt until we set the trap. But I'm in deep and all I did was kiss her… this time.

Chapter Three

OVER THE NEXT FEW WEEKS, Mr. Tall-And-Sexy and I put our plans for decorations in motion. On the weekends, we take the girls on scavenger hunts for materials and supplies.

Today we explore a junkyard in Louisville, Colorado.

On the tips of my toes, I hoist myself up onto the frame of an old, hollowed-out engine area of a rusty truck. I spot the perfect tire for the base of our scarecrow. My feet dangle off the ground as I reach for it. Slightly off balance, my body rocks and I'm falling forward.

Strong hands grip my waist, stopping me from hitting the dirt face first.

Bryan presses against my back, face so close that a slight turn of my head and our lips will merge.

"Be careful." His seductive voice strokes my ear.

We fit together like two puzzle pieces. I bite my lip as my eyes close for a moment. This intimate position isn't good for someone who has been celibate for four years.

He lifts the tire up and out, then steps back. I lower my feet to the ground and turn to face him.

The smirk on his lips confirms what I've suspected: Bryan's purposely pushing my buttons.

"Tag, you're it." Kourtney taps his arm and zips past him.

He covers his face with his hands and counts. Once he gets to ten, the chase is on.

She enjoys spending time with him. Their personalities are so similar, as are mine and Emma's.

Bryan and Kourtney view the junkyard as a playground with endless objects to climb on, hide behind, and to find a scientific way to incorporate into the Halloween decoration theme. Emma and I look at the place as a blank canvas to create works of art.

It turns out to be a really good Saturday.

Monday afternoon, Emma helps me do a classroom art project with the things we found in the junkyard. I notice she shies away from certain classmates.

Jacob Brooks is one of those students, yet he insists *Emma* help him. I try to divert his attention by praising his effort. Emma's opinion is the only validation that satisfies him.

Christy Banks, Julia Johnson, and Melissa Valentine, "the mean girls," are the other students Emma won't go near. They seem harmless to me.

Everyone is super excited about the theme. And I like meeting the parents. Most tend to become guarded when they learn I'm a therapist. Not Max, Penelope's dad. His flamboyant personality is fun to be around. And contagious too. Somehow he manages to get me to shed my controlled exterior and let the vivaciousness rule the throne for a little while.

So far Max has been subtle with his questions about my working relationship with Mr. Hawk. I always steer our conversations to safer topics. Max and I have gone out to lunch twice.

Most parents are supportive and cooperative in helping with supplies for decorations. Then there's the three who deny *my* solicitations. Instead they leapfrog over each other to aid Mr. Tall-And-Sexy.

On Friday, as I wait in front of the school—along with other parents—for the students to be dismissed, the three Horny Toads float their lily pads near me.

"Bryan called me yesterday afternoon. I told him it's okay to come in my garage." Holly Valentine gloats.

Inwardly, I roll my eyes at her wordplay.

"Yesterday, I told Bryan he had to come quickly. My husband was due home any minute." Stephanie Banks tops Holly. The threat of exposure is more exciting than an open invitation.

"I dropped off old clothes to Bryan last night, and he invited me in for a drink. I didn't get home until almost midnight and Simon is pissed." Fake Boobs, aka Madelyn Brooks, trumps them both. "Bryan stretched and pounded me so hard, my lips are swollen, and I don't mean the ones on my face."

I know they're just fantasizing about cheating on their husbands with the same man, but these married women are publicly bragging about being cheaters.

Could there be some truth to their fantasies?

Does he have the energy to screw three women in the same day?

For all I know, he could be a professional gigolo.

This is one reason I don't date. Too many manwhores, not enough monogamous men.

"Hi, Danielle." Max breaks my train of thought.

We air kiss each other's cheeks.

"Hi, Max. How are you?"

"I'm fabulous, honey. Listen, I tried calling Bryan yesterday, but his housekeeper told me he's been out of town for a few days. Do you have a copy of the updated list of materials? I'm going to my in-laws on Sunday. I'll see what they have in their garage."

"No, I don't have a copy, but I'll ask him to send you one. Emma is staying with us until he gets back Monday afternoon. He checks in with me." I try to keep a straight face when I see the Horny Toads' reaction. I'm not a good liar.

Bryan isn't out of town. He dropped off Emma's overnight bag right before I came to pick up the girls.

The ringing of the school bell signals the end of the day. Students run like animals set free from their cages. Kourtney and Emma skip out hand in hand with Penelope.

"Hey, Max. Can Penelope spend the weekend with the girls?"

His smile grows bigger as he takes his daughter's backpack. "Sure, I'll drop her off in an hour."

We leave the Horny Toads frozen on their lily pads.

"Bryan isn't sleeping with those sloppy bitches," Max whispers. "Why would he need other men's wives when there's a sexy single mom slaying his line of sight?" His elbow jabs my side.

The following Saturday, I pick up Penelope and the three of us go to the Hawk's residence. The girls rake leaves into a large mound. Instead of stuffing the bright orange bags, they run and jump into the irresistible pile, scattering leaves everywhere.

Kourtney is shedding her reclusive shell thanks to Emma and Penelope.

I watch them from my seat on the patio as I sip sweet tea and talk to Marie, the housekeeper, and her husband, Willis, the grounds keeper. Bryan *is* out of town this weekend.

"It's so nice to see Emma have friends over for something other than her birthday." Marie has a Southern drawl in her tone.

"I'm surprised Kourtney's made friends so fast."

"How long have you been in Boulder?" Willis asks.

"A few months."

"Have you and Kourtney been sightseeing yet?" Marie stares at my daughter.

"No, I'm still learning my way around."

My cell phone vibrates with an email from Bryan requesting that we meet in his office Tuesday to review our plans. I reply my acceptance and go back to chatting with Marie and Willis while the girls run around the yard on this beautiful fall day.

Monday night, I toss and turn in bed, nerves keeping me awake.

Tuesday morning, I take extra time choosing my clothes. In my office, I watch the clock until it's time for me to leave for my meeting with Bryan.

Ten minutes to noon, I pull into the parking structure of Bryan's office building in downtown Boulder. Inhale, exhale I climb out of the truck and press the key fob to lock the doors.

I enter the building.

"Good afternoon, ma'am. How may I assist you?" The guard behind the desk greets me. On the lapel of his navy blue suit jacket is a silver pin of a hawk.

"Hi." I smile. "I have a meeting with Mr. Hawk. My name is Danielle Edwards."

He taps the monitor in front of him. I look around the lobby. The tan walls are spotless and the floors are polished to shiny brightness. An American flag and the Colorado state flag don the poles next to the guard's cubical. *Guess Bryan's not a professional gigolo.*

Other than the doors that lead to the walkway or parking garage, I see no others in the lobby.

"I sent an alert to his office letting him know you're on your way up."

I turn my attention back to him, and he hands me a keycard with my photo on it.

Where's the camera?

"Wave that in front of the sensor in the elevator and you'll have access to Mr. Hawk's floor," he says.

I turn and take three steps, glancing to the left then right. Looking back at the guard, I catch him staring at my butt.

"Where's. The. Elevator?"

"My apologies, Dr. Edwards." He taps the monitor. "I control the elevators from here."

Wall panels slide open and I walk across the lobby, stepping into the elevator.

"The sensor is to the right, ma'am," the guard calls out.

The white keycard has a hologram logo of a hawk on the front, wings spread wide, talons out to strike. I wave it in front of the smoke-glass rectangle in the elevator. The door closes.

"I didn't introduce myself as Dr. Edwards. How did he know?" I mumble to myself.

I'm not sure what floor the elevator stops on, but I know the breath caught in my lungs is due to the man standing in front of the open doors waiting for me.

Mr. Tall-And-Sexy looks lethal in his brown pants, white shirt and patterned tie.

I make a mental note to Google a nearby adult entertainment store. I will definitely need battery-operated relief after this lunch.

"Good afternoon, Dr. Edwards." His hand touches the small of my back after I step off the elevator. A sensual jolt shoots through me, triggering a reaction from sensitive body zones that are starving for a male's attention. He guides me in the direction of an open office door.

Since Max convinced me Mr. Tall-And-Sexy isn't a manwhore, my nightly wet dreams spill into the daytime, without James in the background.

Bryan Hawk brings out my inner Horny Toad, and it's getting harder to keep her from taking a leap.

"Sir, I'm going down to retrieve your lunch. It just arrived at the security desk," the man sitting behind a desk says, then nods at me. "Good afternoon, ma'am."

"Tell Hatchett I will see him after my meeting," Bryan says.

We walk into his huge office.

A massive desk with a large monitor stands in front of floor-to-ceiling windows while a leather sofa and matching wing chairs offer a sitting area. A ten-seating conference table with five monitors on top takes up a corner in the room. A huge flat screen television is mounted on the wall in front of the conference table. There's a bar off to the side. Everything in this office screams power. Alpha male.

"Have a seat." He walks over to the bar. "Can I get you something to drink?"

"Water, please." My throat feels scratchy.

I sit on the sofa watching him. He pulls a wall panel and it swings open to reveal a stocked refrigerator. Bryan takes out two bottles of water, twists the cap off one, and pours the liquid over ice in a crystal glass. He adds slices of cucumber and a straw.

I take a quick peek at his thighs as he walks toward me.

"Thank you."

I sip from the straw, and my gaze slides over his butt as he turns away. At the bar, Bryan pours himself a glass of water, then joins me on the sofa.

"You never told me what you do." I take another sip of water.

"I own Hawkeye Personal Protection."

And that means what? I raise an eyebrow.

"I provide specialized protection for government officials, foreign diplomats, and CEOs of high-end corporations." He sips the water. My eyes drop to his lips on the rim of the glass, hypnotized. He swallows, then grins, lowering the glass.

"Do you have a lot of clients?" I capture the straw between my lips, lowering my head so the straw slips deeper in my mouth than necessary. Hallowing my cheeks, I suck.

"My clients stretch around the globe." His voice drops an octave.

Bryan shifts in his seat, pulling at the fabric of his pants. The tip of his tongue flicks the rim of his glass before his lips close over it. He takes another sip of water.

My thighs squeeze together and I shift in my seat, every sensitive point of my body heightened by the visual memory of being touched by soft lips.

He couldn't let me win.

Porter walks through the open door carrying a brown restaurant take-out bag.

"Where do you want it, sir?"

Bryan cocks a suggestive eyebrow. Boy, was that a loaded question and I'm zero for three.

He chuckles when I don't respond.

"Conference table, please, Porter."

"Hatchett has been informed, sir." Porter places the bag on the table and leaves, closing the door behind him.

Mr. Hawk stands, offering his hand. He leads me to the conference table.

Setting his glass on a coaster, Bryan pulls out containers from the bag. My stomach grumbles. Skipping breakfast wasn't a good idea.

"I ordered chicken Alfredo pasta and a Caesar salad. Is that okay with you?" He spoons portions onto a plate. The bite-size garlic breadsticks smell heavenly.

"It's fine. I'm not as picky as Kourtney led you to believe." I take the plate he's offering.

Once he is seated, I dive in.

My eyes close; the sauce is perfection. "Hmmm."

"Like it?"

I nod enthusiastically and eat more.

"I'll give you the address of the restaurant. It's not far from the hospital and they deliver."

"Thank you."

"First order of business." He taps the monitor in front of him, pulling up the 3-D version of a decorated classroom. I scoot closer.

Over lunch, we discuss the best way to decorate, check off what's completed and what needs to be done, and we compile a final To-Do List.

The pasta is so good. I have a second serving. I'm a good eater and not ashamed of it. No woman should be.

After we finish lunch, he opens the refrigerator, taking out two slices of plain New York- style cheesecake with fresh sliced strawberries on the side. I melt when he hands me a dessert plate and fork.

We eat our cheesecake in comfortable silence then I help him clean up.

"Sir, you have a call on line three," a female's voice announces from the vicinity of his desk.

"Roger that, Riley."

"Take your call. I have a patient scheduled for two o'clock. Before I go, may I use your restroom?"

He nods and stands, pulling my chair out. I pick up my purse and follow him to the corner by the window. He pushes on the wall and a panel swings open to a full-size bathroom.

"Wave the keycard in front of the sensor to open the door." He points to a small rectangle on the wall similar to the one in the elevator. He backs out and the door swings closed.

His clients have to be paying top dollar for his services.

After I relieve my bladder and wash my hands, I rinse my mouth and reapply lip gloss on my lips.

I wave the keycard in front of the sensor, and the door swings open.

Bryan is still talking. I don't see a phone but I do glimpse the headband of a cordless headphone. He motions for me to give him a minute. I nod and walk over to the window, looking out at the afternoon traffic.

This building is hi-tech. Elevators with keycard access, walls that aren't walls. Who designs those things?

I wonder where Riley sits. Is she pretty? I bet she's gorgeous. I didn't see another desk when I got off the elevator.

"Sorry my call took so long."

I turn around, smiling up at him. "It's okay. I have to get going though."

"I'll walk you to the garage."

At the elevator, Bryan places his hand on a sensor, and the elevator doors slide open right away. He motions for me to enter first, then steps in beside me.

"Good afternoon, sir. What floor?" the voice of Riley asks.

If there were flies in here, several would fly into my wide opened mouth.

"Garage," he says.

I close my mouth.

When the doors open to the parking garage, I step off and walk toward my truck.

"Thank you for lunch."

"It was my pleasure."

Bryan opens my door. I glide onto the seat and wait for him to close the door.

Why isn't he closing the door?

I follow his gaze. The hem of my burnt orange skirt has risen to the middle of my thighs. Reaching out, his fingertips brush the exposed skin. Instant heat flows through me. My head drops back on the headrest as my eyes close and toes curl.

Ever so softly, his lips peck the side of my mouth. Past be damned, I grab his head, bringing his lips to mine. Greedily tasting his mouth.

His fingertips graze up my thighs and they part for him. I refamiliarize myself with his lips until Bryan pulls away and closes the door.

My cell phone chooses that moment to ring. I connect it to the sound system and back out of the parking stall.

"Hi, Danikins. I stopped by your office to see if you wanted to grab a late lunch." Max's cheery voice comes through the car's speakers.

I wait until Dani's Range Rover turns onto the street to execute the perfect about-face and march through the visitors' entrance to my building. Chen is already standing at the reception desk, slipping his cell phone into his pocket.

"The guys are waiting for you, Bry. Let me handle Hatchett," he says.

"Get his ass out of my goddamn building."

"Sir, I don't understand what I did wrong," Hatchett says. "I greeted Ms. Edwards, gave her the keycard, and summoned the elevator."

Unimaginable anger shoots through me. I move before Chen can block me. Fingers tight around the lapels of Hatchett's jacket, I yank him toward the counter.

"You called her *Dr. Edwards,* you fucking idiot. Riley didn't list her as *Dr. Edwards* on my appointment schedule. *And* you were staring at her ass! I watched the whole thing on my monitor."

Chen grips my wrists, squeezing the pressure points in an attempt to make me release Hatchett. Instead, I pull the fuck-up closer. I know his feet are off the floor. We're nose to nose.

Fright shines in the Watcher's eyes.

When it comes to Dani and Kourt, I want them all to fear my wrath.

Dani's smart. She picks up on the littlest things and she can never know the real reason I'm in her life. The fallout would be devastating, and it puts my daughter in danger too.

Chapter Four

TODAY IS HALLOWEEN. I WAKE up an hour early so I can drop Kourtney off at Bryan's and get to the school to decorate the classroom. She isn't a morning person. This is going to be a challenge.

I softly knock on the door before walking into her room. Kourtney is awake and sitting in the middle of her bed. She stretches and yawns. "Good morning, Mommy."

"Good morning, sweetie." I smile and sit on her bed, fingers ready for our daily ritual. Kourtney laughs as I tickle her. "How did you sleep?"

"Like… a… baby," she stutters.

I hug and kiss my daughter.

"Go get dressed. I don't want to be late." She wiggles out of my embrace. "Bryan said he's making a special breakfast." Kourtney hops out of bed and skips out the door, heading to the bathroom.

I shake my head as I walk back to my room. Normally I have to drag her out of bed. Today, the promise of a special breakfast makes her excited about waking before sunrise. Or is it the man who is making the meal that has her so cheerful?

Max and Tom are waiting for me when I arrive at the school. We unload containers filled with decorations onto a hand truck. Bryan recruited five parents to help decorate.

On my second trip back to the truck, Horny Toad Madelyn Brooks approaches me.

"*You're* here to decorate?" Madelyn asks.

Someone sure sounds disappointed. I give her my best fake smile and stack the last container. "If you'll excuse me, I really need to get started." I grab the handle of the hand truck and walk away.

"Bryan begged me to come…" She pauses a little too long. "… help decorate."

Wordplay loses its shock value the more I have to listen to it. Besides, at this hour, I don't want to deal with it. I increase my pace and pray her stilettos prevent her from keeping up. Who wears heels that high to volunteer at their child's school?

Unfortunately, she matches me stride for stride.

Ribbit.

"Bryan and I go *way* back," she croaks. I was expecting the skin under her neck to puff out like a frog's. "We're more than friends, but he doesn't want anyone to know. I *am* married." Her chuckle mirrors a maniacal cartoon character.

Okay, I've had enough and it's only been a few minutes. I stop and face her. "I'm sure he'll be disappointed that you feel the need to discuss this with me. After all, *you're* the one cheating, aren't you?" I leave her standing at the entrance to the corridor.

"Bitch!" Her insult hits my back, yet I keep walking away.

David and Jennifer Hill have joined the decorating crew. The Hill's son Dylan sits next to Penelope.

Bethany Johnson is also here to help. Her daughter is one of the mean girls in the classroom. I didn't see her at Back to School Night.

Bethany is standoffish with me, but she chats with the other parents in the room.

It takes us almost two hours to get the room decorated the way Bryan and I envisioned.

"How did you guys come up with this?" Tom asks, snapping photos of the room.

"When Bryan was a kid, he liked that Halloween story about the headless horseman. We made decorations around that theme."

"These life-size headless scarecrows look great." Max poses with one, and Tom snaps a picture.

"I like the giant pumpkin head." David poses next to it. Tom snaps a picture and turns the viewing screen to me. The homemade green glow sticks inside of the pumpkin head look ghostly. Kourtney came up with that idea. She and Bryan worked on it together.

"This hay looks realistic," Jennifer comments.

"Emma and I experimented with different materials until we discovered that painted and shredded newspaper gave us the best look."

Holly and Madelyn snicker from the doorway, making crude comments. Usually counting to ten helps to control my temper. I'm about to add blood to our Headless Horseman's Haunted Pumpkin Patch.

"Bryan can be *very* creative with his hands," Holly ribbits.

"That man is great with *whatever* he's doing," Madelyn croaks.

And so the innuendo contest begins. I refuse to stand here and listen to them outdo one another. I stack empty containers onto the hand truck. After one final look around the classroom to make sure everything is in place, I grab the handle and walk out the door.

"Did we offend you?" Madelyn asks.

I keep walking.

"Wait up, Danielle," Jennifer calls out as she jogs to catch up with me. "Don't let those two get to you. Madelyn has been after Bryan since our kids were in preschool. Holly's new. She hasn't learned that Madelyn is a bloodsucking parasite. If Holly isn't careful, that leech will latch on to her husband too."

"What about Stephanie Banks?"

"Rumor has it, things aren't happy in the Banks household. Tristan is having an affair. That's probably why Stephanie's joined the Bryan Hawk fan club."

"Emma and Kourtney are friends. I'm not sleeping with Bryan."

"As long as Madelyn sees you as competition, she's going full throttle on chasing you off." Jennifer walks with me to the parking lot. She amuses me with other rumors on the parent gossip line as we load empty containers into my Range Rover. We stop our little chitchat when we spot a black SUV turn into the parking lot.

Mr. Tall-And-Sexy pulls into the spot in front of me. I quickly toss the last container onto my backseat and close the door, setting the alarm.

He climbs out dressed in a Haunted Headless Horseman's costume. The girls begged us to dress up too. I'll put on my Haunted Pumpkin costume now that the classroom is decorated. Tom and Max are dressing up as the Haunted Pumpkin Farmers.

Bryan opens his back door. Emma, Kourtney, and Penelope climb out. They're dressed in matching black crow costumes.

Kourtney runs to me flapping her wings.

I pull out my cell phone to snap pictures. "You girls look adorable."

"Here's your costume." Bryan hands me a backpack. "Marie said she made the adjustments."

I follow him around to the back of his truck and help him unload the bags of treats.

"What's wrong?" he asks.

"Nothing." From the corner of my eye, I see Bryan pause and stare. How does he know something's bothering me?

"The trophy boogers are throwing shade and serving filth to Danielle." Max walks up to the truck. "Bitches lucky I ain't vogue one time in their faces and end it with a shablam! Snap my fingers and walk off like I'm Queen Bee." That earns him a raised eyebrow from Bryan and laughter from Jennifer. Max exhales in frustration, tosses back his nonexistent long hair and translates. "Madelyn Brooks and Holly Valentine are tossing insults at Danikins. I wanted to bitch slap them before I walked away."

The Haunted Headless Horseman nods his head. "Girls, let's go," he commands and marches off with Max, while the rest of us bring up the rear.

"This should be good," Jennifer whispers.

"I hope not."

We follow the leader down the hall to the classroom. The students are outside on the playground getting ready for the Halloween Parade. I send the girls to join their classmates.

Mr. Hawk is deceivingly too calm.

Madelyn, Holly, and now Stephanie stand by the table set aside for treats with "please notice me" looks in their eyes. Bryan walks toward them. Each Horny Toad strikes a pose that pushes out their boobs and toots their booties.

"Good morning, ladies." He starts to unload the bags.

I remain silent, helping him fill the papier-mâché bowls.

Every now and then, he winks and tosses them a sexy smile.

Oh yes, Bryan's up to no good, and I'm not sticking around to see what it is. I fill the last bowl. Before I can escape, he pulls me into his arms, resting his chin on top of my head.

"You did a great job decorating. It turned out better than I imagined." He leans back lifting my chin with his fingertips. His voice drops an octave and takes on a seductive tone. "But then again all I could see that night was you underneath me, moaning my name. Sweat covering your body from the work we put in." He kisses my lips, then holds me at arm's length.

Dumbfounded, I stare at him. My brain can't believe the words flowing past his lips.

He's not finished. A slight bend of his knees and we're eye to eye. "I think we went five hours nonstop that night, right? I hope you're up for the sequel tonight because"—he adjusts himself—"I want to play needle in your haystack again."

I'm too shocked to reply. Or move. All my faculties flew out the window *after* the first thirteen words of his monologue.

He leans in to give me a promising peck on the lips before turning me by the shoulders. His hand smacks my butt. The sound echoes through the room and bounces off the walls.

"Go get that sexy ass in your costume." He picks up the backpack and places a strap in my hand, then pushes me in the direction of the door.

Max laughs and all other conversations come to a halt as I double-time march out of the classroom, seeing red.

He has to know I'm furious with him. It takes every bit of self-control to not walk back in that room and punch him.

Once I change into my costume, I join the students on the playground. Instead of eye daggers, Madelyn tosses verbal insults like a professional.

This is another reason I don't date. Who wants to deal with jealous exes, or in this case, a jealous, married Horny Toad who wants what she can't have?

When the events move indoors, I stand at my post by the classroom door, plotting the best way to castrate that Haunted Horseman strutting around the classroom.

Kourtney, Emma, and Penelope win fourth place for best costume, and Ms. Williamson's class is runner-up and wins a pizza and ice cream party prize for the best decorated second grade classroom. A sixth-grade class wins first place.

Of course that Haunted Headless Horseman adds more fuel to the fire when he makes his speech in front of the entire classroom thanking me for the *hours* of creative inspiration I provided him.

My devious plot now includes a tube of crazy glue and the leftover newspaper hay, once I have his balls in my hands.

You're going to pay for this, Mr. Bryan Kendall Hawk IV.

Chapter Five

KOURTNEY AND I GO TO the mall to buy Emma's birthday gifts. We stop in the food court for a cup of hot chocolate and sit at a table near the play area. Kourtney watches the colorful lights in the water fountain dance to the tunes of Christmas carols. She's excited about our first Christmas in Colorado. Snow started sticking to the ground the latter part of November.

"Hi, Kourty. Hi, Danielle." Out of nowhere, the little brunette slides into the seat next to me.

"Hi, Emmy."

I prepare myself for the next Hawk to sit at our table. I've reduced his acknowledgement to a simple nod if our paths cross in front of the school. Kourtney isn't happy about it.

After a minute, I eye the crowded food court, searching for him. "Where's your dad?"

"He had to work late."

"Are you here with Marie?"

"No. Uncle Vinny."

"Where's your Uncle Vinny?" I ask.

"In the toy store."

Her short answers are killing me. "Does he know where you are?"

"I told him."

"He allowed you to walk all the way over here by yourself?" Seriously? She shrugs her shoulders.

"Emma, did he hear you when you told him where you were going?" She shrugs again. "I don't know."

Children will drive you crazy when they don't give you everything you need at one time. "Why don't you know if he heard you?"

"He was on the phone talking to my dad."

"Emma, the toy store is on the other side of the mall. You walked over here by yourself?"

"I thought I saw Ms. Williamson, so I followed her, and then I saw you guys."

With my cell phone in my hand I stand. I'm not sure who I'm looking for. Christmas shoppers are everywhere. I turn to ask Emma to describe her uncle when a shout rings out across the food court and a dark-haired, bull-of-a-man dressed in a business suit stampedes in our direction.

Shoppers scurry out of his way.

The scent of old dirty socks and fish crosses my nose. The sound of water takes me back to a night when I had to fight for my life.

Chill bumps sprout all over my body.

The cell phone slips from my fingers.

Emma says something, but I block out everything around me. Shoulders squared, I take my boxer's stance and focus on the predator coming at me.

I must protect myself.

I throw two consecutive hooks to his ribs and follow through with a jab to his chin. The force of the blows causes him to stumble back, and I don't give the predator the opportunity to recover.

Most people are surprised at my skills. My size and personality hide the inner kickboxer. I've knocked down many unsuspecting sparring partners.

He's looking over my shoulder. Lips moving. Hands waving. I reach back and uppercut him, my fist connecting in the right place under his chin. He drops to one knee, dazed and exposed. I give him a solid kick in the gut, knocking the wind out of him.

Just as I take a step to turn around, something hard under my shoe throws me off balance. A vise clamps around my ankle. My foot is pulled out from under me. I stumble.

"*Mommy,*" Kourtney calls out. It's the last voice I hear before I crash onto the table.

My eyes flutter open and I look around. White walls. White linens on an uncomfortable bed. Faint beep of a monitor. Mobile bed tray in the corner.

"Kourtney!" I cry out and a sharp pain shoots through my head.

Kicking off the hospital blanket, I swing my legs around to get out of bed. I'm stopped by the IV line taped to my arm.

I reach to pull it out and long fingers clamp around my wrists.

My eyes follow the path of the fingers. Up the muscular arm covered in a lavender dress shirt, continuing to broad shoulders, and stopping at the loosened purple-striped silk necktie hanging around his neck.

"What are you doing?" Bryan Hawk demands. "Don't pull that out."

I struggle against his hold. "We have to find Kourtney."

His fingers tighten. "Kourt's fine. She's at my house. Marie is looking after her."

Scrunching my forehead, I draw in air to ease the pounding in my head. "I remember Emma coming to our table. You weren't with her."

"Lie back and I'll give you the short version of what happened."

I stay where I am. His eyes narrow and he repeats the instructions, this time as a firm command. My head hurts too much to argue and my daughter is safe. I swing my legs back onto the bed. He covers me with the blanket and stands, crossing his arms over his chest.

"You were kicking my friend's ass, lost your balance, and hit your head on the table. I brought you to the hospital."

It's starting to come back to me. I remember fighting a man and something making me wobble.

"No, he grabbed my ankle to throw me off balance. What kind of friends do you have that will render a defenseless woman unconscious?"

His eyes narrow and jawline tightens. "Friends I trust to always have my back," he barks. "There's nothing defenseless about you. *You* knocked *him* down."

My eyes close. I try not to talk louder than a whisper. "I need to get out of here and take Kourtney home." My fingers touch a tender knot on my forehead.

I hear the swoosh from the door opening and the squeak of rubber-sole footsteps on the tile floor approaching the bed.

"Hello, Dr. Edwards. I'm Dr. Ignacio Acosta Jr, a friend of Bryan's. How are you feeling?" His gentle Spanish-accented voice greets me.

I crack open an eye. A dark-haired man with friendly chocolate-brown eyes and a warm smile stands next to the bed. I. Acosta Jr, MD is embroidered in red on his dark-blue hospital scrubs.

"I want to leave." The pounding in my head causes me to inhale and squeeze my eyes tight.

"I've admitted you for overnight observation. You're panting. Is your headache that unbearable?"

"I can't stay. I have no family to watch my daughter."

"If there's no one other than your child to keep an eye on you at home, I cannot discharge you."

"I'll keep an eye on Dani. Plus, Kourt and Emm need to see she's okay." I frown in the direction of the sound of his voice.

"The length of her unconsciousness concerns me, Bry."

"You found nothing on the CT scan, right? You have my word she'll be watched at all times in my home."

"Please stop talking over me." I open my eyes. "Dr. Acosta, I'll sign the papers that releases the hospital from liability. I have the right to discharge myself and I'm exercising my rights. I'm leaving this hospital with or without your permission."

The two men stare at me for a moment.

"Keep a close eye on her for forty-eight hours," Dr. Acosta addresses his friend.

My outburst didn't interrupt their conversation.

Bryan assures him he can handle this.

"If you can't wake her, dial 911. If her vision blurs and the headaches worsen, bring her back right away. I'll have my physician assistant come by the house to check on her in the morning, and I'll stop by in the evening." Dr. Acosta finally turns to me. "You will experience headaches for the next few days. I'll write you a prescription. Do not take the medication on an empty stomach. It will make you sleepy so no driving or operating heavy machinery. Get plenty of rest and don't over exert yourself. The nurse will be in once I write up your discharge orders. I'll schedule a follow-up appointment for the middle of the week. I can place you off work until then."

"Thank you, but I've already planned the time off since my daughter will be on winter break. I'll call in sick in the morning."

He nods and exits the room.

I stare at Mr. Hawk, trying to figure out how I can get Kourtney and myself to our apartment without a fight. "Where's my truck?"

"I had my friend drop it off at your apartment."

"The same friend who put me in here?"

"Kourt wouldn't go near him so Max picked up the girls and Vin dropped off your Range Rover."

The throbbing in my head distracts me from asking more questions. A petite-size nurse walks through the door and immediately starts removing the IV. Gum popping in her mouth, she works fast. Instead of tape and a cotton ball, she covers the puncture with gauze, then wraps a self-adhesive band around my arm.

"You can get dressed while I print your discharge papers and have your medication sent up from the pharmacy." The nurse leaves us alone.

I stare at Bryan.

He raises an eyebrow. It's his annoying way of silently asking a question.

"Leave so I can get dressed," I answer.

"I just gave my word that I'd look after you, so change in front of me or stay here."

"You can't be serious."

"Try me," alpha male challenges.

While I do a mental rundown of the underwear I'm wearing underneath this hospital gown, I frown at him.

You need to get to Kourtney. Who cares if you're wearing sexy underwear or granny-panties?

Peeling the blanket off my legs, I swing them around and slide off the bed. The minute my feet touch the floor my head swims and my knees buckle. Bryan grabs my waist to steady me and I hold the bed for balance. His touch magnifies my instability. I push his hands off.

He takes a couple steps back, but stays ready to catch me if I fall.

To block his view, I pull the privacy curtain. I moan as pain shoots through my shoulder in protest.

Metal against metal, the sound of Bryan yanking the curtain back makes me angry.

"Are you going to watch me on the toilet too?"

He cocks an eyebrow.

My daughter is more important than dueling back and forth with him, and I'm not ashamed of my body. I let the hospital gown slip off my shoulders and float to the floor, landing at my feet.

I stand before him in a soft pink bra and boy shorts panties.

His eyes prowl every inch of me like hands tracing the outline and his mind coloring inside the lines. Bryan's eyes meander my lips, neck, and cleavage. My stomach, hips, and thighs. All the way down to my pedicured feet then back up to the triangle of my thighs.

The clenching of my inner muscle turns into a sexual ache. My nipples harden at the thought of his touch. It's a good thing this hospital room is cold; otherwise he'd know the aroused shiver is because of him.

He takes a step toward me. The heat from his body and the scent of him invade my senses. The pounding headache fades to an offbeat tap. And without permission, my feet take a step toward him. The unsteady beat of his heart pulsates in the vein in his neck. His Adam's apple bobs up and down. His hands grip my waist, pulling me to him.

Kourtney's face pops into my mind, and the rhythmic pounding in my head returns. I step back. "Can you stand on the other side of the room?"

"I'm fine where I am."

I surrender. I can't go toe-to-toe with him.

Someone folded my clothes and placed them on the shelf next to the bed. I reach for them and slowly get dressed under his watchful eye.

Bryan leads me to a chair and helps me put on my shoes. He ties the laces.

"If I'm being forced to stay with you, I need to pick up clothes for Kourtney and myself."

"Give me your keys and I'll have someone bring your things to my house."

"Why must everything be a challenge?"

"It's a challenge because *you're* making it a challenge, Dani."

I sigh. "I prefer to do it myself."

"Then I'll take you to your apartment."

The nurse comes in with a clipboard. "Dr. Acosta is discharging you with these instructions." She reads and I initial every line, showing I understand the orders. I sign the discharge papers. "I will be back with a wheelchair to take you downstairs."

"A wheelchair won't be necessary. I can walk out on my own."

"Sorry, Dr. Edwards. Hospital policy."

The door closes behind her.

"You can always stay," he taunts.

I mumble an expletive under my breath. Alpha male has pushed one too many buttons and my brain-to-mouth filter malfunctions.

His lips twitch. I ignore him and pick up my purse and cell phone.

The nurse reenters with a wheelchair, hands Bryan my paperwork and prescription, and gestures for me to sit. I do as I'm told and follow hospital policy.

Chapter Six

BRYAN OPENS MY DOOR AND helps me out of his truck. We're in front of my apartment building. He cups my head, massaging my temples with his thumbs while his fingers caress the hairs at the nape of my neck.

"Are you okay?" he asks, genuine concern etched in his face.

I search his eyes for a moment then take a deep breath, and nod.

We walk the path to the stairs. He keeps his hand on the small of my back as we climb. Bryan waits as I fumble to unlock the door and follows me inside.

"It'll just take me a few minutes," I tell him and head to Kourtney's room, leaving him in the living room staring at the shelf full of framed pictures.

Her small suitcase is on the top shelf of her closet. I stretch on my tip-toes and reach with my right arm. Pain shoots through my shoulder and I drop my arm, grabbing it.

Bryan stands behind me, in my personal space. I didn't hear him come into the bedroom. He reaches over me, taking down the suitcase.

"Thank you." I step around him.

From the corner of my eye, I watch him as he walks around Kourtney's room. He pauses at the picture frame documenting her first days of school from preschool to present. His fingers brush over trophies and ribbons. He stops and reads her certificates.

I pack an assortment of clothes and grab her teddy bear off the bed. The smile on his face is hard to miss.

Bryan picks up Kourtney's backpack, then taking the small suitcase and bear from my hands, he leaves the room.

I cross the hall to my room. My movements become slow. Bryan comes in and sits on my bed, watching me underneath those long eyelashes. Images of us tangled in the sheets, doing the intimate dance of sexual pleasure, invade my imagination. I close my eyes to calm my raging hormones.

I pack while trying not to look at him.

Bryan takes my suitcase to the living room while I go to the bathroom for our toiletries.

Turning on the light. The shock of seeing a familiar yet battered face staring back at me from the mirror is startling. Gone are the lustful thoughts from moments ago.

The greenish knot on my forehead and silver-dollar-sized blotch on my right cheek will be black and blue by morning. Silent tears pool in my eyes. If I had been seriously injured, what would have happened to my daughter?

I pull the sweater over my head and let the tears fall. My right shoulder will also be black and blue in the morning.

Movement in the mirror catches my attention. Bryan rests against the doorframe, watching me. He closes the physical distance between us in the tiny bathroom. His hands hold my waist, and I stare at our reflection as we face the mirror.

We hold a nonverbal conversation with our eyes.

Bryan's lips brush my bruised shoulder, then my bruised cheek. "I'm sorry."

I nod.

"Kiss me."

I hear the unspoken "please" in his request.

Turning, I cup his face in my hands, pulling his lips to mine. They're soft and the distraction I need from this evening's event. My aches and pains are forgotten. Overshadowed by the euphoric high his lips give me.

He lifts me onto the bathroom counter, stepping between my parted thighs. Bryan slips my tank top free of my jeans. His warm fingers travel underneath and glide up my sides until he cups my bra-covered breasts.

I break our kiss and turn my head to catch my breath. His lips find *that* spot behind my ear; a moan travels up my throat and pass through my lips.

I want him. Right here. But I'm not ready to take that step. The essence of desertion is still too raw.

"Dani," he whispers.

My body tenses with heartbreaking pain. Calling me by that nickname is like ice cold water thrown on me.

"Please stop." I push at his shoulders, overcome with the need for him to stop touching me.

"What's wrong?" His eyebrows form a V.

"I need you to stop."

He steps back and his hands slide down to my waist.

"It's late and I want to check on Kourtney." I push him back further, sliding off the counter and picking up my sweater. I slip it over my head.

Bryan stands in the doorway as I put toiletries in the travel bags.

I follow him out of the bathroom.

We leave the apartment.

The car ride to his house is quiet.

"As soon as we get there, I have to take the medication." I stare out the window at nothing in particular.

"I was wondering how much longer you'd let yourself suffer." He reaches across the console, squeezing my hand. "I'll call Marie and ask her to have something ready for you as soon as we get to the house."

I close my eyes to block out the bright headlights of the oncoming cars.

"Are you okay, Dani? I can stop at a drive-thru."

"Please stop calling me that."

"Why can't I call you Dani?"

"Because I've asked you *not* to," I snap.

I'm jostled against the seat belt as the truck swerves. My eyes fly open. We come to an abrupt stop on the side of the road.

Bryan's hand encloses both my cheeks, turning my head to force me to face him.

"Why can't I call you Dani?"

I stare at him.

The pressure of his hold tightens.

"Why. Can't. I. Call. You. Dani?"

Tears pool in my eyes and I yell, "Nicknames are terms of endearment. It's how you show someone you care about them. You don't care, Bryan. Kourtney is the only one who gives a damn about me."

"I know it may not seem like it, but Kourt isn't the only one." His voice is soft. Tender. Persuasive. "Dani."

A tear escapes my eye and is caught by his thumb. Bryan's smile is sad. "Trust me, it wasn't by choice and it hasn't been easy for me either."

His fingers reclaim the steering wheel. He pulls back onto the road, not explaining the meaning behind those words. There was a time when I'd want to know more, but too many years have gone by. The emptiness of blind trust consumes me.

After we travel a few miles his voice penetrates the silence.

"I'm sorry," he says for the second time tonight.

I twist the ring around my finger and turn my attention to the passing scenery of Boulder. The silence is deafening as we drive toward the outskirts of town.

Bryan pulls into the semicircle driveway. Willis is standing on the bottom step with a smile on his face. He opens my door and offers his hand. "How are you?"

"I've been better."

"Take her suitcase and bag to my room. I've got Kourt's suitcase," Bryan says as he's rounding the front of the truck to take my hand. He guides me up the steps.

"I can share a room with Kourtney."

"I can't keep an eye on you if you're sharing a room with her."

We stop in the foyer.

Marie comes down the hallway with a welcome smile on her face. "Go on upstairs, dear," she says. "I have the guest room prepared for you. I'll bring your tray up."

"Dani's staying in my room."

"I'll bring your tray up to Bryan's room, then." Her Southern accent more pronounced, Marie's voice rings of disapproval.

"I have to check on my daughter first."

"I sat with her until she fell asleep."

Bryan takes my hand once again, leading the way upstairs. His hand is warm and has the texture of manual labor. At the landing, we turn to the right and walk down a hallway. He opens the first bedroom door.

Rushing to the bed, I wrap my arms around her. I feel complete. "Hello, baby."

The mattress dips, Bryan sits behind me.

Kourtney's eyes flutter open. "Hi, Mommy." She yawns and bumps my sore shoulder as she hugs me.

I gasp.

"Be careful, Kourt. Mom's in pain."

"Sorry," she says.

"It's okay." I give her a gentle squeeze, then lean back to kiss her cheek. "I brought Mr. Cuddles." Bryan hands her the teddy bear she's slept with since she was three years old.

Kourtney lies back on the pillow, yawning again. She snuggles with the bear.

"Go back to sleep. I'll see you in the morning." I kiss her forehead. "Are you okay with the lights off?"

She nods, her eyelids losing the fight to stay open. "Mr. Cuddles keeps the monsters away right, Bryan?"

"Yes, he does," his voice cracked.

"Goodnight, Mommy. I love you."

"I love you more, sweetie."

"Goodnight, Kourt," Bryan says, the tone of his voice is emotional.

We sit and watch her drift back to sleep. It feels like the most natural thing for us to do together.

"If you're ready, I'll show you to my room," Bryan whispers.

"Marie went to the trouble of preparing the guest room. I'll feel bad if I don't use it." I flip the switch on the lamp. The room darkens. I follow him out, closing the door behind us.

"Dani, I'm not walking to this side of the house every two hours. There's a couch in my room. You can have the bed."

I didn't realize how big his home was until we walked to the other side. This part of the house appears to be all his. He opens the double doors and motions for me to step in ahead of him. I enter and turn in a circle to take it all in.

His room is the size of my entire apartment.

The masculine bedroom has no traces of a female's touch. His scent permeates the air.

The custom-made bed and frame are bigger than a king and face glass doors that open to a deck.

There's a big fireplace and cozy sitting area off to one side. A big flat screen television adorns a wall in front of two reclining chairs on the opposite side.

"Marie will sit with you while you eat and shower. The bathroom is through that door." He points across the room.

"Going back on your word?" I smirk.

A slight bend of his knees put us eye-to-eye. "Oh, I want to stay and watch you shower, but I can't promise I won't seduce you into sleeping with me, even though I know you're in pain and need to rest. Or, you can have your privacy and let Marie listen out for you. It's your choice, Dani, but decide quickly. Considering how long it's been, I *will* have you tonight and face the consequences in the morning."

The seriousness of his words is magnified by the appetite in his eyes.

"Marie can listen out for me."

A knock interrupts before I give in to the sexual pull. Marie walks through the door carrying a lap-tray in her hands and a frown on her face. She observes how close Bryan and I are standing.

"I'll wake you in two hours." He kisses my cheek and walks out of the room, leaving the double doors open.

"I brought you chicken stew. I hope that's okay."

Marie doesn't wait for me to reply. She walks over to the couch, setting the tray on the coffee table.

I follow and sit down. "It's fine, thank you." My stomach growls before the spoon reaches my mouth.

Marie sits at the other end and pulls knitting needles and yarn from a bag.

I eat the stew in silence, listening to the rhythmic click of the needles and the whispered lyrics of a song she's singing. The sound is comforting. I become entranced by the foreign words.

I look around the bedroom. It's clear Bryan has money. His temperament hides his net worth.

James had a millionaire's persona yet was frugal with his money because he had so little growing up. Grocery shopping was done at different stores on sales days and with coupons for every item in the basket. Even a simple dinner and a movie date didn't happen unless we had coupons. In high school I didn't mind his thriftiness. We had fun finding free things to do. Before he went off to boot camp, we opened a joint savings account. We dreamed of a better life than what our childhood afforded us.

A month after his death, a statement for a separate account came in the mail. I went to the bank to verify the six-figure balance. That same day, I found out I was pregnant.

"Thank you again, Marie. The stew was delicious. I know it didn't come from a can." My stomach is full after only eating half the bowl.

"My mother used to make it for me whenever I was under the weather." She sets her knitting aside. Rising from the couch, Marie strokes my hair in a comforting gesture. She lifts the tray off my lap. "Go shower. I'll turn down the bed and dim the lights."

I get my pajamas and toiletries from my suitcase.

The bathroom is beyond description. An automatic soft light comes on showcasing a deep, extra-large bathtub against one wall. Adjacent is a walk-in shower room enclosed by glass walls. Paneled mirrors rise to the ceiling over the sink and oversized countertops. Next to them, a doorless walk-in storage closet. There are heated towel racks mounted by the shower and tub. When I kick off my shoes and socks, my feet are welcomed by the heated tile floor.

His bathroom looks high tech like his office building. I don't see knobs on the faucets.

I strip out of my clothes, pull my hair into a bun high on top of my head, and cover it with a shower cap.

Bryan's bathroom faces the moonlit, snow-covered Rocky Mountains. It's a lovely sight. Calming. I set my body wash on the tile pedestal and read the options on the control panel, choosing the water temperature and low flow pressure. The water comes out hot—I don't have to wait a few seconds for it to warm up—and it feels good on my skin.

I could get used to this. Maybe staying here for a couple of days won't be such a bad thing.

I stare out at the mountains while washing my body. It's a good thing the mountains are his backyard neighbors; otherwise anyone who uses this shower would be on full display.

How many other women have enjoyed this view?

Jealousy creeps into my thoughts and I wash it away. I have no right to be jealous. He's living his life as I have mine. I step out of the shower, dry off, and quickly dress in fleece pajamas.

A fire burns in the fireplace when I come back into the bedroom. A folded set of covers and two pillows are propped up in the middle of the couch.

The bed is turned down. The overhead lights are off and the bedroom doors are closed. Marie waits for me with a teacup in her hands, steam circling around the rim.

"It's a fresh jasmine and cinnamon brew. It'll help you relax."

"You don't have to stay with me," I tell her as I climb into bed and under the covers.

She hands me the cup and medicine bottle. "Bryan's request, dear."

Marie goes back to the couch, picking up her yarn and needles.

After a few sips I lean back, listening to the click of the wood hitting wood and Marie softly singing. I take another sip and set the cup on the nightstand, snuggling into the pillow.

Bryan's scent is on the sheets. It's my version of how a real man smells. Power. Strength. Spicy. Confidence. Soap. Comfort. Warmth. Sandalwood. Everything rolled up into one Mr. Tall-And-Sexy.

Now that Dani is in bed, I turn off the camera in my room and concentrate on the video chat the five of us are in.

"Vin, are you sure she called you Mr. Tucker? Tell us again what happened," Chen says.

We're trying to figure out what triggered Dani's aggressive attack on my friend.

He moves the ice pack from his chin. "I got an alert from the Watcher that someone was following Danielle. Emm walked away as I was getting the details. I spotted the three of them sitting at a table. The perp was scoping her from that shoe store near the food court. I started for the store and some kid spilled a bag full of candy balls. In all the chaos, people started yelling and jumping out of the way. The perp was heading for Danielle. I was stomping balls as I rushed to head him off. I didn't see her standing in front of me until she said, 'stay away from me, Mr. Tucker' and started punching me. The perp turned the other way when mall security headed toward us. Each time I waved off the guards, she got in a good punch. Man, that one to my chin floored me. It felt like a hit in the sac. Then she kicked me in the stomach. She turned around and stepped on a candy ball that rolled under her foot. I grabbed her ankle to keep her from breaking it or her leg."

"The little boy said something bit him and that's why he spilled the candy," I say.

"His mom brought him to the emergency room like you advised. He has a small puncture wound in his forearm. The perp was across the courtyard. He couldn't have pricked the kid," Ig says.

"What about a dart?" I ask.

"Sweepers didn't find anything like that on the floor," Tony says and moves out of view.

"He wasn't working alone. Have you found anything from the security footage from the mall or the stores?" I ask Vin.

"Not yet, I'm still going through it."

"Bry, I've gone through every detail of information we have on the people in Danielle's life. There's no Tucker in the files." Chen puts on his glasses looking at something on the left of his screen.

Tony sits back down in front of the computer. "If we had a first name, I could run it through the database."

"Her reaction to Vin mirrors the fight or flight response as a result of post-traumatic stress, but we know that isn't the case with Danielle," Chen says. "It could be a part of Edwards's conditioning of her. I'll need more information to make a definite assessment."

An alert pops up on my screen, and a grainy airport image uploads.

"Vin, forward the mall security footage to Tony. Guess who just cleared customs in Los Angeles and is waiting for a connecting flight to Arizona?" I say, making the image available for them to see.

"I knew Kimberly was lying," Ig says. "She's helping Edwards. Are we rolling out the welcome carpet?"

"Depends. Vin, you up for a little interrogation?" I ask.

"I can be in the air within the hour."

"We'll debrief when you get back. Hey. Don't forget Dani's staying in my room, so knock before you barge in."

"I'm dusting off my best kid's birthday party threads." Tony laughs.

"Don't go overboard. She shies away from too much flirting," Chen warns.

"She'll be calling me daddy by the end of Emm's party." He smiles.

"And I'll kick your ass," I warn.

Chapter Seven

I CAN'T ESCAPE THE STENCH OF fish and old socks. It's suffocating me and hundreds of hands grab me, pulling me down.

The scream tears from my throat and my eyes pop open. Panic spreads through my body.

Where am I?

This isn't my bed.

The room is dark except for the moon light glimmering through the glass doors.

"Kourtney," I yell out, kicking the covers off.

His hands clamp down on my shoulders. I shriek and knock them off.

"You're safe, Dani," Bryan whispers.

I blink, several times until my eyes adjust to the dimness. I take a deep breath and give my mind time to catch up.

Kourtney is safe. We're at Bryan's house. No one can hurt us here. Tears of grief begin to flow from my eyes. Bryan's fingers gently brush them away. His tender touch makes me cry harder. My heart aches for the years I've needed a comforting touch.

His warm body slides into bed next to me. He pulls me into his arms and shelters us with the covers. I rest my head on the soft cotton shirt covering Bryan's chest. The feel and sound of his steady heartbeat helps to calm me. It's familiar.

"Go back to sleep, Dani. I'll fight off the bad guys for you." His arms tighten around me. I close my eyes. Relax my body. And will myself to go back to sleep.

★★★

Something soft presses against my ear then Bryan's whispered words awaken me. "The PA is here to check you."

I peek at the clock; it's six in the morning. Falling asleep in his arms kept the bad dreams away. I roll over and Bryan helps me sit up.

The name under the picture on the badge attached to the powder blue scrubs reads Charisse Flowers, PA. I know she's from the hospital; I have the same badge with my name and picture on it.

PA Flowers is a short, plus-size Black woman with a warm smile and gentle touch. Her long dark hair has purple and pink highlights.

She asks questions as she examines me.

I yawn through my answers.

After typing notes on a tablet, she leaves.

Bryan comes out of the bathroom. His wet brown hair is slicked back, and the loosely tied hunter-green robe doesn't hide his body. "Don't worry about Kourt. Marie will make sure she's ready for school." He winks at me on his way to the closet.

"Thank you." I snuggle into the bed, closing my eyes. I fall asleep listening to the sounds of him moving around the bedroom.

Sometime later, a soft knock wakes me. Bryan's footsteps pad across the room.

"May I see my mom?" Kourtney whispers.

"Of course you may. Come on in," he says.

To gage her reaction to seeing me asleep in his bed, I purposely keep my eyes closed as I listen to two sets of feet approach. I hope the bruises on my face don't scare the girls.

"Is she okay?" Kourtney asks.

"She's fine and will be even better in a day or so." Bryan's tone sounds reassuring. "Are you girls ready for a three-week winter break?"

I wait for the answer, but one isn't spoken.

"Dad, can we go ice skating on the pond after school?" Emma asks.

"I'll ask Marie and Willis to take you."

"I've never been ice skating," Kourtney says, her voice laced with excitement.

"We want you to take us," Emma pleads. "You're the best teacher."

"How can I argue with that?" He chuckles. "I'll take you two down to the pond when we get home this afternoon."

I stretch and moan, opening my eyes.

"Good morning, Mommy." Kourtney climbs onto the bed dressed in her school uniform.

Bryan stacks pillows behind me after helping me sit up. He's dressed in a white shirt and platinum black pinstripe suit pants.

"How did you sleep?" I ask Kourtney.

She giggles as I tickle her. "Like a baby."

"Your hair looks cute." I play with the intricately constructed braids.

"Ms. Marie did it."

"Did you sit still or did you give her a hard time?"

A sheepish smile spreads across Kourtney's face. "I tried my best to sit still."

I turn my attention to Emma. Her hair is braided like Kourtney's. "Good morning, Emma. How did you sleep?" I reach my hand out to her.

There's an unhappy expression on her face.

"What's wrong, sweetie?" I cup her chin in my hand.

She stares at my face. "It's my fault Uncle Vinny hurt you."

"I'm fine. Just next time introduce me to your uncle *before* I punch him." I laugh and tickle her.

"I tried… to tell you… it was… Uncle… Vinny." She stutters. The sound of her laughter brings on memories of better times.

I wrap both girls in my arms, ignoring the ache in my shoulder.

"Dani, are you hungry?" His voice sounds off.

I watch him, hoping he looks at me when he finishes buttoning the suit vest.

"No one *ever* calls Mom Dani. She doesn't like it," Kourtney says.

Finally, his gaze meets mine. The suffering in his eyes makes me blink back tears. Maybe being a single parent hasn't been easy on him either. Although the Franklins weren't my real family, I knew what it was like to grow up in a two-parent home. I want my daughter to have that experience. I've dreamed of family time like this, Kourtney with her dad and sister. As much as I tried to get over him, those dreams always included her father. Does Bryan have those same dreams for Emma?

"Yeah, she told me, but I call her Dani because I care about her. And I call you Kourt because I care about you too." He playfully pulls one of her braids. "Go eat breakfast. We'll be leaving in thirty minutes."

Kourtney kisses my bruised cheek, then jumps off the bed and runs out of the room. Emma follows her.

"Have a good day," I call after them.

"You too, Mom." Her voice echoes from the hall.

"Bry…"

He turns and walks toward the closet, cutting me off. Okay, he doesn't want to talk about it. I'll let it go for now.

"You're leaving me to fend for myself?" I speak louder than a whisper so he can hear me.

He steps out of the closet with his suit jacket on. "I have something going on at work that requires my attention. Marie and Willis are here. If you need me, just call. Your number is on the list. Riley will put your calls through even if I'm in a meeting."

I ease back down in the bed and roll onto my stomach. "Remind Kourtney to take the gift bag I left next to her backpack. Ms. Williamson's gift is in there too."

"I'll check on you in the afternoon, Dani." His soft lips linger on my forehead.

Later in the morning, Marie brings in a breakfast smoothie. I tried eating earlier, but chewing food magnified the pounding headache.

My cell phone buzzes while I'm sipping the thick berry-flavored beverage. It's an email from Bryan. He called in sick for me. It feels good to be taken care of.

In high school, James came to visit me the few times I'd gotten sick. He brought me comfort food and gossip about what I'd missed at school. I did the same for him. Boy, the slightest ailment sent him over the deep end and it was up to me to pull him back up.

I swallow a pain pill and go back to sleep.

In the afternoon, my cell phone rings. I reach for it with my eyes closed.

"How are you feeling?"

"Like I've been hit by a tank."

"That's a good way to describe Vin," Bryan laughs. "Sorry it's taking me longer than expected to handle things at work. Do you need anything?"

"I'm fine."

The bedroom door opens after a soft knock. Marie comes in carrying a tray.

"Are you eating?" Bryan asks.

"Marie just walked in with my lunch."

"I'll let you go. Enjoy your lunch."

"Thanks. See you when you get here." I end the call and sit up, stacking pillows behind me.

"Homemade chicken noodle soup," Marie says.

I stare at the big bowl. There's no way I can eat all this.

The chime of the doorbell rings throughout the house.

"Eat what you can, dear. Leave the tray on the nightstand. I'll come back for it in a little while," she says rushing out of the room, closing the door behind her.

I take a tentative sip from the spoon. Not bad. This isn't a canned soup. I scoop up another spoonful and stare out at the view from the glass doors while I enjoy my lunch.

All too soon my eyes begin to droop, but I fight to keep them open. Dr. Acosta wasn't kidding when he said the pain medication would make me drowsy. I try to eat most of the delicious soup, but my eyes won't stay open.

I feel the presence of two little girls standing on the side of the bed, watching me sleep.

"Hi, baby, how was your day?" My voice sounds muffled because my cheek is pressed into the pillow.

"I got a good gift from Karen Patterson."

"What did you get?" I ask.

"A teddy bear diary with a lock and key."

"How was your day, Emma?"

"I didn't like Jacob Brooks's gift."

"What did he get you?" I ask.

"A ring with a shiny pony on it."

"Sweetie, when you get older you'll be happy to get a shiny ring from a boy."

Bryan grunts. "Over my dead body, and not even then."

My eyes spring open. He walks out of the closet pulling a sweatshirt over his head.

How long has he been here? The girls have changed out of their uniforms. I look at the time. It's only two o'clock. They get out of school at two fifty.

"Marie has a snack waiting for you in…" The girls are out of the room before he finishes the sentence.

I throw the covers back and stretch. "What time did you guys get here?"

"About one thirty. I picked them up early to avoid the after school traffic jam."

"I need to get up and go to the pond with you guys."

Bryan stands in the doorway of the closet blocking me from entering. "Ig said not to overdo it. Besides, you heard Emm. I'm the best ice skating teacher."

So he knew I was pretending to be asleep this morning. "I've been in bed all day. My body needs movement. Where's my suitcase?" I squeeze past him.

He holds me by the waist from behind. "Marie unpacked your clothes and, knowing her, she put your underwear in my top drawer and moved mine to the bottom." Bryan's seductive whisper makes my stomach jump, in a sensual way. I lean back, loving the feel of his body against mine.

Knock.

Knock.

I hear the bedroom doors open.

"Danielle, I brought you a passion fruit smoothie for a snack," Marie announces.

Bryan and I pull away from each other like teenagers getting caught doing adult things. I turn around in time to witness Marie scowling at him.

Bryan kisses my cheek and hurriedly walks out of the bedroom.

Chapter Eight

THE POND IS ABOUT A seven-minute casual stroll from the house. The cement path has been cleared of snow. Bryan carries a plaid fleece blanket under his arm. A pair of black ice skates, tied at the laces, dangle over his shoulder.

We pass a one-story house, not too far from the main house.

"You own all this property?" The wooded area, just beyond the pond, is full of winter-bare trees.

He nods. "It took a couple years to build the house and remodel the old one for Willis and Marie. The pond is manmade. We've been here for five years."

Bryan cleans off a spot on a bench for me to sit and watch. He unfolds the blanket, wrapping it around me.

I've asked him more than once how long he's been in Boulder. He didn't answer the first time, yet he so nonchalantly tells me now. A mixture of emotions rolls through me at the revelation. Bryan's being closemouthed about himself. Am I being irrational for feeling hurt that he's being secretive?

And this land. That house. It's bigger than the dream home I designed in my head while cuddling in bed with Kourtney's father. Once he was gone, the house went with him. Or so I thought. I'm staring at it. Temporarily living in it. We were supposed to share a home like this. Is my irritation over the pride Bryan takes in constructing this place justified? Why do I suddenly feel like he's trying to make up for something?

Kourtney's excited laughter draws my attention. I stop living in the past and push aside those thoughts, tucking them away until there's a better time and place to analyze them. What's important in this moment is my daughter's happiness about spending time with her best friend and Bryan.

Bryan helps Emma put on her skates and she takes off, gliding on the frozen water.

He turns to Kourtney, explaining the skate's blade and how to lace the ties of a pair of *brand new* ice skates. How early did he pick them up?

With his own skates on his feet, Bryan guides Kourtney onto the frozen surface, holding both her hands. I hear him tell her the ice isn't smooth like at an ice skating rink.

As he skates backwards, Bryan is coaching and instructing Kourtney.

It doesn't take long before she lets go of his hands to skate on her own. With every one of her slips and falls, I wince and grit my teeth until Kourtney glides across the ice with confidence. Bryan skates near her and once she's more stable, Emma shows her how to do a small jump. Now I'm able to relax enough to laugh and clap in encouragement and take pictures with my phone.

Bryan snaps close-ups of them on his phone and sends them to me.

I'm happy I didn't miss this, especially the ice skating bunny hop the three of them are doing right now. It's really nice to see this side of Bryan. He's a natural with the girls.

A cool breeze flows through the trees. I shiver and wrap the blanket tighter around my shoulders. The sun is sinking lower in the late afternoon sky, a chill is growing in the air.

My smiles and words of encouragement falter. The headache is returning with a vengeance. I try to hide the pain as best I can whenever Bryan glances over at me.

"Hey, girls, it's getting late. How about we head back for hot chocolate?" he suggests.

Kourtney hugs him. "Thank you for teaching me to ice skate."

"You're welcome, Kourt." He hugs her back.

I stand and fold the blanket while he helps them take off and store their skates in matching bags.

Bryan slides his arm around my waist. We casually walk back to the house. Kourtney and Emma run ahead, giggling.

"What time did you pick them up from school?" I ask.

"Not that early." He gives me a sideways glance and I raise a questioning eyebrow. "I picked them up after lunch. We went to the mall to get Kourt a pair of ice skates." He shrugs his shoulders and I raise both eyebrows. "They weren't doing anything today, just partying."

I know there's more to the story.

Bryan and I walk through the side door. I hear the girls in the kitchen asking to help make the hot chocolate. He points me in the opposite direction. "Go up to my room and rest. I'll have Marie bring up your dinner."

I go upstairs, kick off my boots, climb onto the bed, and close my eyes. Sleep comes right away. I dream of a gentle and patient Mr. Tall-And-Sexy teaching *me* other things.

A soft shake of my shoulder and I open my eyes. Dr. Acosta is standing next to the bed. The lamp on my side is on. Outside, the sun has set and the sky is dark.

"Hello, Danielle. How are you feeling?"

"A lot better." I sit up.

He's dressed in a dark blue business suit that looks like it was made to fit his body.

He opens his medical bag. "The PA said your headaches aren't as intense. The pills are helping?" He checks my eyes.

"Yes, they're working."

"Follow my finger with your eyes," he instructs. "Bryan and Marie adhering to your discharge orders?"

My eyes move left, right, up, and down. "Yes. He's been taking good care of me." My eyes cross as his finger taps the tip of my nose.

Dr. Acosta types notes on a tablet. "On a scale of one to ten how bad are the headaches today?"

"A six compared to the ten yesterday."

He asks more questions as he examines my shoulder and the bump on my forehead. He types notes on the tablet, then reminds me to take it easy.

I snuggle down and go back to sleep.

"Danielle, wake up, dear."

Rolling onto my back, I open my eyes. Someone covered me with a warm blanket.

Marie is holding a tray with covered dishes and a glass of iced tea on it. I struggle to sit up and pile pillows behind my back.

"You must eat something. I tried waking you earlier, but you asked me to let you sleep for another hour."

I rub my eyes. I don't remember any of that happening.

Taking the tray from her hands, I place it over my lap and lift the metal covers. "Thank you, Marie. I hope it wasn't too much trouble making pudding."

She brushes my cheek with her hand, a motherly gesture. "It was no trouble at all. Kourtney told me you like banana pudding, but I believe it's more her favorite than it is yours. I was told yours is better." She sits on the couch, pulling out her knitting needles.

"Where are the girls?" I look at the time on the clock above the fire-place.

"They're in the family room playing a board game."

"With Bryan?"

The needles pause and Marie frowns. "He had a business meeting and will be back late." Her lips tighten and tension wrinkles form around her eyes and mouth.

It's best to keep the rest of my questions about Bryan to myself.

Under Marie's watchful eye, I clean my plate and eat half the pudding. Not to toot my own horn, but mine is better.

Marie stores her yarn and needles, retrieves the tray, and leaves the room.

I slip out of bed to use the bathroom, then go downstairs to check on the girls.

"Mommy, are you feeling better?" Kourtney meets me at the bottom of the stairs. She wraps her arms around me.

"Yes, sweetie." I beckon for Emma to give me a hug too.

"Will you watch a movie with us?" Emma looks up at me.

"You two pick out the movie and I'll see if Marie has popcorn."

They run to the family room and I continue down the hallway to the kitchen.

The breath catches in my throat. *This is my dream kitchen.* Every modern appliance I could ever want is in here. Thanks to my foster father, I love to cook. Even the view of the snow- covered yard is as I described it. I'm completely—surprised.

"Do you need something, Danielle?" Marie's concerned question brings me back to the here and now.

"Do you have popcorn?"

"We have microwave popcorn. Is that okay?"

"That's fine."

"It's in the pantry. I'll pop a couple of bags for you."

I sit at the table while Marie goes to the walk-in pantry. I love this kitchen. He couldn't have done a better job.

"We found a movie, Mom," Kourtney says, running into the kitchen with Emma right behind her.

"Tomorrow is my birthday party. Will you and Kourty be here?" Emma asks.

"Of course we will," I assure her. "I'll even help out if you want."

"Yes." Her excitement is contagious and I wrap my arms around her.

Marie pauses mid-step, and a warm smile spreads over her face.

"Want to join us for movie night?" I ask, as she fills a bowl with popcorn and puts another bag in the microwave.

The irritation she showed upstairs is now gone. "I'd love to."

Emma tells me about the plans for her party while we wait for the last bag to finish popping.

Armed with juice boxes and a big bowl of popcorn, the four of us settle down on the sofa in the family room.

The room is cozy. It's decorated in soft tones with bold accents. A massive fireplace adds warmth to the room. A big picture window faces the pond. I would say the family room is the focal point of the house because it looks to be the most used. But there are no framed family photos in here.

The movie the girls picked is one that I've watched a thousand times with Kourtney. We sing along with the characters and act out our favorite parts. Before the end credits roll, the girls fall asleep.

Marie helps me get them to bed.

I run a hot bubble bath in the big tub in Bryan's bathroom and slip in. Leaning back, I close my eyes and relax.

"Dani?"

My eyes flutter open. I stare at the forehead of the man I was dreaming about.

"Are you okay?" he asks. He's squatting next to the tub.

"Yes." I smile, then look down. The bubbles have dissolved and Bryan is staring at my naked body submerged under cold water. "What time is it?"

"A little after one," he says, licking his lips.

I'm instantly aroused.

Cupping my cheek in his hand, he leans in to kiss me. Without hesitation, my mouth opens for him. Our tongues brush.

"Daddy?" Emma's sleepy voice calls from the bedroom.

Bryan exhales a frustrating groan. He kisses my bruised shoulder before standing and walking out, closing the door behind him.

The bedroom is vacant when I come out of the bathroom. I climb under the covers and turn off the lamp on my side.

James's frowning face haunts my dreams.

Chapter Nine

THE NEXT MORNING, I WAKE up alone in bed, but I hear Bryan's voice. I crawl to the edge and watch him pace back and forth on the deck with his cell phone to his ear. Shoulders squared, one hand fisted. Bryan is upset about something.

The bedroom door swings open without warning.

Rotten fish and dirty gym socks assault my nose. I'm taken back to the walkway of my old apartment in Arizona. Leering eyes watching me from an open door. Filthy, stained wife-beater barely covering a sweaty protruding abdomen. Dirty cutoff jeans unzipped and unbuttoned.

"Hey, Bry." The owner of that deep, Italian-accented voice strides into the room.

My defense mechanism kicks in.

He stops in his tracks when he sees me perched on the edge of the bed. "Sorry. I forgot Bryan had company. How do you feel?"

I squint. "How do I look?"

He cases the bump on my forehead and the bruise on my cheek. A teasing smile creeps across his lips. "Like shit."

"Jokes from a little mitch?"

"Mitch? My name's Vin."

"Male-bitch." Adrenaline spreads through my body, overshadowing the soreness in my shoulder. I jump off the bed, prepared to strike.

Bryan steps in the middle of the warpath. I didn't hear him come in. The need to protect myself tunneled my vision.

I'm scooped up by Bryan, carried back to the bed, and dropped on my butt. He's in alpha mode.

I stand, in defiance.

Bryan blocks my path and glances over his shoulder. "Back off," he commands.

Vin takes two steps back.

I storm toward the bathroom.

"What the hell happened?" Bryan asks.

"I don't know..." The rest of Vin's sentence gets drowned out by the door slamming and the click of the lock engaging.

Stomping to the shower room, I leave a trail of pajamas. I blindly select options on the control panel and manage to shove my hair in the shower cap before hot water pours on me like a heavy rainfall from tiny clouds.

I reach for the body wash on the pedestal, pop the top open, and squeeze it until liquid soap oozes in my hand. Right away, the stench that provoked self-preservation is chased away by a more pleasant masculine scent.

Bryan's scent.

Adrenaline ceases to feed my anger. A sensual hunger flows through my veins. Using my thumb, I snap the rounded cap into place, tracing the circumference. The bottle drops from my hands. Essence of sandalwood, Tonka bean, and vanilla wrap around my body like a lover. Bryan's fingers emerge from the mist to slide down my neck. Cup my breasts. Seduce my nipples into hard, brown, sensitive buds.

His imagined fingers flow over the smooth surface of my stomach, spreading the seduction to the triangle of my thighs. One finger brushes that little sensitive nerve. Circling it. Enticing it. My clitoris pulsates with excitement.

Two mystical fingers reach the opening I've allowed only one man to enter. They slip inside. A slideshow plays through my mind as the sexual suspense builds in my body.

In. Out. Fingers slide.

Circle. Circle. A finger traces.

My head falls back. Steamy water drops rain thousands of tiny kisses upon my face and neck.

Close to release, my knees quake. I fall into the hardness of his body. The frosted glass protests as we bump it. I moan, loudly.

Right there. Oh yes, just a little more...

"Dammit! Dani, answer me!"

Pound!

Pound!

Pound!

Bryan's voice chases away the fantasy, breaking up the pleasure cloud. Why is he pounding on the door?

"Dani, are you okay? Unlock this fucking door before I fucking kick it in!"

Thump!

Thump!

The wood creaks in protest.

I whip off the shower cap and cautiously tiptoe across the tiled floor. I reach the door just as another *pound! thump!* Hits the door again. *Creak!* The wood protests louder.

The bathroom door swings open the second I disengage the lock. It ricochets off the wall but is forced to stay open by Bryan's hand. He rushes in with Vin following close behind.

I step back.

Concern and fear battle for dominance on his face. "Are you okay?"

Bryan grabs me, preventing my retreat.

I wince. He's squeezing my bruised shoulder.

"Yes." I squirm to loosen his rough hold.

"Did you fall? I heard a bump on the glass and you cried out. Are you hurt?" His eyes roam over me.

I can't tell him I was masturbating while thinking of him. "I bumped my shoulder on the shower wall. The shoulder you're squeezing."

"Why did you lock the door?"

"I apologize for worrying you. If you two will excuse me..." I'm dripping wet with a towel wrapped around me and two men assessing my alleged injury. Could this be any more embarrassing?

Bryan gestures with his head. Vin leaves, closing the door behind him.

"I want you to step out too." My focus stays on a small white button on his shirt.

"You don't get your preferences when I have to damn near break down the door to get to you."

"Again. I apologize for worrying you, Bryan."

His fingertips gently lift my chin. Most of the tension is gone from his face. "I thought something happened to you and I couldn't get to you fast enough."

Sincerity shines in his eyes. My soul is warmed by his actions.

"I really need to get dressed. Marie's waiting for me to help her in the kitchen."

Bryan steps back until he's leaning against the counter with his arms folded across his chest, feet crossed at the ankle.

He can't be serious. But the set of his shoulders, his body language. The look in his eyes. He's keeping an eye on me.

They say the truth is better than a lie. Let's hope they're right.

Eyes closed, I take a deep breath and whisper the embarrassing truth as I exhale. "I was thinking about you and pleasuring myself the moan you heard was from me about to… I bumped into the glass now please leave." Out of breath, my confession is fast. I hope he understood because I refuse to say it again.

There's a moment of charged silence. I stand in the middle of the bathroom with my eyes shut, waiting for the sound of the door closing behind him. Instead, I'm gripped at the waist and pulled forward into his body.

Bryan's lips go right to that spot behind my ear. My hold on the towel loosens. It drops to my feet as I wrap my arms around his neck.

His hands slide down my wet back to cup my butt, then lift me off my feet. My legs wrap around his waist. The wickedness of his tongue does things to my neck that makes my sex jealous. I'm floating.

The cool marble countertop welcomes the heated skin of my backside. Eyes open, I watch Bryan lower to his knees. From underneath those eyelashes, he questions me with his eyes, silently waiting for consent to proceed.

My legs drape over his shoulders.

Knees relax. My thighs part for him.

He leans in. His tongue slides along my sex.

One. Slow. Long. Lick.

Hypnotized by the sight, I clear my mind and just go with it.

Bryan licks me again. The tip of his tongue swipes the hood of my clitoris.

My stomach jumps.

"You taste like sunshine," he murmurs.

Bryan takes another slow, long lick. And I shake. My fingers tangle in his hair to speed along his pace. His tongue circles my clitoris again while a finger slips inside. My walls grip it. My hips rock, welcoming the feel.

"Did you come?"

"Nooo," I sing.

Mr. Tall-And-Sexy smiles, pulling me closer to the edge. "Do you want to come?" He slides a second finger inside while his tongue flicks my clitoris.

I jump. "Yes!"

"May I make you come?" he asks. Bryan's lips wrap around my nerve bud, tickling it with his tongue. My inner thighs tremble.

"Yes," I hiss. My body prepares for that moment when all else ceases to exist.

He pulls back, just enough where he's no longer pleasuring me, but close enough so I know the pleasure is near. "I need you to promise me something or else I can't make you come."

I part my thighs wider, a blatant invitation. The fervent need for sexual release is intense and I've lost all inhibitions.

He flashes that *sensual* smile. A small wave of anticipation adds to the building pressure of the big one.

"Promise you'll stop fighting my friend." *That* smile coupled with *that* vocal inflection causes a tremor from the imminent orgasm to roll through me.

Releasing his hair, my fingers drift to my palpitating bud.

Smack!

Bryan swats my hand away. "As much as I'd love to watch you play with yourself, I'm not letting you come until you promise not to fight Vin anymore."

I'm even more aroused.

"Please make me come."

Bryan gives my clitoris a butterfly kiss.

I shudder.

"Say the words."

"Please... please, Bryan. I can't... I need to..." I've lost the ability to complete a sentence.

"Tell me, Dani." His lips brush my sensitive nerve. "Say the words."

"I won't fight your friend anymore. *Please!*" My fingers grip the edge of the counter.

He seduces my passage with his fingers. His tongue dances over my clitoris. The pressure is liberated and I climax for several wonderful heartbeats. Bryan keeps me safely on the countertop.

The orgasmic aftershocks are just as pleasurable. I grab his hair, pulling him up. I have to kiss him. His lips meet mine. I need to kiss him. The taste on his tongue is naughty.

He breaks away and stands. A confident smile on his face. Bryan licks his fingers as he backs away. He picks up the towel off the floor and tosses it to me before walking to the door.

Mr. Tall-And-Sexy-Alpha-Male gives me a warning glance, points to the door lock, then leaves me alone in the bathroom.

I've got to get a handle on this thing with Vin. But I must admit, the consequences chased away the aches of years of celibacy.

Chapter Ten

CHILDREN AND ADULTS CROWD THE downstairs for Emma's birthday party. I help Marie keep food and juice boxes on the tables set up in the sitting room and help the face painter draw characters on children's faces in the family room. I use a stencil. I'm not an artist.

Circulating between the two rooms, I talk to parents and do my best to ignore the Three Horny Toads standing in a corner lusting after the man who pleasures me. I'm still on a sexual high. There's an extra bounce in my step.

"Don't overdo it," Bryan warns.

"I love doing this for Emma," I say, shifting a tray of juice boxes to avoid a collision with a boy not watching where he's going.

"Come—with me." Bryan's suggestive tone triggers a quiver that makes me squeeze my thighs together underneath this ankle-length skirt. "I want to introduce you to another friend."

He takes the tray from my hands, setting it on the table.

We walk over to the three well-dressed men standing off to the side in the family room.

"Danielle Edwards, this is Anthony Paul." He gestures to the man with a big, flirtatious smile on his face. "You've already met Ignacio Acosta and Vincenzo Ricci."

"Danielle." Anthony takes my hand.

"Hello." I shake his hand and let go. He doesn't. I tug against his hold. "How long have you guys known each other?"

"Second semester freshman year at CU," Anthony croons.

"Let me see if I can guess your college personalities." I look them over. "Ignacio, you were the innocent-faced ringleader." I yank my hand free. "Anthony, you were the sweet-talking peacemaker." I take a slight step closer to Bryan. "Mr. Hawk, you were the handsome-faced hustler." I place my hand on his muscled arm encased in a fitted lightweight sweater.

He changed for the party. "Vin, you were the mitch who started crap, but couldn't back it up without your friends."

"Ouch," Anthony laughs.

Ignacio claps his hands.

Vin stands up straight. "You can't kick my ass."

I know how to end his little macho attitude. I raise my right pinkie-finger waving it at Vin. "You're boring me."

Vin puffs out his chest. If it were possible, steam would be shooting out his ears.

Anthony steps closer to me. "Damn girl, you've got a pair on you. I don't know too many women who dare challenge Vin."

"Mom." Kourtney pats my arm. "Dylan Hill pulled my hair and messed it up." She holds her hair bow in one hand and points.

"Let's go upstairs and fix it." I lead her out of the family room. "I owe you a trip to the teddy bear store."

"You told me I couldn't hit him again."

"No, sweetie. You have perfect timing."

She gives me a strange look as we walk upstairs.

I grab the brush from the bathroom, and when I come back, she's sitting on the bed with Mr. Cuddles in her arms. Tears trail down her cheeks. I sit next to her.

"What's wrong, sweetie?"

"I'm tired of Dylan being mean to me."

"How's he being mean?"

"He pulls my hair. And sticks his tongue out at me all the time. And one time he pushed me."

"Did you do anything to him?"

"Not since that time I punched him in the stomach for hurting Emmy."

"Have you told Ms. Williamson?"

"Yes, but she said that's how second grade boys show they like girls."

"May I come in?" Bryan knocks and pokes his head around the open door. He comes in. "Kourt, don't cry. Do you want me to fix your hair?"

"No, thank you," she sniffs.

"I may not be as good as your mom and Marie, but I know how to comb hair." He takes the hairbrush from my hand, holding the end with the bristles, and runs the handle over her hair.

Kourtney doesn't laugh.

Bryan sections off her hair, twisting it into a ponytail. The tip of his tongue pokes out the corner of his mouth. He takes the hair tie, wrapping it around the end of the messy ponytail. Taking the hair bow from Kourtney's hand, he fastens it to the top of her head.

"There," he says.

I play along. "Not bad, Hawk."

"I still won't go back."

"That boy won't bother you anymore." Bryan sits on the bed drying her tears with his thumbs.

"How do you know?" she asks.

"I told him he'd have to deal with *me*."

"You did?" Her eyes fill with hope.

He nods. "I had a talk with his dad too."

"Thanks, Bryan." She climbs on her knees, throwing her arms around his neck, kissing his cheek. "You're the best."

The genuine smile on his face makes my heart flutter.

She wipes her eyes with a swipe of the back of her hand and bounces off the bed.

"Let your mom do your hair."

"You said it was perfect." She skips out of the room.

"Thank you. I was going to talk to Jennifer later." I walk toward the door, sensing him a step behind. His hands sneak out, closing it and trapping me between him and the bedroom door.

He narrows the gap between our bodies by pressing me into the cool, hard surface of the door, my back to his front.

My hair is swept to the side as his lips rain titillating kisses on the skin of my neck. His hands slide down the door, then move to my hips. The fabric of my skirt gathers in his hands.

"May I?" The tip of his tongue traces my ear.

The heat builds between my thighs. I moan and nod my consent.

"I need to hear you say it, Dani."

"Yes, you may, Bry."

My skirt rises to expose my thighs, and his expert hand slides inside the front of my panties, cupping me. I look over my shoulder at him and we share a private smile. My hips rock, mimicking the movement of his fingers. An awkward kiss stifles my sounds of pleasure against his lips.

"What's happening?!" My body wonders.

My brain replies, *"You've had two orgasms in one day!"*

I wobble to the bathroom to freshen up.

We leave the room, fingers intertwined, and rejoin the festivities.

"What happened to your face?" Madelyn croaks.

Makeup couldn't hide the bruise or the purple-and-green knot on my forehead.

"I bumped my head on his rock hard…" I pause. My hand runs down his chest, stopping explicitly low on his stomach. His muscles contract under my touch. Bryan leads me away, leaving the Toads to interpret that any way they please.

We join Tom and Max, standing by the window with their daughter, Penelope.

"Do you have a fever, Danikins, or is a Hawk making you hot?" Max presses the back of his hand to my forehead.

"Humm… I don't know what you're talking about." I lean away.

Max gives me duck lips and a quick head tilt. "Humph, you were fine *before* you went upstairs."

"Why are you standing here with your dads?" I ask Penelope.

She shrugs as her eyes cut to the three girls singing on the karaoke machine. I know I should take her over there because that's where she really wants to be, but it's too close to Max's all-seeing-eyes. I spot Kourtney and Emma on the giant Twister mat on the other side of the room.

I take Penelope's hand, tugging her away with me.

Chapter Eleven

ONCE THE GUESTS LEAVE AND the decorators restore the sitting room and family room, Bryan, Marie, the girls, and I sit at the kitchen table. After hostessing for five hours, my head is pounding. I need to go upstairs and pack so Kourtney and I can go home.

The doorbell rings and Bryan goes to answer it.

A few minutes later, footsteps echo down the hall.

"I have Emma's dress. I think she'll love it," a female's voice remarks. "Vinny said to bring sample dresses for a woman and child. He guessed at the sizes."

A middle-aged woman with dreadlocks and hair charms, steps into the kitchen ahead of Bryan, three garment bags draped over her arms.

"Jailynne, this is Danielle and Kourtney. I realize it's short notice…"

"Don't say another word," she interrupts him, shifting the garment bags to one arm. She motions for me to stand and turn in a circle. "I think we'll find the perfect dress to complement your beautiful skin tone and accentuate your figure."

I sense Bryan's eyes assessing me.

The woman turns to Kourtney. "You are a little princess. I have the perfect dress that will bring out those beautiful hazel eyes."

"Kourt, take Ms. Jailynne up to your room. Emm, help her pick a dress. Then you guys come to my room and help Dani pick one."

"That sounds like a plan." Jailynne follows the girls.

"Marie, Dani needs to take her pain meds. Do you have something she can eat right now?"

"I'm okay, Bryan." My protest lacks confidence.

"How about that stew you like?" Marie is already rising from her seat. "I'll warm some and bring it up. Go lie down, dear."

"Kourtney and I are supposed to go home tonight." Even as I say the words, my legs turn to rubber and I feel light-headed. Pinpoints of perspiration coat my forehead.

"One more night, Dani." Bryan moves closer.

My knees buckle and he catches me before I fall to the floor.

Lifting me in his arms, Bryan carries me out of the kitchen and upstairs without saying another word. I don't protest. I like being in his arms. He lowers me onto the bed and I settle with my back against the headboard. Bryan loosens the ankle straps of my wedge heels and slides them off my feet.

His fists and muscular arms support his upper body as he hovers over me. Frowning.

I reach out, using my fingertips to massage the lines between his brows. "How did you know?" I ask.

"When your head hurts, you squint those pretty brown eyes." His lips follow through with a tender peck on each eyelid. "When something's bothering you, your nostrils flare." A delicate peck from his lips touches the tip of my nose. "When you're angry, your lips tighten"—his lips linger on mine—"and you ball your fists." One by one Bryan brings my knuckles up to his lips. He comes closer. Cheek to cheek. Bryan whispers in my ears other things he knows about me.

I giggle and smile. The throbbing in my head becomes a faint pulse. He knows stuff James never took the time to figure out.

I wonder how long my marriage would have lasted if James were still alive. Although he didn't verbalize it, he was anxious about his deployment. And as his friend, I wanted to give him the security he'd always given me. We married on impulse.

James understood what it was like to not have family roots; that was the basis of our friendship. After high school, I went to college. He enlisted in the Army. Our friendship withstood the physical distance, but our relationship didn't. James changed. Gone was the jovial best friend I'd called my boyfriend. The man he became was—two-dimensional. Our dreams were no longer the same. I know now we never should have crossed the line of friendship, even in high school.

"Scoot forward," Bryan says, breaking my train of thought.

I move up and Bryan climbs onto the bed, sitting behind me. My hair is parted and swept over my shoulders. His thumbs draw tiny circles from the back of my neck to the base of my skull. I close my eyes, enjoying the gentle massage. Thoughts of my life with James are forced back into the box inside my mind.

The sound of Marie entering the room, without knocking, rouses me.

She sets the tray on the nightstand. Dishes clang together. The door closes behind her—hard.

Bryan moves from behind me, filling the space with pillows. "Comfortable?"

I nod.

He hands me the tray and perches on the edge of the bed. I look down at the mouth-watering bowl of chicken stew.

I lift a spoonful to my mouth. The next one is offered to him. He accepts.

"You know what would be good right now?" he asks.

I arch an eyebrow.

"Your red beans and rice."

"I'll make you some."

"Cabbage and hot water cornbread too?"

I nod, offering him a spoonful of stew.

The spoon alternates between his mouth and mine until we finish the bowl. I give him the last spoonful and reach for the medicine bottle.

Bryan sets the tray on the nightstand.

I want to move forward, but so much of the past keeps me from being impulsive again. He stares at me. The heartbreak is mutual, and our loneliness is mirrored.

Knock, knock, knock!

Jailynne and the girls walk through the door.

"Mommy. Wait till you see my blue princess dress."

Bryan stands as the girls climb onto the bed. Jailynne lays out the garment bags at the foot and unzips one.

"I'll get out of your way." Bryan leans down, kissing me until the girls giggle.

He pulls away and kisses Emma and Kourtney on the top of their heads before picking up the tray.

"Is Bryan your boyfriend?" Kourtney asks before the door closes behind him.

Unsure how to answer that question, I turn to Jailynne. "So… what do you have in mind for me?"

She pulls out several gowns. I take the first one into the bathroom. Kourtney's never seen me interact intimately with a man. I need to think of how I can explain this without giving away too much.

After trying on nine different dresses, we all agree on the emerald green one. Jailynne and the girls leave the room. In the center of the bed, I stack pillows behind me and lean back, closing my eyes with the intention of resting for only a minute.

My body is floating in a scented cloud of him, drifting in the direction of peace and comfort. A layer of warmth falls over me. I know he's here.

"Lie with me, please," I whisper, needing Bryan's arms around me.

"I thought you were asleep."

One by one, the thud of a heavy pair of shoes dropping to the floor momentarily interrupts the silence in the room.

The warm shield lifts, and Bryan's body slides in next to me.

"I was resting my eyes."

His body shakes from his laughter. "Is that what they call it when your eyes are closed, mouth wide open, and you're snoring?"

"I don't snore."

"My parents raised a gentleman. I won't record you next time and play it back in front of the girls in the morning."

I wiggle until I find a comfortable position. My head on his chest. Leg between his.

"Why didn't you answer Kourt's question?" he asks.

"You heard?"

His fingers slowly run through my hair. It relaxes me.

"Why did you kiss me in front of her?"

"She's seen you kiss a boyfriend or two."

"I'm not one of those single mothers who parade men in and out of my child's life. I don't sleep with every Tom, Dick, or Vinny."

Bryan chuckles. "You didn't answer my question," he points out. "Why didn't you answer Kourt?"

He caught that.

"How *do* we define us, Bryan? Is there an *us*?"

His cell phone rings and he leans away to answer it. "Hawk."

"Kimberly took the bait," someone shouts.

Who's Kimberly?

"Give me a minute." He ends the call, untangling his body from mine. I watch as he scoots to the edge of the bed to put his shoes back on. "Can we finish this conversation later?" he asks, tying the laces. "I need to take care of something."

I crawl to him, wrapping my arms around his shoulders and gently hug him. He stops for a moment. His hand squeezes mine.

"You and Kourt are here now. We can go as slow as you need. But I will kiss you in front of our girls, so come up with a definition for *us.*"

Chapter Twelve

KOURTNEY AND EMMA HOLD EACH other like they'll never see one another again. The two became close in their short time together.

"You girls will get to hang out during the break," I tell them.

"You promise, Mommy?"

"I promise." Over my heart, I draw a cross with my finger then she and I link pinkies. It's something Kourtney and I do to show we'll keep our word. I turn to Emma and kiss her cheek. "We'll see you later, sweetie." I hug Marie. "Thank you for taking care of us."

"You're welcome, dear. Call us if you need anything."

I make sure Kourtney buckles up in the back before climbing into the passenger seat. Willis reverses out of the driveway while Marie and Emma wave goodbye.

Kourtney cries the entire ride to our apartment. I have to admit I already miss being there too. The minute we walk through the door of our apartment, she runs to her room.

The place feels small after being in Bryan's home for three days. The house in Arizona wasn't as large as his, but it was big enough for the two of us. Here, we're tripping over each other. I've had to get creative with the limited space.

I'm happy to be home because my period started this morning. The first day is always the worst for me.

Kourtney sulks around most of the afternoon while I do laundry and clean. She straightens her room, works on the winter-break homework packet, and waters the plants. The only time she's this quiet is when something's bothering her.

Early evening, I find her lying on the bed, holding Mr. Cuddles.

"Are you ready to talk about what's on your mind?" I say from the doorway.

She shakes her head.

"Marie gave me a list of fun places to visit. How about you look them up and decide where you want to go?"

Kourtney frowns. "Okay."

"The list is sitting next to my laptop."

She drags herself out of bed.

Over dinner Kourtney hands me two sheets of paper. I unfold the first sheet. Smiley faces show her favorite destinations. "What's this?" I ask, waving the second sheet.

"It's for Santa. Can we mail it tomorrow?"

"Sure, but when did you start making a Christmas list?"

"It's not just mine." She pushes away from the table. "I'm done eating. May I go to my room?"

I nod and unfold the paper.

Emmy, Kourty and Penny's Christmas List. Item number one, a dog.

I take my cell phone off the charger to snap a picture of the list and send it to Bryan and Max, along with my vetoed items, the dog being first. Our apartment is too small for an animal.

The next morning, we leave early to explore Boulder and the surrounding cities, choosing not to use GPS. We get lost and find our way and get lost again. It turns out to be a good day.

"May I call Emmy?" Kourtney asks before I can get the door open.

"You may call her while I cook dinner."

"What's for dinner?"

I brace myself. She looks so much like her dad when she smiles like that. "What do you have a taste for?"

"Marie's chicken noodle soup," she giggles.

Lucky for me, I know my daughter and try to stay a step ahead. "Marie gave me a container of soup before we left yesterday."

Kourtney's lips tighten. She holds out her hand. "Can I call my best friend now?"

I hand her the phone and walk away patting myself on the back. There's also a container of chicken stew in the freezer too.

I do a victory dance while I warm up the soup, make sandwiches, and toss a salad.

On my way to the bathroom, I pass Kourtney's open door.

She's whispering. "He *is* my mom's boyfriend."

I knock on the door, pretending I didn't hear anything. "Dinner's ready. Tell Emma you'll call her tomorrow."

She and I need to have a conversation about my relationship with Bryan soon.

A few days pass. Bryan and Emma stop by and stay for dinner. If someone were to look through the window, they would think we were a family.

"Dad, can Kourty spend the night?"

"Yes, if it's okay with Dani."

"Please, Mommy. I miss Emmy."

The girls lean their heads together, poking out their bottom lips, batting their eyelashes to plead their case.

"Yes, you can spend the night. Go pack your bag." I couldn't say no.

"Come help me, Emmy." The girls jump up from the table.

"Wait," I tell them.

Using my napkin, I wipe spaghetti sauce from the corners of Emma's mouth.

They run to Kourtney's room.

"Don't forget your toothbrush," I say.

Bryan helps me clear the table.

"Let's go out for drinks."

"What about the girls?"

"We've earned a grownup's night out. Marie will watch them. Let me take you out, Dani."

"Give me twenty minutes to change."

"Take your time. I got this." He gestures to the dishes in the sink and the pots on the stove top.

I head to the bathroom to freshen up, then dash across the hall with a towel wrapped around me.

Bryan and the girls are in the living room with the television turned up loud, laughing at whoever's on the screen.

Rummaging through my underwear drawer, I choose a gray lace thong with a matching bra. In my cramped closet, my hand touches the hanger holding a grape-colored jumpsuit, but the peacock blue knit sweater dress catches my eye. I take it off the hanger and match it with gray, high-heeled boots.

From my jewelry box, I select platinum hoop earrings.

I pull my hair into a messy bun. The bruise on my cheek is fading, but the one on my forehead is still purple and blue. I cover them with makeup and add a clear gloss to my lips. Releasing my hair from the bun, I run the flatiron over it.

Smiling at the image in the full-length mirror, I admire what I see. Max coaxed me into buying this dress the day we went shopping on my lunch hour.

I grab my purse and turn off the light in my room, the bathroom, and Kourtney's room. No one notices me standing in the living room until I pick up the remote and turn off the television.

"Wow, Mom. You look beautiful."

I smile toward my daughter, but my eyes stay on Bryan. The gleam in his eyes says it all.

The girls chat in the backseat of Bryan's Chevy Silverado. I watch the scenery as we pass by, and a sense of melancholy drifts through me. He reaches over to take my hand.

"What are you thinking about?" he asks.

"Kourtney's never wanted to spend the night at a friend's house." I glance back at her. It occurs to me: Mr. Cuddles isn't with her. "I'm happy she has Emma, but I wasn't expecting to feel gloomy."

Bryan kisses the back of my hand without taking his eyes off the road.

Marie is waiting for us when we pull into the driveway. I hug the girls and remind them to behave.

Bryan pulls out of the driveway onto the street. In the side-view mirror, I glimpse Kourtney and Emma jump and high-five each other. Bryan laughs. He's looking in the rearview mirror.

He takes me to a popular club in the heart of Boulder's nightlife. Bryan orders a beer. I order a Midori Sour.

A comfortable silence descends upon us and we listen to the band play. I like all kinds of music except for hard rock, heavy metal, and gangster rap. People are moving and shaking on the dance floor. The tables in the club are filled. It's busy for a weeknight.

Curiosity gets the best of me and I have to ask him. "Did you sleep with any of the Horny Toads?"

"Horny Toads?"

"Those three moms who fall all over you."

"Hell no! I don't fuck other men's wives." The squint of disgust clouds his eyes. "Why would you ask me that?"

"I'm not trying to offend you. It's just that our friendship bothers them."

A sly smile now crosses his face. He reaches for my hand, playing with my fingers. "So that's what we're calling it? Friends?"

I return the smile, intertwining our fingers. "Do you date?"

"Are you asking if I dated as in long term relationships or if I dated as in no strings attached?" He brings our fingers up to his lips.

"Both." My heart pounds as hard as the drummer is beating his drums. "I'm asking both."

"Mostly, I did the no-strings-attached thing. I've taken women out, but they knew what was happening at the end of the night. I've had a friends-with-benefits relationship, too."

My hand pulls away. *Is that what this is?*

"Which relationship do you prefer?" I ask.

"It depends on the woman."

"Do you believe in monogamy?"

Bryan takes a long swallow from his beer bottle. He looks me in the eyes. "Yes, but I haven't always practiced it. I didn't lie to women I've dated. I told them upfront where they stood with me."

I drink down half my Midori Sour. I guess I wasn't expecting him to be so forthcoming. "How long was your last relationship?"

Someone slaps Bryan's shoulder. He turns around glaring. "What are you doing here, Tony?"

"I'm having drinks with two deputies. Hello, Danielle, it's nice to see you again. May we join you?" He waves two people over.

"Do you mind?" Bryan frowns.

"First round's on me," Anthony offers, gesturing with his hands. "What are you two drinking?"

Alpha Male rumbles his reply, but his eyes search the club.

"Can I get a shot of Absolute too?" I ask.

Bryan cocks an eyebrow at me.

I shrug while I answer, "Kid-free tonight."

Bryan's lips turn up in *that* smile. "Shot of Absolute for the lady."

I scoot my chair closer to him, making room for the intruders. His arm hangs over the back of my chair. His casual body language is contagious. I relax as well.

Anthony returns with our drinks and introduces everyone. Bryan takes my drinks from his friend and sets them on a napkin in front of me.

"What are you doing in a club on a work night, Mr. Hawk?" Anthony takes the empty seat across from Bryan

"Having drinks and enjoying the music. Why aren't *you* guys on duty?"

"Got a call about a yummy mummy being harassed by a dirty old man." He lifts his beer bottle and salutes his friend.

"If you're on duty, you don't need this." Bryan snatches the bottle before it touches Anthony's lips. "Fast hands for a dirty old man."

"He has to make up for his other deficiencies," Anthony whispers for everyone to hear.

"No deficiencies here." Bryan holds up his hand pointing to the index and ring fingers.

I laugh along with the guys, getting the joke. Rumor has it, if a man's ring finger is longer than his index finger, he has a long penis.

"Old wives' tale." Anthony grabs for the bottle. Bryan moves it out of reach.

I toss back the vodka from the shot glass, not giving the liquor time to sit on my tongue. It slides down my throat. I take a long drink of the Midori Sour as a chaser.

The antics at the table stop.

Bryan's eyebrows meet his hairline. He shifts in his chair. "Do you want another?" he asks, his voice deep and sensual.

"No, thank you." I watch him watching me. "One is my limit."

"Don't be a lightweight." Ernesto motions to the waitress passing by. "Can we get another shot of Absolute?"

"The lady said one is her limit." The tone of Bryan's voice makes the atmosphere drop to minus twenty degrees at the table. The casual body language now a façade. Alpha Male is ready to attack. I glimpse the retreating back of the waitress.

I squeeze Bryan's thigh, hoping to calm him.

"What part of law enforcement are you in?" I turn to Anthony. He too looks ready to pounce.

"Sheriff's department," Valerie answers and elaborates on her background until the friendly conversation around the table resumes, but the banter seems forced.

The band starts to play '80s music.

"Come on, Danielle. Let's hit the dance floor and show these people how to move." Valerie sways in her seat.

I want Bryan to take me to the dance floor. Instead, he asks if I'm ready to leave, which I'm not.

Once the band takes a break, and the DJ takes over, Valerie and I make our way to the crowded floor. Since our date got interrupted, I want to dance for the rest of the night.

It's been a while since I've been to a club. James never wanted to hang out with me and people from my study group after finals. He'd mope around the apartment as I got dressed. He'd remind me to not accept drinks unless I watched the bartender pour it. He never said have fun. Instead he'd compliment me on how I looked, tell me don't let random strangers dance all up on me, and not spend any money unless it was an emergency.

When Ernesto shows up on the dance floor, I chance a quick glance over my shoulder. Bryan and Anthony have their heads together in what appears to be a deep conversation. The song is an up-tempo beat and I keep my movements tame and the distance between Ernesto and me friendly. Valerie's dancing with a man whose height puts him at her boob level.

The song morphs into a Michael Jackson song. It's like the DJ played it just for me. I get into my groove and turn my back on Ernesto to face Bryan.

Bryan looks up. Our eyes connect. My movements losing some inhibitions, I dance and lip-sync the words to him."

He sits up. Watching me. A sexy smile spreads across his face. His gaze doesn't leave mine, even when his friend leaves him at the table alone.

Anthony two-steps to the dance floor, then dances with a woman near me.

I wink at Bryan and turn back to the dance floor.

The smile on Anthony's dance partner's face and come-hither look is all the encouragement he needs to gyrate on her butt.

The DJ mixes in a reggae beat. Closing my eyes. I rock my hips side to side. And imagine Bryan on the dance floor with me.

Opening my eyes, I turn to face him. Pleading with him, through body movements, to join me. Bryan rises out of the seat like he's hypnotized. He steps onto the dance floor, wading through the other dancers. His eyes never leave mine.

When he reaches me, he hesitates, looking unsure of what to do next. I take his hands and place them on my hips.

"Dancing is like having sex, but on the dance floor." I whisper in his ear until he rocks with me, catching the rhythm. I turn around, my back to his front.

We stay on the dance floor for the rest of the night rocking and grinding on each other. *Having sex on the dance floor.*

★★★

We have a holiday tradition of buying our tree seven days before Christmas, and this year is no different. After I pick her up from Bryan's house, Kourtney and I go to the mall to do a little shopping, then stop at a nearby lot to get a small tree.

We return to our apartment late in the evening. She's fallen asleep. I rouse her and help her climb out of the truck.

She yawns and stretches and stumbles a bit. "What about the tree?"

"I'll come back and get it." I grab our shopping bags.

"Can you carry it by yourself?" Her feet drag as she walks toward the stairs.

"It's not heavy," I tell her.

When we get to the last step, I notice our front door is cracked open. I drop the bags, pick up Kourtney, and run down the stairs to the truck.

"What's wrong, Mommy? Why is the door open?"

Fueled by anger, I make an impulsive decision.

"Here, baby." I set the timer for ten minutes and hand her my phone. "If I'm not back when the alarm goes off, call 911. Don't unlock the doors or get out of the truck until I come get you. Do you understand?"

"Yes, Mommy." Tears pool in her eyes.

I go to the back of my truck and pull out a baseball bat before handing her the keys. "Lock the doors and don't open them for anyone." I give her a kiss on the cheek, then close the door. The alarm activates.

I jog back to the apartment building and up the stairs. Using the tip of the bat, I push the door open and step into the living room. I flip the light switch.

Nothing happens.

I give my eyes a second to adjust to the darkness, then move around the living room with the bat in position, ready to swing at the first thing moving.

It takes only a minute to search the kitchen and dining room.

My feet kick or step on things scattered around the floor. I don't have time to ponder what they are. In a few minutes, Kourtney's calling for help.

I make my way down the dark hall to the bathroom at the end of the hallway. I use the bat like an arm to search it as best I can with no lights.

In my room, I search the closet and underneath the bed. In Kourtney's room, I do the same.

On my way out of her room, I relax the bat at my side. But it's too soon. The bat is knocked out of my hand at the same time someone jumps me from behind. My attacker covers my mouth and nose with something wet and soft.

I rush backward, slamming us into the wall.

She grunts.

I reach behind me until my fingers tighten around hair. I pull as hard as I can as darkness consumes me.

Bryan's Interlude

WHILE I WAIT FOR THE satellite image to load, I think about last night. Dani and I went back to her apartment. Normally I take the lead, but there's something about her that stops me from doing what I'm trained to do. Rules and protocol fly out the window. I want her to decide when we have sex. She's still guarded, understandably so. But it was a turn-on to watch her struggle to maintain control as we dry-humped like teenagers. She's different from the more experienced women I've been assigned to extract information from.

I left her apartment at two in the morning, hard and frustrated, with the smell of her all over me.

Too bad my shadow showed up at the club, prompting Tony, Ramirez, and Summers to back me up. I was unarmed and had given Porter and Mitchells the night off. I have to hand it to my team; Dani had no idea something was wrong.

My shadow's getting bold with her stalking. Her curiosity draws unnecessary attention. I'm surprised Dani didn't see through her act at Back to School Night. I'll have to put a stop to it soon. Yes, my relationship with Dani and Kourt is different, but she need not know that.

The satellite image finally finishes. My jaw tightens. I stare at the monitor.

"You're cold you bastard. Dani's not in North Carolina and I'll keep you hunting until *I'm* ready for you to find her," I say to Edwards's image.

He landed in Canada over a week ago and is back on American soil. Thanks to Kimberly's obliviousness, now I'm able to track his every move. I breathe a little easier.

If he'd gotten to Dani and Kourt before me, things would've escalated and my daughter would be a pawn to use against Phantom.

Every move Edwards makes mirrors traitors seen in a Hollywood movie or television show. I know Dani has what I'm looking for. She just doesn't know it.

We've searched the apartment in Arizona and the house she bought once they moved in. Sweepers searched the apartment here in Colorado. We're looking for anything that opens the disk drive on Edwards's laptop.

The stolen top-secret information isn't stored on the hard drive, and without access to the driver, I can't figure out the external hard-drive he used. Edwards built that dinosaur laptop with nonworking USB ports and no button to open the driver. For eight years, I tried everything in my arsenal to bypass the last security block. I'm stuck.

My cell phone rings. "Hawk," I answer without checking caller ID.

"At twenty-one hundred hours a 911 call from Kourtney Edwards was received and broadcast over the sheriff radio. She said they got home and their front door was opened. I've been unable to communicate with Corporal Dial. Sweepers ETA six minutes. Phantom's Sheriff Units are en route. I'm ten minutes out," Lieutenant Colonel Anthony Paul reports.

The background noise of the wailing siren emphasizes his words and triggers the urgency for me to get to Danielle and Kourtney—quick.

"I'm on my way. Locate Corporal Dial. Instruct him to have his ass in my office at zero six hundred hours or I'll put a bullet in his fucking head."

I thought I'd made it clear to every Ghost, stupid mistakes will not be tolerated. U.S. Phantom Military is a global success because we are trained to pay attention to every detail.

This assignment is too personal to leave it in the hands of incompetence. I fight horrific visions of my girls' lifeless bodies lying somewhere dark and bare.

Squashing the panic that threatens to take over, I open my desk drawer, pull out my firearm and holster, grab my keys and cell phones, and I'm out my office door.

"Bravo. Hotel. Four. Charlie. Two," I shout before closing the door. Everything in my office shuts down and arms itself.

"Riley, alert Major Ricci to an emergency call. Rendezvous at Kalmia Avenue."

Porter rushes toward the elevator. The doors close before he reaches it. I'll make sure Paul doesn't hurt him. I can't wait.

"Roger that, sir. What floor would you like?" Riley asks.

"Garage."

I slip my arms through the holster straps.

Disengage the magazine.

Check the ammunition; slap it back in place.

Take the safety off.

Rack the slide.

My gun is hot.

I holster my weapon.

Inhale.

Exhale.

I say a prayer, bolting through the elevator doors the minute they slide open. I press the button on the key fob. The Camaro's engine thunders and the driver's door opens.

The wheels spin on the concrete as I accelerate out of the parking garage.

I ignore traffic laws and whip through the streets of downtown Boulder. Being pulled over is the least of my worries. Our vehicles have specialized government plates.

My building is fifteen minutes from Danielle and Kourtney. I need to get to them in *five*.

My military cell phone syncs to the car's audio sound system. "Call Lieutenant Colonel Paul," I command.

The sound of his phone ringing bellows through the speakers.

"I'm four minutes out. The Sweepers are on the scene and one Phantom Sheriff's unit," Paul reports.

"Danielle and Kourtney?" I ask, crossing the double-yellow lines to get around stopped traffic.

"Summers doesn't see anyone. Sweepers are combing the area. Give them a minute."

"They may not have a minute. Corporal Dial is supposed to watch them when they're in that damn apartment. There should *not* have been a fucking emergency call." My fingers tighten around the steering wheel, my car crossing back over the double-yellow lines.

"Bry, I feel you. I will *not* let anything happen to them. What are you driving?"

"Camaro."

"Any available units near Sixteenth and Pearl. Sheriff's escort needed to Kalmia Avenue for a two, zero, one, three, silver-gray Chevy Camaro. License plate Bravo. Hotel. Alpha. Whiskey. Kilo. Zero. Four," Paul announces over the sheriff's radio.

I push the Camaro through a yellow light that's about to turn red.

A Boulder County Sheriff's unit pulls alongside of me when I cross Nineteenth Street. We acknowledge one another, then he falls behind.

Up ahead another sheriff's unit waits in the intersection while blocking traffic.

"Any communication with that corporal?" I ask.

"Negative. Corporal Dial's not at his post."

"Death is the only excuse he gets for neglecting his duties."

"I'm here. Kourtney's in the back of the Range Rover. Corporal Summers is trying to get her to open the door. Danielle went into the apartment with a baseball bat."

"Locate her." I disconnect the call and sync my personal cell phone. "Riley, connect Dani's phone."

"Hel-lo?" she stutters, answering on the first ring.

"Kourt, I'm on my way. Don't be afraid. My friends are there to help you. Do you see Tony?"

"Yes."

"Do you see Vin?"

"He's getting out of his truck."

"You can open the door for one of them."

"Mommy said I can't until she comes back," she cries harder. "I'm scared."

"Don't cry, baby girl. I'm coming. Stay on the phone with me."

To keep her calm, I hum an old lullaby.

When I make a right onto Kalmia and park, I scan the area with my eyes while running in the direction of the white Range Rover with a Christmas tree tied to the roof.

Bystanders gathering in front of other apartment buildings. Neighbors looking out their windows. Two Boulder County Sheriff Units blocking off the street. Three Phantom Sheriff Units in front of the building, emergency lights flashing. Two black Phantom Suburban trucks inconspicuously parked, one on each corner. Major Vincenzo Ricci's Suburban parked in the middle of the street.

Sandwiching my phone between my shoulder and ear, I draw my weapon, put the safety on and holster it again.

I tap the back window. Kourt's lying on the backseat. She looks up and my heart drops. Her fear punches me in the gut. I'm doing a piss-poor job of protecting them.

"Unlock the doors, Kourt," I say into the phone. "I'll take the blame."

The car alarm deactivates. I open the door. She jumps into my arms and buries her face in my neck.

"Are you hurt?" I ask.

Her body shakes. I can feel her rapid heartbeat against my chest.

Major Ricci comes toward us. His face is serious. This can't be good. I put Kourtney on her feet and spot a pair of ear buds on the floor of the truck. "Listen to music while I talk to Uncle Vinny."

Quickly plugging her ears, I connect the cord to my phone, press the kid's music app, and turn up the volume. I keep a protective arm around her.

"The intruder parked three blocks down, near the park, and dropped this." He holds up a picture of Danielle and Edwards on their wedding day. "Corporal Dial's body was found by the Sweepers."

"Danielle?" I ask.

"Unconscious in the apartment."

Fuck! The move from Arizona was clean. I personally made sure of it. I sent decoys to Oklahoma and Nevada. And I planted fake, searchable information on the internet linking her to Tennessee and North Carolina.

I scan the area again. This time I spot my shadow parking where she thinks she can't be seen.

"I want a conference call with Captain Valentine and Major Chen, tonight. Interview the Watcher on duty."

I pass Kourtney to him. She pulls away, leaping back into my arms, snatching out the ear buds. "Baby girl, I need to help mom. Go with Uncle Vinny, please."

She shakes her head, burying her face in my neck again. "I'll stay in the truck and wait for you guys."

"I need to know you're safe. I can't help mom and worry about you too. Please go with Vin." I nod for him to take her.

She screams and fights against him, landing a solid heel kick in his upper thigh. He shifts his legs to block the heel headed toward his package and adjusts his hold on her to keep from getting put out of commission.

"Take her to my house. Have Summers tail you. Stay until I get there," I yell over Kourtney's screams of protest.

Running to the apartment building, I step over scattered shopping bags and stuff as I climb the stairs.

Phantom Security Team, dressed in Sheriff Deputy uniforms, aim flashlights toward Kourtney's room.

Paul is bent over a motionless Danielle. I drop to my knees beside her.

"Is she okay?" I ask. She's on her stomach with one arm tucked underneath.

"She's breathing. No visual head trauma. And I don't see blood. I called

Acosta."

I look up at the two corporals. "Why aren't the lights on?"

"All the light bulbs have been removed," Ramirez replies.

I take the flashlight from the corporal and use it to find my way to the kitchen. Pulling out my handkerchief, I open the drawer where I know the spare light bulbs are kept.

"Is she still unresponsive?" Major Ignacio Acosta Jr walks through the door carrying a medical kit and a flashlight.

I screw in a bulb and turn on the lamp closest to where Danielle lies on the carpet.

"Sir, look at this." Corporal Ramirez points to a cloth on the floor just inside the door.

Paul stands, pulling a pen out of his shirt pocket and uses it to pick up the cloth.

Acosta examines Danielle.

"Chloroform." Paul sniffs the cloth again.

"She put up a fight," Acosta says, pointing to her hand. He's turned Danielle onto her back. Her fist is full of blond hair.

I grab an evidence kit from Acosta's bag.

"Where's Kourtney?" Acosta asks, as he continues to examine Danielle.

"Ricci's taking her to my house. I checked her; she's fine."

"Corporal Dial is dead." Paul puts on gloves and opens the small plastic bag for me.

I drop hair samples inside. "He left his post before calling it in. I want to know why."

"I'll have Sweepers in here after you guys leave." Paul seals the bag and opens another.

"Put Porter on Danielle's detail." I swab underneath her fingernails.

"Roger that, Colonel." Paul seals the bag after I drop the cotton swab inside.

I run a lint roller up and down her body and drop it in the bag Paul is holding open.

Acosta takes out an ammonia capsule. "Are you moving her again?"

I shake my head. "We'll view the footage from the cameras later, but until we know who was in here, Dani and Kourt are staying with me. I'm sending you two on a recon mission in North Carolina. Riley will contact you with the details. Ricci and I will pull double duty with Delta Team as backup. Debrief when you get back."

Paul collects the evidence bags and drops them in Acosta's medical bag.

I lift Danielle off the floor, carrying her to the sofa. Acosta cracks open the capsule and waves it under her nose.

Chapter Thirteen

THE STRONG SMELL OF AMMONIA burns my nose. Turning my head away from the offending scent, I open my eyes.

"What the hell were you thinking, coming in here with a damn baseball bat, Danielle?" Bryan shouts.

He called me Danielle. He's mad.

I'm on the sofa in Bryan's arms, and he's visibly trying to curb his anger.

"Is Kourtney okay?" I ask.

"Why didn't you wait in the truck with her? Or just drive straight to the house?"

"Where is she?" I try to sit up. He pins me with his arms.

"She's fine. Vin's taking her to the house." He cups my cheek in the palm of his hand. "You have *me* now. And my friends. You don't have to do everything yourself."

I glance at the people crowding my tiny living room. Anthony in his uniform and two deputies standing beside him. Ignacio's still wearing hospital scrubs.

I sigh in defeat.

"Danielle, I need to take a report. Are you up for that?" Anthony perches on the love seat, pulling a black leather notepad and pen from his breast pocket. The radio attached to his vest crackles. He lowers the volume.

Nodding, I slide off Bryan's lap and hold his hand. I try not to look around at the mess in my living room that Ernesto is photographing.

Ignacio hands me a glass of cold water and says he'll be back.

I take small sips while Anthony's pen moves over the paper of the notepad. I try to give as much details as I can remember.

When Ignacio returns, he's carrying the shopping bags I dropped and a brown paper bag from a twenty-four-hour pharmacy store nearby. I watch him unload packs of light bulbs. Bryan tells him where the step stool is stored.

Ignacio restores light in the living room first, then the kitchen and dining room. He takes the step stool and light bulbs down the hallway, the deputy following him.

Okay, I admit to myself, I took a thoughtless risk. But in my defense, I've been independent for far too long. Sitting back waiting for someone to come to my rescue was a thing of the past the minute my foster father put a pair of boxing gloves on my hands. My independence was a constant thorn in James's side.

Anthony rises from his seat. He's finished questioning me. They leave my apartment.

I walk around the living room. My foot kicks a broken picture frame. I bend and pick it up off the floor. It's a picture of me holding Kourtney the day I brought her home from the hospital. The sight becomes blurry.

Bryan wraps his arms around me, letting me cry. Sobs make my body convulse.

I feel vulnerable. Something I haven't felt in a long time.

I feel violated. Something I've never felt.

I feel safe wrapped in Bryan's arms. Something I've been combatting since our paths crossed in that classroom. And I'm tired of denying how much I've yearned for him to comfort me.

"Come back to the house with me. I want you guys to stay with us for a while. We'll come back tomorrow, clean up, and make a list of what's missing."

My shoulders drop as I walk to my room. I scrummage through the mess and find a change of clothes to pack, then go across the hall to Kourtney's room. The intruder didn't touch her room, which brings me some peace of mind.

Bryan waits for me in the living room. The whispered fury in his voice lets me know the person on the other end of that phone call is being chewed out. He disconnects the call when I walk into the room. He takes the bags from me and I follow him out the door. He locks it behind us.

Bryan leads the way down the stairs to my Range Rover. His head moves left to right like he's looking for someone. The neighborhood is quiet except for the bark of a few dogs and a car pulling into the carport across the street. A handful of neighbors stand in the walkway of their apartment building staring our way.

I point to the Christmas tree tied to the roof of my truck. "What should I do with that?"

Bryan opens the back door of my truck. "We'll find somewhere for it."

He tosses the bags onto the seat. "I'll follow you." He's frowning. Something is troubling him.

I rise on my tiptoes and kiss his cheek. "You look good in glasses."

He wraps his arms around my shoulders. Although he chuckles, his body remains rigid.

I embrace him around his waist. "Thank you for coming to our rescue."

His lips peck the crown of my head.

I squeeze him tight and something hard presses into my arm. "What's this?" I step back and lift his left arm. The black holster and the back end of a gun illuminate the seriousness of my actions tonight. I take in his appearance. "Why are you carrying a gun?"

"It's late. Let's go." He hands me the keys to my truck.

I take a page from his book and raise an eyebrow. An unspoken question.

"I'll do whatever I have to—to protect you and Kourt." He holds the door open for me to get in. Discussion over.

In the rearview mirror, my eyes follow him to a shiny Camaro. He has the Suburban, the Silverado, and a Camaro. Bryan must have a thing for Chevy.

We drive down the street, leaving the looky-loos behind. The Camaro's headlights shine bright in my rearview mirror. He stays on my bumper the entire drive to his house.

I go straight inside and let him and Willis worry about the tree.

I head upstairs to check on my daughter.

Kourtney's on her side with her arms around the pillow. Eyes puffy and her nose red. We'll talk about what happened in the morning. I kiss her cheek, lay Mr. Cuddles by her side, turn off the lamp, and leave her bag on the dresser on my way out the door.

Across the hall I check on Emma.

Her lamp is still on too. She fell asleep with a book in her hand. I mark the page and set the book on the nightstand. I kiss her cheek and turn off the lamp.

My feet drag as I shuffle to the other side of the house. Bryan is pacing the floor with his phone in his hand when I walk through the open door. He set my overnight bag on the foot of the bed.

"Whoever broke in was searching for something." His phone is on speaker, and its Vin's voice I hear.

Bryan watches me. "I'll call you back." He pockets his phone. "Don't be mad at Kourt. I wanted to make sure she wasn't hurt and to get her away from there. That's why she unlocked the doors."

"She trusts you, as she should."

"I'm going downstairs to my office." He turns and leaves, no further discussion.

The beeping of a truck backing up and loud voices of men shouting wake me the next morning. I'm still in my clothes and alone in the room. Bryan's side of the bed is undisturbed.

After a hot shower, I patter down to the kitchen.

"Good morning," Willis shouts over the noise of drills and hammers. He pours coffee into the cup in his hand.

"What's all that?" I motion in the direction of the sounds coming from outside.

"They're getting ready for the party tomorrow night."

Marie steps out of the laundry room with a basket of towels. "You couldn't sleep in either?" she shouts, that Southern drawl making her words sound like a song. "Would you like breakfast?"

"I'll find something."

"Don't argue with her, you won't win," Willis shouts before walking out the kitchen.

"Sit. I made French toast." Marie sets the laundry basket on the counter.

The faint sounds of giddy giggles from two girls running toward the kitchen drown out the noise outside. Kourtney has the biggest smile on her face when she passes through the doorway. Emma hugs me with one arm.

"How did you sleep?" I ask.

"Like a baby," they shout together, tickling each other, struggling to do so with shopping bags in their hands.

"You guys went shopping this morning?"

"We're giving each other manis and pedis for the party tomorrow. Bryan took us shopping."

"Four shopping bags worth?"

Bryan walks into the kitchen. He winks at the girls on his way to the sink.

Marie sets a plate and bowl of fruit in front of me.

"Danielle, can we do your nails when you're done eating?" Emma asks.

"Sure. Where do you want to do it?"

"The family room," she says as they run out of the kitchen.

"Don't come until we call you, Mom," Kourtney yells.

Bryan sits next to me, plucking a grape out of my fruit bowl with his fingers. "I cleared my schedule. We can go to your apartment anytime you're ready."

He's a little more relaxed this morning.

"What are the girls up to? Emma got a manicure kit for her birthday."

He bites the fruit. "I've been sworn to secrecy and you know I'm a man of my word." He leans over to kiss me, then slips the grape-half into my mouth with his finger.

Marie leaves the kitchen, forgetting the basket, her words muted by the sounds of construction.

"Where did you sleep?" I ask.

"Did you miss me?"

I pick up a melon cube with my fingers, flicking it with the tip of my tongue. "Nope." I lick the tasty, ripe fruit. One. Slow. Long. Lick. Gazing into his eyes. Painting on a sexy smirk, I wrap my lips around the square and suck.

Bryan shifts in his seat and bites his lip.

Bryan three. Danielle one.

I pick up another piece; he captures my wrist in his hand. He takes the green cube from my fingers with his teeth. I lean toward him and bite the half poking out from his lips. Juice runs down his chin. I stop the flow with my tongue, feeling the rough stubble of hairs on his chin.

He shudders.

Who knew finding creative ways to eat breakfast could be a turn-on? I don't think I'll ever be able to eat honeydew melon, cantaloupe, and red grapes without getting aroused. Don't even get me started on the syrup-covered French toast. The knife and fork go untouched.

"Danielle," Emma calls.

"I guess they're ready for me. Are you coming?"

Bryan looks at his crotch, then at me and shakes his head.

I take my dishes to the sink, rinse them, and put them in the dishwasher.

"Now we're even." I kiss his cheek on my way out of the kitchen. I float down the hallway, triumphant. When I walk into the family room, the girls are standing in front of a tall Christmas tree, the top third sparse of decorations.

"They got their Christmas tree yesterday too," Kourtney says.

"What did you do with the tree I bought?"

Emma points. "Look out the window."

The small tree is decorated and sitting in the yard, its base covered in snow.

"We decorated that one, too," Emma sings.

"Mom. Are we really staying for the holidays?"

"Yes, we are."

"You promise?" She crosses her heart with her finger then holds up her pinkie.

I cross my heart too and link my pinkie with hers.

The girls go back and forth whispering in each other's ear until Kourtney nods.

"Mom? Isn't Bryan your boyfriend?"

Unprepared to answer her question, I change the subject. "How about I help you guys finish decorating the tree and afterwards, we do our nails?"

Bryan enters the room carrying a stepladder.

While we finish the tree, Bryan and I talk to Kourtney about the break-in. She's afraid to be in the apartment. Bryan assures her we can stay here as long as we need. He will not let us go back until he makes it safe for us to be there.

Once the tree is finished, I cover the coffee table with old newspaper and teach them how to pamper their hands and feet. Bryan sits on the sofa snapping photos of us on his phone.

I'm not a fan of young girls wearing colored nail polish on their fingers so I coat their nails with a clear polish and let them go crazy with colors on their toes. The shoes they're wearing are closed-toe.

Bryan and I pick up lunch on our way to my apartment. Vin left a note on top of a bundle of unassembled moving boxes and a box of industrial strength trash bags by the door.

We spend a comfortable afternoon finishing our conversation from the other night while we clean up. I pack my important, irreplaceable items including my portable safe to take back to his house.

After I confirm nothing's missing, we load up his Silverado and head back.

During dinner, Bryan receives a phone call and storms out of the house.

I'm holding a dirt-covered shovel as I stand over the hole disturbing the beautiful green grass. It's a warm spring day and I'm alone in the military cemetery in Arizona.

The shovel drops from my grasp. I pull at the wedding ring stuck on my finger, with tears of regret and pain making trails through the patches of dirt on my face. I tug harder. It won't budge.

Bryan appears at my side. He smiles, and not just any smile, it's that same mischievous smile his daughter is known to give when she's up to no good.

Lifting my hand, his lips close over my fingertip. They inch up my ring finger until it disappears in his mouth. His textured, wet tongue swirls, making every part of my body want the same attention.

Bryan's lips relax as his teeth grip the ring. I slowly retract my finger. The weight that's been anchoring me is gone. I'm light. I'm free.

We lace our fingers to keep me from floating away.

Bryan lets the ring fall from his mouth.

In ultra-slow motion, the band flips over and over, the sun's light reflecting off the gold. It falls into the hole.

Cling! The ring bounces onto James's shiny mahogany casket.

Ding! The ring bounces again. It's the sound of the bell at the start of a boxing match.

Ping! The casket's lid flies open. James's angry gaze fixates on me. His lips move, but no words are spoken. His arm rises, a gun pointed at my chest. A flash of fire and smoke shoots from the muzzle. Bryan pulls me into his arms.

My eyes fly open. I'm clutching my chest. My whole body shakes as my mind replays the dream.

Crickets call out to each other, and an owl hoots from somewhere in the wooded area. The sound of an unfamiliar nocturnal animal echoes in the night.

Bryan mumbles and rolls over onto his side, facing me. He's asleep. The room is cast in shadows from the moonlight piercing through the glass doors, but I can see him. His face is relaxed and those long eyelashes are at rest. His lips are parted and he's breathing through his mouth. The covers lie around his waist. He's shirtless.

I scoot closer to him, resting my head on his pillow. I know I shouldn't, but I reach out and run a finger along his strong jawline, the stubble prickling my fingertips.

His eyes open.

"I'm sorry. I didn't mean to wake you," I whisper.

"Everything okay?"

"Had a bad dream."

He reaches out, pulling my body against his. "Do you want to talk about it?"

Talking is the last thing I want. I press my lips to his. My tongue slips between his soft lips. I let this kiss answer his question.

Gently, I push his shoulder until he rolls onto his back, and I roll with him without breaking the kiss. I straddle his hips, pressing my body into his, the remnants of the dream chased away.

Resting my hands on his chest for balance, I sit back. For a moment, doubt clouds my mind and body. I've only initiated sex once in my life and my heart is fighting to break free from my chest.

His silent, sexy smile encourages me to keep going.

I grasp the hem of the sleep-shirt and arch my back. Bryan sits up and helps me pull the cotton material over my head. Carnal instinct takes over. The need for skin-to-skin contact washes away self-doubt. My breasts brush the skin of his chest and my sex aches for a touch only he can give me.

Bryan rolls me onto my back and rains kisses on my face and neck. He moves down my body leaving wet caresses from his tongue on my skin to cool in the air in the room. The path glides along the center of my abs to the apex of my thighs.

Bryan kisses me through my panties. Teasing me. Making me squirm. The ache growing more intense. He does not linger. The warmth of his body leaves me.

"Dani…"

I open my eyes, not because he called my name, but because of the emotional restraint I hear in his voice.

Bryan stands at the foot of the bed, the front of his pajama pants failing to contain his erection. The tip peeks out from the waistband hanging low on his hips.

Words are unnecessary. He will stop if I don't want this. He respects my body, and the decision is mine.

Every reservation I've had about him since that day at Back to School Night is erased. The memories of lonely nights evaporate.

I want this.

I want him.

I want us.

I reach for him.

Bryan steps out of his pajama pants, and the sight intensifies the longing in the core of my being. He crawls onto the bed. We lace our fingers as he settles in between my legs. He touches his forehead to mine and stares into my eyes. What I find in his eyes gives me peace and reassurance that this is more than a friends-with-benefits relationship. This is not a booty-call.

Untangling one hand, he trails his fingers over the side of my body, reaching between us to guide himself to my passage. The secret words he whispers make my stomach jump and my body ignite with lust. My eyes close.

His hand reconnects with mine as he rocks into me. After years of celibacy, my walls welcome him home. My muscles stretch and mold around him.

"You haven't been with anyone since…"

My eyes pop open. With a slow twist side to side, I shake my head before he can finish asking the question.

His hazel eyes search mine. He leans in, his lips against my ear. "You make me want things I've never wanted before," he whispers, and then his teeth clamp down on my earlobe at the same time he pushes into me.

My breath pauses.

My focus divides between the sensual pain pulsing through my lobe and the satisfying pleasure of Bryan inside me. Reclaiming me.

No longer do I hear the sounds of nature outside. What invades me is the warmth of his body against mine. The emotional connection of our coupling. The taste of his tongue as he kisses me. We guide each other on the path toward an erotic ending.

We explore each other's body. Set a rhythm that arouses our souls and feeds my heart. I rock my hips while Bryan rolls his. I roll my hips while he rocks his.

I like it when Bryan shortens his strokes to bring me to the brink of an orgasm, then shifts his hips to go in long and deep.

I like controlling Bryan's sounds of pleasure.

When I stroke down on him, he growls.

I circle my hips and drag my nails along his skin. Bryan moans.

When I rock my hips, nibbling on his ear, he groans.

I grasp his butt and squeeze, Bryan grunts.

When I caress him, he sighs.

I lock my ankles around him, and Bryan whispers naughty things in my ear. The tremble of culmination starts from my center. He strokes my G-spot gradually. Thighs quiver. Walls clench and release him. My hips circle quick and fast, brushing my clitoris against him. The contrast between slow and steady, quick and fast drives me to that orgasmic crest. A sense of Zen pours through my being. I hum and moan his name.

Bryan's body trembles. Mouth against my neck. A shudder goes up his back as he orgasms. His strokes are faster. Harder. He laces his fingers with mine. Our bodies rock together. I whisper visually graphic words in his ear and Bryan comes; my name becomes his creed.

He pulls out, rolls onto his side, cuddling me in his arms. "Talk to me, Dani."

"I'm okay."

A memory flashes of a time when after-sex cuddling was just as intimate as the actual act. The talks we had. The plans we made for our family. That was eight years ago. My tears fall onto his chest. His arms tighten around me. I don't have to say it out loud. He understands. Those talks are what I miss most of all.

It's hard to put into words how happy I am being with him.

We stay like this, listening to the nocturnal sounds.

My resolve firm, the tears dry up. I roll away, pulling off the wedding ring and setting it on the nightstand. I'm free from what that piece of jewelry symbolized in my relationship with James. Friendship. Connection.

I now have that and so much more with Bryan—and want to absorb as much of it as I can. My leg stretches across him. I straddle his hips and rain kisses along his neck.

"I'm ready for the sequel." I capture the tip of his ear between my teeth.

I make love to Bryan until we fall asleep, legs and arms tangled, our lives forever connected.

Chapter Fourteen

I *S WAY TO THE MUSIC PLAYING on the stereo, as I get dressed for our* *wedding. James really outdid himself with this CD mix. He hasn't made me* *one since I moved here to Arizona. This one is different from the ones I used to* *fall asleep listening to. He's blended the songs together so it seems like one song is* *playing for hours.*

James whispers in my ear. His words echo in the background of the music. *"Don't trust anyone. I'm your only friend."*

I turn around, but he's not there. I'm in the cemetery standing over his grave. *Bryan's with me.*

James floats out of the casket, stepping into the light. A gun in his hand, aimed *at Bryan. Shots ring out. Bryan falls to the green grass.*

I gasp. My eyes fly open searching the room for him.

It was just a dream, I chant to myself until my heart beats at its normal pace.

Today is the holiday party. Instead of waking up happy after the night and morning I shared with Bryan, my dream darkens my mood. The wedding band is still in the place I put it. There's an invisible string attached to it and my finger.

Bryan is already up and dressed. He's sitting on the couch with papers in his hand, and talking on the cell phone. Steam swirls above the rim of the coffee cup on the small table in front of him. He's watching me.

"Hold on a second," he says into the phone and pulls it away from his ear. "Everything okay, Dani?"

Nodding without making eye contact, I climb out of bed and walk toward the bathroom.

"I'll call you back," Bryan says. He meets me at the door. "Did you have another bad dream?"

"I'm fine."

He reaches for me, but I step around him, closing the door in his face. I don't regret what I shared with Bryan, and I want more nights, and days, with him. I'm just in a weird headspace right now. Hopefully as the day progresses, I can shake this feeling.

The girls and I have a lot to do, so I don't waste time in the bathroom. I take a hot shower and go through my body-moisturizing regimen. Bryan is back on the phone when I come out. I quickly dress in a pair of wine-colored winter leggings and a flannel button-down shirt with one of Bryan's black wife-beaters underneath. I hurry downstairs to the kitchen. We have a nine o'clock hair appointment and it's ten minutes to eight.

The girls are already eating breakfast.

"Good morning. How did you sleep?" I ask.

Kourtney and Emma wink at each other and rush me. "How did you sleep?" They tickle me.

"Like a baby." I laugh, wiggling away from them. "Okay, tickle twins. Let's get a move on it. We have a hair appointment in an hour. We have to look our best for Bryan's party."

Kourtney squints her eyes at me.

"They'll be gentle," I tell her.

Marie places a plate in front of me. "Willis will drive you. It's the last weekend before Christmas, and the mall will be crowded." She's upset about something.

I bite into a turkey sausage link. "We'll leave as soon as I finish."

The girls take their dishes to the sink and race each other out of the kitchen.

Marie frowns. "You've got a glow about you this morning." Her disapproval is magnified by the drawl. Maybe she's old fashioned in her beliefs regarding an unmarried couple having premarital sex.

Are we a couple? Is that how I'm defining our relationship now? Does he see us as a couple? I'm not foolish enough to think he loves me just because we've been intimate.

Lost in my thoughts, I don't hear Vin come in the kitchen until he speaks.

"Had a good night?" He opens a cabinet, fighting a knowing smile that wants to break free. Just his presence puts me on the defensive. The remembrance of a scent makes my stomach roll and fist clench.

"Leave her alone, Vin," Marie warns.

With a coffee cup in his hands, he turns around, a smirk on his face. Vin walks toward me. Fish and old socks hover in the recesses of my brain. I push back in the chair and stand to face him head on.

He looks down at me. "Which one made you glow? Tom, Dick or…"

I sucker punch him in the mouth. The coffee cup in his hand crashes to the floor. Marie yells something that doesn't penetrate my fighter's brain. I concentrate on the tank wiping his mouth and nodding his cocky head. He's about to make a move.

Bryan charges through the door. I don't take my eyes off my enemy though.

"Danielle!" Bryan bellows.

With Vin momentarily distracted, I throw an unsuspected punch to his chin and get ready to use his momentum against him. I take a step to the side.

Bryan rushes me, stepping in between us before his friend can retaliate. He throws me over his shoulder, fireman style. I flip Vin the bird as I'm carried through the door, kicking and screaming.

Marie's yelling at Vin. I don't understand what she's saying. Her Southern drawl is too thick. And she's not speaking English. Plus Bryan and I are shouting at one another too.

"I never promised not to defend myself," I pound on his back with my fist.

Bryan stomps up the stairs, unfazed by my attempts to squirm off his shoulder. Everything is his fault.

He slams the bedroom door behind him and stops in front of the bed. He lifts and launches me at the rumpled covers. If I weren't so mad, I'd be impressed by his strength.

I bounce onto the center of the bed.

"Your caveman act is unnecessary," I hiss, scooting to the edge of the bed.

"Shut up, Danielle!" He paces back and forth, stopping long enough to throw his suit jacket over a leather reclining chair.

"That was a private conversation between you and me. That's not something you tell your friends!"

"Don't give me some bullshit explanation for your actions."

"My actions? What about yours?" I throw the accusation back at him. He pauses and looks at me.

"Bring her back down here so we can settle this." Vin's voice carries from downstairs.

"Come up here if you're man enough, stubby," I yell back.

Bryan moves so quickly I don't see him coming. His hand clamps over my mouth. "Shut. The. Fuck. Up." His voice is calm. He stares into my eyes.

When he drops his hand, I stand, forcing my way past him. He grabs my waist, pulling me back and sitting me on the bed.

I stand and throw a hook to his ribs then a jab to his jaw. He blocks both and even the one aimed at his chin. His fingers enclose my fist and Bryan shoves me back onto the bed.

Scooting back, I kick him, getting him square in the chest. He stumbles and falls to the floor, but recovers quickly. Like a warrior. He lunges himself at me.

Reflexes are spot on. I roll out of the way.

Bryan grabs me. We wrestle on the bed until he pins me down.

"Why are you fighting me, Dani?" Bryan asks.

I don't respond. Instead I jerk underneath the weight of his body.

"Stop. Moving."

His command adds fuel to the anger roaring inside me. Channeling that energy, I gather the strength to throw him off and land a good punch to his temple. This time it connects. I move to get off the bed.

Bryan leaps on top of me, pinning me down again. I push against his shoulders, trying to get him off. With my nails, I dig into his flesh through the mustard-colored dress shirt, tearing the expensive cotton material.

He captures my wrists in one massive hand, holding them above my head. His free hand pulls and tugs, then yanks off his striped tie. He wraps the silk cloth around my wrists and ties it to a post in the headboard.

Oh, I'm beyond pissed now.

"You've worn that ring for eight years because you made a promise to…"

"Don't you dare speak his name. James didn't tell his friends about our private moments. He didn't allow his friends to speak to me like that. And he certainly treated me a lot better than you ever have."

Bryan's sinister chuckle sends a chill through my blood. "Name one of his friends, Danielle."

He waits for me to respond, but I can't. In all honesty, after high school, I only met one of his friends. And that was after James deployed to Iraq.

"If you weren't so closed off, you'd know the dynamics of close friendships. My friends are my ride-or-die. We have no secrets." His voice is so menacing, I pause to look at him.

He's surpassed angry.

Self-preservation kicks in and I fight, squirm, and wiggle underneath him, shutting out the back and forth banter. With all my upper body strength, I pull against the restraint around my wrists.

"Stop before you hurt yourself," he barks.

Keep fighting.

Protect yourself.

Legs open, I lock my ankles in the middle of his back and squeeze his ribcage between my thighs as tight as I can.

He breaks the hold. Rolls off. Flips me onto my stomach. And lies on my back.

"You're acting like a child and not like the educated woman I know you to be."

He struggles to control me.

Keep fighting.

Protect yourself.

"I brought you up here to defuse the situation." His lips brush my ear.

When you're up against the ropes, free your mind and look for your opponent's weak spot, then go in for the kill. My foster father's voice comes to mind.

I jerk back, head-butting Bryan. The weight of his body falls off me. I pull myself up onto my knees, biting at the tie wrapped around my wrists.

A vise clamps around my ankles, yanking me back.

Humph. I fall to my stomach. My wrists out of reach. He pulls the Ugg boots off my feet and jumps onto my back.

"Please don't make me kill one of my best friends for hurting you," Bryan whispers in my ear.

"I'll kill him for you."

He growls. "Abdicate the thrown, Danielle," Alpha Male warns, hovering close to my head.

"No," I shoot back, defiance speaking for me.

"I'll keep you tied to this bed all day," Alpha Male threatens.

I use his position to my advantage and head-butt him again.

"Shit," he shouts.

I climb onto my knees, planting them on the mattress and sidekick him off the bed. Bryan, caught off guard, hits the floor. Hard.

I pull at the silk around my wrists with my teeth. In the background, I hear the tinkle of a belt coming undone. The knot in the tie loosens a little.

He grips my ankles. I'm yanked back so hard my chin scrapes the bed sheets. An after-burn smolders on my skin. My ankles are now restrained like my wrists.

Bryan's beside me. A dark and dangerous alpha male stares me in the eyes. I try to head butt him. He twirls my ponytail around his hand and gives it a quick yank. His eyes are void of emotion. His face, within inches of mine, takes on the appearance of a predatory animal.

For the first time in my life, I know the real fear of being defenseless. And it's Bryan who scares me.

Slowly, he unravels my hair from his hand. I'm flipped onto my back. Pain shoots through my wrists.

The stillness in the room makes me shiver.

Blood from Bryan's nose flows over his lips, down his chin, and stains the torn dress shirt he's wearing. He doesn't bother wiping away the blood. Small red, crescent-shaped marks tarnish the spots where my nails tore through the material of his shirt and broke the skin. The corner of his bottom lip is swollen and also bleeding.

Bryan climbs off the bed, unbuttoning the shirt. Pulling it tight, he covers my face with the shirt. Physically I know I can't be suffocated, but the mental feeling is sobering.

The sound of water running in the sink wafers through the door. Immediately my mind goes to being waterboarded. I fight the panic and draw on my mental strengths as a boxer.

"Untie me from this bed, Bryan," I shout.

No response. For all I know, he could be standing over me with a pitcher of water. I jerk and wiggle, and use my mouth and tongue. The shirt covering my face, blocking my vision won't budge. My foster father didn't teach me to defend myself once I'm literally defenseless. That's because he always told me not to allow myself to be put in a situation where I am defenseless.

Bryan's silence is eerie. I wait for the sounds of him moving around the room.

Nothing.

His stealth mode brings on a new level of fear. I'm trained to see and hear my opponent attacking. His demeanor is cold and unfeeling.

The tears begin to flow. "Please, untie me, Bryan. Please." My helpless cries fill the room. "Please," I sob. The need to curl into a ball is strong, but he's in control. I'm at his mercy.

Minutes seem more like hours. Finally, my ankles are set free. The shirt is lifted off my face. Restraints around my wrists loosen, then disappear. My hands are placed on my stomach.

I open my eyes.

Bryan's hand shakes as he reaches for my face. Instinct has me flinch away from his touch. He just showed me a side he's kept hidden.

My tears flow heavier and I turn away from him, curling into a ball.

The bedroom door opens then closes.

The sound of Dani crying on the other side of these doors is slaying me. Today, she met the monster within. The one that lurks within every member of Phantom. Mine was dangerously close to going too far, and that scares me.

Danielle isn't the enemy.

What the hell was I thinking?

Only she can make me lose control.

Inhale. Slowly exhale.

Would I really have followed through? Or was I just trying to scare her into giving up the fight? The line is blurry. I can't see the answer.

Leaning against the door, I try to pull myself together. Tony and Ig are back from their mission and we were supposed to meet in the office at nine, but I really should go back in there and apologize.

Kourt's voice stops me. She sounds like she's coming up the stairs.

"Where's my mom?" her voice trembles.

"I'm sure she's getting ready so you guys can go," Willis replies.

I take another deep breath and step away from the door to head her off. I'll calm her fears first. Before the day is over, I have to apologize and hope Dani forgives me. Deep down, I need it. I've always needed it.

Chapter Fifteen

WIPING THE TEARS FROM MY eyes, I sit up and put the ring back on my finger. Even though that burden crashes down on my soul, I welcome it. It's familiar.

Blinded by tears and stumbling from the weight, I make my way to the bathroom. Sobs cause my body to vibrate as I splash water on my face.

There's no way the Bryan who made love to me would manhandle me in the light of day. But he just did.

For years I abstained from sex and should have waited longer. Gotten to know him *before* things got complicated.

Okay it happened—now what do you do? Defiance asks.

I'm done crying like a helpless woman.

Good, keep going, Defiance encourages.

Take Kourtney and disappear!

Sounds like a plan, Defiance confirms.

I dry my face and leave the bathroom.

The closet door slams into the wall from the force of my determination to leave this house. My suitcases are in the back. I grab one and carry it back to the bed. The second suitcase I fling onto the mattress.

Like a tornado, I whip through the closet, sweeping up my belongings. Leaving empty hangers swinging on the rod or falling to the hardwood floor. Empty drawers are left tittering in their slots. All the while, I curse the day Bryan Kendall Hawk IV strolled into my life.

I drop clothes, shoes, and accessories from my arms into the open suitcases, not caring if they're neat and orderly.

The bedroom door opens. Immediately my shoulders square, ready to face my opponent. Back heel slightly off the ground. Weight mostly on front foot. Knees bent. Elbows down and in. Fists up. Chin down. I'm ready to fight my way out of here.

Marie walks into the room, raising her hand in surrender when she sees me. I relax my stance and march back into the closet.

"Why are you packing?" Marie asks.

"Kourtney and I are leaving." I come out of the closet with my arms full.

Her disapproving frowns and tone were warnings I didn't pick up on. I got caught up in the fantasy; turned a blind eye to the reality.

"Don't leave," Marie begs.

"We can't be here."

"That apartment isn't safe for you and Kourtney."

"We'll stay at a hotel until I decide my next move."

"Mom, we can't leave. You said we're staying for the holidays and the party is tonight." The hurt tone of her voice pulls at my heart. I've never seen her so happy since we moved to Colorado.

Kourtney's standing in the doorway watching me. *What do I do?*

Emma runs in, wrapping her arms around my waist. "You can't miss the party, Dani. Please don't leave."

"You promised, Mom." It's not a reminder. It's a statement. Tears pool in her eyes as she stares at me. I haven't broken a promise to her, and she's letting me know this is one she'll hold against me if I do.

Emma squeezes me tighter and I wrap my arms around her. I don't want to disappoint them, but that's a part of life.

The girls are not at fault. They don't deserve this. I count to ten as I exhale.

"We'll stay for the party." *But we're leaving in the morning.*

Marie touches my arm. "Willis is waiting downstairs. I'll unpack for you."

"Please move my things to the other guest room for tonight." An escape plan is forming in my head, I lead the girls out of the room.

We put on our coats and leave the house to get ready for Mr. Hawk's holiday party. In the car, I call the hair salon, changing our appointment to later this afternoon. We head to the mall first.

I make a point of staying out all day to avoid Bryan. His back-to-back calls go to voicemail. I delete his text messages and emails without reading them.

We return a few hours before the party is scheduled to start. I have Kourtney and Emma bring their dresses to the guest room and lock the door. I get them dressed first then touch up their hair and send them to

Emma's room until I'm ready to go.

The lighting in the bathroom is perfect. I apply the basics of makeup standing in front of the mirror. Instead of allowing the hair stylist to give me a fancy up-do, I told him to straighten my hair and turn the ends under.

I unlock the bedroom door for Marie. She's already dressed for the festivities. The party started an hour ago.

I slip into the emerald curve-hugging gown with a V that reaches down to the small of my back. Marie zips the hidden zipper.

From far away it appears as if I'm wearing a strapless gown that leaves my back bare. Up close the sheer, flesh-tone material is visible.

I step into my heels and put in my simple diamond earrings.

"You look beautiful, Danielle."

"I don't feel beautiful, but thank you, Marie."

"You and Bryan will work things out." She gently squeezes my hand the way my foster mom did when I was upset.

I thought Marie was against my relationship with him. What could have changed her mind? Whatever the reason no longer matters. Kourtney and I are out of here in the morning.

I grab my clutch and wrap and go to Emma's room.

"Mom, we're staying for the holidays, aren't we?" Kourtney asks.

"Come on, girls, we're already fashionably late." I will not lie to my daughter.

"You didn't answer the question." When she frowns like that, she looks so much like her father. My heart hurts.

"Kourt. Can we get through tonight and worry about tomorrow, tomorrow?"

Her mouth twitches. "May we wear lip gloss?"

This morning knocked me off my game. I vaguely remember the questions she asked while we were at the makeup counter in the mall. She knows I'm not an advocate of young girls wearing cosmetic products. We don't have time for a battle of the wills. I open my clutch and hand her the tube of clear lip gloss. "Don't put on too much."

Kourtney hesitates. She must have expected me to say no. She takes the tube. They rush into the bathroom and I follow to supervise them. When they're finished, we go downstairs to put on our coats and leave the house to join the party.

The four of us walk the covered lit path to the enclosed gazebo constructed for tonight's event. Whoever Bryan uses to decorate did a beautiful job outside. Even the first row of bare trees is lit by clear lights. The path is covered with a white material that matches the tented archway.

A young man dressed in old-fashioned white tails and top hat stands at the door to collect the guests' coats. I keep my wrap.

The outside was beautiful, but the inside is a winter wonderland of white satin fabric draped around the room, twinkling clear lights and branches painted white to add to the ambiance. Crystal icicles hang from the ceiling. Splashes of green, red, blue and silver showcase the beauty of the season. The subtle scents of pine, cinnamon, and vanilla add warmth to the room. The grand floor-to-ceiling green noble fir stands near the entrance. Guests stop for a quick photo shoot in front of the tree. It's decorated with white poinsettia leaves, big champagne- colored balls, white ribbon, and clear lights.

Tom, Max's husband, snaps a few pictures of us.

Vin is the first person I spot. He's at the bar with a drink to his lips, while Anthony and Ignacio talk to two women off to the side.

The woman standing next to Anthony is laughing. On second look, I recognize her. She's the woman he danced with at the club. Tiffany is her name. I think.

Ignacio smiles but looks preoccupied. The woman in front of him is all but doing jumping jacks to get his attention.

Max sits at a table, talking with his dining companions. I assume the vacant chair next to him is for Tom.

"Willis is waiting for me. Try to have a good time, dear." Marie pats my shoulder.

Bryan has a lot of business associates. The women are wearing gowns and dresses of different lengths and colors. The men are dressed in black tuxedos of various styles.

I continue to search the room until I see him.

Bryan is talking to a raven-haired woman in a shiny silver dress too short to be called a cocktail dress. Her body language screams, *I'll gladly screw you in this room full of people if that pleases you.*

The Horny Toads could learn from her. She has his complete attention. I check the room again to make sure those Toads are not here. Their antics are the last thing I need tonight.

The buffet table is to the left. I escort the girls over to it. The selections are mouth-watering. I haven't eaten all day. My breakfast was ruined… Never mind, I won't dwell on this morning.

While I help the girls put food on their plates, a hand touches the small of my back. My body stiffens and the hand retracts as if burned.

"You are beautiful, Dani," he whispers.

Kourtney and Emma turn around.

"Wow. Girls." He kisses their cheeks. "You both look like princesses."

"Daddy, what happened to your lip?"

I turn and look at him, fighting the smile of pride threatening to break free. *Yeah, Daddy, tell them how much of a jerk you are.*

"I played a little too rough with a friend today," he tells her, and his eyes briefly look my way.

"You look nice, Bryan." Kourtney nods appreciatively.

He turns around like a model on the runway, giving us a three-sixty view of him in his tux.

"Come on, girls, I see three open seats." I walk away from the buffet table, happy someone chose that moment to stop and chat with him.

"Are these seats taken?" I ask the couple sitting at the table.

"No. They are not. Please sit. Join us." The man rises out of his seat.

A waiter brings me a glass of wine and lemonade for the girls once we're settled at the table. The centerpiece is made of three big, shiny red balls stuffed with holly leaves and berries. The laser-engraved message on the balls reads: Happy Holidays from Hawkeye Personal Protection.

"You are exquisite." The gentleman stares at me.

"Thank you. Your wife is beautiful too."

The woman offers me a quick nod, but her eyes watch the room.

"Excuse me, sir. I like your accent. Where are you from?" Kourtney smiles at him.

"I'm from Saudi Arabia."

"Really!" She sits up in her chair.

Oh boy, here we go.

"Did you know Saudi Arabia has the world's largest sand desert and you have a king, not a president like we do?" Everything she's ever read about his country will be the topic over dinner. "Why aren't you wearing your traditional robes?"

I give him an apologetic smile. Kourtney can be a walking, talking wealth of knowledge and endless chatter when the topic interests her.

"For security reasons, when I travel, I dress in business attire." He looks around like a spy in a movie. He beckons with his index finger. "Can you keep a secret?"

Kourtney and Emma lean in, nodding like bobble-head dolls.

"I am Jawad bin Ali Al Omran. Crowned Prince of Saudi Arabia," he whispers.

Kourtney's fork drops to her plate. For once, my child is stunned silent.

I spittle in my glass of wine, slam it on the table, thankful the glass didn't break, and reach for my wrap off the back of the chair, covering my chest. I don't want to offend Bryan's guest.

"How do you ride a camel?" Emma's question makes him rear back and laugh.

His laughter is infectious, soon the whole table is laughing with him.

"Danielle, you do not have to cover for my sake. I understand American women do not cover themselves like they are required to in my country. Your appearance does not offend me."

I keep my wrap on anyway.

Wait! We haven't introduced ourselves. "How do you know my name?"

His indulgent smile piques my interest. "I make it my business to know beautiful women."

Kourtney and Emma begin to riddle him with questions, preventing me from finding out how he knows who I am.

Emma's interested in the horses and camels and any other animals associated with his country. Kourtney's interested in the land and the government. Her inquiries about the king, surprise me. Prince Jawad answers their questions, even the one about why he's allowed to have many wives. Their conversation isn't interrupted by the dishes being taken away, or by the delicious desserts served.

"I see you've met *my* girls." Bryan stands above me.

The prince looks at me, his eyes hiding something.

"Yes, I have, Mr. Hawk. I find her charming and lovely."

Bryan comes around to stand next to me. I gaze up at him.

"She's stunning," he says, not taking his eyes off me.

The girls giggle.

Tension creeps into my body as his hand hovers over my shoulders, but he doesn't touch me.

"I've had the pleasure of dining with your three beautiful girls."

"Formal introductions are not needed then." That is the voice of a possessive alpha male.

"You must bring them with you on your next travels to my country. They will be my guests. I would love for them to experience my culture and traditions firsthand." His eyes shift to me then back to Bryan.

"It will be awhile before I travel East." Bryan's tone drips of a warning.

"Perhaps they can travel without you. I would be more than happy to arrange it and they will be safe with me."

There's more going on than an invitation to Saudi Arabia.

"If you'll excuse us, Prince Jawad, there are people I want to introduce them to." Bryan pulls out my chair offering his hand.

I rise unassisted.

Bryan walks over and pulls out Kourtney's and Emma's chairs too.

The prince stands, taking my hand in his. His lips brush my knuckles. "It was a pleasure, Danielle. I hope to see you again. Soon." He turns, bowing to Kourtney and Emma.

I was expecting Bryan to throw a punch. Instead he leads us away from the table.

Throughout the night we're introduced to different business associates. Bryan keeps his hand near the small of my back without touching me. I excuse myself after a few minutes of polite conversation.

If I played mind games, I would flirt with other men to prove I am not, nor will I ever be *his girl*. But I learned a long time ago how to choose my battles. Tonight I choose not to fight with Bryan. Instead, I plot my retreat to win the war. So for now, I'll play the role of arm-candy. Tomorrow, Kourtney and I will be ghosts.

Bryan and his friends take turns dancing with the girls. Kourtney shies away from Vin and I don't encourage her to interact with him. She lights up when she's dancing with Bryan.

I dance one song with Ignacio. He is the only one of Bryan's friends I can handle tonight.

Max cuts in the second the song ends. "What's wrong, sweetie?"

The music starts and we move side to side on the semi-full dance floor.

"I'm fine, Max." I stare at his bright orange bowtie.

He stops moving and waits until I look up.

"I know a bad example of a contour face and a beat face. Something's up, Danikins. When you're ready to talk, call me."

Tears pool in my eyes. I blink them away. "Thanks, Maxie."

I rest my head on his shoulder, letting him twirl me around the dance floor. In the middle of the second song, he dips me, trying to coax a reaction. My soul is too sad to give anything more than a fake smile and forced laughter. He knows I'm not being genuine.

When the song ends I make a beeline for the bar, ordering an Electric Lemonade. A blue drink for my blue mood. I've been wasted once in my life. Tonight there's a good possibility it will happen again.

I gulp the first drink and get the bartender's attention. I put a hefty tip in the jar. She adds an extra splash of light rum in the second drink. I guzzle that one down in less than a minute. An instant buzz filters through my brain, easing some of the tension. *The next one I promise I'll sip and enjoy. The first two didn't settle on my taste buds long enough for me to say I like the drink.*

As I motion for the bartender, I spot Bryan heading my way.

I've avoided being alone with him all evening and he's not coming with the intentions of introducing me to another business associate. The girls aren't with him. I turn away from the bar.

"May I have this dance?" Anthony steps in front of me.

I glance back at Bryan. His mouth turns down in a frown, eyes squinting.

I see why some women like playing mind games. It gives them power, and right now, I have the power to ruin the night for Bryan, but at the expense of his friendship with Anthony. Mind games are for Horny Toads. I'm twenty-seven. An adult. I don't need negative attention.

"No thank you, Anthony." I walk around him and search for Kourtney and Emma.

I find them dancing with Ignacio. Emma reaches for my hand and we form a quartet dance circle.

Around eleven thirty, Emma yawns first, then Kourtney. I use that as an excuse to leave the party before it ends. I wait for the girls to say good night before taking their hands. We retrieve our coats. I know Bryan is watching me. I sense it. The girls and I leave the gazebo.

Walking up the path toward the house, Kourtney and Emma rub their sleepy eyes. The air is crisp and chilly. We're the only ones outside.

If I hadn't had those two drinks and that glass of wine, Kourtney and I could leave tonight. She's more agreeable when she's sleepy and I could have convinced her to let me off the hook with the promise.

Out of nowhere, a raven-haired woman steps in front of us.

"Hello."

"Hello," I mimic.

"Bryan puts on a great party, wouldn't you agree?"

Where is she going with this?

"How long have you been with him?" she asks.

Uneasiness chills me. I try to step around her, but she blocks me.

"Where are you going, Dani?"

I freeze.

She opens her coat, showing me the gun in her hand. I recognize that shiny dress. She's the one Bryan was talking to when the girls and I walked into the party.

I pull Kourtney and Emma behind me. "What would you like to talk about?"

The alcohol in my system is preventing me from coming up with a plan of action. I'm always clearheaded when I'm in protective mode. Just another example of the bad decisions I've made since he came into my life.

She smiles. "How about we start with your boyfriend?"

Is she one of his no-strings-attached relationships that ended too quickly for her tastes?

I have to get the girls to safety.

"Since you want to talk about Bryan, it's only fair that he's in on this conversation too." I turn to Kourtney and Emma, not giving the woman a chance to interrupt. "Girls, run and tell Bryan…" I glance back at her, raising a questioning eyebrow.

"Kimberly."

She's Kimberly?

No time, Danielle, focus.

"Run and tell Bryan Kimberly wants to have a discussion with him."

I push them in the direction of the gazebo.

"Run." I watch them scurry off, wondering if I can kickbox in this dress, these heels and buzzed. I plant my feet, ready to test my abilities. I grip my gown… Pain shoots from between my shoulder blades up the back of my neck. My vision blurs and I'm falling forward.

Chapter Sixteen

M Y WRISTS AND ANKLES ARE immobile. I'm lying on my back, spread-eagle, and it's chilly in here. There's an old musty scent in the air, like the room sat closed-up for a while. I keep my eyes closed and listen. An airplane flies overhead and crickets sing to one another.

"Bryan is a master."

I don't recognize this female's voice. She's Russian.

"He knows how to get exactly what he wants. And how to get what he needs."

She's somewhere near my feet. I open my eyes, blinking until they focus. Particles of dust float in the single bright lightbulb hanging overhead.

My gown does little to give me warmth. Rope has me tied down to a table. The room is in shadows. I refuse to panic.

Kimberly saunters into my line of sight, gun in hand, the raven hair replaced by a long auburn ponytail. The silver dress is gone, in its place a long-sleeved black sweater and dark blue jeans.

"I'm not with Bryan." I keep my eyes on her, not the gun.

"Of course you are. He just hasn't fucked you into submission, then interrogated you."

"Why would he interrogate me?"

"Isn't he the best fuck you've ever had?" She walks around the table. My eyes follow her. "He's the best I've ever had," she chuckles. "I can see why Amelia fell in love with him. He knows his way around a woman's body. That's how he gets us to reveal our secrets. But once he gets what he needs, he moves on to the next."

"If this is about him, what do you want from me?"

"Bryan has something we need."

"I don't get why I'm here."

I lose sight of her as she walks behind the table.

"Let's just call you an incentive for him to give me what I came for."

"I'm nothing to Bryan."

"I've watched him with you. He's emotionally attached to you. You're nothing like Amelia. She was stupid."

"Who's Amelia?" I ask, the cold air making me shiver.

"Bryan used her like he's using you. He's the reason she killed herself. Bryan wants something from you, Dani. He's..."

The room goes black.

Voices all around me begin to shout. Quick flashes of fire from gunshots pierce the darkness. The rope around my ankles and wrists come undone. I'm pulled off the table, onto the cold cement floor.

"Put this on," Bryan whispers in my ear.

My arms slide through sleeves and I'm instantly warm. His scent makes me exhale. I try to stand, but I'm pulled back down to the floor.

"Stay down," he commands.

Something thumps behind me and rapid gunshots go off beside me. I jump and cover my ears. Frightened.

"I'm hit!"

I know that Italian accent.

Medical training takes over. My fingertips search the floor around me until I find him. I roll up the jacket sleeves and my hands roam over him finding the wet spot. I apply pressure.

"Hold your fire!"

I recognize that voice too. It's Anthony.

As sudden as it started, the gunfire stops. Three flashlights turn on. My eyes try to adjust to the limited lighting.

The three men remove what look like sunglasses from their eyes; they're still dressed in tuxedos. My hands are pressing into Vin's shoulder, his eyes are closed, but the rise and fall of his chest assures me he's alive. His sunglasses are pushed back on his forehead.

"Stay awake, you ogre." *Who got shot while rescuing me.* They all came to my rescue, again.

"I think you mean big tank," he chuckles.

"Now you're pushing it." I laugh with him, and tears trail down my cheeks.

"Dani, do not move your hands," Ignacio commands. "Bry, is the room secured? I need to check Vin."

"Dani, are you okay?" Vin asks. His eyes are open.

I nod.

"Did she hurt you?" Vin asks.

I shake my head. He's genuinely concerned about my well-being.

"Left flank clear," Anthony says from somewhere near the left side of the room.

"The room is secured," Bryan replies from the right side of the room.

Ignacio holds the small flashlight between his teeth and pulls gloves and bandages out of a pack around his waist. He walks toward us. "Dani, on three, move your hands." He drops to his knees near Vin's head. "One. Two. Three."

I raise my hands, and Ignacio presses down on Vin's shoulder with one hand while the other moves over his body.

I try to stand, but the room spins.

"Hey, Bry! Dani don't look too good." Vin's voice sounds distorted.

I feel my body slumping to the floor.

The comfortable firmness and familiar scent makes me feel secure as I open my eyes. I'm in Bryan's bed. He's standing at the closed glass doors. Shirtless. One hand in his pocket. An amber-colored drink in the other. The flames in the fireplace make the hawk tattoo on his back look like it's flying.

The lamp on his nightstand is on.

"How's Vin?" I sit up and scoot to the edge of the bed. I'm still wearing his tuxedo jacket. Vin's blood has been cleaned off my hands.

"He's fine. Ig patched him up." He drains the glass.

"What about Kimberly?"

"She's been detained."

"What do you want from me?"

Bryan turns to face me. "I don't know what you mean."

"Kimberly said you want something from me."

He shakes his head.

"What does she want from you?"

"She was blackmailing one of my clients with sexually explicit photos. Someone stole them. She thinks it was me."

"Who's Amelia?"

Bryan crosses the room to sit at the foot of the bed. He turns so he's slightly facing me. "Amelia is Emm's biological mother."

My eyebrow arches.

"The guys and I were sitting around after a party one night. I asked if they wanted to make extra money working for me. They thought I was joking because we were pretty wasted. The next day, I showed them my business records. I'd started an escort business and needed help. My clientele was growing and my escorts were traveling the world."

Is he serious?

"A Prime Minister called, offering ten grand to train his young mistress. He'd heard that I trained the girls who worked for me. I told him no. He doubled his offer. I accepted and he sent Kimberly to Colorado. The guys looked after the business while I taught Kimberly how to… please a man in bed."

He's lying.

"A few years later, Kimberly asked if I could help her friend who needed money to finish school here in the States. Amelia had little sex experience. She picked up quickly and I liked hanging out with her. But she mistook sex for love and friendship for a relationship. She got pregnant on purpose, thinking she could force me into marriage. I told her I'd take care of my child, but I wasn't interested in a relationship. Emma was a week old when Amelia dropped her off to me, then killed herself. I closed the escort business and opened Hawkeye Personal Protection."

"Why didn't you tell me about Amelia?"

"What was I supposed to say? My daughter's mother killed herself because I didn't want to be with her? Would you have wanted anything to do with me if I said that?"

I stand and walk to the bedroom's double doors.

"I would never intentionally hurt you. This morning I was frustrated. I handled you instead of the situation. I was wrong." His tone expresses remorse and something else I can't identify.

I face him. "I promised the girls we'd be here through the holidays. It's the least we can do for them after everything else. I want you to stay out of my way and I'll stay out of yours while we're here. The beginning of the new year, Kourtney and I are gone from your life. For good."

I close the doors behind me.

I'm being chased through the woods by a pack of dogs I can't see. Every time I look back all I see is darkness. Their growls and barks haunt me. I know the dogs are there and they're closing in.

Up ahead a debilitated wooden shed stands lonely in a moonlit clearing. My legs pump faster. I get inside and slam the door.

Thump!

The dogs bang into the side of the shed, making it shake, and pieces of the rotten wood ceiling and dust rain down on me.

Inside are three more doors. No windows.

Outside, the dogs growl and bark and howl, clawing and tearing at the wood.

I stare at the three doors and choose one.

Behind the first door is the living room of my first apartment in Arizona, before I moved in with James. The Hawaiian flower scent welcomes me. I kept potpourri burners around the apartment. The sweet scent masked the stench of fish and old socks coming from the apartment next door.

Music from a CD James made me in high school is blasting on the stereo. I step into the room to turn down the volume—and freeze. James sits on the brown loveseat still in the Army dress uniform he wore for our wedding. On the floor in front of him, a naked auburn-haired woman on her hands and knees, her lips wrapped around his penis. An identical James, in an Army combat uniform, thrusts in and out of her from behind. Another woman lies sleeping on the sofa. I can't see her face, but I know her. Hurt and anger fill me. I run back through the door, into the old shed.

The dogs made small holes in the wood; I can see their eyes and teeth. There are four of them. Blue eyes. Brown eyes. Chocolate eyes. Hazel eyes.

I open another door.

I'm in a war-torn neighborhood surrounded in chaos. Black smoke clouds the sky.

Turned over cars on fire.

Homes shattered.

Children crying.

Women mourning.

Men bleeding.

The chemical scent in the air burns my nose and makes my eyes water. Somewhere in the distance, I hear a comforting rhythmic clicking and words spoken in an unfamiliar dialect while soldiers of all hues march through the debris-littered streets. Frightened citizens scurry out of their way.

Four bullet-riddled bodies lie in the middle of the street. I know these men and I run to help them. One by one, I turn them over.

Anthony.

Ignacio.

Vincenzo.

Bryan.

A shadowed figure moves toward me, beckoning me. With a wooden knitting needle, she points to something in my hand.

I look down.

Bryan's gun. I'm holding Bryan's recently fired gun. Guilt spreads like an out-of-control wildfire through my heart. I drop the gun as I back away. Turning, I run from the shadowed figure following me. The door slams in its face.

The dogs are almost inside the shed. The holes are large enough for their heads to poke through. The four dogs bare their sharp white teeth. Foam dripping from their mouths.

I reach for the knob of the third door.

I step into the darkness expecting to be cold. The warmth is comforting. Inviting. Safe.

I turn in a circle. All I see is darkness, yet I'm not afraid. Three-year-old Kourtney, in pajamas and holding Mr. Cuddles, stands by my side. She's crying and reaches for me to pick her up.

The voice of Bryan whispers in my ear. "I'm asking you to trust me."

I nod.

"When I tell you, run toward the sound of my voice."

Behind me, I hear the wood of the shed give way. Bryan yells for me to run. He promises he'll keep us safe, but I have to trust him and not ask questions.

Something bursts through the door. It's not the dogs; it's someone more evil. I cradle my daughter to my chest and take off. Bryan tells me not to look back, to run faster.

Behind me, I hear the dogs growling like they're attacking the dangerous being.

Bryan's voice guides me through the darkness. My feet move on the unseen ground. I know we're secure and he wouldn't let anything happen to us.

Three-year-old Kourtney slowly grows older, still holding Mr. Cuddles, and cradled in my arms. The call of Bryan's voice is the driving force that keeps my feet moving through the darkness.

A bright light shines ahead and his outline appears inside it. He's waiting for us. Arms open. The snow-covered Rocky Mountains in the distance.

I run into his arms.

"I got you," he whispers. We're enclosed in his embrace. "My girls are safe now."

Chapter Seventeen

THE GUEST ROOM IS LAVENDER scented to match the décor. It's like the other rooms on this side of the house. No floor-to-ceiling glass doors, but there's a window seat that faces the pond. I've been sitting here staring out the window since I woke up from that dream.

A crew arrived at sunrise to start the cleanup and demolition of the gazebo. Bryan's been outside with them.

Around seven thirty, Kourtney and Emma run back and forth between the two rooms. I shower and get dressed and go to the family room. My mind and body are tired, but I want to assure the girls that everything is okay, even if I don't feel it.

We go through our tickle routine first.

"You guys want to talk about last night?" I ask.

"Nope. Daddy talked to us when he made breakfast," Emma says.

"What did he tell you?"

Kourtney presses the button on the remote to pause the television. "He said he didn't invite that lady to the party and asked her to leave."

"She thought you could make him talk to her," Emma adds.

"I have errands to run. Do you want to come with me?"

"Bryan's taking us ice skating."

"Will you be okay without me?"

Kourtney frowns. "Yes. Mom."

"Okay, see you later." I kiss the girls and leave before I run into Bryan.

The boxing gym is my first stop. It's not crowded this morning. I usually work out in the evenings and Kourtney sits in the observation room with my laptop.

Today, I visualize the punching bag is Bryan and do my best to beat the crap out of him.

"You lose form and technique when you're angry," Willis says from behind me.

I grab the bag to stop it from swinging back on me and turn around. "Did he send out a search party?"

Willis laughs. "No, I work out here too."

I turn back to the bag, get into my stance, and aim for imaginary Bryan's kidneys. "I've never seen you here." I grunt with each hard hit.

"I work out in the mornings." Willis steps behind the bag and holds it steady while I pulverize it with more combinations. "Stay focused, even though you're angry. And pull your left elbow in more. Here, let me show you."

We trade places. Willis takes his stance and starts by showing me how my elbow looks then how it should look. He points out the difference in the power behind each punch.

I watch as he goes through more complex combinations. Willis is good. He hits like a professional.

We trade places again. "Chin down, elbows in, shift your weight and follow through," he coaches.

Willis and I move around the gym, working out and talking boxing. In the ring, I surprise him with how well I execute kickboxing techniques.

I leave him at the speed bag and head to the locker room to shower and change. There's last minute Christmas shopping I need to do.

For thirty minutes I circle the parking lot at the mall. I use the time to call an old college classmate and cash in a favor.

A black SUV backs out of a stall near the entrance and I pull into the spot. It doesn't take long to pick up the gifts I came for, so I sit in the food court and nurse a grilled chicken salad and a cup of hot chocolate until thoughts of Bryan bring tears to my eyes. I need another distraction before I turn into a blubbering mess.

With shopping bags in hand, I walk over to the movie theater and buy a ticket for a holiday comedy. Laughter and buttery popcorn are what I need right now.

I leave after the end credits.

As I drive in the direction of Bryan's house, I admire the festive holiday decorations on both sides of the road. Kourtney and I used to go all out. The lawn full of ornaments. Every room in the house filled with Christmas… The high-beams of a car from oncoming traffic veer into my lane. I'm blinded. I turn the wheel to the right to get out of its path. Blinking to regain sight, I press hard on the brakes. A horn blows. My peripheral vision catches a dark shadow passing my window. Tires squeal on asphalt. Constant honk of a horn. A black SUV blocks the blinding lights from crashing into me. The car with high-beams veers back into its lane, metal scraping metal, it clips the black SUV in front of me.

I take my hand off the horn, too shaken to do anything else.

"Are you okay, ma'am?" A young man knocks on my window.

I nod without looking at him. He returns to his SUV. The engine of his truck thunders as it makes a U-turn. He speeds off in the direction of the high-beams.

Somehow, my phone is in my trembling hand. My finger hovers over Bryan's number. I don't remember picking it up. I take deep breaths setting the phone back in the holder.

Decorations forgotten, I pull back onto the road in defensive driving mode until I pull up in front of Bryan's home.

Marie opens the front door. She tells me the girls are upstairs in bed and Bryan just left. Light spills into the darkened hallway from the door of his home office.

I walk upstairs, put the bags away, and go check on the girls.

I knock on Emma's door first. Kourtney never falls asleep right away.

"Can we read for a little while?" Emma asks.

"Sure. What would you like to read?"

She pulls a book from under her pillow. On the cover are pictures of horses and ponies. A pony was number two on their joint Christmas list.

I kick off my slippers and climb in next to her. She opens the book. We cuddle as she reads out loud. I help her sound out unfamiliar words and tell her the meaning so she will remember them. Halfway into the second chapter, Emma's eyes close at the end of a sentence. I mark the page before setting the book on the nightstand.

My attention gets captured by a drawing in her sketchbook. I pick it up. Emma's working on a picture of the four of us out by the pond. For an eight-year-old, she's a good artist. I hope Bryan nurtures her talent.

She yawns. "I love you. I want you and Kourty to stay forever."

"I love you too, sweetie."

It's true. I love this little girl like she's my own. I climb out of her bed and tuck her in, kissing her forehead.

Across the hall I knock on Kourtney's door. As expected, she's awake, and on my laptop.

"I know I'm supposed to ask, but you weren't here and I wanted to look at pictures of Saudi Arabia." She closes the website.

I place the laptop on the nightstand. "It's okay. I know you don't abuse your privileges."

"Why was your laptop in the guest room?"

"I'll sleep in there until we leave."

"Because you and Bryan had a fight?"

My child is observant and quick.

"What did you hear?"

"I heard Mr. Vin say bad words, then Mr. Willis asked us to help him find his gloves by the pond. I think he just wanted to get us out of the house."

"Bryan and I need a timeout."

"Boyfriends and girlfriends have time out?"

"Bryan isn't my boyfriend."

"He kisses you on your lips. *All the time.*"

Her dramatics make me laugh.

"Why isn't he your boyfriend?"

"Get some sleep. We have a long day ahead of us tomorrow."

"Lie down with me?"

"Sure, baby, for as long as you want."

I climb in and we snuggle each other.

"Why don't you answer my questions about Bryan?"

"I know you're hoping Bryan and I end up together, but it's not going to happen, Kourt."

"Why not? I like Bryan and I know you do too. You kept looking at him at the parent meeting. You smile big when he's around. Except for last night." She yawns. "Emmy and I want to be sisters."

"You are sisters." Tears well up in my eyes. "Best friends are like sisters."

"We want to be real sisters." She yawns again. "Please don't be mad at him anymore." She snuggles closer. "When you smile a lot, I know you're happy."

I turn off the lamp so she can't see the tears fall from my eyes.

I wake the girls before sunrise. Today we're going to a winter amusement park a few hours from Boulder. It's a place marked off on Kourtney's list.

I've learned that Colorado weather is unpredictable. I'm bringing along extra clothes.

Marie packs a sack lunch. She's going with us.

I go outside to load up my truck. It's been moved into the garage. I open the hatch and see an emergency roadside kit and a note from Bryan that says he hopes we have fun. His Silverado is gone.

"Bryan filled your tank, checked the tires, brakes, and fluid levels."
Willis walks into the garage. "There's a backup cell phone in the glove
compartment too."

The girls, Marie, and I head out. Less than an hour into the drive,
Kourtney and Emma fall asleep and Marie turns down the radio.

"Bryan cares about you."

"I got the impression you didn't approve of our relationship."

"In all the years I've known him, I've never seen Bryan with a woman.
I mean I know he's been with women, but you get it, don't you?"

I nod.

"This is so out of character for him. He always seemed to be missing
someone. I've suspected it was Emma's mom. He's never talked about
her. I don't even know her name. There are no pictures of her around the
house. And you still wear your wedding ring even though your husband
has been dead for years. It worried me that neither one of you were ready
for a relationship. I care about you guys. I don't want to see either one
get hurt."

"Thank you, Marie."

"Willis told me to mind my own business and warned me not to med-
dle. But I do want to tell you one thing my mom told me before I
married Willis. And after that, I will let you two figure things out."

I quickly glance at her.

"A man who truly loves a woman will go to the extreme to protect
her. The methods may not always be to our liking, but in the end, it's the
motive behind his actions that makes us forgive them. The way Bryan
tore out of that party when the girls told him about that woman showed
how much he cares for you."

My heart flutters. "How did you meet Willis?"

"We met in a hospital."

I raise an eyebrow at her, then turn my focus back to the road.

"You learned that from Bryan," she laughs. "Willis was at a bar in New
Orleans with his squad. I was there with my fiancé, Pierre." She sighs.
"Pierre and I were arguing. I didn't know it, but Willis was paying attention to us. I remember telling Pierre I wouldn't marry him and next I
woke up in a hospital room. Willis was sitting next to my bed, holding my
hand. He introduced himself."

"What happened?"

"I don't know."

"What happened to Pierre?"

"I never saw him again. Willis and I married two months later. I was eighteen. He was twenty-three."

"That fast?"

She laughs. "Young people nowadays don't grow up with the values we did in my day. And I grew up in the Deep South."

"Your Southern drawl is cute. It's more pronounced when you're mad."

She agrees.

"Do you guys have children and grandchildren?"

"Our daughter died several years ago. She was our only child."

I take a second to look at her. Marie's eyes become misty and I regret my question.

"I'm so sorry for asking such a painful question." I reach over and pat her hands folded in her lap. "How long have you worked for Bryan?"

"Emma was a year old when he hired me to babysit. Me and Willis didn't become full time until after the house was finished."

Marie and I spend the rest of the drive getting to know each other. She asks me about Kourtney's father. I tell her about my relationship with James.

The next morning back at Bryan's house, I leave notes on Kourtney's and Emma's pillows and go downstairs to leave one in the kitchen for Marie. I'm going to the apartment to wait for a delivery.

Marie startles me. "Would you like something special for breakfast? The girls asked me to make snowman-shaped pancakes."

"No, thank you. I was about to leave you this note." I wave the folded piece of paper in my hand. "I'll be back before you're off the clock this afternoon."

Turning to leave, I bump into Bryan and stumble back. He grabs my waist to steady me. He's dressed in a business suit.

"I have a meeting. I'll be back by ten," he says.

I step around him and leave him watching me walk down the hallway.

Every bump and creak in the apartment makes me jump. I left a message for the apartment manager and the owner about installing a security system before we come back next week. Sleeping with a baseball bat in the bed with me is an option too. I look around the apartment, noting spots where I can stash other baseball bats.

James told me I was being foolish when I insisted he install extra door locks and window locks that rainy night I fled my apartment building and moved in with him. He promised to keep me safe, but that doesn't mean I felt safe. There's a difference.

Hopefully I can put up a brave front so Kourtney doesn't notice my apprehension. Maybe I should look for an apartment in a gated community. Knowing the grounds are patrolled would give me a little peace.

Wrapping Christmas gifts is how I start my morning. My cell phone is a hotline. I let Bryan's calls go to voicemail and answer the others. I know he and I need to talk. I'm just not ready.

Midmorning, there's a knock on the door. I tiptoe over and peek through the peephole. It's the express delivery company with the package I've been waiting for.

A part of me expects Bryan to show up at my door.

I call Marie to check up on Kourtney and Emma. She tells me Bryan took them to see a movie. I read off a list of ingredients needed to bake cookies this evening. She puts me on hold to check the pantry then comes back to let me know what I need to pick up from the store.

For the rest of the time at the apartment, I concentrate on typing notes in my patients' files and check work emails, replying to some and flagging others. Part of the agreement for me to take this time off, I have to keep in touch with patients who need counseling during the holidays.

I let my boss know that I will see a few patients on January 2nd and email Vanessa the list of appointments to schedule, then shut down my laptop.

It takes several trips to load the gifts in my truck and lock up the apartment.

On the way to the grocery store, a catchy song plays on the radio and I turn up the volume. The lyrics ignite a yearning in my heart and the emotion in the singer's voice speaks to my soul. I know what it's like to want to give yourself to someone, but to be uncertain they will take care of your heart. It takes ultimate trust to drop my guard and make myself vulnerable to anyone. I wanted that with Bryan. I wholeheartedly gave him something James never had. The most valued piece of me. We have history. I didn't realize how lonely I'd been until we moved here. My world has been shaken off its axis.

I find a spot at the far end of the lot and listen to the rest of the song. A black SUV pulls in next to me. Turning the car off, I press the button on the key fob to arm my truck and go inside humming the chorus of the song. I want what the singer's singing about. Love's tenderness and to know love's devotion.

There are no shopping carts or hand baskets available. My reusable bag will have to do. Lucky for me, everything I need is on one aisle.

I squeeze past impatient shoppers to get to aisle seven, baking supplies. As I turn the corner, I see Max picking up a box of salt substitute off the shelf.

"Last minute grocery shopping too?" I ask.

"Tom's family doesn't believe in complying with a simple respondez, s'il vous plaît. I have five extra people coming for dinner tomorrow. And get this"—he frowns with fake despair—"they each have special dietary needs. What are you doing here?"

"I'm picking up a few things. Baking Christmas cookies on Christmas Eve is a tradition for Kourtney and me."

"Sweetie, what's going on with you and Mr. Hawk?"

"I don't want to talk about it."

"Aw, Danikins. Please tell Maxie what's going on. Do I have to cut him for bringing tears to those brown eyes?" His knuckles brush my cheek. "I watched that man watching you at the party. Every opportunity he had to interact with you, no matter how small, he lit up brighter than a fairy, and you dimmed his light each time you walked away. You're both miserable. Use your training as a psychologist. View the issues a different way." He pulls me into his arms. "Heads up. Horny Toad at six o'clock," he whispers.

Stepping out of his embrace, I take a peek. "What happened to her?"

"Collagen and Botox withdrawals." He smiles "And those roots are as dark as my Uggs." Max blows a kiss and waves. "Happy Hol-Hoe-Days."

Holly Valentine offers a weak smile before pulling the hood of her sweatshirt over her head.

Something's not right. It surprises me when she walks right by us. Holly's never missed an opportunity to drop an innuendo about Bryan. Perhaps when she's not with Madelyn she's not as brave.

"I'm horrible." Max snickers.

"I wonder what's wrong."

She turns left at the end of the aisle.

He smacks his lips. "I told you she's going through withdrawals."

I playfully tap his arm. "I'm serious, Max."

Max does his famous dip and toss of his nonexistent long hair. "Me too, Danikins. Withdrawals ain't no day at the spa."

"Where's your holiday spirit?"

"Take a look through your own camera lens, Danikins. Where's your holiday spirit for Bryan?"

"I better get back. Don't forget we promised to take the girls to the spa." I pick up a box of organic food coloring.

Max smirks. "I wouldn't dream of breaking a promise. Call me and we'll plan the details." He leans in and air kisses my cheeks. "Merry Christmas, Danikins."

"Merry Christmas, Maxie."

I pick up the rest of the items I came for and weave my way to the front of the store. In the express checkout line, I spot Holly two lines down, wiping her eyes.

The girls burst through the backdoor laughing and brushing snow off their jackets. A few seconds later, Bryan walks through covered in remnants of snow.

"What have you two been up to?" I ask.

Kourtney and Emma hide behind me.

"We ambushed him with snowballs," Kourtney says.

"What's this for?" Emma points to the counter.

"Christmas cookies. We can leave out some for Santa," Kourtney tells her.

"Yeah?"

"Go hang up your jackets and hats, then wash your hands." My eyes follow them out of the kitchen.

Bryan steps into the laundry room. He returns minus a jacket and cap, wiping his face with a towel. "Can we talk?"

"What do we need to talk about, Bryan? You said you were frustrated."

"Is that all you heard?"

I exhale. "Bottom line, you're not interested in long-term relationships…"

"You're condemning me for a conversation I had years ago?"

"You said the same thing at the club."

"We were talking about my past!" He stares at me. "This is about you…"

The excited laughter of two girls racing each other down the hallway stops him from finishing his sentence.

"Are you helping us make cookies too?" Kourtney runs over to him.

"I wouldn't miss it."

"Kourty says you do this every year." Emma picks up a bottle of specialty candy sprinkles. "What kind are we baking?"

"Sugar cookies. You can make them any color and decorate them any way you want." I hold up the cookie cutter collection I started when I was pregnant with Kourtney.

We spend our late afternoon singing Christmas carols, baking and decorating cookies. Relationships and broken promises are put on the back burner as we get into the spirit of the holidays for our girls.

Sweet scents perfume the air and the kitchen counters are filling up with decorated cookies cooling on parchment paper. We're running out of space.

"Daddy, I'm getting hungry."

"Me too," Kourtney chimes in.

"I can call my elves and ask them to bring dinner a little early."

"You have elves?" Kourtney asks.

"They visit Emm and me every year." He smiles at her and winks at Emma. "Go get cleaned up while I help Dani clean the kitchen."

Kourtney runs over to Bryan, throwing her arms around his waist. I know he sees the sadness in my eyes because I see the same emotion reflected back at me in his.

"Thank you for letting us stay," Kourtney says.

He picks her up, kissing her cheek. "You're welcome, sweetheart."

She jumps out of his arms and follows her friend.

The kitchen isn't that messy. I made sure I cleaned any spills and swept the flour off the floor after Bryan showered the girls with a handful. The few dishes in the sink won't take two people to wash, but Bryan and I clean the kitchen in silence.

"You can fight. So what. Why is it your first reaction to Vin?"

I walk out of the kitchen.

Chapter Eighteen

THE WINDOW SEAT IS A place of comfort and solace. I draw my knees to my chest, wrap my arms around my legs, and stare out the window.

In foster care, the possibility of being moved always hovered in the background. If he were alive, James would attest to that. He'd been in four different foster homes since he was three years old. Even though I wasn't moved from their home, I didn't view the Franklins as permanent people in my life until I was in my late teens.

James and I had our ups and downs, but nothing close to the emotional turmoil I'm having with Bryan. I've cried more than I did when I learned James was dead.

Max suggested I become a voyeur, peeking through the camera of my life.

The Christmas lights outside the windowpane add depth to the darkness that I use as a backdrop. I take a step behind the camera and start from the beginning. I know exactly why I didn't keep my word. Suppressed resentment from the void he left in my heart. The morning he walked out the door, I was on my own. The foundation to my inner fortress set. The walls went up. My world became my child and giving her the best life I could as a single mother. And being the best therapist to those in need. But even the strength of the walls couldn't keep out the loneliness. Moving to Boulder, being here with Bryan, my fortress was infiltrated with permission. This time will be different, I convinced myself, yet here I am. Sitting on a window seat taking a close look at how we got to this point.

Vin, a panicked man, is desperate to find his best friend's child. He's not stampeding. He's walking with a purpose and spots Emma with a woman he doesn't know. Not only does the woman block him from the child, she throws the first punch. She throws all the punches.

In the bedroom, Vin asks a simple question. There's no malice behind his words. He even looks concerned. Yet she responds with aggression. He immediately backs off when told to do so and is the second one through the bathroom door when they thought she was hurt.

She demeans his character before she even knows him and pushes a sensitive button for all males young and old, straight or gay. The size of a man's penis is a matter of pride. She uses that knowledge to taunt him.

In the kitchen, she uses double entendre to defend her behavior, but she broke her promise any way it's viewed. The woman threw the first punch. He isn't the aggressive one. He starts off with harmless teasing but ends up reacting to her behavior.

What is it about Vin that triggers such aggressiveness?

The answer appears on the backdrop. I come from behind the lens and look at him head-on.

Those leering eyes that undressed me whenever our paths crossed. His lack of appropriate clothing every time I dropped off the rent check. The stomach-turning odor of rotting fish and old socks slapped me in the face when he opened the door.

Vin's body-size and threatening presence reminds me of Derek Tucker. The manager of the apartment building I lived in when I first moved to Arizona. Mr. Tucker was a predator. The suggestive words and innuendos he used every time we conversed kept me guarded. I slept with a baseball bat near me.

When I lived in that apartment building, finding a parking spot on the street was next to impossible and I didn't like parking in the assigned stall. The lighting in the underground structure was horrible.

One rainy night, I stayed late with my study group. I was going to spend the night at James's, but he didn't answer when I called. I drove to my apartment, looked for a parking spot on the street, then finally pulled into the parking structure. As soon as I got out of the car, Mr. Tucker came at me. Forcing me against the door. His hands groped my breast. From the smell of his breath, he'd been drinking liquid courage. His bravery got him cracked ribs and a broken nose once I stopped punching and kicking him.

I uncurl my limbs and walk across the room to get my cell phone. My fingers brush across the screen as I scroll through the contacts until I find the number I'm looking for.

"Hi, Danikins," Max answers on the second ring.

A sob escapes my lips and I drop to the floor the minute I hear the nickname. Bryan was right: I don't know what it's like to have true friends. But I'm learning.

Between weeping and stuttering, I tell my friend Max the short version of my twenty-seven years of life.

The chime of the doorbell rings throughout the house.

"Kourt, can you get that?" Bryan calls from downstairs.

I make it to the landing when she reaches the door. Her laughter fills the foyer. I reach the bottom step and laugh too, my soul is no longer heavy. After a two-hour phone therapy session with Max, I feel better.

Standing in the doorway, wearing elf hats with elf ears are Bryan's three best friends. They're holding insulated bags. One elf's arm is in a sling decorated with tiny red-nosed reindeers.

"You guys are so cool." Kourtney hugs Ignacio and Anthony before running back to Bryan, taking his hand.

A strange look crosses Vin's face.

Bryan has a fire burning in the fireplace in the family room and Christmas music playing on the surround sound speakers. We unpack a smorgasbord of food and drinks.

The adults reminisce about our Christmases when we were eight years old. I tell stories about my holidays with Mr. and Mrs. Franklin. The girls explain how they came up with their joint Christmas list and which gifts they hope they really get.

I watch how Kourtney interacts with Ignacio and Anthony. She's comfortable around them but shies away from Vin. That strange look crosses his face each time he tries to joke with her and she withdraws.

I also notice who Kourtney is sitting next to—Bryan.

"Danielle, what do you want Santa to bring you for Christmas?" Emma giggles.

"Emm, who do you want to read the story?" Bryan asks.

"Uncle Vinny." She skips over to the bookshelf and skips back to her uncle. "Come on, Kourty. Uncle Vinny is the best reader. He makes up funny accents."

Kourtney turns to me. Uncertain.

Vin watches me too. It's obvious she's taking her cues from me. He pleads with his eyes. He wants her to trust him like she does the others. I see it now. He cares about us and Kourtney's mistrust bothers him.

If I hadn't been so determined to knock down the memory of Derek

Tucker, I would have seen Vin's nothing like him. Vin is a harmless teddy bear who needs a hug once in a while.

"Go ahead, Kourtney. Go listen to the story." I tell her.

She doesn't move, and everyone in the room gets quiet.

"It's okay, sweetie." I smile.

She takes a tentative step in Vin's direction, glancing at Bryan first then back at me.

Her next step is taken after our encouragement. Now she keeps her eyes on Bryan. It's his assurance she seeks to take the last step.

"Do you want to sit next to me too?" Vin asks.

Kourtney gives a slight nod.

He winces as he pulls his arm out of the sling and reaches out to her. Once she's settled next to him, Vin opens the book and starts the classic Christmas story with an exaggerated Transylvanian-like accent.

A year ago, I couldn't convince her to take a picture with Santa and now she hugs these men like they've been a part of her life since birth. She looks to Bryan for security and validation. My baby has come so far. For the two steps forward she's taken to expand her comfort zone, she will take five steps back if I cut them out of our lives. Is that really fair to her?

I carry a load of dishes to the kitchen. Bryan follows with food containers. We stop and stare at each other for a few seconds. I break the connection going back to the family room for more dishes.

Bryan and I pass one another going back and forth. At one point, I bump into him in the doorway of the family room.

"Mommy. You and Bryan are standing under the mistletoe. You guys have to kiss."

When did Vin finish the story?

"Kiss her, Daddy."

"Go ahead. Smooch and make up," Vin's making kissy sounds for emphasis.

Emma and Kourtney snicker.

"Time for bed, girls," Bryan says.

"Aw, come on. Can't we stay up a little longer?" Kourtney whines.

Bryan shrugs. "Fine, but Santa won't come if you're still up."

They scurry out of the family room.

"Wait, we have to leave cookies and milk for Santa." Kourtney stops at the bottom of the stairs.

"Shower and put on your pajamas, then come back down," I tell them.

They race up the stairs while I go to the kitchen. I rinse and load the dishes in the washer, then turn it on and store the leftover food in the refrigerator.

"How many cookies do we leave for Santa?" Emma runs into the kitchen, Kourtney right behind her, both dressed in matching pajamas.

They couldn't have showered that fast. Kourtney loves the water. I usually have to make her get out.

Kourtney climbs on the counter, getting the Santa plate I brought from the apartment.

Emma opens the refrigerator, reaching for the carton of milk.

They put a half-dozen cookies on the plate and pour milk in a Santa glass. I help them carry the tray to the family room.

The girls run around saying good night to everyone.

Kourtney runs to Vin last, hugging his waist. "Uncle Vinny. That was the funniest Christmas story ever."

He picks her up in his good arm. "I'm glad you liked it, Kourty Bear."

She kisses his cheek before hopping down.

"I'm right behind you," I call after them.

"Mommy, may I sleep in Emmy's room?" She's dancing on the middle step.

"Only if you two go to sleep and not play around." I walk out of the family room.

"You're falling for her, Bry," Ignacio says.

I pause on the first step to hear his response.

"Never thought I'd live to see the day *the* mighty Hawk falls fast and falls hard," Vin teases.

"Look who's talking. *The Tank* got crushed by a seven-year-old," Anthony taunts.

"Kourty Bear would rather stay in a dangerous situation than to come with me to safety. That wasn't cool. So yes, she did something your weak-ass could never do. Get me to tone it down." He laughs.

"Don't make me choose between you and Dani ever again. That goes for all of you. I guarantee you won't like my choice."

"Bry, I'm the last one to give relationship advice, but since you're my brother from another mother, it's my duty to tell you—grow a pair as big as hers and take a leap."

I rush up the stairs before they see me.

I check Kourtney's bathroom, then go across the hall to Emma's. The girls are in bed, covers pulled up to their chins. They watch me with hope-filled eyes.

Shaking my head, I stand in the doorway to the bathroom. "Get out of bed and take real showers."

They turned on the water, but forgot to at least wet their towels.

One at a time, they take a shower and brush their teeth.

In bed, Kourtney and Emma play tug of war with the covers until I've had enough with their shenanigans. They settle down.

For the past few nights, Kourtney's slept without Mr. Cuddles in her arms. He's fought off the monsters and watched over her while she slumbered since she was three years old.

When I go back downstairs the men are in the foyer eating cookies and fastening their coats. The gifts from Kourtney and me in their hands.

"We got the presents out of your truck for you," Bryan tells me.

"These cookies are good." Vin talks with his mouth full. "How do I get some all to myself?"

"If you're on Santa's good list, I'll raid the bakers' stash for you."

"Some of us are better than others." Tony winks at me.

I go to the kitchen and put a dozen cookies in plastic storage bags for each elf. There's still a lot left.

"Good night, Dani. Merry Christmas." Ig hugs me, taking a bag of cookies from my hand.

Vin gives me a one-arm bear hug. "Welcome to the family, Dani." He too takes a bag of cookies.

"Go easy on him, Dani," Anthony whispers as he hugs me. He takes the last bag of cookies. "Merry Christmas, little sis."

Bryan opens the door for them.

"Merry Christmas. Drive safe." It doesn't bother me that they are calling me Dani. It feels good to be thought of as someone's little sister. "Thank you for tonight."

Bryan and I watch them drive off before closing the door.

"Can we talk, in the family room?" Bryan asks, gesturing with his hand.

"Yes, I'd like that." I promised Max I would talk to Bryan once the girls went to bed and we got the gifts under the tree.

The lights are off, but the fire burning in the fireplace provides enough light for me to see the four monogramed Christmas stockings hanging on hooks attached to the mantel and all the presents around the tree. The coffee table had to be moved to accommodate the boxes and gift bags.

"We went a little overboard this year," Bryan says, rubbing the back of his neck.

I perch on the sofa. He sits near yet leaves space. Bryan looks down at his hands and fidgets. He takes a deep breath, holds it and releases it, lifting his head. He stares into my eyes.

Vulnerable. That was the look in his eyes I couldn't identify. Bryan looks unsure and vulnerable.

"None of them were you, Dani."

"I don't understand."

"Those women. Amelia. I didn't want a relationship with them."

I can sympathize.

His long eyelashes accentuate the longing in his eyes. "Only you."

"I *know* how anguish alters a person's behavior. It's why I specialize in grief counseling. The levels of pain a person experiences at the loss of someone you feel connected to, deep in your soul it's…" I shake my head, unable to find the words. "This constant tug of war between us makes it easy for me to push you away. I don't want to get too close then have to deal with you leaving us."

"I'm not going anywhere."

"You say that now, but…"

"*I'm not leaving*," he proclaims.

Deep down I believe him. His words are spoken with so much power, why wouldn't I? But there's still the issue of the other day.

"You scare me, Bryan. You stripped me of the ability to defend myself."

"Hearing that doesn't make me proud. Causing you pain doesn't make me feel like a man. I'm sorry, Dani. I was trying to stop you from getting hurt and hurting yourself. I went too far."

I watch the flames flicker and dance in the fireplace. And listen to the wood crackle. The silence is comfortable after days of tension. Even the atmosphere in the house seems light.

"What do you want from me?" he asks.

"I want you to be my friend. I want you to censor what you tell your friends about us."

"For you, I will. And for the record, we've always been more than friends." Bryan reaches for my hand but pulls back before he touches me. He wants that physical link with me but is unsure if I'll welcome it. I see it in his eyes. "Tell me what you need from me."

I close the space between us, covering his hand with mine. "I need to know our relationship is going somewhere and I'm not just another one of your no-strings-attached flings."

He winces. "I apologize if I gave you that impression. I want this. Do you?"

"I need to feel safe."

He leans in. "Your trust means everything and I won't abuse it again. But I need you to listen and not challenge how I protect you. You can take a step back. I'm always here for you and Kourt even if it seems like I'm not."

We lace fingers.

I squeeze his hand.

"What do you want right now?" he asks.

"I want to know you."

He sits back on the sofa, pulling me with him.

"What do you want to know?"

"What's your favorite color?" I rest my head on the fluffy cushion behind me. I draw my legs up and stare into the fire.

"It used to be blue, but I became partial to light brown."

I smile. "Why the change?"

He laughs and I lay my head on his shoulder.

"Dani, who's Mr. Tucker?"

"How do you know about him?"

"In the mall, you called Vin, Mr. Tucker."

I take a deep breath. "Derek Tucker attacked me a few months after I moved to Arizona," I begin to tell Bryan the whole story.

Chapter Nineteen

CHRISTMAS MORNING THE GIRLS BURST into the room, bouncing on the bed. Bryan and I sit up. Surprised.

"Wake up," Emma shouts.

"Come see what Santa left for us," Kourtney yells.

Bryan roars, tackling and tickling them until they're lying between us, breathless from laughing. I prop myself up on my elbow and watch them.

"You two know it's five thirty in the morning?" he yawns.

"Uh—yes," Kourtney says, smacking her lips.

Bryan drops a pillow on her head. "Let's lie here for an hour, then go downstairs."

Kourtney peeks from underneath the pillow. "Mom? Are you guys still on a timeout?"

"The timeout is over," I tell her.

"Dad? Is Dani your girlfriend?" Emma asks.

Bryan gives me the questioning eyebrow. I grin.

"Dani's my girlfriend."

The pillow flies off Kourtney's head as the girls wiggle-dance in the bed.

"Mom. I saw a *big* present by the tree for you." She uses her hands and arms to emphasize the size.

I jump out of the bed. "Go brush your teeth and wash your face. Last one downstairs is a rotten egg."

The girls scramble out of the room. Bryan drops back on the bed covering his face, mumbling.

I throw on his robe over the pajama top and boxers I borrowed. In the bathroom I grab a spare toothbrush, doing the fastest face wash and teeth brushing in history. I beat the girls to the top of the stairs.

We race to the family room like a wrecking team, reading names on the tags and tossing boxes to one another. Kourtney picks up a small black gift bag with distinctive monogramed initials in purple. She looks for a name. The breath catches in my lungs and I grab the bag from her, shoving it in the pocket of the robe. I hand her another gift in exchange.

Bryan turtle walks in, running his fingers through his bed-hair. He tosses me a pair of socks as he plops down on the sofa. I sit on the floor in the middle of the chaos to slide my feet into the thick cotton men's crew socks.

Kourtney hands him a gift and goes back to the big one with her name on the tag. "To Kourty-Bear from Uncle Vinny," she reads before clawing at the wrapping paper and peeling off the tape in the center of the box. The sides unfold and a life-size, brown grizzly bear cub stuffed animal gives a realistic roar. Kourtney hugs it. "I'll name him Uncle Vinny Bear because he's big and tough."

"Vin has a new fan," I whisper and Bryan nods.

"To Fala-Emmy from Uncle Vinny," she reads, taking her time to unwrap the gift. Kourtney chants for Emma to hurry and open it. The sides unfold and a life-size white-and-black spotted miniature pony stuffed animal neighs. It's the Falabella pony in the book Emma and I are reading.

"Vin spent a small fortune on their gifts." I run my fingers through the soft mane of the tail.

"Open your box, Mom."

I jump to my feet and step over discarded wrapping paper to get to my big box. "To the Featherweight from Vinny the Tank," I read the tag out loud. With childlike excitement, I rip off the wrapping paper. "Oh, my... I can't believe him," I laugh, holding the flaps open.

"What is it?" Bryan asks, craning his neck to see.

I step aside so they can see the life-size punching bag on a stand, with Vin's smiling face painted on. Also inside are a pair of hot pink boxing gloves with matching boxing shorts and robe. I pick up the Feather-weight Championship belt.

"Will it fit in the apartment?"

Bryan rises from the sofa, walking around the mess in the middle of the floor to get to the fireplace. He takes my Christmas stocking off the hook, bringing it to me, then reclaims his spot on the sofa without saying a word.

I go sit next to him. The girls stop opening gifts to watch us. I reach inside and pull out a set of keys and remote fob.

"Emm and I want you and Kourt to move in with us."

My lungs stop functioning for a heartbeat.

"I know it's fast, but it feels right," Bryan says.

"We're getting to know each other again. What if it doesn't work out? I have a one-year lease. What would I do with our furniture? We have to think about the girls. I'd have to talk to Kourtney first, her opinion is important…"

His finger presses against my lips, silencing me. "This will work because we want it to. Give me a copy of your lease. I'm sure I can get you out of it, and if I can't, I'll write a check for the balance of the year. Bring whatever pieces of furniture you want, we'll make it fit. Hey, Kourt." Bryan keeps his eyes on me but is talking to Kourtney. "I asked your mom if you guys would live here with Emm and me. She says she has to ask you first."

Kourtney hops over opened boxes and piles of torn wrapping paper to sit between us, squirming until we make room for her. "My answer is yes."

"We can read together every night." Emma sits next to me.

Uncertainty and doubt begin to fill my heart and mind. "What if it doesn't work out?"

His smile spreads to his eyes. "I'll move out. You and the girls can have the house."

"I don't know." I stare at my hands.

Bryan stands, then squats in front of me. He takes my hand, placing it against his shirt, over his heart. I feel the steady pounding against my palm.

"It's not just us who gets hurt if…"

Bryan kisses me, forcing away the fear of the unknown. Exorcising the ghosts of our past. The emotion behind his kiss speaks volumes to my soul. He's *ready* to commit.

We get so lost in our nonverbal communication, we forget the girls are sitting next to us until they giggle.

Bryan rests his forehead on mine. "Only you," he whispers.

I cup his cheeks in my hands. "Only you," I repeat.

"Sooo," Kourtney sings. "Are we living here?"

"Yes," Bryan and I say simultaneously.

"Good." She jumps up from the sofa. "Let's open more presents."

Emma hugs me and follows Kourtney.

"You have a gift from Marie, Mommy."

Bryan returns to his spot next to me, wrapping his arm around my shoulder. Kourtney brings me the wrapped box. Inside is a book of Marie's family recipes.

I thumb through the pages. "I think I'll make the red velvet cake first."

Bryan leans over, pressing his lips against my ear. "I'll lick the bowl while you lick the spoon?" His deep sensual voice strokes the embers still burning after our make-up sex-session early this morning. "Come help me start breakfast. Our guests will be here any minute."

I let him pull me to my feet. "What guests?"

"Uncle Vinny spends the day with us," Emma says, shaking a box.

"Ig and Tony are spending the day with us too. Usually they visit their families." He stops in the doorway. Bryan lifts my chin with his fingertips. "May I kiss you under the mistletoe?"

My hands slide up his arms as I rise on my tiptoes, giving him a lingering peck.

Our audience cheers and claps.

Bryan leads me to the kitchen. I pull out the small black gift bag from the pocket of the robe and hand it to him.

"You gave me your forgiveness. Sex by the fire. Great sex in the shower. And oh yeah, a travel kit. Plus, you agreed to move in..."

"Look inside."

He reaches in and pulls out a pair of Sex-Dice encased in provocative packaging. The day after we went to the club I found an adult entertainment store. No longer wanting battery-operated relief, I bought something we could play with. One die names the gratification of the receiver. The other die names how the gratification is given. There were lots more to choose from. I figured I'd start off slow and work my way up to the more explicit ones. I forgot the gift bag was in the hatch until I saw it in Kourtney's hands.

"Can we play tonight?" I ask.

"Want to play right now?" He lifts me onto a countertop, kissing me.

I run my fingers through his thick hair, deepening the kiss.

"Break it up, you two."

We pull apart and look to the kitchen's entrance.

Vin leans on the doorframe. "People eat in here. Didn't you guys do that after we left?"

I push Bryan back and hop down.

"That's none of your business." I go to Vin, rising on my tiptoes to kiss his cheek. He has to lean a little for me to reach. "Thank you for the punching bag."

He blushes. "You're welcome, Champ."

And just that fast, Vin and I establish an unspoken truce.

Tony strolls into the kitchen. "I gave her a gift certificate to the firing range. She may mistake you for the dummy and shoot you in the ass." He hugs me.

"Why can't you two give practical gifts?" Ig walks in, kissing my cheek.

"What did Ig give you?" Vin asks.

"An extra-large first aid kit." I laugh. "Thank you, Ig. I'll carry it with me at all times."

"Gag gifts aside." Ig pulls out a red envelope from the back pocket of his designer jeans. "This is from the three of us." He hands it to me. "It's more of a gift for Bry though."

I open the envelope. My mouth drops.

"What did you guys give her?" Bryan peeks over my shoulder.

"A private shopping spree at that lingerie store in the mall, tomorrow at three," Tony gloats.

Bryan walks around the kitchen high and low fiving his friends. "What's her limit? I'll kick in on it."

I exit the kitchen, shaking my head. I don't think I'll ever understand their friendship.

I wait until Dani and the girls go upstairs to question Tony.

"Did you find any information on Derek Tucker?" I ask.

"Sorry, Bryan. I ran his name through the Arizona database. No Tucker lived in that building."

"She said she cracked his ribs and broke his jaw. Did you search the records of the hospitals in that area?"

Tony nods. "A Stephon Greene flatlined on the table the night Dani said she had an altercation with Tucker. He had a broken jaw, cracked ribs, and a fatal stab wound in the gut."

I lean against the counter. "She didn't say anything about stabbing him."

"I checked the police database. That night, an emergency call came in from a bar five blocks from Dani's apartment building. Steps it's called. A Caucasian male had been stabbed. Six one. A hundred and ninety-five pounds. Brown hair. Brown eyes. According to witnesses, he was already drunk when he stumbled into the bar. He went to the restroom, came out holding his side, and collapsed on the floor."

"Any idea who did it?"

"The case remains unsolved. But there's one interesting fact though. The owner told the detective Greene met up with an African American

Army Soldier two or three times a week there."

"Let me guess. The soldier's description matches Edwards," I say.

Tony touches his nose.

"His description somewhat matches Vin's. Did you upload the medical files?" Ig asks, stirring a sauce in a pot.

"Yep. I'll forward it to you." Tony pulls out his phone.

"I'll see how far back the bar's security cameras' archives go," Vin says checking the oven.

"What about the apartment building's management company? Any record of a Tucker managing the property?" I ask

"That's the thing. Greene was a Hollywood B-List actor slash stuntman in Arizona filming a movie. The building wasn't managed by a company. The building went through a quick sale two weeks after Dani moved in. It was owned by Elijah Hopper."

"Why does that name sound familiar?" I ask.

"I thought so too, so I have Riley doing a search."

Tony cracks his knuckles and takes a deep breath. That's never a good sign. He's about to tell me something I don't want to hear.

"I checked phone records, utility company records, cable company records. Other than the water, which the building owner pays, no other utilities or services were turned on in that apartment." He looks me square in the eyes.

"Does Greene have any ties to this case besides Edwards?" I ask my friend.

"No."

"Then she wasn't lying about the attack, Tony." I rub my neck out of frustration.

We all know what he's thinking, without actually saying it.

He shrugs. "I didn't say she was. I'm just presenting the facts."

That unwritten law between bros is being tested. This isn't the first time our friendship's been stretched because of a female. And it won't be the last. We are the Elite Team. To stay on top, we have to trust each other in the field and off. No matter how I feel about Dani, we're still working a case. I have to treat it as such and consider all the possibilities. But Tony still has to present more facts to sway me.

"Anything on the driver of the car that tried to run Dani off the road?" I ask.

"His name is Yang Ma-han. American born, but paid to cause an accident," Ig says.

"By whom?"

With one hand, Vin lines up croissants on a pan. "A female. He didn't get a name."

"Is he telling the truth?"

Vin throws me a *you know better than to ask me that* look.

"I have to hand it to Porter. He managed to shoot out the car's tire and stop Yang from getting away on foot without backup." Tony turns over the sausage in the frying pan.

"That's why I want him on Dani's security detail."

"Bry, did you tell her your parents are coming?" Ig turns down the fire under the pot. If he were sitting he'd be flapping his wings. Instead he's moving around the kitchen like a madman.

I shrug. "Thought I'd wing it."

Tony slaps my shoulder. "Bro, have I not taught you anything?"

"Mom and dad will be happy to meet my girlfriend." No one looks at me. I push away from the counter and finish slicing fruit. "You guys think I should tell her?"

Next to me, Vin pulls a pan out of the oven and closes the door with his foot. "Your funeral."

The girls haven't stopped talking about how much fun it will be to live in the same house since we came upstairs to get dressed.

The smells coming from the kitchen float up the stairs and make my mouth water. Who would have thought all four of them were competent in the kitchen?

I wonder if I can convince Max to go lingerie shopping with me tomorrow. Probably not, he has family visiting.

"Dani. Emm. Kourt. Breakfast is ready," Bryan's voice carries from downstairs.

The girls bounce down the stairs ahead of me. The best gift Bryan and I gave them today is their perception of sisterhood.

The front door swings open. "Merry Christmas, everyone," a woman shouts.

Three people, loaded with wrapped gifts and wearing heavy winter outerwear, step inside.

"Grandma. Grandpa. Aunt Jessi," Emma screams, jumping the last two steps, running to them.

The trio drop the gifts on the bench by the door to hug her.

Kourtney waits for me to catch up. She grabs my hand.

I'm floored.

I wasn't expecting to meet his family so soon.

"I forgot to mention that my parents and sister come every Christmas. They stay until New Year's Day."

New Year's Day? Okay floored doesn't come near what I'm feeling. Dumbfounded should cover it.

Bryan takes Kourtney's free hand, guiding us over to his family. "Mom. Dad. Jessi. This is Dr. Danielle Edwards and Kourtney. Dani. Kourt. This is my mom, Nancy. My dad, Bryan. And my sister, Jessica."

I recover from the temporary shock. "It's nice to meet you."

Bryan looks a lot like his dad, but he has his mother's hazel eyes and brown hair.

Nancy and Jessica give me warm handshakes and hugs. His dad ignores my outstretched hand.

Bryan's mom stares at Kourtney, then hugs her. Kourtney returns the hug. What surprises me is Kourtney isn't put off by Nancy's display of affection after just meeting her.

"It's nice to meet you, sweetheart," Nancy says to Kourtney.

"It's nice to meet you too, ma'am."

Kourtney turns to Bryan. "Your dad's name is Bryan too?"

"Yes, young lady. What's your dad's name?" The person she asked isn't the one who answered. The venom in his voice makes her step back like she's getting out of the strike zone.

I move in front of Kourtney ready to put him in his place, but Bryan picks her up.

"My name is Bryan Kendall Hawk the Fourth. My dad is Bryan Kendall Hawk the Third. It's a tradition in my family."

"When I say Bryan, which one of you will answer?" She looks nervously at his father.

"You will address me as Dr. Hawk," he rumbles.

Kourtney shrinks back even though she's safe in Bryan's arms.

Marie and Willis enter the house through the side door, interrupting the unladylike words about to roll off my tongue.

"You're spending the day with us too?" Emma asks.

"This year we didn't go see my family," Willis tells her.

Kourtney slides out of Bryan's arms and quickly walks over to Marie. "Merry Christmas. Thank you for the teddy bear blanket and beginners knitting set." She hugs the motherly woman.

"You're welcome, dear," Marie cups her face. "And thank you for the homemade potpourri jars. I love them." She turns to Bryan's family. "It's good to see you guys."

They each give her a warm greeting.

"Let's go in for breakfast," Marie tells Kourtney and Emma. "After we eat, Willis has a surprise out back for you."

"Behave, Bry," Nancy says, warning her husband. She hands him her coat, scarf and hat. "I'm so glad you guys are joining us for breakfast, Danielle." She takes my hand as we walk toward the formal dining room. Jessica follows.

The décor of the room is something you'd see in a diplomat's home. Burgundy-painted walls with a pure white ceiling. Windowless with two gold chandeliers hanging overhead. A fourteen-seat cherrywood table. The upholstery of the high-back chairs matches the drapes that frame the main entrance. The other entrance leads to the kitchen.

Dr. Hawk blesses the food and we pass the dishes around.

"Boys, you outdid yourselves this year." Nancy looks around the table. She insisted on sitting next to Kourtney, who is unusually quiet. She coaxes timid smiles and one-word replies from Kourtney.

"You're a lefty too?" Nancy asks, holding up her own hand to show she's also left-handed.

Kourtney nods while her eyes cut to Bryan. I gaze at him too. My heart threatens to beat out of my chest and his fork pauses for a second.

"Kourty sits next to me at school, Grandma. We had to switch seats because we kept bumping elbows."

Nancy winks. "Your dad had that same problem when he was in elementary."

"How was the drive?" Bryan asks.

"Beautiful as ever. Winter is my favorite season. What part of Colorado are you from, Danielle?" Nancy asks.

"I grew up in California and moved to Arizona when I graduated from college. I enrolled in the graduate program in Tucson. We moved here in July."

"You have a college degree?" Sarcasm drips from Dr. Hawk's lips.

I throw the sarcasm right back. "Your son introduced me as *Doctor* Danielle Edwards. I have a Psy.D. in Clinical Psychology."

"How old are you?" Jessica asks. "I'm sorry, that was rude, but you look so young."

"I'm twenty-seven."

Her eyes grow big.

"I took classes at a Junior College while I was in high school. When I graduated at fifteen, I started at a University as a sophomore."

"Your parents must be very proud," Nancy says.

Willis fails to suppress a smile.

"My mom died in childbirth and I never knew my father."

"What a shocker," Dr. Hawk grunts. "Does she even know her father?" He points at Kourtney.

"That's enough, Dad." The calmness in Bryan's voice contradicts the threat behind his words.

I don't miss the glances passing between Bryan and his friends. Alpha male and his pack are on alert.

"Remember, you're a guest in *our* house."

Sneering in my direction, Dr. Hawk huffs. "Our?"

Bryan jumps out of his chair, hammering the table with his fist. Dishes clatter and clink as the vibration rattles them. Kourtney and Emma jump in their seats.

Kourtney has never been exposed to testosterone-driven hostility, and from the looks of it, neither has Emma.

"Come, girls," Marie says. "Let's go see Willis's surprise."

"Leave your dishes. I'll get them," I say.

They jump to their feet, bumping the table. Dishes rattle again as the girls try to get away as fast as they can.

The room is quiet except for the clink of Jessica's fork hitting the china plate. The unfriendly atmosphere in the room hasn't curbed her appetite.

I look around the table, and my gaze lands on Nancy. Now I know who Bryan inherited that angry-calmness from. The way she's staring at her husband has me cowering in my chair.

Bryan leans over, kissing my cheek. He finally sits in his chair.

I pick up my dishes and rise from my seat, going around the table to get the others.

Vin sits up straight, a knowing grin on his face. I approach Bryan's father.

"Dr. Hawk, I would appreciate it if you'd refrain from insulting me in front of Kourtney and Emma. You and I can do that in private any time you'd like. But let me warn you, sir…" I step a little closer. He looks up, clearly unsure what to make of me. "When I feel threatened, I get physical. I've been boxing since I was eleven years old. My skills have improved over the years. Ask Vin."

I carry my load out of the dining room.
Out of one frying pan and into another!

Chapter Twenty

INSTEAD OF GOING BACK TO the dining room, I walk down the hall to go upstairs and get my jacket and cap. When I make it to the landing, familiar hands come down on my shoulders guiding me toward his bedroom. I didn't hear Bryan sneak up behind me.

He kicks the door shut and turns the lock once we're inside.

"What are you doing?" I ask.

He pulls out something from his pocket, makes a fist, and starts shaking his hand. *Clack, clack, clack.* The dice roll around in his palm.

My inner muscles contract. "Bryan, we can't play with those right now."

"Why not?"

"You have a house full of people."

"Okay, a quickie then." He tosses the dice over his shoulder and reaches for the button on my jeans before they hit the hardwood floor.

Bryan has my jeans unbuttoned, unzipped, and down around my ankles by the time the last die stops rolling.

His hand slides into the front of my panties. "Hmm. Someone's getting excited."

I reach for the button on his jeans. "Okay, a quickie." I walk backward unzipping his jeans, pushing them down along with his boxer briefs.

The back of my knees bump the bed and I fall onto the comforter. Bryan pulls off my shoes, socks and jeans, while stepping out of his.

He holds up my ripped panties.

"When did you do that?"

"Boys' Club secret. Don't miss your appointment tomorrow. Make sure you buy stuff that leaves little to my imagination and is easy to rip off."

Crab crawling onto the bed, I watch Bryan remove his shirt, tossing it to the floor.

"I thought for a quickie, you kept half your clothes on?" I say.

"Not the way I want one with you."

I get on my knees, pulling my shirt over my head, unhooking the back clasp of my bra, letting it fall to the bed. I cup my breasts in my hands and rub my nipples until they tighten under my stimulation. Feeling bold, I stick two fingers in my mouth, sucking them.

His eyes take on a lustful gleam. The tip of his tongue is captured between his teeth.

I ease my fingers out and trail them down my chin. My throat. My cleavage. My stomach. They continue downward until they're between my thighs.

Bryan watches as I pleasure myself. His Adam's apple bobs up and down. My eyes close. Sounds of pleasure flee my throat to express the desires boiling within my sex. Bryan's deep, sexy voice directs my actions. Hips circling and rocking against the glide of my fingers. The sensation becomes intense and I use both hands to push myself to a climatic end. Erotic pictures of us play like a slideshow in my mind.

My eyes open and follow his hand as it slides up and down his length to the same rhythm set by my fingers sliding in and out of me.

Our eyes connect as the heat takes over, but my body isn't satisfied. I need him. Inside me. And I will not starve myself of this craving.

I crawl to the edge of the bed, kissing my way up his defined torso to his soft lips. Thrusting my tongue into his mouth. Bringing him down upon me.

The soft down comforter welcomes my back. My tongue shows him what my body wants while my hand reaches between us, guiding him into me.

Arms and legs close around him. I circle my hips against him, chasing after that orgasm.

"Slow down, Dani," Bryan pants.

I squeeze him tighter.

All rational thoughts.

Gone.

All sense of discretion.

Bye-bye.

The desperate need for the ultimate release takes over. I don't care what I do to get it. I don't care how I get there or who hears me. I need it.

Quick.

Hard.

And deep.

Bryan's tongue traces the shell of my ear. He's letting me run the race on my own. This time the tingling starts in the depths of my sex. The flame igniting every cell in its path, like trails of gunpowder heading to one destination.

Bryan thrusts into me and bites down on my earlobe, causing everything to happen at once.

My mind goes blank.

My heart stops beating.

My eyes roll back.

My toes curl.

I float into the abyss of an orgasm. The pleasure is unimaginable. Indescribable. All consuming. Every part of my body is stimulated by the pleasure of coming. A jolt of electricity makes me clench, then my body goes limp and I release Bryan from my death grip.

He lies unmoving on top of me while my lungs work overtime. His weight presses me into the mattress.

"Are you okay?" Too caught up in my own pleasure, I forgot about him.

His body shivers, but he doesn't answer me.

My eyes open in alarm. "Bry?"

He doesn't respond.

He's hurt. What do I do? Do I call for help? I push on his shoulders.

His arms move and he pulls himself up. I realize why he hasn't answered.

"Are you laughing?" I ask.

I push him off me.

How did we get in the middle of the bed?

Bryan rolls onto his side, laughter stealing his ability to talk. I try to move away, but his strong arm pulls me to him, spooning me.

"I'm... sorry," he stutters.

Insecurity rears its ugly head.

"I have been screwing since I was sixteen and never have I heard a woman cuss that much while she's coming."

"I don't cuss."

"Ohh baby. You were cussing so much you came up with new phrases."

I don't remember saying anything, but then, I don't remember how we got in the middle of the bed.

"That by far was the *best* quickie I've ever had." Bryan laughs.

His guffawing makes my body shake.

"If you keep laughing, I guarantee you'll never get another." I pull away and climb out of the bed.

Tears fall from his eyes and he holds his stomach. "I'm not... laughing… at you."

I gather my clothes from around the bed and glare at him. He rolls onto his stomach. I stare. Surprised by the sight.

"Bryan! Your shoulder. Your back." The clothes drop from my hands as I look at my nails.

Ten, long, red welts mar the hawk tattoo on his back, from his butt up to his shoulder blades. Small beads of fresh blood highlight the puckered skin. The unmistakable imprints of my teeth mark his shoulder.

"I consider them badges of honor." He buries his face in the comforter as a new round of cackling takes over.

Bewildered. I tread to the bathroom, closing the door behind me. That hunger for an orgasm was never in the books I read. I wish I had a friend to compare notes with. I wonder if Max's experiences are similar.

Bryan is sitting on the edge of the bed in his underwear when I come out of the bathroom. "I don't know why my dad is being an ass, but if you don't want him here, I'll tell him to leave."

I cup his cheek in my hand. "I would never ask you to do that, but please don't make me promise not to defend Kourtney or myself."

His lips press into the palm of my hand. "It's my job to defend you guys."

"Maybe we should tell them."

"I will, but not during the holidays."

"I don't want you or your friends to harm your father." I trace his lip with my thumb.

Bryan nods.

"*If* I need your help, I'll let you handle your dad."

"Deal."

"I'm going to see what Willis got the girls." I pick up my bra, shirt, and jeans. My dilemma is that all my clothes are in the guest room. I have no panties. I could go commando, but that is uncomfortable in jeans.

"You didn't pack everything the other day. Check the drawer for underwear or wear a pair of mine." Bryan smiles.

I kiss him and carry my clothes into the closet to get dressed.

When I come out, I hear Bryan in the shower humming a tune. A memory flashes in my mind of him walking in on me in the shower. Headphones covering his ears, singing that R&B classic, he didn't know I was already in the bathroom.

I leave his room and go outside.

Kourtney is wearing a helmet and sitting behind Willis, her arms around his waist. They're gliding over the snow on a snowmobile. Emma claps her hands as they go by.

"She's safe." Marie pats the empty spot next to her on the bench. "He wouldn't let anything happen to her. Or you."

We watch the snowmobile circle the pond. I wrap my arms around the motherly housekeeper for a quick second. "You have been so kind to us. I can't thank you enough."

"No need, dear. You and Kourtney are a joy to have around." She shifts and slightly turns to look at me.

"Will you feel that way with two extra people in the house? Bryan and Emma asked us to move in."

Her smile could light up a dark night. "Of course I will." She squeezes my hand. "So you and Bryan worked things out?" There's a teasing twinkle in her eyes.

I fight the telling smile, trying to break free.

"Thank you for the gift certificate to the Hot Springs Spa. I can't wait to be pampered for a whole day." She changes the subject. "Willis was excited when he pulled out the autographed boxing gloves from the box. How did you get them?"

"I cashed in a favor."

"He took down all his old military boxing trophies from the mantel and put the gloves up in their place."

"When we worked out together, he didn't mention boxing while in the military."

Marie looks away. "It was a long time ago."

The snowmobile pulls up a few feet in front of us. "That was fun," Kourtney shouts. "Thank you, Mr. Willis."

"My pleasure, Miss Kourtney."

"You should try it, Mommy. Mr. Willis is a safe driver."

"Go for a ride," Emma shouts. "It's fun!"

"I think I will."

I use the running board for leverage and throw my leg over the seat. Willis hands me a helmet.

"Hold on tight. I don't have to go slow like I did with the girls," he shouts, revving the engine.

I grab the passenger grips and we take off. Snow spews behind us. We head toward the woods near the pond.

Willis takes me on a tour of Bryan's property. I see the size of our audience has grown when we emerge from the trees. They're standing out in the yard. Bryan hops on behind me when Willis gets off. He teaches me how to operate the snowmobile and soon we're gliding over the snow-covered ground. I love being in control of the powerful machine with my man behind me. Trusting me.

Bryan tells me he had a not-so-subtle conversation with Dr. Hawk before coming outside. His dad chose to stay inside.

Vin trash talks from the sidelines while he watches his friends show off their skills on the snowmobile.

Jessica and Nancy join in on the fun and take a turn.

Bryan shows his bravery by teaching the girls how to operate the snowmobile and rides along with them. I grit my teeth the entire time, hiding behind Vin. While I'm using him as my shield, I take the time to apologize to him for my behavior.

He tells me, "If I ever catch up with Derek Tucker, I'll finish what you started." The promise in his words is clear.

From the corner of my eye, I see Anthony chuck a snowball at Jessica. I turn and run for the house. Nancy and Marie are right behind me. From the safety of the family room, we watch them. It is an every-man-for-himself snowball fight. No one is immune. Vin is right there in the middle of the battle giving it as good as he gets. Kourtney and Emma work as a team and are holding their own.

Once Ig calls a cease-fire, everyone comes inside. To warm them up, I make hot chocolate with whipped cream.

In the afternoon, the girls sit on the floor in the family room playing a board game. Nancy, Jessica, and Marie help me transfer toys and gifts from the family room, upstairs to the girls' rooms. The men are glued to the basketball game on television.

I step in front of the screen and demand they help carry the heavy gifts upstairs. We get into a battle of the wills until I grab the remote, switch to a cartoon channel, and run.

I banish Marie from the kitchen. Nancy helps me prepare dinner. We use the time to get to know each other.

I was a little worried she would question me about Kourtney's father. Instead she tells me she was a stay-at-home mom until Bryan went off to college. Now Nancy volunteers at a convalescent home. I laugh at her stories about the frisky gentlemen she's paired with.

After dinner, Bryan walks his friends out. Marie and Willis go home. Jessica helps me clean the kitchen while the girls give Nancy a manicure and pedicure in the family room. Dr. Hawk retires to one of the downstairs guest rooms.

Once the kitchen is clean and the food put away, Bryan moves my suitcases back to his room. I put fresh linens on the bed and straighten the room for his sister.

Bryan gets the girls tucked into bed early and turns in too.

Jessica, Nancy, and I sit by the fire in the family room with a bottle of wine. They entertain me with stories of Bryan, the overachieving, competitive sports fanatic who had female and several male classmates falling all over him. *Some things never change.*

Close to one in the morning, we call it a night and I drag myself upstairs. Bryan is hugging one of my pillows.

I wash up and pull on a sleep shirt and panties. I slide in next to him and pull the pillow from his arms, replacing it with my body. He holds me close like he's never letting me go. I close my eyes happy to bask in the warmth of him.

Chapter Twenty-One

WITH SHOULDERS SLUMPED, KOURTNEY SITS on the side of the bed when I come out of the bathroom.

"Good morning, sweetie. How did you sleep?" I ask.

"Morning, Mom."

I frown. "Did you sleep like a baby?"

Her shoulders rise and fall in one fluid motion.

"Did you eat breakfast?" I ask.

"I wasn't hungry."

"Kourt, what's wrong?" I sit next to her.

"Is Dr. Hawk going to live here too?"

"No, he's visiting for a little while."

"What's a little while?"

"They'll be here for a week."

"Do we have to stay while he's here?"

"Not if you don't want to. Talk to me, sweetie. What's wrong?" I cup her chin.

Her lips begin to tremble and tears roll down her cheeks. She climbs onto my lap.

I wrap my baby in my arms. "Do you want to tell me how you're feeling?"

"I'm sad."

"Can you tell me what's making you sad?"

"I heard Dr. Hawk say mean things about you."

"Was it the truth?"

She shrugs her shoulders.

"What's one thing he's said that makes you sad?"

"He said you're a gold digger."

"Do you know what a gold digger is?"

"I thought it meant someone who digs for gold, but I don't think that's what he means."

I kiss her temple. "You're right, one definition is someone who digs for gold like when we went to that ghost town in Arizona. Do you remember?"

Kourtney nods.

"The other is a way to define a person who pretends to love or care about someone that has a lot of money or valuable possessions."

"Why would he call you a gold digger?"

"I don't know. We just met yesterday. What's another thing he said that makes you sad?" I hug her tight, hoping the next thing out of her mouth isn't a racial slur.

"He said you're a whore."

I was more prepared for the racial slur.

"Do you know what that means?" I count back from fifty. *No seven-year-old needs to know the definition of a whore regardless of their IQ.*

Kourtney shakes her head.

"That word is used to define someone who sells their body for money. And it's an inappropriate thing to say about anyone."

"I heard Dr. Hawk say he bets you're a whore off the street who needs money to support your kid. A gold digger after Bryan's money. I don't want to be here if he's going to say those things about you." She sniffs.

"We can go back to our apartment if that's what you want."

"Is the apartment safe?"

"We can go to a hotel if you don't feel comfortable staying in the apartment."

"Can my sister come with us?" I rock my baby girl, letting her cry it out. I want to absorb her pain and replace it with the courage to overlook ignorance.

An internal conference is going on between my heart and mind. Dr. Hawk is ruining my daughter's holiday.

Once Kourtney's calm enough to slide off my lap, I wipe her tears and cup her cheeks. "I'll get dressed and go downstairs to tell Bryan we're going to a hotel. You go pack." I kiss her nose.

She leaves the room, the door closing softly behind her.

To kill him is predictable. He is Bryan's father so I'll keep that in mind, but I'm going to hurt him really, *really* bad.

I stomp my way into the closet, surprised the house isn't quaking with each step. My butt-kicking clothes are yanked from a suitcase. Foregoing the body-moisturizing regimen, I get dressed.

The boxing gloves stay in the gym bag. I want fist to skin contact. They'll be able to recognize him. *After* the swelling goes down. When I'm done, Dr. Bryan Kendall Hawk the Third will think twice before saying anything derogatory about me loud enough for my baby to hear.

Twisting a scrunchie around my hair, I leave it in a high, messy ponytail on top of my head. I grab the tape from my gym bag and start wrapping my hands and wrists. My mind filters through quick, effective combinations meant to hurt, but not do too much damage.

The tape roll drops to the floor.

The bedroom door slams behind me as I stomp my way to the stairs. In repetitions, I ball a fist then relax my fingers, testing the strength of the tape.

Bryan reaches the bottom step the same time I make it to the landing.

"Get. Out. Of. My. Way." I jog down the stairs.

"I'm not stopping you. Just give Emm time to get in the family room before you have a talk with my dad."

I stop two steps in front of him, which puts us brown eyes to hazel eyes. "Did you hear what he said?"

"No. Emm asked me what a whore is."

"She heard him too?" I try to duck under his arm.

He blocks me from getting past. "The offer still stands."

"This is your home, Bryan. I won't ask you to make your family leave."

"Our home," he corrects. "If Mom and Jessi want to stay, I'll drive them back to Colorado Springs when they're ready."

"Kourtney doesn't want to stay here. We're checking into a hotel."

"Baby, do you mind if I talk to Kourt?"

Emma calls out, letting us know she's in the family room.

He steps back.

I stretch my arms.

Bryan follows me down the hallway, mimicking the roar of a crowd and talking like an announcer at a boxing match. "Looking sexy in black, black. Leggings, leggings. And red, red tank top, top, top. Firm round ass, ass, is the undisputed Featherweight Champ…"

I stop in the doorway of the kitchen. Bryan walks into me, ending his announcement of the fight.

Marie's chasing Dr. Hawk around the kitchen table with an old-fashioned, wooden rolling pin in her hand and circling it above her head. "How dare you call Danielle a gold digger whore, you old fart!" She's moving fast and her Southern roots are more pronounced. "I'm gonna knock some sense into that hard head of yours!" She's rounding the table in hot pursuit. *Boy is she angry.* If she wasn't so hell bent on clobbering Bryan's dad, I'd laugh at how her drawl is distorting her words.

"Son, control your housekeeper." He scurries around the table like the rat he is.

Bryan's hands pat my shoulders. "Sorry, Dad, that's the lady of the house's job."

Marie takes a swing at the rat from across the table. He squeals. Nancy and Jessica stand back laughing.

The seriousness of what's going on in the kitchen calms me down enough to take control of the situation. I step in Marie's path. She stops chasing, but does not holster her rolling pin weapon.

"Why are you here? You're off until the first?" I pull at the tape, unwinding it from my wrist and hand.

"I left my scarf yesterday. I heard Emma ask what's a whore," she huffs and scowls at her intended victim. "I knew that knucklehead said it loud enough for them to hear."

"Thank you for coming to my defense, Marie. I can take it from here." I look across the table. "Have a seat, Dr. Hawk. You and I need to talk. One on one." I turn to everyone else in the kitchen. "Can you give us a minute, please?"

Marie takes another swing before storming out the back door still holding the baking utensil and speaking in a dialect similar to French. She forgets her coat and scarf, and leaves the door wide open. She's rounding the side of the house. I bet the snow's melting from the heat emanating from her body.

"Bryan, please go give Marie her coat before she gets sick."

He kisses me, then grabs her things off the hook and runs out the back door. Also leaving it open.

Nancy and Jessica laugh their way down the hallway.

"Okay, Dr. Hawk, what's on your mind?" I walk over and close the door, then plop down in a chair, balling the tape in my fist.

"I know your kind and I want you to leave my son and granddaughter alone. Find someone else to sink your claws into." He sits in the chair across from me, breathing like he ran ten miles in under a minute. *Oh wait. He did.*

"Dr. Hawk, do you know me? Do you work at one of the two banks I have active accounts with? Do you sign my paychecks? Do you have access to my credit information? Do you have hidden cameras in my apartment?"

He shakes his head, still breathing hard.

"You met me yesterday. How do you know I'm a whore off the street? A gold digger? Have *you* been sleeping with a whore? Perhaps you have a gold digger as a side-piece and you can't get rid of her."

He gawks. "Of course not!"

"How else do you explain your qualifications to define me as a *whore off the streets who needs money to support my kid? A gold digger after Bryan's money*?" I keep repeating his words so he understands just how demeaning his remarks truly are.

"How long have you known my son?" The indignation is evident in his tone.

I have to be careful how I answer this. "Long enough to know his place in our lives."

"You've known him a few months and now you and your daughter are living here. That's *awfully* fast, don't you think?"

"You have a valid point, Dr. Hawk. But I still don't see how you've come to the conclusion I sell my body and am in need of your son's financial support."

He glares at me the way a parent looks at their child, waiting for a confession of guilt.

To gain the upper hand, I give him what he wants. "Yes, it is *awfully fast*. But it's a decision the four of us made. Besides, don't you think your son is intelligent enough to spot a gold digging whore when one crosses his path?"

"My son is thirty-four years old. *Dr. Edwards.* He's never exposed his daughter to one of the notches on his belt. Nor has he introduced us to one. Not even Emma's mother. Why would he change his ways for you?"

"Would you feel better if I told you Kourtney and I don't need your son's financial support?"

"Show me proof and I'll rest better."

He's a dad looking out for his son and granddaughter; I respect that. The rage now replaced by mutual parental understanding.

"If that's what it takes, fine. The papers I need are upstairs." I leave him at the table and go upstairs to Bryan's room.

My safe is in the back of the closet. I punch in the code and take out two files. A photo falls to the floor. I pick it up and open a file. Taking a moment, I look at the loose pictures. A jolt of sadness shocks my heart and I blink away the tears. He was so happy and I was coming around. We were making plans. Three years later, he was gone.

Where's the other photo? There should be three pictures of us from that day. One is missing. With the back of my hand, I wipe away the tears.

I don't have time to do a thorough search in the safe. Dr. Hawk is waiting. I move the two photos to an envelope at the bottom of the safe along with Kourtney's official birth certificate and social security card. I close the safe and it automatically locks. I push it back in its spot.

I return to the kitchen and sit next to Bryan's father.

"I'm a private person but willing to make an exception because I would never want to come between you and your son. Before I give you these, may I ask you a question?"

He raises a questioning eyebrow. *So that's where Bryan gets it.*

"Does the color of my skin affect your opinion of me?"

"Hell no!" He genuinely sounds offended. "You are a beautiful, attractive Black woman, Dr. Edwards."

"There is one thing you must trust me on, since there's no other way to prove it. Kourtney's father is the only man I'd been intimate with and I was nineteen at the time. My husband and I were childhood friends, yet I waited until after I was married to have sex." I hand him the files. "Kourtney receives monetary support monthly. Every penny goes into a trust account *I* set up. I've worked since I was sixteen years old and learned to save my money. My husband spent only what was necessary and put the rest away for a rainy day. There was a good amount of money in his savings when he died. I owned my home in Arizona. You will see, it sold in August and I invested part of the money. I'm a licensed *working* therapist by choice, Dr. Hawk." I rise from the table, walking out of the kitchen.

Chapter Twenty-Two

BRYAN, KOURTNEY, AND EMMA ARE about to walk out the side door.

"Where are you three going?" I ask.

"We're making a snowman," Emma answers.

"One bigger than Uncle Vinny." Kourtney smiles up at me.

"So we're staying?"

She nods. "Bryan made me feel better." She's holding his hand.

"You guys have fun."

Nancy jumps up from the sofa as I walk into the family room. "Are we hitting the sales, ladies?"

"We should have been at the mall at five this morning." Jessica folds the sales paper in her hands and jump to her feet.

"There's some work I need to finish, so I'll pass." I'm not in the mood to shop. I know I have that appointment, but I'll reschedule.

"Work!" They snort.

"Come on, Danielle. Let's go shopping," Jessica whines. "When's the last time you went shopping with just the girls?"

Does Maxie count?

"You're going *with* us," Nancy demands. "Bryan will look after the girls."

I raise an eyebrow.

"My son Bryan. Now go change into comfortable shopping clothes. Come to think of it, what you're wearing is fine. Jessica takes sale shopping to the extreme. We may have to jump in when she fights other shoppers or the salesclerks. And don't bring a big purse." She turns me by the shoulders and pushes me in the direction of the door.

It would be fun to go shopping with them.

"Danielle?" Dr. Hawk walks into the room, handing me the folders. "I can see it's not just your beauty that attracts my son. You're smart. Independent. And financially savvy. I'm ashamed of the way I spoke about you. Especially knowing your little girl and my granddaughter overheard me. My children are adults, but I still want to protect them from the world. You'll understand when Kourtney is an adult. Please accept my sincerest apology."

I hold out my right hand. "Truce, Dr. Hawk?"

He takes my hand in both of his, then kisses my knuckles. "Truce. And please call me Bryan."

"You wouldn't believe he's the Superintendent of Schools in our city district from the way he's been acting," Jessica comments.

"I'll help entertain the girls. I owe them an apology too."

Feeling accomplished, I run upstairs, laying the folders on the nightstand and going into the closet to change. My clothes are still in suitcases. I open the big one and scramble through the mess until I find a pair of jeans and a heavy sweater to wear.

After I put in my gold stud earrings, transfer my driver's license, credit cards and cash to an across the shoulder wallet-purse, I grab my keys and cell phone.

On my way down the stairs, I hear Willis yelling, his voice booming from the family room. I walk in that direction, but Nancy and Jessica catch me under each arm, pulling me in the opposite direction.

"Wait, let me tell Bryan I'm leaving." I walk across the hallway to the side door and step out onto the deck. "Hey, I thought you guys were building a snowman."

Bryan is ducking behind the Christmas tree while the girls throw snowballs at him from behind the giant lawn ornaments.

"I thought so too," he laughs throwing snowballs back at them.

"I'm going shopping with your mom and sister."

"Have fun." He ducks out of the way of a precisely pitched snowball. The smile of pride on Bryan's face can't be missed. His daughter's got a good arm.

Nancy and Jessica wait for me inside the garage. "Let's go shopping, ladies."

Nine hours later, tired and hungry, I turn onto Bryan's street.

"I can't believe I spent that much money." Nancy looks over her receipts for the tenth time since we left the mall. "He'll kill me when he opens the credit card bill next month."

"Dad will fuss, but he'll never lay a hand on you." Jessica smacks her lips. "My little brother *will* lay hands on Danielle. *And* other things. I can't believe the guys paid to have the store shut down for you."

"I thought it was a joke until the manager locked the doors." I peek at Jessica in the rearview mirror. "Your girlfriend's going to love what you bought."

During the shopping spree, Jessica told me about Samantha, her long-term partner.

"Hey, I'm not the one who purchased sheer lingerie. At least most of my lady parts are covered. Bryan can rip off your flimsy stuff with one good tug," she laughs.

I'm not sure this is an appropriate conversation to have in front of your boyfriend's mother. But she bought racy underwear too. Nancy even picked out a few pieces for me.

"I have to find somewhere to hide my bags before your dad sees them."

"Let's go in through the back." I suggest. "We can sneak upstairs and no one will notice. Hide your packages in Jessica's room."

I pull up to the curb in front of the house. Like a professionally trained special ops team, we infiltrate the house. Undetected. Each carrying shopping bags in both hands. At the top of the stairs, they go to the right; I go left.

In the room, I go straight to the closet and empty a bottom drawer. I hide the lingerie in there, the other bags I leave on the bed.

My team meets me at the top of the stairs to celebrate completing a successful mission. Single-file, we march down to the family room.

The girls have dolls and doll clothes scattered around the coffee table and floor. Bryan senior's hair is in tiny pigtails and he's holding a doll in his hands. I'm tempted to snap a photo. Jessi beats me to it.

"What have you guys been up to?" Nancy asks.

Kourtney and Emma fall over laughing.

"We played a trick on grandpa." Kourtney holds her sides.

"I asked Kourty to call me grandpa if that's okay with you?" He climbs to his feet.

My eyes water at the thought. Kourtney has a grandfather in her life.

"I'm taking my granddaughters to the Play 'n' Fun Center for dinner tonight. Who's going with us?"

Bryan walks into the room. "You're not taking my girls anywhere looking like that."

Hawk family night is a fun adventure. We're the last to leave. The girls are exhausted and fall asleep before we pull out of the parking lot.

I fight the sleep battle all the way home.

As I climb out of the Suburban, I watch the garage door coming down and a dark-colored SUV drive past.

I say goodnight and go straight to bed.

Bryan wakes me early in the morning to tell me he's taking the girls out for the day. I roll over, nod, and go back to sleep.

Around noon, I take a shower and raid his side of the massive walk-in closet. Dressed in sweats and one of Bryan's sweatshirts, I go downstairs to fix myself lunch. The house is quiet.

He sends me a text message to let me know they'll be home before dinner.

I unpack my suitcases, then lounge on the sofa in the family room reading a book I ordered earlier this month.

At five, I start warming up dinner.

Bryan, the girls, and his parents return just as I turn off the oven.

"Where have you guys been all day?"

"I'm going to have a teddy bear room," Kourtney says.

"She wants a teddy bear theme bedroom. We went to see an interior decorator. They'll start right after the New Year," Bryan says.

"This is how my room will look." She pulls a brand new iPad from her backpack, slides her finger across the screen, taps it and turns it around, showing me the 3-D design of her bedroom.

I shoot eye daggers at Bryan and he knows why.

"I'm going to have a pony bedroom." Emma also pulls out a brand new iPad from her backpack.

Laser beams shoot out my eyes at Bryan.

He raises his hands. "I didn't buy them." He points to his dad.

I turn my glare on Bryan senior.

He hands me a wrapped gift box.

"You should see all the teddy bears Grandpa picked out for my room."

"I'm getting lots of ponies."

"Girls, I'm going to end up in the dog house with Danielle if you keep talking," he whispers.

"You and Mommy can't be in the dog house. Where will Trevor sleep?" Kourtney frowns at him.

"Who's Trevor?" I ask.

"Trevor is our Labrador Retriever." Kourtney informs me matter-of-factly.

Nancy laughs as Bryan senior turns red. My fists clench. And their son takes two steps away from me.

"Ratted out by my granddaughters."

"We rescued him from the pond," Emma adds.

"You mean pound," Kourtney corrects.

"We pick him up tomorrow. The man said he's house trained and everything. Huh, Kourty?"

Bryan senior looks like he's hoping the floor will open and swallow him, right now.

"Excuse me." Willis stands in the doorway. "Bryan you have a phone call."

He chuckles and follows Willis. "Saved by a call."

"Well, will you look at the time? Girls, how about we go out back and see where Trevor's dog house should go." Bryan senior walks out of the family room tugging the girls along with him. "You two keep it up and I'll be eating dinner in my room."

Nancy plops down on the sofa laughing.

"Is he for real?" I ask.

"It's his way of apologizing."

"He knows he can't buy love?"

"Yes, he knows, but he's fallen in love with your beautiful little girl. We both have and we'll spoil her like we spoil Emm. He asked what she wanted for Christmas since we didn't get her anything."

"Bryan, Max and I purposely vetoed pets and expensive tablets."

"Take solace in knowing my son put his foot down with the electric scooters."

I collapse on the sofa with my unopened gift still in my hands. "Why couldn't he put his foot down for the dog?" I close my eyes. "I don't indulge Kourtney's every whim. Do I want to know what's in here?" I set the box on my lap.

"I'll give you a hint. The girls have one too." She laughs harder when I glare at her.

"Baby, I'm going out of town." Alpha male stands at attention in the doorway.

"Is everything okay?" I ask, rising from the sofa.

"Business."

"When are you leaving?"

"Now." He does an about-face and marches toward the stairs.

I follow.

"Can I help?"

He doesn't answer.

"Do you want me to help you pack?"

He keeps marching up the stairs.

"Bryan!" I raise my voice.

He finally stops and turns around.

"I asked you a question."

"I'm sorry, baby. I didn't hear you. My mind is elsewhere."

Something's off!

"Is everything okay?"

"Yes, baby."

I don't believe you.

"Baby, go get dinner on the table. I'll be down in a minute."

I turn around and go back down the stairs. *There's more to this business trip than he's saying.*

Nancy helps me set the table in the kitchen. We're already eating when Bryan comes in, dressed in a designer business suit.

"You're leaving?" Bryan senior asks.

"Urgent business trip."

"How long will you be gone, Dad?"

"Not long, honey." He kisses the top of Emma's head. "I'll be back by the thirty-first." He kisses the top of Kourtney's head and his mom's cheek. He walks around the table and shakes his dad's hand. "Keep an eye on my girls."

"You know I will."

"Baby, walk me to the garage." He holds out his hand.

I excuse myself from the table.

We walk down the hallway without speaking. At the door he turns to me.

"Baby, I'm asking you to please stick around the house while I'm gone."

I blink at him, tilting my head to the side. "I made plans to take the girls to the spa with Max and Penelope tomorrow."

"Call the spa and have someone come here, baby."

That's the seventh time he's called me baby. Not once has he said my name since announcing he's going out of town.

My lips twist. "Fine, I'm sure I can improvise."

He pulls me into his arms. "Thank you." His phone vibrates in the hand against my back. "I'm leaving now. I'll be in the air within the hour," he answers, then pulls his mouth away from the phone to give me a quick peck on the lips. "I have to go."

He walks to his truck talking on the phone. Before he climbs into the driver's seat, Bryan turns around. "You may not be able to get in touch with me, but if anything comes up, call Vin."

"What about Tony and Ig?"

"They're pulling double duty. But Vin is off work, baby."

He still hasn't called me Dani or Danielle. Bryan quickly backs out the garage.

On my way back to the kitchen, the front door opens. Jessica walks in. Her eyes are red and puffy like she's been crying. "Was that Bryan?"

"Yes, he's leaving for an urgent business trip."

If I wasn't trained to notice body language, I would have missed Jessica's slight pause in step.

"I forgot I was supposed to call a patient today. I'll be in for dinner in a few minutes." She walks back out of the house.

I tiptoe to the door, pressing my ear against it.

"What's up, Bry?" *Pause.* "Really? When?" *Pause.* "Do you think it's him?" *Pause.* "Yes, I'll keep an eye out."

If the holster I felt hidden under his jacket when I hugged him isn't enough to convince me, that cryptic conversation does. I know this is more than an urgent business trip.

I toss and turn in the big empty bed before giving up trying to sleep. Not wanting to leave the sanctuary of the warm bed to get my laptop, I pick up the one Bryan left sitting on his nightstand. It's slow to load, but thankfully, not password protected. The laptop makes a sound like the bell at a boxing match and the driver drawer opens on its own.

Curiosity gets the better of me and a plan develops in my mind. I search the hard drive for files. Bryan doesn't have anything saved on this laptop. *What does he use it for? It's very old.*

After connecting to the Wi-Fi, I open the web browser and research ideas for a home spa day. I'm not calling in professionals.

Why would Bryan ask me to stay home? Something has him spooked. If he's not going to tell me what it is, I'll find the answer on my own.

I shut down the laptop after writing out a list of supplies needed and lie back, allowing my plan to come together.

I set the alarm for six thirty. Phase one of my plan begins over breakfast. I smile to myself and hug Bryan's pillow.

Chapter Twenty-Three

WHILE NANCY HELPS ME PREPARE breakfast, I tell her about a romance series I read last year. Just like I guessed, she loves to read and the series I'm telling her about will capture her attention the second she reads the first paragraph. It has erotic elements and it's written by one of my favorite authors. I give her the first book in the series. Before I put the food on the table, Nancy goes to their room.

Phase one complete.

Jessica declines my invitation to join our home spa day. I can cross the second phase off the list. She takes her breakfast to go.

I hand Bryan senior the list I made last night and sweet-talk him into going shopping and taking the girls with him.

With everyone distracted, I can search Bryan's home office for clues about his trip. I close the door behind me and start with his desk.

My hand touches the mouse pad and his computer turns on. A hawk glides onto the screen, talons out ready to strike.

Unfortunately, this computer is password protected. After the third attempt, I stop trying to guess his password.

Next, I try to snoop through the drawers of his desk.

They are locked.

I move to the file cabinet and storage cabinets.

They're also locked.

I try the closet.

It's locked too.

The search of his office is starting to frustrate me. The drawers, cabinets, and closet have no key slots or keypads. They don't even have knobs.

I could try to pry them open.

My hand rests on the mouse pad while I reach for the letter opener. The hawk on the screen disappears and the image of a handprint begins to load. In my peripheral, a light slides up and down near my left hand.

I look. The mousepad is a scanner. I quickly snatch my hand away, the image stops loading. An error message pops up on the screen across the partial scan of my palm. At the moment, I stop trying to play super-sleuth before I do something that I can't undo. I leave Bryan's office.

In the kitchen, I start making the red velvet cake.

A little before one o'clock, Max and Penelope ring the doorbell and our spa day begins.

First on our list is a light lunch followed by the cake.

We put on swimsuits, robes, and slippers. With towels wrapped around our hair, we give each other hand and foot treatments using a homemade scented sugar rub.

Next we do manis and pedis.

"Where's Mr. Tall-And-Sexy?" Max asks, guiding the nail brush over my toenail. I chose neon green.

"Last minute business trip." I'm polishing his toenails royal blue.

"Why aren't we relaxing at the spa, letting professionals pamper us?"

"Bryan asked me to stick around the house while he's gone."

"Stick around the house, huh?" He twists his lips. "So you've decided to be a good girl and play nice?"

"I thought it would be fun to do it ourselves. The girls are having fun."

"You worked things out and now wittle hawk's making you his wittle house-woman?"

I smack his foot. "It's not like that, Maxie."

"Tell me what it's like, Danikins?"

"The break-in at my apartment shook him up. I told you he was carrying a gun." I sneak a peek at the girls to make sure they aren't paying attention to our conversation. They've gone neon crazy on their toes and nail art crazy on their fingers. "Bryan needs to know we're safe while he's away."

"What will he do after the holidays?"

"We're not going back to the apartment. He asked us to move in with them."

"That was fast."

I don't reply.

"Do you love him, Danikins?"

My shoulders rise and fall. I don't meet his gaze.

The nail brush in his hand pauses mid-stroke. I watch him from underneath my lashes.

Maxie smirks. "He loves you."

The nail brush finishes the trek down my toenail.

"How do you know?"

"Bryan looks at you the way I look at my husband. And I'm deeply in love with Thomas."

"It's too soon to talk about love…"

"Where is it written that love comes with years? Why can't love be instant and unexpected?" He points the nail brush at me. "Why can't you love him after only knowing him a few minutes? I've known Bryan for a long time, Danikins. He's in love with you."

I glance over at his daughter. She's animated as she talks to her friends. She has inherited so many of his mannerisms.

"Bryan's dad got the girls iPads," I say to change the subject.

The Maxie tangent begins. I'm not telling him about the dog yet. That information will be my next subject changer if the conversation goes back to my feelings for Bryan.

Once our polish dries, we ditch the robes. Apply an avocado face mask. Put cucumber slices over our eyes. And relax on the chaise lounge chairs in the family room in our swimsuits.

Sounds of a tropical island play on the surround-sound speakers. I turn up the heat in the family room to give it a tropical feel. We sip fresh-squeezed lemonade from coconut cups with colorful umbrellas. Floor lamps give the illusion of sunshine.

Someone clears their throat. I lift a cucumber slice off one eye. Vin's standing in the doorway, his arm in a navy blue sling.

"Good afternoon. Would you like some lemonade?" I ask.

"I would love some," he chuckles, pulling at the collar of his sweater.

I pick up the bell resting by my hand, giving it a shake. *Tingle-ling-ling-ling.*

Bryan senior walks into the room wearing flower print board shorts, a dark tank top, and flip-flops.

"Yes, Ms. Danielle?"

"Please bring our guest some lemonade." I reapply the cucumber slice.

"Yes, ma'am. Right away."

Vin laughs. "You made him your mitch?"

"He's earning the right to spoil the girls."

"Will I have to serve you dinner for bringing their dog home?"

I sit up, peeling off both cucumber slices.

The full-grown Labrador retriever sits by Vin's leg, panting.

"Bry asked me to pick him up."

Kourtney and Emma jump off their chairs, their cucumber slices falling to the floor. They run to the dog.

"Welcome home, Trevor!" Kourtney hugs him.

He barks and starts licking the avocado off their faces. His happy wagging tail is a blur behind him.

Emma looks over her shoulder. "Penny, come meet Trevor."

"You got them a dog?" Max yells at me.

"Blame that man." I point to the culprit walking through the door carrying a coconut cup on a tray.

"Daddy, can we go to the shelter and get a doggy like Trevor?" Penelope's little voice rings out over the barking dog. Trevor's licking the avocado off her face too.

Home spa day is interrupted by the newest member of the household. *Yippee.*

Before I lie down for the night, I go back to Bryan's home office to see if the partial handprint is still on the screen. Thankfully it's gone. I don't know what explanation I could have come up with if it was still there. Unplugging the computer was my backup plan.

I fall asleep dreaming about a hawk's eye watching me.

In the morning, Bryan senior and the girls go outside to put together Trevor's doghouse. A waste of time if you ask me, he wouldn't sleep in the laundry room for one night. Kourtney and Emma camped out in the family room with Trevor so he would go to sleep.

I spend the rest of my morning cleaning the house and doing the laundry. It's not a task I feel obligated to do, these are chores I'm happy to do. I'm fulfilling a secret desire, taking care of my man and our children.

Nancy curls up in a chair in the sitting room reading the second book in the series. I doubt she slept last night.

While I wait for the clothes in the dryer, I research local shelters. I find two I want to donate our furniture and old clothes to, once we move in here.

Bryan senior and the girls pick up take-out for dinner.

As expected, Trevor shuns his doghouse and falls asleep in the family room while Nancy sits on the sofa still reading.

I sleep on Bryan's side of the bed, missing him. His scent on the sheets is like phantom fingers caressing my inner thighs. Softly. Sensually. Sexually. Just the smell of him brings on the phantomlike feel of him sliding into me. He seeks the spot that makes my inner walls quake.

The scent of him caresses my throbbing clitoris. My toes curl. My hips circle. My back arches off the sheets. I moan his name.

Six o'clock flashes at me when I open my eyes. It's been a while since I've had a sex dream like that.

A room-temperature shower cools me off.

Trevor is whining at the bedroom door when I come out of the closet wearing jeans and one of Bryan's sweatshirts. I splash a hint of his cologne on me so I can keep him with me all day.

Trevor trots alongside me as I walk down the stairs. We turn toward the kitchen and I stop. *What's that sound?*

Trevor's ears stand up. We listen to the rhythmic *tap, tap, tap* on the wall. The sound is coming from the hallway near the downstairs guest rooms. *Tap. Tap. Tap.*

"Ohh yes. Big B. Just like that." Nancy's throaty enthusiasm travels down the hallway.

I cover my ears and run for the kitchen, the dog right behind me.

Throwing open the back door, I step onto the patio. Trevor runs down the steps into the backyard. I fight off the visual image my mind tries to conjure up of Bryan's parents doing the *biggity-bang-bang* this early in the morning.

When they come in for breakfast, Bryan senior looks like he hasn't slept all night. Nancy's skipping around the kitchen greeting everyone with warm hugs and kisses. Jessica and I share a knowing smile when Nancy picks up the third book in the series and goes to the sitting room with a cup of coffee in her hand.

Kourtney and Emma beg and plead until Bryan senior gives in and hooks up the brand new gaming system they conveniently forgot to tell me he bought. The three put in a dancing game.

Jessica leaves the house saying she has errands to run.

I go upstairs to the bedroom to finish patient files and return calls. While reading over the notes for the patients I'm scheduled to see on January 2nd, I realize I'm missing a flash drive. I check my briefcase, my purse—I even check the suitcases. The drive isn't here.

The last time I had it, I was saving my notes on it on Christmas Eve. I bet it's still sitting on the table in the apartment. I put on a pair of Uggs and pick up my keys off the nightstand.

On the way to look for Nancy, I stop and get video of Bryan senior dancing with the girls. He's winning.

Nancy hasn't moved. *I think I created a monster.*

"I'm going over to the apartment. I left something I need for work."

She nods her head, not taking her eyes away from the book. Her finger twists her hair. She's biting her lip.

With barely any traffic on the road, I make it to my apartment in twenty-three minutes. The flash drive is on the table next to my digital recorder. I place my keys on top of it so I won't forget it when I leave.

"Might as well pack while I'm here."

I toss my purse on the table and assemble moving boxes left over from when Bryan helped me clean up after the break-in. Kourtney's room is where I start.

I pack her old books and toys, and sort through the clothes in her closet and drawers. The ones she can't fit anymore are packed in the boxes. I write the name of the shelter on the side.

The time flashes on the clock in her room. I've been here for two hours. But I'm in the zone. I go back to the living room, assemble more boxes, and head to my room.

The closet will take me the longest, but that's where I'll start. I reach for...

An uneasy feeling in the pit of my stomach makes me hesitate opening the door. A cool breeze sweeps across my cheek. I look to the right. The bottom half of the blinds swing. The last time I was here I know I made sure the windows were closed and locked.

The boxes in my hand start to shake. I take a few steps back from the closet door. The hairs on the back of my neck stand up. The uneasiness spreads, urging me to get the hell out of here. I drop the boxes, running from the room.

I grab my purse, keys, flash drive, and the digital recorder.

I open the door.

"*AAH!*"

"Are you okay?" Vin asks, standing in front of me.

"You scared me."

"What are you doing here?"

"I can ask you the same question."

"I stopped by the house. Nancy said you were here. I came to see if you needed help."

"What can you do with one arm?" The base of my skull tingles. I glance over my shoulder in the direction of my bedroom.

"Are you sure you're okay, Dani?"

"Yes. I need to go. I'm sure the girls are hungry."

"Dr. Hawk was ordering pizza when I left. You and I can go somewhere for lunch if you want."

I lock the door behind me. "Thanks, Vin. But I can't today. I have to finish my patient notes. Can we go to lunch another day?"

"Sure. Just let me know when." He walks me down to my truck and stands at the curb watching me drive off.

Before I turn the corner, I look in the rearview mirror. Vin's running back toward the apartment building.

I make the block and park on the side street.

I wait.

Someone dressed in black comes running from the stairs. They cut to the side of the building and run away. A few seconds later, Vin comes running from the stairs. He's shouting into his cell phone, his sling twisted around his neck, his clothes disheveled.

I check my rearview mirror. The prowler is already halfway down the block.

A black SUV, traveling fast, speeds up the street. I duck down as it zooms past me. My truck rocks in its wake. I peek over the dash. Vin's tires kick up smoke as he peels away from the curb, flying up the street.

I put the truck in drive and head in the opposite direction, but still checking the rearview mirror. The prowler and both trucks disappear.

My finger presses the button on the digital recorder. I record my thoughts as I head back to Bryan's house.

I stop recording when I turn onto his street. Willis is standing in the open garage like he's waiting for someone. He presses the button to close the garage door after I pull in. Before the door comes all the way down, a black SUV drives past.

Chapter Twenty-Four

A KISS FROM SOFT LIPS WAKES me. My body knows him.
"Hello." I open one eye.

"Bed got lonely without me?" Bryan asks.

"They were frightened by the storm."

One girl is wrapped in each arm and Trevor, the oversized scaredy-cat, sleeps at my feet.

"What time is it?" I yawn.

"Four in the morning." He lifts Kourtney off my arm and walks around to his side.

I gently pull my arm from under Emma and scoot us back to make room. He lays Kourtney next to Emma and climbs in, turning off the lamp.

"How long have you been home?"

"About an hour," he yawns. "The storm delayed my flight. Hey, the red velvet cake is delicious."

"Thank you. How was your trip?"

"Good." He reaches across the girls for my hand.

"Did everything work out?"

"Mmm-hmm."

"I missed you."

"I missed you more, baby," he murmurs.

That's nine, still no Dani or Danielle.

The next time I open my eyes, it's because there's a weight on my chest, and doggie breath assaulting my nose.

Trevor's upper body is draped across me. I turn my head to see the clock: six thirty. His previous owners must have woken up early to let him out.

"Should I be jealous?" Bryan chuckles.

"He needs to go out."

Bryan rolls out of bed. "Come on, boy."

The dog leaps over the sleeping girls and jumps off the bed. He barks and runs out the door.

I roll over and close my eyes.

As I feel myself drifting off, *buzz… buzz… buzz*. The sound startles me.

I sit up. It sounds like it's inside the wall. The buzzing stops.

I snuggle under the warm blankets, and my body relaxes. *Buzz… Buzz… Buzz*.

It's coming from the closet. I get out of bed and open the closet door, trying to pinpoint the whereabouts.

The buzzing stops.

I wait.

Buzz… Buzz… Buzz.

Bryan's winter coat shakes. The offensive buzz is coming from the inside pocket. I search it until my hand encloses the culprit. A cell phone, but it's not the one he normally carries. POTUS flashes on the caller ID.

Should I answer?

Trevor's bark makes the decision for me. They're already upstairs.

I put the phone back in the coat pocket and get back in bed before Bryan and Trevor come through the bedroom door.

Trevor jumps on the bed, circles a few times, then reclaims his spot at my feet.

Bryan walks over to my side of the bed, kneeling. "I was thinking. Let's start off the New Year right. How about the four of us go pack up the apartment today."

The buzzing in the walls starts again.

"Go start the shower, baby. I'll join you in a second," he says, kissing me until I'm squirming from the heat simmering between my legs. The buzz becomes an annoyance in the background.

Bryan peels the covers back and helps me out of bed. I dash to the bathroom. The buzzing starts again. I press my ear against the door the minute I close it.

"I was away from the phone." *Pause.* "Zero three hundred hours." *Long pause.* "I left sweepers there to finish up once I got the call." The sound of his voice comes near the bathroom door.

I run to the toilet pressing the button for it to flush, then go over to the sink. He doesn't come in. I tiptoe back to the door.

"The report will be in your in-box within the hour. Thank you, sir."

I hate one-sided conversations.

Before leaving the bathroom, I get the water started in the shower. When I open the door, Bryan's hands are empty.

"It's a quarter after seven. We have about fifteen minutes before the girls wake. How about a quickie in the shower?" He pulls me against him, his erection poking me in the stomach.

"Daddy, why do you need a quickie?" sleepy Emma asks.

"Help me out," he whispers.

I shake my head, trying not to laugh out loud. It's a good thing his back is to the bed; otherwise he'd have to explain why the front of his pajama pants is poking out.

"I was telling Dani we need to take quick showers, so we can go pack up the apartment."

"Nice save," I whisper.

"I'll have a quickie in the shower too," she yawns.

I giggle into his chest and he squeezes my butt.

"Wake up, Kourty. We need a quickie so we can go pack the apartment."

Unable to hold it any longer, I laugh and step around him to get my cell phone off the nightstand.

I unlock the screen as I walk into the bathroom, closing the door behind me.

Once the search box opens, I type POTUS.

The phone almost slips from my hand. Was Bryan really talking to the President of the United States?

We make it to the apartment a little after nine. Tony and Vin meet us here with moving boxes of various sizes and shapes.

After checking the closet, I let the girls help me pack Kourtney's room. They play around more than anything.

I go back and forth, carrying boxes to the living room. Bryan and Tony carry the heavy ones.

Once her room is finished the guys breakdown her bedroom furniture and take it out to the men from the shelters. I don't know how Bryan convinced the directors to pick up boxes, furniture, and appliances on such short notice.

One-armed Vin and I pack the living room and kitchen while the girls sit in the empty bedroom playing games on their tablets. I question him about how he spent his afternoon yesterday. He's wearing a turtleneck.

Vin says he had a physical therapy appointment and is sore today.

My room is the last to be packed. All my reasons for stalling are no longer valid. Bryan is right outside if anyone is hiding in the closet.

I open the door, peek inside, and begin to sort through my clothes.

By three thirty, the entire apartment is empty. The guys' trucks are full of boxes and a few pieces of furniture. It's time to turn in the keys to the manager and get my security deposit back.

Bryan somehow got me out of my one-year lease without paying off the balance. He walks with me to the manager's apartment.

"I'm all packed." I hand over the keys. This guy isn't the one I met when we moved in back in July.

The manager walks away from the door, returning with an envelope. "Sorry to see you leave." He nods at Bryan.

I snatch the envelope and march away.

"Dani, what's wrong?" Bryan catches up with me.

"Nothing."

He spins me around to face him. "What's. Wrong?"

I sigh. "Something's going on. I see the looks and nods passing between you and the people around us. Tell me what it is."

"Nothing's going on, baby. You're imagining it."

"Bryan, stop bull-craping me! Someone was in my apartment yesterday."

"Baby, I'm telling you, nothing's going on. I called the owner yesterday to tell him you were moving out and to have your deposit ready. He wanted the manager to check the condition of the carpet and walls before he issued the check. I gave him permission to enter the apartment. But what were you doing here yesterday? I asked you to stick to the house while I was away."

"I left something here that I needed for work."

"I thought you were on vacation."

"We're calling it working from home."

Bryan wraps his arm around my shoulder, walking us toward his truck. "Come on, baby, we're hungry."

And he's back to calling me baby.

The ride to the house is quiet. Kourtney and Emma are riding with Vin. I don't want to start the New Year off fighting with Bryan so I put my suspicions on the backburner for now.

Nancy reluctantly put down the book to help me prepare a late lunch. Bryan senior says he's been trying for hours to get her off the sofa.

I season ground turkey to put on the indoor grill. I haven't had a beef burger since I was two months pregnant with Kourtney, but I have a taste for a really good one now. Too bad I didn't take any out yesterday.

We make man-size burger patties and regular ones.

I put together a veggie platter and a fruit platter, and fill bowls with chips. Bottles of beer sit on ice in a bucket and I make a big pitcher of sour-cherry lemonade.

Nancy and I help the girls make their plates, then stand back. Hungry men raid the kitchen. Instead of sitting at the table, they lean against the counter with their legs crossed at the ankles.

"Emmy, how do you celebrate on New Year's Eve?" Kourtney asks.

"I'm asleep. What about you?"

"Mom cooks our favorite foods. We sit on the sofa and watch the shiny ball drop in New York."

"I want to do that. Daddy, can we do that?"

"It's up to Dani." He's piling jalapenos on his second chili cheeseburger.

"I'll need to make a list of everyone's favorite food and find a party supply store."

"I vote for more turkey burgers. You put 'yo' foot in these patties." Tony takes a big bite of his burger.

Emma stops chewing. "You really put your foot in this?" She looks at me, wide-eyed.

I laugh. "No, sweetie. That's just an old saying. What Uncle Tony means is the burger tastes really good."

"Okay. Well, you put 'yo' foot in 'yo' spaghetti too." She bites her burger. Ketchup gathers in the corners of her mouth. Her tongue licks away most of it. I wipe away the rest with my napkin.

"Do you want me to make spaghetti for you tonight?" I ask.

She nods.

Jessica walks over to the counter. She's wearing a skirt and blazer.

Ignacio is right behind her in one of his tailored business suits. "I'll help you cook," he says.

"I'll take the girls to the party supply store for decorations and noise-makers," Bryan senior offers and Vin says he'll go with them.

"Okay, so tell me what you want to eat." I pull out Marie's shopping list pad trying to write food requests, but everyone is speaking at the same time.

"Wait! One at a time, please."

One by one, they give me their food requests.

"Bry, you didn't tell me what you want to eat." I get up from my seat.

Bryan's eyelids droop and he bites his bottom lip. Those hazel eyes start at my feet and slowly travel up my body.

In my reality, the earth freezes and it's just Bryan and I in the kitchen. I feel every layer of clothing melt away under the gaze of his eyes. Somehow I end up in his arms, his lips pressed against mine, our tongues doing a familiar dance.

"I told you two," Vin interrupts. "People eat in here."

I come back to the real world when everyone laughs. I step out of Bryan's embrace. Embarrassment warms my cheeks. I go to the walk-in pantry to get away from the laughter. Making a grocery list doesn't take long. Marie keeps the house well stocked, but I take a few minutes to think about what just happened. It was like I was in a trance. He didn't utter a word yet I was pulled to him.

Bryan and Anthony take the grocery list and go to the store.

Nancy and I discuss the book series while we clean the kitchen and start chopping vegetables.

In the evening, I send the girls to their rooms to take a nap so they won't fall asleep before we ring in the New Year. It's been a long day for me too. I go upstairs with intentions of taking a nap, but my mind won't rest. Bryan is definitely hiding something. I get out my recorder and sit on the couch taking notes as I listen to the account of my life since the appearance of one Bryan Kendall Hawk the Fourth.

"What are you listening to?"

I didn't hear Kourtney come in. I turn off the recorder and look at the clock. *Where did the time go?*

"I'm listening to some notes."

She climbs onto my lap.

Kourtney does this when we need to have a heart-to-heart talk.

"Does Bryan like you, Mommy?" She takes my left hand, twisting the wedding ring around my finger.

"Yes, he does."

"Is he going to give you a ring?"

"I don't know, sweetie. Why do you ask?"

"Jacob Brooks said a man is supposed to give a woman a ring when he likes her. That's why he gave Emmy the pony ring."

Jacob will be a broke man if he follows that theory for the rest of his life.

She looks up at me with curious eyes. "Why do you still wear this one?"

"I don't know. I guess out of habit."

"Do you think Bryan's waiting for you to take it off?"

"That's a good question."

"I think you should so he knows you like him too."

I hug my baby girl. In her own way, she's telling me it's time to let go of the past and open myself to a future with Bryan.

The thought no longer troubles me. It's a weight I need to shed for the New Year.

I slide her off my lap and walk over to my jewelry box to search for an old gold chain. Once I find it, I take the ring off my finger and put it on the chain. I hand it to Kourtney when I sit her back on my lap.

"You have to promise not to lose it. You can wear it around your neck or put it in a special place."

"I promise not to lose it." She draws a cross over her heart and we link pinkies.

The bedroom door opens.

"How are my girls?" Bryan strolls in, picking up Kourtney, giving her a hug.

She holds up the chain. "Mommy gave me her ring."

Bryan's eyes squint as he looks at the ring twirling on the chain in front of him.

"The wise Mr. Jacob Brooks says when a man likes a woman he's supposed to give her a ring." I wink at Kourtney."

Suddenly, the biggest smile spreads across Bryan's face.

"Kourt, go wake up Emm and meet us downstairs. I need to talk to Mom for a second."

"Okay." She jumps out of his arms, skipping out of the room, closing the door.

The second the latch catches he lunges for me. I jump off the couch before he can grab me.

"What's the matter, Bry? Little Jacob Brooks knows more about wooing a woman than you?" I laugh, dodging his hands, and make a dash for the bedroom door.

Bryan grabs me by the waist lifting me off my feet.

"You think that's funny," he laughs in my ear, walking back to the bed.

We fall onto the comforter and he pins me down with his body.

His fingers tickle me.

I laugh and squirm, trying to get away from him.

"Apologize."

"No!"

He tickles me.

"Apologize."

"Bryan. Please. You'll make me wet my pants." *Did I say that out loud?*

His fingers are relentless on my sides and under my arms.

"Apologize or I will make you pee on yourself right here."

"Okay! Okay. Stop tickling me first."

His fingers still.

"I'm sorry you're using your daughter to get close to a woman."

For a quick second he frowns, then tickles me until I yell uncle. He releases me and I sprint to the bathroom.

It's Bryan's fault that I have to wash up and change clothes, before we go downstairs holding hands. He teases me for not being able to hold it long enough to get my pants down. I see handcuffs and a bowl of warm water in his future.

Nancy and Ignacio have the buffet already set up in the family room. Marie and Willis join in on the festivities.

We eat and party the night away. Bryan senior shows off the dance skills he's learned from the video game. Trevor is showing off some dance moves Kourtney taught him. *He's growing on me.* It doesn't take much coaxing to get Bryan to dance with me. We keep our moves family friendly. His friends heckle him about losing his two left feet all of a sudden.

At ten minutes to midnight, the girls pass out party favors. I turn on the television, and Bryan hands everyone a glass of champagne. Kourtney and Emma get sparkling apple cider.

I smile at the people who welcomed my daughter and me into their lives. Kourtney and I are ending the year part of a bigger family unit. We count down.

Ten.

Nine.

Eight.

Seven.

Six.

Five.

Four.

Three.

Two.

One.

"Happy New Year!"

Horns sound off, confetti rains down on everyone.

Bryan dips me back; his kiss is a promise of every tomorrow of his life. He leaves me light-headed and hopeful.

It's a free for all.

I throw my arms around Marie first, then Willis. Bryan senior and I give each other an extra squeeze. Nancy kisses both my cheeks before she hugs me. Jessica and I hug and laugh. She asks if I'm wearing any of that flimsy underwear for her brother to rip off later on. Vin and I smile at each other before I wrap my arms around his waist. I wait for Ig to put Emma back on her feet, then give him a hug. Dropping to my knees, I hug Emma, showering her with kisses all over her face. I lean away from Tony's fish lips, grab his chin, turn his head, and kiss his cheek. I glimpse Bryan holding Kourt to his chest. The impact of what he's experiencing shows on his face and it makes my heart flutter. He pulls me into their hug. I take Kourtney in my arms to wish my baby a Happy New Year.

A whistling sound followed by a big boom goes off. We turn to the picture window in the family room. Another whistling sound followed by a boom and colorful lights dance in the darkness out by the pond.

Trevor whines and howls.

A whistle sound…

"Incoming!" Vin yells.

The lights go out. Ig tackles Kourtney and me to the floor. Bryan lunges for Emma, dropping to the floor, covering her with his body.

Marie and Nancy drop near the sofa holding on to each other. Bryan senior falls near the fireplace with Jessica.

Vin and Tony duck down near the window.

Why are they overreacting to fireworks and where's Willis?

A piercing whistle, unlike the others, fills the night air. The boom that follows shakes the house. Bryan shouts something, but I can't make out what he's saying. Trevor's howling in my ear.

Tony and Vin military crawl out of the room.

Bryan pushes Emma over to Ig who is hovering over Kourtney and me. Bryan runs out of the family room.

A ground-shaking boom follows another whistle.

We yell out.

Trevor howls louder.

"Easy boy," Ig tells him.

Bryan's crouching down in the doorway of the family room. I can't make out what's in his hands.

"Stay down," Ig orders and pushes Emma closer.

I wrap the frightened girls in my arms, protecting them with my body.

Ig military crawls over to the doorway. Bryan hands him something. They stick to the walls, heading toward the stairs. I hear another whistle and brace for the impact. The boom causes the Christmas tree to sway. Glass ornaments crash to the hardwood floors. Shattering.

Another whistle and rapid popping sounds. I don't know if they're gunshots or firecrackers. The boom sounds far away. More colorful lights shine in the window.

Consecutive popping sounds fill the night air. It sounds like their coming from upstairs. And still colorful lights dance in the window, but just as sudden as they started, the fireworks stop. An eerie silence follows.

The fire crackling in the fireplace provides light in the room. A mixture of wonder and fright mirrored on all our faces. No one moves or says a word.

Bryan and Ig come in empty-handed, and the lights come on.

"Everyone can get up now," Bryan says. He's in full-out alpha male mode.

The girls run to him.

"Daddy, what was that?" Emma cries.

He squats to hug both girls. "Someone was setting off fireworks near the pond." His voice and flared nostrils tell a different story.

Ig's demeanor mimics Bryan's. They're on alert.

"Where did Uncle Vinny and Uncle Tony go?" Kourtney looks toward the front door.

"They went to see who was lighting the fireworks," alpha male answers.

"That's enough excitement for tonight." My knees shake as I get to my feet. "Let's get you two into bed."

"Dani, may I sleep in Kourty's room?"

"Yes, you may."

"Can Trevor sleep in the room with us?" she asks.

"Sure, the scaredy-cat can sleep in the room too."

I take the girls' hands leading them out of the family room. As we're walking up the stairs, I see a panel in the wall under the stairs slide open, Willis walks out talking into his hand.

What in the hell just happened?

Chapter Twenty-Five

WALKING OUT OF THE BATHROOM, I find Bryan naked and kneeling in the middle of the bed. A fire burning in the fireplace. Soft instrumental jazz music wafting through the surround sound speakers in the room.

"I rolled the dice," he says. "I have to give you a sensual massage." A clear bottle filled with a honey-colored oil in his hand. Mr. Tall-And-Sexy pats the comforter. "On your stomach." The tone of his voice has me wet with anticipation already.

I drop my robe and crawl to the center of the bed. The ends of two red scarves are tethered around posts in the headboard, another is draped across the pillows.

I hesitate.

"Why the scarves?" I pick up the one on the pillow, letting the silky material glide across my palm.

"Do you trust me?" he asks.

Do I?

Of course I do.

I nod.

"On your stomach, arms in front of you."

I lie on the warm cotton comforter, arms stretched in front, and my head rest on the vanilla-scented pillowcase.

Bryan wraps the free end of a silk scarf around one wrist and secures it with a knot. He kisses the back of my hand. "Is it too tight?"

I shake my head.

He binds the other wrist with the second silk scarf.

"Think of a number between one and one hundred," he says, straddling my hips.

"I don't remember reading that in the rules."

"I'm giving it my own spin. A number between one and one hundred, please."

"Eleven."

"Why eleven?"

"Aside from Kourtney, I have eleven important people in my life now."

"Okay, eleven," he says and covers my eyes with the silk scarf, fastening it at the back of my head. "Tonight, you'll have eleven orgasms." His lips brush my ear with each word spoken. "You won't be able to touch me or see me."

Wait! "What!?" I tense.

He slides down the back of my legs, grasps my ankles, and pulls me until my arms are stretched even more.

My body stiffens from the tension. My breathing becomes heavy. I fight the panic threatening to ruin this massage. Images of the last time I was tied to the bed play through my mind.

"Are you okay?" he asks.

I shake my head and whimper.

I feel the heat from his body lying next to me. His lips upon mine.

"Dani, it's not my intention to leave you tied to the bed or harm you. If it's too uncomfortable, just say stop, and I will. You're safe with me. Okay?"

"Okay," I barely whisper.

"May I begin?"

I nod.

"I need you to say it," he says, kissing me.

I want to deepen the kiss.

I want to touch him.

My body wants more.

"May I begin?"

"You may begin."

I hear a cap top pop open, his palms rubbing together. His slick hands press down on my shoulders, kneading in circular motions. Bryan doesn't apply too much pressure. Tension slowly evaporates from my body.

His hands move to my back. They meet at my spine, slide up, span out and around. Bryan repeats the motion. The warm air of his breath falls on my neck and shoulders. The oil heats my skin. My scalp tingles and I sigh.

Bryan moves to my lower back to continue the cycle. Hands meeting in the center, slide up, span out and around. Soft breeze from his mouth. Oil heats. Tingle. Aaah.

His hands disappear and are replaced with his mouth. He glides his tongue across my skin. The contrast between fingers and tongue is so arousing. My body melts into the comforter.

The spot behind my ear is tickled by his tongue and I feel the wetness flow for my first orgasm.

Pop. The bottle's top opens. Three warm lines are drawn on my butt. The thickest being the one seeping into my crack. Bryan massages the silky liquid in. His hands push my cheeks up. Out and open. Down and closed. The oil seeps in deeper.

The thrill runs through the back of my knees. Hedonistic lips rain kisses up my spine to the base of my neck. An erotic breeze warms a path down the center of my back.

His massaging hands continue the cycle. Up. Out and open. I tingle now between my thighs. Erotic breeze in the valley of my butt. The two heated sensations collide in the intersection as the small waves of a sensual orgasm roll through me.

"That was beautiful," he whispers.

Bryan moves down while his fingers massage the inner skin of my partially parted thighs.

I groan.

Bryan blows tiny circles on my skin, followed by his tongue. One thigh then the next. The carnal suspense brushes the passageway to the place he calls Sunshine. My body trembles through a third orgasm.

"I wish you'd picked a higher number," he whispers.

Pop.

My body's still trembling. Oil flows down one leg to my toes and up the other leg. Bryan's massive hands massage it into my skin. Soft nibbles on the back of my knee, he blows and Sunshine flutters.

A warm tongue swipes the back of the other knee; he blows. The pleasure is so sultry the fluttering transforms into a fascinating orgasm.

"If I had more chances, I'd see how many ways I could make you come just by licking the back of your knees."

Both his hands press into my legs, pushing up. Fingertips slide down them. The stimulation is repeated. Breeze up one leg and down the other. Bryan lifts my right foot. Starting at the tips of my toes, he massages them using light circular motions working his way down to the heel. The sole of my foot warms from his breath.

I wiggle.

He switches feet to once again start at the tips of my toes. I'm so turned on. I feel the wetness between my inner thighs.

"You're doing good, Dani. I'm turning you over."

His oil-coated hands grip my hips and I'm rolled onto my back. The scarves must have crossed. They don't have as much give as before.

With his mouth, he makes love to each toe and the skin in between. The waver starts in my pelvis. He reverses the massage for the other foot. Ending with a slow. Long. Sexually explicit lick of the sole. I growl through a feverish orgasm.

Pop.

Bryan grasps my knees, dragging his fingers down my legs, then kneads my calves. Inch by stimulating inch upward, the breeze from his mouth ignites the oil, his tongue spreading the flames. The massage travels up to my thighs. They part for him. A blatant invitation to taste me.

Bryan chuckles.

The throbbing in my center increases. I know he'll taste me. Touch me. I'm prepared for it. My inner muscles clench in anticipation of it.

He reaches the triangle.

Pop.

Warm oil slithers onto my clitoris, zigzagging up my stomach, across my breast, up to my neck and back down. Silky liquid circles each nipple.

The room's atmosphere causes my sex to burn in the most sensual of heat. Bryan grips my inner thighs spreading them wider. He brushes the triangle with strokes from his tongue. The air from his mouth heats the outline.

His tongue dips into my navel.

Wait!

Hold!

Up!

I pull against the scarves. Burning.

That's it!? That's all he's going to do?!

If my hands were free, I'd grab his head, forcing him back down there and holding him down until I reach orgasm number eleven.

My need for him is almost painful. His massive hands cup my breasts, squeezing them. His fingers roll my aching nipples. I cry out at the pain and pleasure. They're extra sensitive lately. The oil scorches them. His teeth clamp down on my nipple.

"Aaah." I pull against the restraints around my wrist.

His tongue flicks the captured morsel. My back lifts off the bed shoving my breast up as my body sizzles through an orgasm.

"Please, Bryan!" I beg.

The pleasure-pain consumes me.

His massage moves up to my shoulders and neck as he slides up my body.

Pop.

I've lost count; I'm not going to reach eleven. I'll pass out from over-stimulation.

The oil coats my arms and hands. The massage begins with my under-arms. The sensation makes my toes curl and Sunshine clench. He blows to heat the oil.

One by one each finger gets drawn into his mouth. My palms are licked. No skin on my hand is left unexplored. Bryan spends an extended amount of time on the ring finger of my left hand. He moans.

Slithering down my body, his lips find mine. He kisses me.

Slowly.

Sexually.

Intimately.

I taste the sweet cinnamon flavored oil. Bryan's tongue thrusts, circles, and explores every inch of my mouth.

Images of him thrusting, circling, and exploring every inch of my sex trigger a scintillating orgasm.

"Mmm, I gave you the outline and your sexy mind colored it in," he whispers in my ear.

He settles between my legs. His erection touches my overheated clito-ris. I wiggle and rock, squirm and circle, trying to get him in a position that will give me the friction I need to come.

"Find my rhythm, Dani," he says in my ear. "Stop squirming and con-centrate on relaxing."

He waits until I'm still.

"Relax your toes."

"Your legs."

"Your knees."

"Your thighs."

"Your hips."

"Your back and stomach."

"Your ribs, chest and shoulders."

"Your arms, hands and fingers."

"Your neck."

"Your chin and mouth."

"Your nose, eyes and brows."

"Your face."

"Listen to my breathing; see if you can match it," he whispers.

I listen for each inhale and feel each exhale.

Inhale, smmmh.

Exhale, ahhhhh.

I slow my breathing until we're functioning as one. My heart beats to his rhythm. The thumping sensation starts throughout my body, heading to the same destination. Our breathing picks up sensual-speed.

I experience an ebullient orgasm.

"That was so hot, Dani. I've read about people having an orgasm that way."

He shifts; unfamiliar words are spoken against my ear. The deep, masculine tone and inflection are sexy. Steamy. The flow, sultry.

I concentrate on the vibrations of the words and the emotion behind them. Just the thought of what he's saying gives me a naughty orgasm.

Bryan scoots down my body. His sensual breeze heats the path until he's there, his shoulders pressing my thighs wide open.

"You're so wet," he says with humor.

He kisses my southern lips. A sweet, soft peck. His finger slides in, rubbing the roof of Sunshine.

Something starts to happen right away. My instinct is to close my legs, but his shoulders are in the way.

"Relax. Enjoy it. Don't fight." His voice sounds far away.

The constant contact of his tongue brushing the hood of my clitoris keeps me climbing.

What's happening?

I pull against the silk scarves.

My shoulders leave the bed.

Abs crunch.

Slowly my fingers capture the atmosphere in a tight grip.

My toes curl as my body shakes.

I stop breathing.

The pot top flies off.

A geyser shoots out of me for a tidal wave of an orgasm.

Bryan hums his approval.

My shoulders drop back onto the bed. Body unresponsive. Brain foggy.

I vaguely acknowledge him entering me.

He lifts my leg, hooking it around his hip, drawing circles within my center, stroking that bundle of nerves inside me.

"Come on, give me number eleven," he chants.

"I can't." Unable to coax movement from my hips.

"Give it to me." His fingers brush my scorching clitoris. My hips buck, shocked by a volt of electricity.

Renewed, I match him thrust for thrust. Circle for Circle. He elevates me into an extraordinary eleventh orgasm.

Bryan thrusts faster and harder, his own release imminent.

I pull my knees up, locking my ankles in the center of his back. The headboard taps out the pace.

He growls, somehow freeing my wrists without losing his rhythm. Bryan pulls me up with him, sitting me on his lap.

With each upward thrust, he brings me down on him. I clench my walls to grip him as tight as I can.

His body tenses. A low rumble comes from his chest, growing louder. Every contraction of his release is felt in the depths of my sex. He's holding me tight. I continue to clench and release around him, milking him for every drop.

We collapse on the bed, both breathing hard. I welcome the weight of him on top of me.

"Do you think anyone heard us?" I kiss his shoulder.

His chuckle resonates through me. "I'm sure they heard us across the state of Colorado."

"If I could lift my arms right now I'd punch you."

Bryan climbs off me. I reach up, removing the silk scarf to watch him walk into the bathroom. I love looking at the tattoo of a hawk on his back. Its wings span from one shoulder to the other. The scratches aren't red anymore.

I hear water running in the bathtub. He passes the bathroom door several times, moving around.

Bryan walks back into the room. My gaze meanders across his strong shoulders, chest, and defined abs. My second favorite part of his body is now flaccid and hanging from a trimmed nest of pubic hairs, flopping side to side with each step he takes. My favorite part of his body are those muscular thighs and long muscular legs. He is Mr. Tall-And-Sexy.

"What are you smiling at?" he asks.

"You." I smirk. "Where do you work out? I want to watch."

"I have a gym at work and one off the garage. Willis put your Vin dummy in there."

Scooping me up in his arms, he carries me into the bathroom and helps me into the lavender-scented water.

He lit white candles.

"I'll be right back," he tells me and goes in the room.

Returning with a bottle of champagne and two flutes, he hands me a glass. Bryan fills my flute first, then his, and climbs in behind me. He sets the bottle on the floor beside the tub.

Ting. Bryan taps his glass against mine. "Happy New Year, Dani."

"Happy New Year, Bry."

I sip the sweet champagne. "What language were you speaking?"

"Arabic."

"What were you saying?"

"I'm so happy to have you in my life. You're the only woman I desire. I want to give you new experiences, mentally, physically, emotionally, and sexually. I will always treasure you."

I lift his hand to my lips, kissing his knuckles. "How long have you had those arrows on your ribcage?"

"Four years?"

"What do they stand for?"

"My baby girl."

Over my shoulder, I gaze at him. The sadness in his eyes can't be missed. His lips peck the tip of my nose.

We sit in mutual silence.

I take a deep breath hating to kill the mood, but I need to ask. "Bry. Why won't you tell me what's going on?"

He exhales.

I wait for him to say something. I try again. "You overreacted to the fireworks. Please tell me why."

"Those jerks put our house in jeopardy." He nibbles on my ear.

I move away from him so he can't distract me from this conversation.

"It's winter, Bryan. Would the trees really have caught fire?"

"With the right kind of accelerant, yes, trees can burn even during a Colorado winter. I've seen all kinds of things happen year-round."

"Are we safe? Kourtney and I. Are we safe here in Colorado with you?"

"You guys are always safe with me."

I stare into his eyes. "Are you telling me the truth?"

"I have no reason to lie to you, baby."

He had me up until he called me baby. I'm not going to press him for answers now, but we will finish this conversation later.

Bryan reaches for me and I move back into his embrace. His arms tighten around me as I relax against him, sipping champagne.

I wake up with my head on a pillow, naked underneath the warm covers. Bryan changed the comforter.

It's almost three in the morning and he isn't in the room. The lights are off in the bathroom. I don't remember falling asleep.

I roll out of bed, put on my robe, and leave the room to check on the girls.

The house is too quiet and all the lights are off. Usually the track lighting that runs along the baseboard of the wall from one side of the upstairs to the other is on. Bryan said he installed it so Emma could always find her way to his room in the middle of the night.

Trevor lifts his head when I open Kourtney's door. He's lying at the foot of the bed.

The girls fell asleep with the lamp on and Mr. Cuddles between them.

"Watch over them, Trevor," I whisper patting his head.

On my way out of the room, Bryan meets me at the door. He's dressed in black cargo pants, black turtleneck, and wearing black military-style boots.

"What are you doing up?" I ask.

"Checking on things."

I hear footsteps and voices coming from downstairs.

"Who's here?"

"Tony. Vin. And Ig. Go back to bed, Danielle," he commands.

I take a second to absorb the way he's dressed, his posture, and short answers. Bryan is in alpha mode. Now definitely isn't the time to challenge him. I nod and walk by. A quick glance back and I see the gun holstered in the center of his back.

Yeah, we're safe with you, but now, I'm convinced something's going on.

Chapter Twenty-Six

A SMALL RED SORE ON MY ring finger is the source of the ache that wakes me out of my sleep this morning. I remember dreaming of fighting off a pack of dogs. I must have scratched myself in my sleep.

I get a bandage out of the medicine cabinet.

Bryan is asleep, lying on his stomach, one arm above his head, the other hugging his pillow with his left hand tucked underneath. The covers slipped down to his hips. I don't know what time he finally came to bed. I pull the blanket up to his shoulders. He stirs but doesn't wake or change position.

I get dressed in the closet, then go down to the utility room to get the carpet sweeper and cleaning supplies, taking them to the family room.

After the fireworks, everyone went to bed. I thought Vin, Ig, and Tony went home too, until I heard them downstairs. There's another guest room next to Bryan's parents and two rooms in the attendants' quarters off the laundry room.

I close the doors to the family room so I don't disturb anyone.

Each time I pass the picture window, I stop to stare out at the yard. Something's missing, but I can't put my finger on it.

The shards of broken glass from the tree ornaments sparkle in the sunlight. Broom and dustpan in hand, I start to sweep up the pieces. It hits me. I know what's missing. I stand in the window.

The small tree is gone. And the snowman Bryan and the girls made the other day. The lawn ornaments are also gone.

Marie steps out the door of their house. She strolls up the path bundled in her winter coat and scarf. I watch for her reaction to the bare spots in the yard. She looks up and sees me standing in the window. Marie waves. I return the gesture and wait. She doesn't pause.

She comes in through the side door.

Maybe she'll tell me what's going on.

I quickly finish cleaning the family room and go to the kitchen.

"Do you know what happened to the Christmas tree in the yard?"

"Willis was up early this morning taking down decorations," she says, opening the refrigerator.

"I was up pretty early too. I didn't see him in the yard."

"Were you up before sunrise?"

I shake my head.

"Willis is always up and piddling in the yard before sunrise no matter what time he goes to bed." Her hands are loaded with bell peppers and onions.

I guess it's possible that Willis moved the tree, but I don't think he'd dismantle the snowman without asking the girls first. He knows how much they loved building it with Bryan.

"Was that the first time someone set off fireworks out by the pond?" I ask.

"Willis and I usually visit his family for the holidays so I don't know what went on around here. It wasn't until Emma was four that Bryan spent Christmas in Boulder. They used to travel then end up in Colorado Springs with his parents. This is the first time I've ever seen him happy during the holidays. I know it's because of you and Miss Kourtney."

"Let me put away the cleaning supplies and I'll help you make breakfast."

After returning the cleaning supplies to the closet, I wash my hands, put on an apron, and start chopping the onions and bell peppers for Marie. She's peeling and cutting potatoes.

"Now that you and Kourtney are all moved in, are there any changes you want to make?" she asks.

"This is a big house and I know it's not easy keeping it clean by yourself. Let's sit down this weekend and divide the chores."

"It's going to be great having a woman around here. Hopefully you can make Bryan's room more feminine friendly," she laughs.

"I actually love Bryan's room, but you're right—it needs a woman's touch here and there. I won't make any drastic changes. Yet." I elbow her. "And I'll certainly do it little by little so he won't notice."

We laugh. Men can be territorial when it comes to their space. She's right though, Bryan's room is very masculine, and subtly adding feminine things will be a challenge. We talk about redecorating other parts of the house.

James would have a mitch-fit whenever I added things to his apartment. Lord help me if I moved or organized his cluttered desk filled with papers, computer equipment, and blank CDs.

I go to the refrigerator and take out sausage links and bacon. Marie sets two frying pans on the stove and fills a pot with water. I turn on the fire.

We work well together in the kitchen. It's been a dream to cook on this six-burner stovetop.

"Should I do biscuits or toast?" Marie asks.

"Definitely biscuits. Those buttermilk ones if you have any."

The smells in the kitchen make my mouth water and my stomach growl. Last night, I ate a lot. I even tried the asada tacos Ig made with homemade salsa.

I stand at the counter cracking eggs into a bowl. Marie sets the whisk near me and turns the bacon.

I tilt the bowl and whip the eggs, staring out the window. In my peripheral, someone dashes through the bare trees. Squinting, I focus. It's not the guys out in the wooded area; they're in the family room with the girls and Jessica, watching the parade. Bryan and his parents are closed off in his home office. Could it be Willis?

I turn my attention back to the eggs, pouring the mixture into the pan. Marie hums as she moves around the kitchen.

Once I turn off the fire under the pan of scrambled eggs, I leave the kitchen.

"Breakfast is ready," I call out, standing in the hallway.

I help the girls make their plates and get them settled at the table before I put food on mine.

"Uncle Vinny, did you find out who was lighting those fireworks?" Emma bites into a piece of crispy bacon.

"No." He sits across from her after pouring creamer into his coffee.

"The colors were pretty, but the sounds scared me," Kourtney says as she spreads jelly on a biscuit. "I hope they don't come back."

"They won't," Bryan says, walking into the kitchen behind his parents.

"The holidays started off rocky and ended with a bang," Bryan senior jokes, spooning smothered potatoes onto his plate.

"So, you're coming back next month?" I ask him. A change in subject is needed.

"I want to see my granddaughter's science project. She showed me her notes," he says spooning grits into a bowl.

"Bryan and I would love for Kourt to come with Emm for spring break," Nancy says, sitting next to me, a full plate in front of her.

"Please, Mommy. I *really* wanna go to Colorado Springs."

"I'll give it serious consideration. Spring break isn't until April."

"I can't believe you're going back to work tomorrow, Danielle. It's Thursday," Bryan senior says.

"The holidays are hard for some people. I've stayed in touch with a few of my patients. They need a face-to-face session. I'm not going in on Friday."

"Do you have a full schedule tomorrow?" Jessica asks.

"No. I have a two-hour break between my morning and afternoon patients."

"How about we meet up for lunch?"

"I would love that. We can go to that Italian place near the hospital."

"It's a date."

While I eat breakfast, I watch Bryan and his friends. Without drawing attention to themselves, they check their cell phones often. The only time they engage in the conversation going on at the table is when asked a question. Their replies are short. No emotion behind the inflection. And they offer no further explanation. Nor do they encourage more questions.

I wonder if I'm the only one who notices Vin isn't wearing a sling this morning. And they're all wearing dark colors.

Before we finish breakfast, Tony, Ig, and Vin excuse themselves from the table and leave.

"We better get going too. I want to get home before the game comes on," Bryan senior says. The legs of the chair scrape the floor as he pushes back from the table. He picks up his wife's dishes along with his and carries them to the sink.

The rest of us rise from the table. I go with Bryan and the girls to help his parents load up their car. Jessica helps Marie clean the kitchen.

"I know you didn't have this much when we came, Nance." Bryan senior struggles to fit a suitcase in the car.

"Yes, I did. You forgot how you packed the car." She bumps my shoulder before hugging the girls.

"I'm going to miss you, Grandpa," Kourtney says, wrapping her arms around his waist.

"I'll miss you too, Kourty. We can video chat anytime you want to talk."

"Don't forget you promised to take us horseback riding." Emma wraps her arms around him on the other side.

"There's a stable not too far from us." Bryan senior hugs her back, then walks over, wrapping his arms around me. "My son is a happier man with you in his life. My granddaughter is thriving because of you and Kourty. Thank you." He kisses my cheek.

My eyes water with tears. Words fail me.

"Drive safe. Call when you get in," Bryan says. He shakes his dad's hand and kisses his mom's cheek.

We watch them climb into the car and pull out of the driveway. The girls run to the edge waving goodbye. Trevor barks and jumps up and down.

"I'm going to the office," Bryan says. He walks into the garage with his hands in his pocket. I've never seen him go to work in casual clothes. A few minutes later, he backs out in my truck.

Why is he taking my Range Rover?

I look back in the direction of Bryan's parents. They make a right at the stop sign. A heartbeat later, a black SUV pulls away from the curb, heading in the same direction.

"Mommy, will you watch us play with Trevor in the backyard?"

"I was going to unpack the boxes in your room. Can you guys wait until after lunch?"

"I'll keep an eye on them," Willis offers. He steps out of the garage.

"Stay where Mr. Willis can see you at all times," I tell the girls.

"Danielle, I have an appointment. I'll be back by dinner." Jessica is backing out of the garage in Bryan's Silverado.

An idea pops into my head.

I go back inside ready to get Marie out of the house for a little while. When I step into the foyer, she's walking up the stairs with the laundry basket in her hands. That's even better. I go to the wall near the stairs and feel my way from one end to the other, searching for the door.

I remember Bryan pushed and pulled on the wall panels in his office. There's nothing on the wall for me to pull, so I push on it.

Light bulb moment. I run upstairs to get the keycard. The one the guard gave me that day I went to Bryan's office. Marie is in the upstairs supply closet, humming a tune. She won't be able to see me.

I hurry down the stairs and wave the keycard in front of the wall. Nothing happens. Face up and face down, from one end to the next, I slide the keycard on the smooth surface of the drab-colored wall.

Nothing happens.

I give up, for now, and go upstairs to Kourtney's room.

Three weeks of sleeping in messed with my internal clock and I'm almost late for work. Bryan tried to convince me to call in sick. He was nibbling behind my ear. Last night he came home in a better mood and it trickled over to this morning. Willpower and dedication to my job, got me out of bed before I gave in.

No time for breakfast, Marie made me a smoothie to temporarily satisfy my hunger while I'm with patients all morning.

By eleven I'm checking my watch and my stomach is having a loud conversation with me. Jessica said she would meet me here.

I search my purse and desk for a bag of nuts or a piece of candy. The desk phone rings right when I find a fun-size candy bar.

"Dr. Edwards," I answer, cradling the receiver between my shoulder and cheek, leaving my fingers free to rip open the wrapper.

Silence.

"Hello?" I take a bite.

"Is this Danielle Edwards?"

"This is Dr. Edwards."

I hope I'm not smacking in the caller's ear.

"That's not what I asked," he says. "Is your name Danielle Edwards?"

The voice sounds familiar.

"Sir, I've told you, I'm Dr. Edwards. How may I help you?" I toss the last of the candy in my mouth.

"Is this Danielle Tatum-Edwards?"

The line goes dead.

My heart stops.

"Danielle, are you okay?"

I look up. Jessica is standing in the doorway, concern in her eyes. I put the receiver on the base.

"I'm fine. Are you ready for lunch? I'm hungry." I stand, ignoring the warning bells going off in my head.

My coat is on the hook near the door. I pick up my purse and we leave my office.

Jessica and I walk to the restaurant around the corner on Pearl Street. The small Italian restaurant is bursting with smells of fresh baked bread and homemade sauces. Checkered tablecloths cover the square tables; black-and-white photos of Italy decorate the walls. The heated enclosed patio is packed, but we're seated right away, inside.

The waiter brings a basket of warm, mini garlic bread sticks and our side salads. I don't need a menu. I order the Chicken Alfredo pasta.

"What were you doing downtown this morning?" I bite into the hot, buttery, garlicky, fresh bread. Hmm, I momentarily close my eyes in appreciation for the homemade treat.

"I had a business meeting."

"I thought you were on vacation." I toss the rest of the yummy grain in my mouth and reach for another.

"It's turning out to be a business vacation."

"What business are you taking care of while on vacation?" My mouth is full of bread. I have table manners, I'm just hungry. Usually I get like this the week before my period, but I'm not craving foods covered in gooey red sauces. Like french fries smothered in ketchup or hot wings dripping with wing sauce or a wet chicken burrito drenched in red sauce.

Tears pool in her eyes. "I'm moving my practice here to Boulder. I met with the hospital board this morning and finalized the paperwork. Iggy's been helping me."

I take a break from stuffing my face to give her my full attention. "Do you want to talk about it?"

"Samantha broke up with me," she cries.

"I thought things were good between you two."

"She's fucking her therapist."

"She's what?"

"You heard me." Jessi looks down at her hands.

The waiter brings our food and another basket of delicious mini bread sticks. Jessica asks if I want to share a bottle of wine. I decline. This is a workday for me. She orders a glass.

"I sent a locksmith to the house."

"Can you tell me what you hope to accomplish by locking her out?"

"Please don't shrink me right now, Dani. I need a friend, not a therapist!"

I shovel pasta in my mouth, thinking of a plan a friend would come up with. This is one area where I'm greatly lacking experience. Being advanced in high school had its pros and cons. The biggest con: I was too young to hang out or go on dates so I didn't have girlfriends to do catty stuff with.

"Okay, Jessi, after lunch, let's drive to a home improvement store in Colorado Springs. We'll need industrial glue, spray paint, and two cordless electric staplers."

"Why? What are we doing?"

I mimic my daughter's mischievous smile and tell her what I have in mind. We finish our lunch plotting revenge, knowing we'd never follow through, but it feels good to plan someone's demise. It's therapeutic.

We walk the long way back to the hospital, laughing at our outrageous scheme.

"So you're an OB/Gyn?" I ask.

"One of the best in the state." She pats herself on the back.

"How soon will your practice be up and running? I'm due for a PAP and need to get on some form of birth control." I link my arm with hers as we step off the curb in the crosswalk. "It's getting close to my period so I can start the pill right away."

"Danielle! You've been sleeping with my brother and not using *any* birth control? Not even condoms?"

I hang my head in shame. "We haven't been having sex that long." I realize I sound like an uninformed teenager.

"Don't give me that bull. You know the consequences of having unprotected sex," she chastens.

Bryan and I haven't talked about our sexual status. I know I'm STD free. He hasn't said how many women he's slept with. Considering he trained women to be escorts or mistresses, I assume he's into the double digits.

He hasn't used a condom with me. How many others hasn't he used one with?

"Danielle, if the past few nights are any indications of how often you two have sex…"

I stop walking.

She stumbles back.

"You heard us?"

"Who hasn't heard you guys? Well, the girls. And dad. He sleeps like a log. I got horny listening to you have multiple orgasms the other night."

"I'm sooo embarrassed," I sing, closing my eyes.

"Don't be! My little brother knows what he's doing. Mom didn't think a woman could climax that many times in one night. Dad's in trouble."

I groan.

"What's the first day of your last menstrual period?"

I pull out my cell phone to check the calendar. "December ninth."

"How long have you been sleeping with my brother?"

"Two weeks." It's also on my calendar.

"Let's go," she says, pulling my arm.

"Where are we going?" I reluctantly let her lead the way.

"To run tests and examine you. It's still early, but it doesn't hurt to check you out."

I stop walking, the action so abrupt, she bumps into me and we almost topple over.

"Too early for what? Check me for what?" I screech.

"You could be pregnant, Danielle," she says matter-of-factly and yanks me forward.

Chapter Twenty-Seven

JESSICA ASKS FOR THE USE of an exam room and a technician to process lab work. I go into the restroom and pee in a specimen cup. She draws blood.

"I have a patient coming in fifteen minutes. Please come to my office when you get the results." I leave the exam room in a daze.

Bryan and I haven't gotten to this point in our relationship.

I silently get off the elevator and walk to my office, unaware of my surroundings. I take a moment to pull myself together, then read over my notes. Ms. Stewart is one of my least talkative patients. Based on our telephone sessions over the holidays, I have questions prepared.

I stand and greet her when Vanessa, the intern, escorts Ms. Stewart into my office.

No matter what's going on in my life, I'm able to push it aside and give my patients the full attention they deserve. Today is no exception.

For an hour, Ms. Stewart and I discuss the loss of her son. She was against him joining the military, but he did it anyway. Her behavior has been erratic since learning of his death and she is under court order for therapy.

Once her session is over, I have no distractions and my mind runs through the "what ifs."

What if I'm pregnant?

What if he leaves?

What if he doesn't want the baby?

Termination isn't an option for me.

My next patient is escorted through the door. For once, I'm happy I scheduled appointments close together. I need the constant distraction from the what ifs.

"Good afternoon, Mr. Brumfield."

When the last patient of the day leaves my office, I no longer fight it. I let my tears run free. Surely the results are back by now.

"Why are you crying, Danielle?" Jessica asks.

I didn't hear her come into my office. My eyes open and zero in on the medical file in her hand.

"I checked with Vanessa to see when you were free." She comes in and sits across from me.

I muster up the courage to sit up straight and square my shoulders.

"Just say it."

"You're pregnant."

I close my eyes and let my forehead drop to the desk. *Thump.*

Will this rollercoaster ever end?

"I'd like to examine you and start your prenatal care. Your iron level is a little low. That is if you want me to be your doctor."

I nod with my forehead still on the desk.

"Let's go back to the exam room."

I follow her out of my office, tears running down my cheeks. Physically, I know I'm walking. I know I'm on the elevator. I don't feel it though. My body's on autopilot.

In the exam room, I step behind the screen to undress and put on a hospital gown.

As I climb onto the table, I come to terms with what's happening, nine years later. *I'm pregnant.*

Jessica goes through the standard pelvic exam.

I cry. Not because I'm pregnant. I'm fighting a losing battle against feeling disconnected. Last time, I didn't share my pregnancy highs and lows with anyone. I was dealing with too many emotions. This time, there are people I call friends. They're my friends because of Bryan. Will they abandon me too?

"I'm going to give you a vaginal ultrasound. We won't be able to see much. I just want to pinpoint the placement of the embryo."

I nod.

Jessica inserts the probe, moving it around and tapping the keyboard while looking at the monitor. I try to keep still.

"Do you want to see?" She turns the monitor, not waiting for a response.

She points to a small circle at the top of the screen. "That's the life you and Bryan created." Her excitement pushes me over the edge.

I cry harder, drifting further away from him. Again.

Jessica withdraws the probe and turns off the machine. "I need you to sign release forms so I can contact your doctor in Arizona. How many pregnancies have you had?"

"One."

"Was Kourtney full term?"

I nod my head.

"Did you deliver vaginally or by cesarean section?"

"Vaginally."

"Dani, don't condemn my little brother just yet."

"Please don't tell him or your parents."

"I'm your doctor. I cannot disclose any information without your consent. And you guys aren't married so he can't make demands." She squeezes my hand. "That's my niece or nephew you're carrying. I wouldn't do anything to jeopardize the health and safety of either one of you."

I take my feet out of the stirrups and slide off the exam table. On autopilot, I get dressed. Before leaving, I sign the release forms without reading them. Silently I leave the exam room with a heavy weight on my shoulders. I reach for my ring finger, but there's no ring for me to twist.

Back in my office, I force myself to concentrate on typing patients' notes in their files and leave exactly at the end of my shift.

Jessica sent me an email to let me know she called in a prescription. I stop at the pharmacy, then head home—unsure if it will be my home much longer.

The girls are in the family room. Kourtney's reading a book. Emma's drawing a picture.

"Hi, you two. How was your day?"

Emma smiles up at me. "It was good."

"No, it wasn't. We got in a fight over the TV. Ms. Marie won't let us watch it now." Kourtney slaps her book closed.

"Have you guys finished your homework packet?" I ask.

"I finished mine last week. Emma still has three pages."

"No, I don't, Kourtney. I finished today."

"That's enough, you two. I will check both packets after dinner. I'm not feeling very well. I'm going upstairs to lie down for a little while."

"Can we watch TV?"

"Not until Marie says you can. Please get along for the rest of the evening."

Kourtney opens her book, tearing through the pages until she finds the one she was on. Emma opens her sketch book. I head upstairs, take a shower, and put on a pair of comfy pajamas. Crawling under the covers, I cry myself to sleep.

"Dani, is everything okay?" Bryan shakes my shoulder.

I clear my throat. "Yes."

"Are you getting sick? Emm said you're sick. Do you want me to call Ig?" His hand touches my forehead.

"No."

"Dinner's ready. Marie made fried chicken. Are you coming down?"

I open my eyes and read the numbers on the clock. I've been asleep for three hours.

"Not hungry."

"The girls are worried about you."

I sigh. "Okay, give me a minute and I'll come down."

He kisses my forehead and leaves the room.

I drag myself out of bed and throw on sweats and one of Bryan's sweatshirts to hide the evidence. Mentally I know I'm not showing. Emotionally I'm due any day.

I join them in the kitchen and go through the motions of a happy family dinner. All the while, I push food around my plate. In the background of my reality, the girls are complaining about going back to school on Monday.

Bryan is watching me; I sense it.

After dinner we sit in the family room and play a board game. I cover my nonexistent baby bump with a throw pillow.

At eight thirty, I take the girls upstairs and get them ready for bed. Bryan takes Trevor for a run.

Since the New Year's Eve fireworks, Kourtney and Emma want to sleep in the same room. Even though they were at odds this afternoon, they put aside their differences to sleep in the same bed tonight.

They don't ask me to sit with them. Mr. Cuddles is placed on a pillow between them. I leave the door cracked so Trevor can take his place at the foot of the bed when he gets back.

I put my pajamas back on and climb into bed, facing away from the bedroom doors. "Take a deep breath and relax your body," I chant to myself. But relaxation and sleep elude me. From as far back as I can remember, I don't think I've ever felt as lonely as I do right now. Who do I have to talk to about this? Where do we go from here? Is history going to repeat itself or will we rewrite it like I thought we'd began to do?

The door opens then closes. I remain still, listening to him move around the room. I keep my eyes closed hoping he thinks I'm asleep already.

He goes into the bathroom and I hear the water running in the shower room. The tears I've been fighting all evening start to seep through my closed lids.

Relax and go to sleep. I chant to myself. I'm too emotional to relax my body.

The bathroom door opens. I crack my eyes open: the room is dark. No moonlight shining through the double glass doors. He pulled the shades down over them.

Through the darkness, I watch Bryan pad to his side of the bed. The covers shift as he climbs under and scoots close to me.

"Dani. Please talk to me. I can't help you unless you tell me what we're dealing with."

I can't say anything.

"Tell me what you need."

"I need you to hold me." My voice is so low I don't know if he heard me until the warmth of his body is against mine.

He spoons me.

"Talk to me," he pleads.

I can't.

With his lips against my ear, he whispers, "I love you, Dani."

Covering my face, I sob into the palms of my hands. Bryan's arm tightens around me.

"Whatever it is, we will face it together."

"I'm pregnant." I blurt it out.

He's reaching over me. Then I hear the click of the switch on the lamp. My hands are pried away. "You think I'll find an excuse to leave."

I look up at him.

"You think I'll let you push me away so you can go through this pregnancy alone," he says.

I don't have to answer. He knows what I'm thinking.

Bryan smiles as his hand slips under my pajama top, resting on my stomach. "I love you and we're adding to our family." The excitement shows in his eyes.

"I love you too."

He leans down, softly brushing his lips over mine. "Tell me what you want."

We talk about his sexual history and the number of women he's slept with. I'm relieved to know he always uses condoms, but his number is well into the double digits. He gets tested regularly.

We talk about us having more children. Bryan wants the baby. Termination was never an option for him.

Bryan and I finally get over the impasse and finish the conversation we started three months ago.

Around one in the morning he raids the kitchen. My stomach is growling. We talk until sunrise and decide to wait before we tell everyone about the baby, including the girls. He hopes it's a boy because he's outnumbered by the females in the house. Trevor doesn't count because the dog's loyalty can be swayed by a doggie treat. Bryan says he will be happy if we have another girl though. He wants her to have my brown eyes.

Bryan vows to travel this journey with me and he's happy his sister is my doctor. He's going to take care of me, starting with taking the girls to work with him so I can get some rest.

I wake up in the afternoon and go downstairs to the kitchen with the tray of dishes. Jessica is at the table typing on her laptop.

I hug her from behind, kissing her cheek. "Good afternoon."

She squeezes my hands.

I put my prenatal vitamin and iron pill on a napkin and go to the sink to rinse the dishes and stack them in the dishwasher.

In the walk-in pantry, I pull out ingredients to make buttermilk waffles.

"Hello, Danielle. I was going to wake you and make you eat something. Are you sick?" Marie walks out of the laundry room. "You didn't eat last night."

"I ate dinner at one in the morning, but I'm really hungry now."

"Sit down, let me prepare something for you. What would you like?"

"I can fix it, Marie. I don't want to disrupt your routine."

"Nonsense, dear. Tell me what you want."

"I'd really like waffles with warm maple syrup, scrambled eggs, and crispy bacon." My mouth waters at the thought.

"So?" Jessica gestures to the pills on the napkin.

I know what she's asking, but I'm not making this easy for her.

"So what?" I open the refrigerator, pouring grape juice into a small glass.

"Oh come on," she sings. "You know what I'm asking."

I feign innocence. "I have no idea what you're asking." Smiling, I sit across from her.

"Did you tell Bryan?" she shouts. The griddle hits the counter top. "Sorry, Marie. I didn't mean to startle you. Danielle's bout with amnesia is infuriating."

"Would you like waffles too?" Marie asks.

"No, thank you." Jessica turns to me. "I'd like an answer from Danielle."

I swallow the pills and drink all the juice before I answer. "Yes, I told him."

"And?" she growls.

"And what?" I laugh.

Her hand hits the table. "Danielle! Don't make me reach across this table and strangle you."

"He told me he loves me and our family is growing."

Marie gasps.

"You cannot tell anyone, Marie. We're waiting to tell everyone."

Jessica squeals, jumps to her feet, and runs around the table. She almost knocks me out of the chair, throwing her arms around me.

Marie drops the griddle and rushes to me, embracing me the way a mother would embrace her pregnant daughter. She wipes her eyes and goes back to preparing my brunch. The two demand minute-by-minute details on how I told him and his reaction.

Marie joins us at the table after she sets a plate-sized buttermilk waffle in front of me. I drown it with the maple syrup, then dig-in with enthusiasm. I answer their questions between each forkful of food. When I tell them Bryan said he's traveling this journey with me, Marie fans her face to keep from crying.

For dinner, I convince Marie to surrender the kitchen to me so I can make one of Bryan's favorites, red beans and rice.

The rest of the weekend we unpack the last of my boxes and get the girls ready for their return to school. Bryan confesses to telling his friends about the baby. I confess to telling Marie. She's constantly feeding me.

Sunday evening Jessica receives back-to-back phone calls from Samantha.

I answer her phone, moaning.

"Who is this? Where's Jessi?"

"Jessi's mouth is full at the moment, but I'll gladly give her a message after I come." I pant and moan.

Bryan snatches the phone out of my hand, disconnecting the call. He throws us a disapproving frown.

Jessi and I fall on the floor laughing. I wish I'd done this in high school.

Chapter Twenty-Eight

MONDAY MORNING IS A BIG change for all.
I've been in and out of Emma's room three times trying to get
the girls up and ready for school. I'm also getting myself ready for work.

After the fourth time going in and pulling the covers off, I'm about to
explode. Alpha male steps in.

"*Girls.* Get out of bed. Brush your teeth. Wash your face. Get dressed
and let Dani do your hair, then go down to breakfast."

His voice carries to the other side of the house. The next time I go to
check on them, they are dressed.

Bryan and I agreed that I'll drop them off in the mornings and he'll
pick them up after school. This morning I go into the school's office to
do a change of address and add Bryan to Kourtney's emergency card. I
also add Jessica, Marie, Willis, and Bryan's friends.

I add myself to Emma's emergency card and walk the girls to class.

"Good morning, Ms. Williamson. How was your vacation?" I ask.

She ignores me and greets another parent.

I kiss Kourtney and Emma. "Have a good day. I love you."

A few blocks from the hospital, I'm stopped at a red light and I check
my rearview mirror. A black SUV is a few cars back. It looks like the one
that pursued the prowler in my apartment. The light turns green. I drive
five blocks and turn into the hospital's employee parking lot. The SUV
keeps going straight.

Vanessa Larson waves to me. She's standing by her car. She greets me
when I get out of my truck. Her start time is an hour before mine. She
must be running late today. Together, we walk to the entrance of the
hospital. When I get to my desk, I receive a text from Max. He's bringing
lunch to my office today instead of us going to a restaurant.

We survive the first week of Operation Return to School. Bryan now
wakes Kourtney and Emma in the mornings. Not because of their back-

to-school blues. He's doing it so I can get a few extra minutes of sleep.

On the desk in his home office, I find a bunch of books on pregnancy. He's writing notes in the margins, which I think is adorable and I love him even more. Marked on the calendar is the date and time of my first prenatal appointment at the end of the month.

After a few tweaks here and there, the four of us settle into a daily routine.

As we walk across the street heading to the medical building, Bryan tells me about the things he's reading in the baby books. I tease him about acting like a first-time dad.

Jessica reviews my medical file from Arizona and goes through the checkup. We hear the baby's heartbeat and Bryan has the biggest smile on his face.

"How far along are we?" he asks.

Jessica looks up from the monitor. "Would you like to see?"

Bryan nods enthusiastically.

She turns the monitor, pointing to the circle at the top of the screen. "The fetus is measuring at about eight weeks, which means you guys conceived somewhere between"—she types on the keyboard—"December twentieth and December twenty-fifth."

"He's our Christmas present," Bryan says, grinning at the monitor.

"He?" I ask.

One of his eyebrows arches and he holds up two fingers.

Jessica prints a picture, handing it to her brother. "That's enough with the sappy sentimental crap. Get out of my exam room."

Bryan uses a towel to wipe the gel off me and helps me down from the exam table. He keeps his hand on the small of my back as he walks me across the street, back to my office, locking the door.

"What are you doing?" I ask.

He stalks toward me. I step back until I bump into the wall. Bryan lifts me. My legs wrap around his waist.

"What I wanted to do the first time I came to your office."

Please do, Mr. Tall-And-Sexy.

Kourtney's birthday is on a Tuesday this year. Bryan wants to throw her a big party the Saturday before.

When I veto a decorator, Kourtney and Bryan lock themselves in his office to plan without me. I'm told its teddy bear themed and that's all.

Every night after dinner, they go to his office and Bryan is being annoyingly smug. The girls are getting a kick out of watching him taunt and tease me about his superior party planning skills.

"Do you have time for lunch?" he walks into my office after knocking. "The special decorations I ordered came in. They're at the mall. We can grab lunch there."

"I don't have any patients today. I'll email Dr. Stevens to let him know I'm leaving early." I type the message before shutting down the computer and locking up my office. "Let me take my truck keys to Jessi. She rode in with me this morning."

I dash across the street and give my keys to Isabel, Jessica's receptionist. "Please tell Dr. Hawk I'm riding home with Bryan."

"Not a problem, Dr. Edwards. Have a good weekend."

Bryan pulls up in front of the medical building. I spot a black SUV parked at the curb a few cars up.

"What did you order and why couldn't it be delivered to the house?" I ask, climbing in and securing my seat belt.

"Last minute purchase," he says, pulling away from the curb.

The windows on the Black SUV parked at the curb are tinted dark. I can't see inside when we pass it. I keep an eye on the side-view mirror. The truck doesn't pull away from the curb. I turn my focus back to Bryan. He assures me the extra decorations are essential to the bear theme.

We walk through the mall holding hands and come up on the Baby Store. Bryan stops to look at the window display.

"When can we buy things?" he asks.

"Let's wait until I'm seven months and we know the sex of the baby."

Disappointment flashes in his eyes.

"Okay, you can buy one thing and that's it."

He drags me inside.

We stroll up and down every aisle. He inspects items before settling on what he wants to purchase. I guess I should have been more specific. Our baby's custom-made crib and mattress will be delivered in three months.

"I thought you'd buy a bib that says I Love Daddy or something like that." I pull him toward the door. "Considering the amount of money you just spent, that thing better change diapers in the middle of the night."

Bryan kisses the back of my hand, following me to the Teddy Bear's Cave store.

"Do you think Kourt will always be obsessed with stuffed bears?" he asks carrying the packages out of the store.

"She'll grow out of the fascination when she discovers boys aren't ugly boogers. But Mr. Cuddles will always be her first teddy bear love."

"I hope she never grows out of it," he mumbles.

Dylan Hill has been less touchy-touchy and more verbal about his feelings for Kourtney. Ms. Williamson was right: Dylan likes her and its driving Bryan crazy.

We find a table in the food court. I order a double cheeseburger loaded with extra mustard, extra tomatoes, extra, *extra* pickles, grilled and raw onions and a side of steak fries.

"So you're eating red meat now?" he asks.

I shrug. "I stopped eating it when I was pregnant with Kourtney. It made my stomach turn. But I have a taste for it now. I should have known something was up when I didn't think twice about eating those asada tacos on New Year's Eve."

When Bryan sets my food in front of me, I take a big bite and hum in appreciation. I don't encourage conversation. Instead I grunt my answers to his questions as I eat. I know my chosen form of communication is frustrating him, but holding a conversation is interrupting my meal. I plan on consuming every morsel in front of me.

"Had enough?" Bryan asks when I push my plate away.

"I'm stuffed." I lean back. "But can we get an ice cream cone before we pick up the girls?" I check my watch.

"What flavor do you want?" He stands and picks up our tray.

I smile a sweet, innocent smile. "Butter pecan, pecan praline, and black walnut with whipped cream, chopped nuts and extra caramel."

He shakes his head and walks away from the table. I get that familiar throbbing between my thighs, watching his easy stride across the food court to get ice cream.

It's amusing to watch other women react to him. *My man looks good in his suits, doesn't he?* I must send a thank you note to whoever tailors his clothes.

My smile fades. Two women elbow each other and follow Bryan to the ice cream shop. They smile at him when he opens the door like the gentleman he is. One purposely tries to brush her body against his, but he quickly moves out of the way. *Look, but don't touch, ladies. Mr. Tall-And-Sexy belongs to me.*

I laugh at their attempts to get his attention. In the end, they leave the store without cones or his phone number.

My mouth waters as he walks back to our table, and it's not because of the scrumptious waffle-bowl he's carrying on a plate. My eyes follow the movement of his thighs with each step he takes. Bryan knows I'm checking him out. I don't hide the fact that I'm mentally undressing him.

"What's the extra spoon for?" I ask, scooping a spoonful of the delicious trio in my mouth.

He reaches with his spoon. "I thought we could share."

I move the bowl. "Get your own, Hawk," I say, my words muffled by the ice cream on my tongue.

"You're joking, right?"

I give him a serious look while shoveling more ice cream in my mouth. "I'm joking, babe." I offer him some from my spoon. "Do you think I can eat all this after the burger and fries?" *Okay I can, but he need not know.*

I alternate between feeding him small portions and shoveling heaping spoonfuls in my mouth.

We finish the ice cream and leave the mall to pick up the girls. Bryan hides the packages in the floor storage compartments in his Suburban. On the way, I question him about my missing Vin dummy. I went to the gym off the garage yesterday evening to work out, and it wasn't there. He claims he doesn't know where it is.

My boxing gloves and shoes are also missing. I found walking tennis shoes and a book about safe exercises for pregnant women in my workout bag. My boxing gym membership has been temporarily revoked until October.

I leave Bryan in the truck on the phone while I stand with Max in front of the school.

Now that I'm craving red meat, we make plans to go to the Steak House for lunch soon. I let him think my change in diet is due to the amount of sex I'm having on a regular basis.

"Are you ready for the invasion of the Horny Toad Trophy Wife tomorrow?" he asks.

"Don't you mean wives?"

"Girl, where have you been?" Max slaps my arm. "The Croaking Trio is down to a Solo. Mrs. Holly Valentine will be *Ms.* Holly Valentine in two more months. She's been cut off financially except for Melissa's school tuition. *Ms.* Valentine has to get a"—he does a dramatic pause—"job and is exiled from the lily pad." He covers his mouth in mock surprise. "*Mr.* Stephanie Banks dipped his oil stick in *Mrs.* Madelyn Brooks's Cathoe-lac. The two were in the backseat of his brand new two thousand fourteen Sex'us SUV parked in the office building's parking garage. Guess Mr. Banks don't have a lock and key on his dipstick like his wife thinks." He snaps his fingers. "There's evidence of the *alleged* affair on the top four social media sites." He pulls out his phone showing me the video and photos.

"Who took these?" I gasp.

"The husband of a part-time professional photographer."

My eyes threaten to pop out of their sockets. "You didn't, Maxie."

"Oh my dear, Danikins. Maxie's serving Halle Berry award-winning realness with those stills of Mrs. Brooks and Mr. Banks with their dirties on display in the parking garage of the same office building my husband works in. I spotted that dye job red mop bobbing up and down when I was trading cars with Thomas."

The bell rings and I hand Max his phone. Students pour out of the gate, running to their parents or nannies.

"Mom, why are you picking us up today?" Kourtney asks.

"Surprise." I hug them. "See you tomorrow, Max." I air kiss his cheeks.

Ms. Williamson is standing at the entrance staring our way with her top lip curled, nose scrunched. She's throwing an eye dagger and it's aimed right at me.

I guide my girls to the parking lot.

"Mommy, why don't you want a birthday party this year?"

I wait for them to climb into the back of the Suburban and buckle their seat belts to respond. "It's not fair to ask our friends to come to two separate parties a few days apart. Besides, my birthday is on the fourteenth. No one wants to come to a birthday party on Valentine's Day."

I close the door and get in the front seat.

Bryan pulls out of the parking space joining the traffic jam to get out of the lot.

"We can cancel my party so you can have one," Kourtney offers.

"Or you guys can have a party together," Emma suggests.

"Thank you, sweetie, but I wouldn't dare let you give up your party for me, or ask you to share the spotlight."

"Don't worry, girls," Bryan chimes in. "I have something special planned for Dani."

"What is it?" Kourtney asks.

"Yeah, Mr. Hawk. What did you plan?" I ask.

"I'll tell you when she's not around." He winks at them in the rearview mirror and blows me a kiss.

The girls try to guess his plans and he plays along, saying things like, "I didn't think of that," or "that sounds good, I may have to do that."

We make it out of the parking lot and head home. I look out the window, ignoring their little game.

A shadow in the side-view mirror catches my attention. I sneak a peek at Bryan. I can't see his eyes because of the shades, but I know he checks the mirrors when he drives. Does he notice the black SUV about three cars back too?

Tonight I'll tell him about the mysterious truck following me.

A catchy tune comes on the radio. "Turn that up," Kourtney shouts. "I like that song."

Bryan cranks up the volume. I look over my shoulder. Kourtney and Emma are bobbing and wiggle-dancing, singing along to the song. Even Bryan is bobbing his head in time to the beat.

They keep the music turned up as we head home. Every now and then, I check the side-view mirror. We're still being followed, but not as close.

When Bryan makes the left turn onto our street, a few seconds later the SUV also makes a left turn.

Usually Bryan pulls in front of the steps when he drops the girls off. This time he pulls into the garage. I turn around, watching the truck drive past the house as the garage door comes down. The girls jump out and go inside. Bryan walks around and opens my door.

"You looked bothered when you came to the truck with Emm and Kourt, Did something happen?" he asks.

"Ms. Williamson is upset with me."

"What do you mean?"

"She's been ignoring me since school resumed. Today she was glaring at me."

"The sun was probably in her eyes."

She was glaring. I felt it.

We walk inside the house. I go upstairs to change out of my work clothes so I can help them get ready for the party. Much to my dismay, I'm ordered out of the garage and gym until tomorrow.

Bryan and Willis park the vehicles on the street and move the equipment in the gym.

It takes mommy guilt to be allowed to decorate the formal dining room. It's where the snacks and food will be served because it is the closest room to the garage.

I'm happy Bryan is doing everything for Kourtney's party, and I understand why he's overcompensating, but I'm feeling left out. This is the first big party she's had and I have a small roll in it.

After dinner, Bryan leaves to hang out with his friends. I take the girls in the kitchen to pump them for information.

"You'll have to come up with something better than ice cream sundaes." Kourtney licks her spoon. "Bryan promised us something good to keep his secret."

Emma nods her head in agreement with strawberry ice cream smeared all over her mouth.

Chapter Twenty-Nine

SATURDAY MORNING, BRYAN AND HIS friends turn the gym and garage into a bear's den. I'm given a tour before the party starts.

Small piñata beehives filled with candy hang from the ceiling with cardboard bees buzzing around. The children have to win clues to get their chance at breaking one open. Grizzly bear cutouts sit in different areas around the two rooms.

What scares me is the mini zip-line over the river of foam fish, and the tree-climbing wall. Bryan rented crash mats and his friends will supervise those areas.

At one o'clock the doorbell rings, signaling the start of the party.

I move around making sure the children enjoy themselves and their parents are comfortable. Holly and her daughter are here. I go out of my way to make her feel welcomed. She seems sad and I want to help if she'll let me.

Stephanie socializes with other parents and throws eye daggers at Madelyn. I know it's wrong for me to celebrate someone's comeuppance, but Madelyn deserves it!

Madelyn moves between the gym, garage, and dining room looking for a friend to talk to. No married woman will socialize with her and the handful of married dads steer clear of her.

Uncle Vinny bursts into the gym dressed in a grizzly bear costume. Personally, I would have gone with a teddy bear, but since I wasn't a part of the planning, I keep my mouth shut.

After the guests leave, I find Bryan in his home office pacing the room, on the phone, and packing a bag. I lean against the doorframe.

His face is a mask of calmness. He doesn't see me in the doorway.

Listening to his end of the conversation, I've deduced that he's going somewhere. I wait until he's off the phone to make my presence known.

"Another urgent business trip?"

He turns around. I've caught him by surprise. His eyes shift to the open duffle bag on his desk, then back to me.

"I will be back by your birthday."

I step into the office and close the door behind me. "What do you do?" I sit in a chair in front of his desk, glimpsing two guns inside the bag.

Without taking his eyes off me, Bryan moves to his desk, lifts the duffle bag, and sets it on the floor, out of sight, before sitting in his chair.

"We've been over this. I own a personal protection company."

"I know that, Bryan. But what do *you* do?"

"It's self-explanatory."

I smile: he's on the defensive. "What does the owner of a personal protection company do?"

"Dani, if this is your round-about way of asking where I'm going, just ask."

I laugh. "It's not. But since you brought it up… Where are you going?"

"A client needs to travel to an unfriendly area and requested I personally handle the logistics of his security."

"Is that a normal part of your services?"

"For certain clients, yes."

Even though I can't see the bag, my gaze shifts in its direction. "And you need to take weapons?"

"Yes."

He offers no other explanation.

I stand, walking around the desk. Bryan touches the monitor in front of him. The screen goes black. The bag is pushed under the desk, by his foot. He turns to face me.

"Why the vague answers? Is what you do confidential?"

"For the protection of my clients, what I do is highly confidential."

"Is it dangerous?"

"Sometimes."

"How will I know if something happens to you?" Now that we're together, I don't want anything to take him away from me. From us.

"You've been on the emergency contact list for a long time." He guides me onto his lap.

I know he's hiding something, yet in his arms, I find everything I'd been searching for since childhood. Something even James could not give me.

Serenity.

Wednesday night the girls and I stay up past their bedtime addressing Valentine cards for their classmates and wrapping the gifts they bought.

I oversleep Thursday morning and forget to buy cookies for the classroom party. The school has a four-day weekend starting tomorrow and they are celebrating today.

I call Jessica. "Can you pick up two dozen Valentine's Day cookies on your way in?"

"Sure, Dani. I'm leaving the house now."

My first patient is always on time. I sip a breakfast smoothie while we have our session. Mr. Brumfield is grieving the loss of his wife after sixty-five years of marriage. They were high school sweethearts. She died four months ago. He refused to let his children touch any of her belongings. He went as far as barring the windows and doors so they couldn't come into the house. We've been making headway. Last week he allowed his youngest daughter to come in and help him pack his wife's clothes to donate to a shelter.

I like Mr. Brumfield. He's a good man. He reminds me of Bryan, protective of the people he loves. I'm sure he was a good husband and is a great dad.

He's been holding back in his sessions. I don't pressure him. I allow my patients to set the pace of their therapy and gently push them when they plateau. When he's ready, he'll open up.

Vanessa sits a vase filled with Amethyst Temple Lilies on my desk after Mr. Brumfield leaves.

"They were delivered to the reception desk," she says.

It's been a while since I've gotten anything for Valentine's Day. James used to make me mixed CDs and write love poems. Sliding the letter opener under the flap, I pull out the card.

Do You Miss Me, Danielle?

My smile fades. This isn't Bryan's handwriting.

The desk phone rings.

"Dr. Edwards," I answer.

"Dr. Edwards?"

"Good afternoon."

"Do you miss me?"

"Who is this?"

The line goes dead.

I know that voice.

My phone rings again.

"Look, either you tell me who you are, or stop calling."

"Dani, this is Jessica. Is everything okay?"

"Yes, everything is fine. I got a prank call."

"How many times have you gotten a prank call?"

I lie. "Once."

"If it keeps happening alert hospital security."

"I will. What's up?"

"Isabel's coming over to pick up patient lab results. Do you want me to send the cookies with her?"

"Yes, please. And thank you for picking them up."

I throw the card in the trash and take the vase of flowers to the family waiting room.

Isabel knocks on my office door right when I finish typing notes in Mr. Brumfield's file. I shut down the computer, lock up my office, and leave for the day.

With Bryan out of town, I'm covering for him at the classroom party. He volunteered to help even though we already completed our volunteer hours for the school year. I know he signed up just so he could keep an eye on Jacob and Dylan. Bryan's going to be a bear when the girls start dating. I pray I'm having a boy for his sanity.

As I reach for the cookies on the back seat, I spot Holly sitting in her car crying. I go over and tap her window. "Holly, are you okay?"

No response.

I try the handle. The door opens.

Holly's right arm rises. The muzzle of a small gun rests on her temple. She's looking straight ahead, tears rolling down her cheeks.

"He left. No warning. No goodbye. He packed up and left," she says.

"Holly, look at me," I plead, pulling my cell phone out of my pocket.

"I have no money. No way to support myself. And no way to support Melissa. I have no friends."

"Holly, look at me right now!" I command.

Slowly, her head turns. She looks at me, but it's like she's looking through me. There's no light in her eyes.

"He doesn't want us anymore," she cries.

I take a small step to the right and press the emergency call button on my phone.

"Lower the gun, Holly."

"I take care of myself. I let him bring other men and women into our bed. Our home is clean. I don't question his whereabouts. And he leaves me."

"You're hurting and you want the pain to stop."

Her dead eyes blink.

"All you want is for the pain to stop," I repeat.

She nods.

"I know what it feels like to have someone walk out on you. If you let me, I can help you find other ways to stop the pain, Holly. Options where you don't have to hurt yourself and leave Melissa here without you."

From the corner of my eye, I see a black SUV pull into the parking lot. I can't break the connection I have with Holly to see who's in the truck.

"You and I can find a way to make the pain go away," I tell her.

She blinks her eyes.

"Can you lower the gun first?"

"Why do you want to help me? We're not friends."

"Holly, we've never tried to be friends. I'm willing if you are." I smile and take a quick breath. She lowers the gun to her lap.

Her finger is still on the trigger.

"I'll go first. Hello, I'm Danielle Edwards. Kourtney Edwards is my daughter. We moved here from Arizona at the end of July."

I wait for her to respond.

"I'm Holly Valentine. Melissa Valentine is my daughter. I'm from Littleton."

"I took Kourtney to a place in Littleton over the winter break. We did rock climbing and zip-lining. That's where she got the idea for her party."

"I've taken Melissa there a couple of times."

Great, she's responding.

"I am a therapist at the hospital," I tell her.

"You're too young to be a therapist."

"I graduated high school at fifteen." I smile bigger. Her finger relaxes on the trigger.

"I'm a housewife, but I completed the program to be a paralegal."

"My daughter is obsessed with teddy bears."

"My daughter's obsessed with monkeys."

We laugh. The front passenger door moves. I keep her focus on me.

"I'm a widow."

"My husband just left me."

I don't give her a chance to dwell on that fact. "My husband was in the military. He died in action."

"My ex-husband is a real estate broker."

"He makes good money?" I ask.

She nods.

"My husband was my only friend until he died."

"All my friends are fake housewives."

Feigning indignation, I say, "Don't put me in the same category as Madelyn and Stephanie, please. I mean I know we're just becoming friends, but come on. Fake housewife?"

Holly chuckles. She sets the gun on the passenger seat. "Okay, I have one friend who isn't fake."

Dramatically, I drag my hand across my brow. "Thank you. Now where was I? Oh yes, I grew up in foster care in Los Angeles."

"My parents still live in Littleton. I have an older sister."

"Holly you came up with options."

She looks confused.

The passenger door cracks open, someone wearing a white long sleeve shirt reaches in lifting the gun off the seat.

"You said you have no financial means. As your friend, I'm telling you to sue your husband for every penny you and Melissa are entitled to. You said you have no way to support yourself. But you completed paralegal training so do the final steps and be a paralegal. We've already established you have one real friend. You said you're alone, but you have family in Littleton."

"Oh my god. Was I really going to kill myself?" She cries into her hands.

"No, Holly. You thought suicide was your only choice to ending the pain. We found another way."

She sobs.

I place a consoling hand on her shoulder. And look around.

There's an ambulance pulling into the parking lot behind Boulder Police patrol cars. I'm surprised the sheriffs didn't respond. One police officer is out of his unit talking to the two men dressed in black suits. The other officers are blocking the entrance to the parking lot, parents stand in the driveway, trying to get a view of the activity. Another police officer is slowly making his way toward us. He's just out of Holly's line of sight. I also see Dr. Barrett, the school's principal.

"Holly, are you aware that you were holding a weapon to your temple?" I ask her.

"Yes."

"Can you tell me what your intentions were with that weapon?"

"I was going to kill myself." Her words are muffled by her hands.

I gently remove her hands from her face. "Do you still want to kill yourself?"

"No." She looks me in the eyes.

"Can you tell me what you want to do now?"

"I want to move back to Littleton with my parents, get a job and keep in touch with my friend."

"Holly, do you understand I am a licensed therapist?"

"Yes."

"Because you admit to having thoughts of killing yourself and you came close to acting on it, I'm sending you to the hospital by ambulance." I motion for Dr. Barrett to come closer. "I can contact your parents. Littleton is forty-five minutes away. If you give your consent, Melissa can come over for a play date until they get here."

The principal is within earshot.

"Melissa can go to your house."

He nods, acknowledging he heard her.

"Holly, I'll call ahead and arrange for Dr. Stevens to meet you in the emergency room. He's head of the Behavioral Science Department. He will decide if you need to be admitted or if you can go home with your parents. As your friend, ethically, I cannot make that determination."

The officer steps back and I help Holly out of the car. We embrace for a moment, then walk with our arms around each other to the waiting ambulance.

She asks me to call her sister and gives me the phone number.

"Thank you, Danielle."

"My friends call me Dani."

She hugs me. "Thank you, Dani."

Once the ambulance pulls out of the parking lot, I step out of earshot of the spectators to call Dr. Stevens. I give him a brief synopsis. He assures me he'll be waiting for Holly in the emergency room.

I give my statement to the officer in charge, then go to Dr. Barrett.

"If Melissa comes to school tomorrow it is my professional recommendation that the school provide counseling for her. I know how these parents gossip. I'm sure she will hear about what happened from the other students."

"I informed the parents that Mrs. Valentine fainted and was refusing medical attention. I hope that appeases their curious minds." He winks.

I get the cookies from my truck and go to the classroom. Ms. Williamson is a little nicer today, but it's forced.

The girls are quiet on the ride home. Normally Emma gives a minute-by-minute recap of her day. They loosen up as we make pizza bagels for snack and by the time they turn on the gaming system, the three girls are friends.

Holly and her sister come to the house to pick up Melissa. They decline my invitation to stay for dinner and thank me for the intervention.

The girls and I go to bed early.

Snuggled under the warm covers, my body relaxes and I'm in the twilight between consciousness and sleep. *"Do you miss me?"* His voice infiltrates my sleepy mind.

"I know that voice," I murmur.

Chapter Thirty

"HAPPY BIRTHDAY!"

I open my eyes. Kourtney, Emma, Bryan, and Trevor stand by my side of the bed with a picnic basket.

"Thank you." I sit up. "Happy Valentine's Day."

"Happy Valentine's Day!" They shout and shower me with rose petals of many colors.

"We're having a picnic breakfast in bed, Mommy."

After I use the bathroom, wash my face and brush my teeth, the four of us sit on the bed.

The basket holds banana slices and warm muffins. They filled a thermos with hot apple cider. Bryan hands me a small glass of cranberry juice with lots of ice, a prenatal vitamin, and iron pill.

Over breakfast, the girls tell him about their play date with Melissa. I'm happy they got to know her outside of school. Melissa really is a sweet child. Emma was surprised to learn Melissa loves monkeys. It looks like the trio will be a quartet soon.

The girls race out of the room when the doorbell rings.

Bryan joins me in the shower.

"What's the real reason Melissa came over for a play date?" he asks.

"I guess I can tell you since technically I'm not Holly's doctor. Her husband left. She and Melissa have no money. Holly wanted to kill herself. I helped her figure things out. If it were left up to me, I'd kick his butt, make him withdraw every penny in his account and give it to his wife and daughter."

Bryan turns off the water and hands me a warm bath towel.

He raises an eyebrow.

"He told her he didn't want her anymore," I explain.

Bryan raises both eyebrows.

"Jessi taught me sometimes people need a friend, not a shrink."

"Should I be nervous?"

"Only if you plan on leaving me." I give him a playful punch in the gut.

"I'm never leaving you again, Dani." His tone is so serious. Emotional. It makes my eyes water.

My thumb traces the line of his bottom lip. "I know you won't. You're going to love me when I can't see my feet and my ankles are swollen?"

"I'll love you when your boobs sag down to your knees and you put your pants on backward."

We laugh as we walk into the bedroom.

"Big Daddy, we're ready for Big Mama's next birthday present, over," Emma announces. I look around for her.

Bryan passes me and picks up a walkie-talkie from the nightstand. "Roger that, Sweet Pea. We'll be down in a minute, over."

"Roger that, Big Daddy. Over and out."

"Big Daddy? Sweet Pea?" I ask.

He holds open a white spa robe. "I heard you tried to bribe my recruits again. Almost got them to give up the goods. I upped the ante and made this fun."

I drop my towel and he helps me into the soft cotton robe. In the closet he hands me a bra and a pair of panties, then tells me to sit on the couch and wait for him.

I do as I'm told.

When he comes out of the closet, he scoops me up in his arms, carrying me out of the room and down the stairs. The doors to the sitting room are closed.

"Close your eyes, Big Mama," he says.

With anticipation and excitement vying for the dominant feeling, I cover my eyes with my hands.

"Surprise!" Kourtney and Emma shout, and Trevor barks.

The sitting room is transformed into a spa and hair salon.

"Go get pampered. I have last-minute details I need to take care of." He lowers me to my feet, kissing my lips. "Cuddles. Sweet Pea. Big Mama is in your hands. Take care of my girl until I get back."

They salute. "Yes, sir."

He salutes back holding in his laughter.

I'm waxed and exfoliated, and given a pregnancy massage, followed by a facial, manicure and pedicure.

Supervised by Marie, the girls make me a grilled chicken stuffed baked potato, kale salad, and tart strawberry lemonade for lunch.

Once I finish eating, my hair is washed and conditioned, blow dried and pressed, flat ironed and styled in an intricate sophisticated ponytail.

Kourtney picks up the walkie-talkie. "Big Daddy, this is Cuddles, do you copy?"

"I copy, Cuddles."

"Big Mama's noodles are cooked."

"Roger that. The dresser just pulled up. You and Sweet Pea go get ready, over."

"Roger that Big Daddy, over and out."

The adults in the room laugh.

The doorbell rings.

"Hey, Cuddles. How long have you and Sweet Pea been training to use walkie-talkies?"

"Da— I mean Bryan got us cell phones, but it took too long to type a text."

Jailynne, along with two men, stand in the doorway to the sitting room. One man is holding a garment bag and the handle to a rolling suitcase, the other is balancing red boxes in his hands.

"Happy Birthday, Danielle." Jailynne kisses my cheeks. "These are my assistants Pascual and Joshua. We're here to get you dressed."

I follow Jailynne to a downstairs guest room. She blindfolds me, then takes off my robe. I'm helped into something smooth and silky against my skin. It feels like a dress.

The fabric is pulled on both sides. I'm turned around several times and told to hold still. And stand up straight.

It seems like forever before I'm helped out of the garment and my robe slipped back on. The blindfold is removed.

Jailynne hands me a red box. "Go upstairs and open it."

I giggle and shake the box on the way up to our room. I perch on the edge of the bed, slide the ribbon off, and lift the lid. A small red envelope rests on top of red tissue paper. I pull out the card. It's Bryan's handwriting.

> *According to a psychologist, red lingerie means you're a passionate, energetic, and a driven lover. I know firsthand this describes you.*
>
> *B*

I peel back the paper.

Inside I find a red half-bra with ribbons instead of straps. Matching thong and garter belt. And thigh high stockings.

Careful not to mess up my hair, I freshen up and stand in front of the full-length mirror in the closet to dress in the lingerie.

I feel sexy. The ultra-sheer material will leave little to Bryan's imagination. Hell, it leaves little to my imagination, and I look good.

A mischievous smile spreads across my lips as I turn to admire the view. This goes perfect with what I have planned for him tonight.

I put back on the robe. Joshua comes up to do my makeup. He keeps my face light and natural, but makes my brown eyes stand out with a rosy-smoky-eye.

When Pascual knocks on the door, I follow him back to the guest room.

Mindful of my makeup, they blindfold me. Once again, I step into the garment. This time it's zipped up the back. Someone puts earrings in my ears, a necklace around my neck, and a bracelet around my wrist. I'm helped into the highest pair of heels I've ever worn.

The blindfold is removed and I turn around, staring at myself in the full-length mirror. I'm dressed in a layered red dress. The first layer hugs my body and is an inch above my knees. The sheer second layer is baby doll styled with loose sleeves. And I'm wearing red designer heels the same color as the dress.

A ruby and diamond jewelry set compliments the look.

I gasp.

Jailynne hands me another envelope. My hands shake pulling out the card.

Red is fire. It symbolizes confidence and courage, love and prosperity.
Red is energy and desire, passion and pleasure. Wearing red you demand
attention.
I see you, Dani.
B

Bryan walks up behind me, handing me a single long-stemmed white rose. "This white rose signifies remembrance and new beginnings. You will always be celebrated."

He's wearing an immaculately tailored black suit, black shirt, red tie with matching hankie, and black designer shoes.

"Ready?" he asks.

I nod.

He takes my hand, looking me up and down. "Thank you, Jailynne."

Bryan leads me to the door, and I barely have time to yell out, "You did an amazing job as usual."

"Big Daddy to Cuddles and Sweet Pea. Do you copy?" he talks into the walkie-talkie in his hand.

"We copy, Big Daddy, over," Kourtney responds.

"Big Mama is ready, over."

"Roger that, we're on our way. Cuddles, over and out."

We walk into the family room where Marie is waiting for us.

"Oh, Danielle," she cries, wrapping her motherly arms around me.

The girls come into the family room wearing matching pink dresses, tights, and pink patent leather shoes. Marie braided their hair and fastened pink bows on the ends. They look adorable.

Kourtney and Emma hold out long-stemmed pink roses. "Pink means we appreciate and admire you," they recite.

A camera captures the moment. I hadn't noticed the photographer.

Marie takes the roses and we have a photo shoot before putting on our coats, then walk out the door.

Willis is standing at the opened door of a black SUV limousine. "Happy Birthday, Danielle." He gives me a fatherly hug, something he's never done. A quick flash of sadness momentarily haunts his eyes.

I kiss his cheek. "Thank you, and Happy Valentine's Day."

He closes the door after we're settled in the back. He opens the driver's door and climbs in behind the wheel.

Willis drives us to a restaurant at the base of the Rocky Mountains.

We're shown to the Glass Terrace. We have the room to ourselves. It's a table for four with a spectacular view of the snow-covered mountains.

The reflection in the windows from the flames of the orange candles makes the room feel intimate. Two small, red gift bags sit on the table next to eighteen long-stemmed yellow roses. Each rose has a card on the stem. A single word, written by Bryan on each card.

Enthusiastic. Passionate. Beautiful. Gentle. Gracious. Loving. Caring. Friend. Mother. Generous. Protector. Ambitious. Warm. Intoxicating. Cherished. Trusting. Home. Forever.

I open the envelope resting on top of my napkin.

Just a few of the words I use to describe you.

B

Waiters bring in the first course.

Over dinner Kourtney tells us about the Valentine's Day cards and gifts they got from their classmates yesterday. "Jacob Brooks gave Emmy a bracelet."

"Where is it?" I ask.

"I traded it for candy," Emma whispers.

Bryan laughs. "That's my girl."

"Dylan Hill gave me a ring," Kourtney says, wiping her mouth with her napkin.

"Where is it?" Bryan squawks.

"I ate it," she answers matter-of-factly.

"You ate it?"

"Yes, it was a watermelon candy ring."

"I thought Dylan was an ugly booger." Bryan sets his knife and fork on his plate.

"Dylan wants me to be his girlfriend."

"Listen, I don't want either of you accepting any more rings or bracelets from boys unless I say you can."

"Not even candy ones?" Kourtney asks.

"No."

"Why?" she asks.

"Because I said so."

"Why do you say so?"

His shoulders grow tense.

"Kourt, what Bryan is trying to get you to understand is that at your age, jewelry should come from family, not little boys in the second grade."

Please don't make him go alpha male. My eyes plead with her. We finish the third course in silence.

"When can we accept jewelry from boys?" Kourtney asks when the waiter brings in the next course.

I thought this conversation was over. Why is she pushing the issue?

Bryan sits up straight, puffing out his chest. I have to teach the girls the art of when to stop pushing him.

"How about we take this grade level by grade level?" I suggest, to prevent him from going crazy. "So tell me more about this walkie-talkie language. How did you guys learn to use them while Bryan was away?"

"We had secret video chats with Da— I mean Bryan."

We get through the fourth and fifth courses with no more talk about jewelry from eight-year-old boys.

"Big Daddy, this is Doc. Do you copy? Over."

"I copy, Doc, over."

"Ducks are in a row and all accounted for, over."

"Copy that, Doc. ETA thirty minutes, over."

"I've got eyes on you. Doc over and out."

"Da—I mean Bryan, we didn't learn the ducks one." Kourtney's eyes cut to me.

"Doc made up that one." Bryan's trying to suppress a laugh.

He hands each girl a gift bag.

"Happy Valentine's Day," we say to them.

They squeal and pull out red boxes. We got them earrings with a matching necklace. Their birthstone sits in the middle of their favorite animal.

I hand them their gift for Bryan. Inside the black leather wallet are pictures of the girls, Trevor and me. In the money slot they put homemade coupons.

Bryan pulls out the coupons, reading the deals, then slaps one on the table. The girls jump out of their seats to give him hugs and kisses. It's the perfect time to tell them about the baby. I reach for his hand, placing the other on my stomach.

"Kourt. Emm," I begin.

"Mom's having a baby," he blurts out.

Emma slides off his lap, walking around the table. She's been quiet all evening. I wonder if she's feeling okay. I pull her onto my lap.

"You're having a baby?" Kourtney whines.

"Yes, Cuddles. You'll have a baby brother or sister sometime in September," Bryan tells her.

She rolls her eyes.

"We better get ready to go," Bryan says. Kourtney climbs off his lap. He pushes his chair back. "But before we do." He hands me a long-stemmed red rose. "May I have this dance?" He offers his hand. It's shaking like he's nervous.

Emma slides off my lap.

"There's no music," I tell him.

He gestures behind me. I turn around to see a man sitting on a stool, an acoustic guitar in his lap.

He wasn't there when we came in.

The girls giggle and hold hands.

I take Bryan's shaking hand. As soon as we step onto the floor, the guitarist plays a ballad. Bryan leans down, pressing his cheek to mine, and sings the first words to the song along with the guitarist.

This is the happiest I've been in a long time. I've always been in love with this man in my arms. I was too scared to admit it. *We've always had a solid connection.*

Chapter Thirty-One

ON THE RIDE HOME, I rest my head on Bryan's shoulder, our fingers intertwined. His palm is warm and moist. The closer we get to the house, the more he fidgets and the girls bounce in their seat.

Willis watches me in the rearview mirror.

Bryan has given me so much today. I will forever cherish this birthday with him. All residual of doubts about him, about us, were wiped away the moment he sang the first two words of that song.

We pull into the driveway. Bryan has to stop Kourtney and Emma from jumping out before the limo stops. Willis comes around and opens the door, and they bolt for the house carrying my yellow roses.

"Do you want me to carry you?" Bryan asks.

I shake my head.

He lifts my chin kissing me. I open my mouth, encouraging him to deepen the kiss. His private Valentine's Day gifts are upstairs and I can't wait to give them to him.

"Let's take this inside." He steps out reaching in to help me.

We walk arm in arm into the house. Bryan helps me off with my coat. I take his hand leading him to the stairs.

"Let's sit in the family room," he says, guiding me in the opposite direction.

When we walk into the room, my heart stops. I inhale and look at the smiling faces of the people standing in our family room. Once my brain has time to catch up, I turn into Bryan's chest and sob.

He embraces me.

"Happy Birthday, Dani," Bryan senior whispers, rubbing my back.

I step into his arms and cry on his shoulder while his son keeps a protective arm around my waist.

One by one, I'm passed around. Hugged and kissed.

"Mmm—hmm," Anthony sings, stomping his feet for emphasis. "Twenty-eight *shoo* looks good on *you*, little sis."

By the time I'm passed to Max, I'm a blubbering mess.

"You're my friend so I know I can say this." He begins. "Girrrl! Shed another tear and I'm gonna…" He pauses, looking at my feet. "Are those…" He points and prances in place. Max picks up my foot to get a closer look. I hold on to Bryan's arm for support and balance. "He got you…" Max does a real, shocked face. No drama. "You lucky hag!" He drops my foot. "Shed one more tear and I'm mopping those Sew Out Tha Box heels off your feet. You serving fish in all this. Tears ain't a proper accessory, but those ruby glitters are sickening."

Bryan clears his throat.

Max sighs and glares at him. "I told her she looks good and if she keeps crying, I'm taking home those thirty-five-hundred-dollar heels *you* bought, and her ruby and diamond jewelry is stunning."

Tom elbows Max. "I'll bring your shoes back. Max doesn't have room in his closet."

Max and I laugh, as we hug each other. We went on a shopping adventure on Monday and I helped him hide his new clothes in Tom's closet.

"You are *so* getting fucked in those heels tonight," Max whispers in my ear.

I pull away and swat his arm. Bryan hands me his handkerchief as I step into the arms of the next person. Bryan's arm circles my waist.

"How are you feeling?" I ask Holly.

"I feel better. Thank you again for yesterday. Melissa loved playing with Emma and Kourtney. Once we're settled in Littleton, I'd like it if you guys would come visit us."

"We'd love to. I can research therapists in the Littleton area?"

"Dr. Stevens already gave me referrals." She sighs. "I also want to apologize to both of you for my behavior at the beginning of the school year."

"Holly, if you need anything please let Dani know and I'll make sure it happens," Bryan says.

"Mark came by this afternoon. He gave me a check and said he'll transfer money into my account every month."

"I thought I was going to have to use my kickboxing skills on him."

Holly and I laugh while Bryan mumbles expletive threats involving my ass if I do. He admitted to hiding the Vin dummy; the only exercise he'll approve is walking or a marathon of sex.

Bryan ushers me to the next people waiting. Marie and Willis. They both have tears in their eyes. It's a warm and loving embrace, full of emotion.

The singing voices of four girls make me turn around. The adults join in.

Kourtney, Emma, Penelope, and Melissa are wheeling in a cart, holding my favorite cake. Vin is helping them.

It's a Bridal White cake with a pastel green double border and lettering. The scent of the Buttercream icing makes my mouth water. The cake is covered with mint green candles. It's from my favorite bakery, Hansen's Cakes.

Kourtney must have told him we spent my birthday weekend in Los Angeles and I always got a cake from that bakery.

Bryan steps behind me, wrapping his arms around my waist. Ig and Tony lift the cake. "Make a wish." Bryan's lips brush my ear.

I wish my first birthday with family and friends and the man I love will never be forgotten. I open my eyes, take a deep breath, lean over, and blow out the candles.

"What did you wish for, Mom?"

Kourtney and Emma giggle uncontrollably. *They've been giggling all day.*

"Her wish won't come true if she says it out loud," Willis chimes in.

"I bet I know what she wished for," Bryan says from behind me.

Everyone in the room gasps. The girls squeal, jumping up and down holding each other.

I look around. What are they reacting to? I turn around.

My hands shake as I cover my mouth, muffling my scream. Bryan's on one knee, an open square crystal box in the palm of his quaking hand. Inside, nestled on a red satin pillow is a princess cut diamond solitaire on a solid platinum band. Unassuming yet powerful.

Me.

"You bring out the passion, energy, and drive in me. You have my complete and utter attention. I've remembered you every minute of every day we've had and I look forward to adding more. You have my admiration and appreciation." He hands me an orange rose. "We've bridged that gap. I want to begin and end my day as your husband until I take my last breath. I love you, Danielle Lauren Edwards. Will you marry me?"

Everyone else in the room ceases to exist. I drop to my knees, the rose falling to the floor. I cup his cheeks in my hands. "Yes, I'll marry you," I whisper.

He throws his head back and exhales. Bryan takes my left hand and slides the ring on my finger, kissing it, then me. He wraps me in his arms like he's never letting me go.

Our girls join us, sharing this hug. Family and friends applaud us. I hear the shutter of multiple cameras going off. I hear sniffles.

"You guys are the best birthday helpers." I rain kisses over the girls' faces and the man in front of me.

"Daddy promised us something super good," Kourtney giggles. "A weekend trip to Anaheim, California."

Wait! Did she call him daddy? My eyes shoot to him. The smile on his face and tears in his eyes take my breath away. He's looking at her.

Emma picks up my rose. "We told you to come up with something better, Mommy."

I grab her, squeezing her tight. She called me mommy.

We stand with the girls in front of us.

"We have one more announcement to make." Bryan places his hand on my stomach. "Go ahead, girls. You don't have to keep this secret."

"Mommy's having a baby," Emma yells.

"Please let me be the one to tell Madelyn," Max begs. "Please, please, please!" He's jumping up and down like a little kid.

"Be gentle when you break the news," Bryan says.

Nancy and Marie rush over to me, Jessica and Max following behind. They want to talk wedding details. Champagne and cake are served.

I notice Willis staring out the window wiping his eyes. I excuse myself from the wedding planners and go to him, resting my head on his arm.

"Are you okay?"

He puts his arm around me. "I'm fine. Just being a sentimental old man."

"May I steal my fiancée away from you?"

"Of course you may," Willis says and kisses my cheek before I take Bryan's hand.

He leads me over to the sofa. Once I'm seated, he picks up a cake plate off the coffee table. "Did I give you something you've always wanted?" He feeds me a piece of cake.

I smile, nod, and chew.

"Are you happy?"

The goofy grin on my face isn't enough, so I nod.

"I truly love you, Dani."

I break off a piece of my birthday cake, feeding it to him. "I love you more, Bryan."

We walk our guests out around eleven. Mom and Dad retire to the downstairs guest rooms. The girls go straight to their rooms, happy to be going to California next weekend.

Jessica leaves with Tony and Vin. "I hope you two are finished by the time I get home," she comments on her way out the door.

Ig offers to drive Holly and Melissa home.

I take Bryan's hand and lead him up the stairs, putting an extra swing to my hips. In our bedroom, I go to my nightstand, pulling out his first gift. I hand him the card.

He reads it out loud, "Beside this man, is the woman who loves him … Dani."

His eyebrows meet his hairline and his eyes bug out as he unwraps the box.

"Read the inscription," I tell him after he pulls out the watch.

"Only you."

We think alike: those are the first two words to the song he sang to me tonight.

"Pick a number between one and one hundred," I tell him.

"Five," he laughs, playing along. He sets the titanium watch on the nightstand.

"That's an awfully low number, Mr. Hawk. Do you want to shoot for a higher number?" I untie his silk necktie.

"Nope, I'll stick with five."

I unbutton his dress shirt, kissing his chest as I go.

"Why five?" I undo the cufflinks, placing them on the nightstand next to the watch. My hands slide up his smooth chest, pushing the shirt off his shoulders.

"We'll be a family of five," he says with confidence.

His lips turn up in that sexy smile as I unbuckle his belt, unbutton his pants, and pull down the zipper.

His pants drop. I hook my thumbs in the waistband of his boxers. A good tug, and they join his pants at his feet.

With a little push on his shoulders, Bryan sits on the bed.

"Dani, that's a six-figure watch."

I squat to remove his shoes and socks, pants and underwear.

"I know." Rising, I take his hand and lead him to a leather recliner.

"Why?" he asks.

I had to get creative with the restraints. I tied several mint green silk scarves together. They run under the chair and come up on either side. Before I answer his question, I secure his wrists. He hasn't noticed the full-length mirror in front of the chair. His eyes are fixed on me.

"That particular watch is timeless. Like my love for you."

I swing my hips as I saunter over to the sound system. Soft, sensual music fills the room. Closing my eyes, I sway to the beat, getting into the groove, and dance my way across the room toward him undressing as I go.

My words for him. *Salacious.*

My striptease for him. *Erotic.*

My dance for him. *X-rated.*

My moves for him. *Yearning.*

"Something new?" he asks.

I wrapped the ribbons of the bra around my body like rope, attaching the ends to the garter belt.

"You should know. You bought it. And I love the ruby glitters."

"I wanted to unwrap you tonight." His eyes are glued to the movement of my hips.

I turn around, sitting on his lap. "Tonight I'm unwrapping you. And your lucky number is five. Count."

My butt circles slowly in his lap while he counts. The lap dance stops when he moans five.

"Aw, baby, how I wish you'd chosen a higher number," I tease.

"This isn't fair, Dani."

"Tell me to stop." I bend over, pulling out the timer I hid in a box of goodies under the chair. "I asked if you wanted to aim for a higher number."

Setting the timer for five slow minutes, I alternate between gyrating and grinding on his lap to the sexy beat of the music. I let the reflection in the mirror drive my movements. Bryan's hums and moans fuel my need to test his limits.

The timer rings.

Reclining the chair, I drop to my knees between his legs. I pull out the next goodie from the box and put it in my mouth. I reach for the remote and turn on the television and reset the timer.

A quick glance over my shoulder assures me the camera is positioned correctly. Bryan's shocked expression is priceless. One slow swipe of my tongue measures his length. He's blessed by that old wives' tale. His ring finger is definitely longer than his index finger.

Bryan jumps and hisses.

I give him a seductive smile and open my mouth to show him the green vibrating tongue ring.

A deep torturous moan filters through his lips and his head drops back. The beat of the music continues to fill the room.

Inside I sing a siren's song. "I want you to watch us on the screen." Wow, that came out confident and sexy in my ears.

He lifts his head, eyes on the television.

I kiss the tip of his penis before taking in as much of him as I can. My hand grips the rest.

"Oh shit, Dani," he moans.

I keep my eyes on him, my mouth and hand stroking his hard length.

"That feels so damn good."

His words massage my sexual confidence.

The timer dings. He's panting and his penis is dancing.

To enhance his enjoyment, I reach in the box and slip on the vibrating finger and reset the timer. My finger glides up and down his penis. Bryan's fingers curl into a tight fist as he struggles to keep control. The power to drive him crazy, sexually, is the reason I went to great lengths to plan tonight's sex-session.

Opening my mouth, I capture his penis. I find his million-dollar spot and massage it with my finger. His hips shoot off the chair and he thrusts deep in my mouth. His thighs strain from the position.

I keep my eyes on him to gage the exact moment he orgasms so I can stop before he ejaculates. Bryan does a stomach crunch. I didn't think it was possible, but his penis grows in width and he begins to chant a single word.

The timer rings.

I release him. The sweet-salty taste of pre-cum is left on my tongue.

Tremors run through his limbs. I turn off the vibrating finger, dropping it back in the box.

His watchful eyes go from the screen to me, back to the screen.

My hips rock-and-roll to the sensual beat of the music. My fingers hook around the scrap of material of the sheer, red thong. Inch by sexy inch, I peel it off.

The heated gleam in Bryan's eyes makes my inner muscles contract and I need to feel him inside me.

I climb onto the chair backwards, straddling his hips, careful that my heels don't puncture a hole in the leather.

"You ready?" I ask him.

He shakes his head.

Way to go, Dani! I mentally pat myself on the back and give him a moment to recover, the heat level of my sex rising from the view on the television. I see the glisten.

"Are you ready, now?"

He nods his head.

I set the timer, position him at my opening and I drop on him, hard and fast using my inner walls to clench his length.

"Again please," he begs when the timer dings.

I put five minutes on the clock and turn around to face him. I kiss Bryan, making love to his mouth with the tongue ring still vibrating in my mouth. He breaks the kiss, gasping for air.

I appease his request, but go slow. I want to feel every inch of him inside me.

The timer dings. I don't move. Our connection is so much more than the act. The sound of our breathing rivals the soft music coming from the speakers.

I ease off him and get the new Couple's Dice out of the box. These have position numbers on one die and location on the other.

Releasing his wrists, I drop the location die on the floor.

I look down, then do a provocative dance on my way to the bed.

The last die falls from my hand. I look down, then cat-crawl onto the mattress.

I look back at him. Mr. Tall-And-Sexy smiles at me. I give him a questioning eyebrow. *What are you waiting for?*

"Want to soak in the tub?" He kisses my shoulder.

Still catching my breath from that last orgasm, I nod my head. "Mm-hmm."

Bryan climbs off the bed, going into the bathroom to turn on the water in the tub. Somewhere after the third time of preventing him from ejaculating, I lost being the one in control. Every man has his limits and I pushed him to his.

Bryan strolls back into the bedroom. One by one, he pulls my heels off, dropping them to the floor.

"Hey. Be careful with those. They cost a lot of money," I playfully scold him.

Bryan chuckles and shakes his head, gesturing to the expensive watch on my nightstand. He unhooks the straps of the garter and rolls the stockings down my legs, followed by the garter belt.

He pulls my arms to sit me up. The tip of his tongue is caught between his teeth as he unwraps the ribbons of the bra and unhooks the front clasp. His penis stirs. I know he can't be ready for another round that fast. Bryan has a healthy sex drive, which is a plus because with this pregnancy, I'm horny all the time. Just the thought of him makes me wet. I'm not calling uncle anytime soon. And before sunrise, I plan on using the other goodies.

With expert fingers, he takes off my jewelry.

I smack his hand in protest when he reaches for my engagement ring. "I'm never taking it off."

Bryan lifts me off the bed and carries me to the bathroom. With excellent balance, he steps into the tub, lowering us into the hot, soothing, bubbly water as it fills the tub.

I sit between his legs, leaning back on his chest.

"I can't wait for you to be my wife."

His words uplift my soul.

"Kourtney called you daddy."

"I've been daddy ever since I let them in on my plans. She didn't ask, she just said it and hasn't stopped."

"I want to adopt Emma."

"We can file the paperwork when you're ready."

"My afternoon is light on Tuesday."

"Kourt's a Hawk now," he says.

"How do we do it?"

"We'll go through the process."

We sit in silence, listening to the music playing on the speakers.

"You bribed them with a weekend in California huh?" I ask.

"Yep, you forced me to go big."

"Our girls played us, Bry. And I'm sure it was all your daughter's idea." I laugh. "I love the rides, but I can't get on the big ones."

"You won't be getting on any. We'll go back when the baby is old enough." He nibbles the spot behind my ear.

"I'm holding you to it." I lean my head to the side giving him better access. "Thank you, Bry. Thank you for giving me the best birthday present." I hold up my hand admiring the sparkle from the diamond in my engagement ring.

"When do you want to get married? I don't want to wait until after the baby is here, but I don't want to rush you either."

"I want the four of us to be a family all on the same day." I run my hands up and down his arms.

"Your wish is my command." He begins to roam my body with his hands. "What other little naughty toys do you have hidden?"

I turn around facing him, a cat-that-ate-the-canary smile on my face. This is my kingdom and I want my throne back. "That's my secret."

Max and I went to lunch last week. I told my friend about the things I've read in books and wanted to try. He fell out of his chair laughing. After he picked himself up off the floor, we had a no-holds-barred talk and he helped me plan this special Valentine's Day gift.

"When we get out of the tub, I'm using that tongue thing and finger on you," Bryan promises.

I open a side compartment near the tub and pull out a waterproof vibrating finger and vibrating rubber duck too. "I *so* wanted you to pick a high number."

Chapter Thirty-Two

BRYAN AND I MEET AT the courthouse Tuesday afternoon to file paperwork and apply for a marriage license.

I research the seven-day weather forecast for Anaheim, California, and take the girls shopping after school. On our way back to my truck, I see a black SUV parked five stalls down and two men looking our way. A chill fills my body. The need to protect my girls overcomes me and I get them fastened into their seat belts right away.

"Hey, baby," Bryan says, walking up to the truck. "What are you guys doing here?"

Tony is walking beside him.

"Pre-trip shopping." I glance back in the direction of the guys in the SUV.

They're gone.

"Tony, I'm riding home with my girls."

"Hey, thanks again for helping me pick out something for my aunt. I can't believe I forgot her birthday."

Bryan walks me to the passenger side, opening the door for me.

I wait until we get home to try and convince him I'm being followed. When I tell him about the phone calls and the trucks, he tells me to question the other therapists at the hospital to see if they're receiving prank calls too. And he blows off the black truck as me seeing something that isn't there. SUVs are popular in Boulder, they are the ideal vehicle to tackle the mountain roads, and therefore I'll notice them more than other cars.

Wednesday morning Bryan asks me to come to his downtown office. He introduces me to his attorney and explains the documents I need to sign. He wants to make sure I'm taken care of in the event something happens to him before we're married.

Once his attorney leaves, Bryan pulls me into his arms, staring me in the eyes. He's trying to communicate something without using actual words.

I don't understand.

Bryan kisses the palm of my right hand, then places it on his dress shirt, over the steady beat of is heart.

"This hand unlocks my world." He says it with so much raw emotion, I know the reason behind it is important and eventually he'll explain.

In the afternoon we meet at the girls' school for the regional science fair finals. Kourtney wins first place in the second grade division and fifth place overall. She's going to the state finals. Dad drove from Colorado Springs to be here and is her biggest cheerleader next to Emma, Penelope, Dylan and me.

Bryan proudly stands by Kourtney as she accepts her trophies and certificates. This is a photo moment that I couldn't resist capturing. I'll frame it and give it to him for Father's Day.

Thursday morning, Bryan and I meet with the court appointed mediator to review the applications.

"That was fast," I tell him when we leave the court building.

"It's a simple process since we're their only living, biological parents."

Since I have the day off, Bryan and I go for walk along Pearl Street. I buy him lunch and we sit on a bench people watching. We talk about our wedding ceremony and reception. The guest list for the actual ceremony is small, but the list for the reception is long. There's one person in particular Bryan wants to invite.

We decide to surprise the girls and pick them up from school together. Max makes us laugh as he recounts Madelyn's reaction to the news of our engagement and pregnancy.

Holly joins us standing in front of the school.

The croak of the Horny Toad interrupts us.

"So, I hear you professionally and successfully trapped him." Madelyn's frog legs carry her over to our cluster. "That was fast. I would say congratulations, but I'll wait for the results of the paternity test to come in. I've seen her prowling around your friend." *Ribbit.*

"Give it a rest. Bryan never wanted you," Holly chastens.

"Says the woman who tried to kill herself because her husband doesn't want her."

Bryan pins my arms to my side, preventing me from throwing a punch.

"I suggest you move along, Mrs. Brooks. My fiancée *will* kick your ass."

A frazzled Dr. Barrett approaches. "Mrs. Brooks. I need to see you in my office. Now. Mrs. Banks. Mrs. Johnson. You need to accompany Mrs. Brooks." He looks at me. "Dr. Edwards, may I have a private word with you?"

We step out of earshot of the other parents.

"I want to personally apologize and let you know that our school has zero tolerance for any acts of racism."

I lean back into Bryan, tears pooling in my eyes.

"I assure you the students involved will be dealt with accordingly. Emma reported what was happening, and I quickly put a stop to it," he says. "Kourtney was not physically harmed, but she's been unusually withdrawn since the incident happened thirty minutes ago. Ms. William-son was not at school today and the substitute did not have control over the classroom."

I don't understand. Kourtney isn't the only Black child in this private school. Hell, she isn't the only ethnic child, so why would she be targeted?

I've taught my child to be colorblind.

I've taught her that the texture and length of a Black woman's hair does not make or break her beauty and there's no such thing as good hair. Hair is hair anyway you comb it.

I've encouraged my child to expand her vocabulary and not judge people by the words they use. Instead, understand the context of the words.

I've taught my daughter to embrace her heritage and be open-minded and respectful of others. To expand her view of the world and not seclude herself within her surroundings.

What did they say to my baby? Did she know what they meant? Did they know the meaning behind their words?

Children are taught prejudices. Learning acceptance and tolerance is a choice.

Bryan speaks, bringing me back to our reality. "Thank you, Dr. Barrett. We will discuss it with the girls and let you know if we're pulling them out of the school."

"I hope it doesn't come to that, Mr. Hawk." He sighs, clearly at a loss of how to make this better. "I'm truly sorry, Dr. Edwards." He touches my arm.

I can only nod. Words fail me at the moment.

The bell rings.

I face the entrance, searching for my baby. I see her running from the school's office like she's being chased. Emma's right beside her. My soul aches at the sight.

"Kourt. Emm," Bryan calls out to them.

I hold my arms open. Kourtney leaps into them wrapping her arms and legs around me, burying her face in my neck. Emma wraps her arms around my waist burying her face in my side. Tears roll down my cheeks.

"Let me carry her," Bryan says taking Kourtney in his arms. He holds her against him as she sobs on his shoulder.

We walk away with our girls. Supporting one another. Comforting each other.

I open the backdoor to the truck. For once, the crowd of parents, students, and teachers are quiet as they stand in front of the school watching us. Emma climbs in and I climb in next. Bryan hands me Kourtney. I secure the seat belts around us.

This is happening to Emma too, and I wonder what Bryan has taught her about different ethnicities.

I don't hear the truck starting. I don't notice us driving away from the school. Sobs and sniffles fill the silence in the truck as we head home. I rub my girls' backs, while I think of how we will get through this. The therapist in me gets overpowered by the emotion of being a mom, but I fight the urge to tell Bryan to turn around and take us back to the school so I can have a talk with those moms.

My girls need me and I'll be strong for them.

Bryan pulls into the garage and opens the backdoor, reaching for Kourtney. She goes to him, crying harder in his arms. Emma and I hold on to each other as we climb out.

The four of us go straight to our room. We climb onto the bed. Tears roll down Bryan's cheeks as he embraces his daughter like he's trying to absorb her pain. The sight is unbearable and I hold Emma tighter.

It takes a while, but we calm down enough to have a family discussion about the incident at school today and how, as a family, we will face it together.

At six o'clock in the evening the doorbell rings. Minutes later, someone knocks on the bedroom door.

"Excuse me." Marie sticks her head in the room. "You guys have company downstairs."

"Who is it?" Bryan asks still holding on to Kourtney.

"Friends." She smiles. "They're waiting for all of you in the family room."

We climb out of bed and wash our faces before going downstairs.

Standing in the family room are our friends. Tom, Max, Penelope, Holly, Melissa, David, Jennifer, and Dylan.

Tom is holding boxes of pizza and Holly has a plate of brownies. Dylan's holding three bouquets of purple wildflowers. Max is wiping real tears from his eyes.

"Bryan, promise me you won't pay a visit to those parents."

He's still furious and trying his best to hide it.

"I can't make a promise I know I'm not going to keep. Those kids hurt her, Danielle. The image of my baby girl's face when she ran through the gates keeps playing over and over in my head. She was running for her life and you're asking me"—his finger jabs his chest—"her father, not to do anything. That's a lot to ask of me." His voice cracks.

He starts pacing. I've never seen him like this. Bryan in dad mode is more dangerous than the alpha male. And that worries me. He's thinking with his emotions. I go to him, wrapping my arms around his waist, hoping physical touch will calm him down enough to think before he acts.

"I feel the same way. But if we retaliate, we give them power over us. Do we teach our children to rise above ignorance or do we teach them to stoop to an ignorant level? We're a biracial family. How we handle this sets the tone for how we handle other incidents of racism that are sure to come our way."

"Interracial, biracial, homosexual, bisexual, that's society's ignorant need to label everything. *Not ours. We're a family.*" The timbre of his voice makes me shiver.

He's barely holding it together. I hold him tight until he starts to calm down.

"I *need* you to understand this promise goes against my duty and my job to protect *my* children from idiots. I won't kick their doors in and demand an apology. But eventually I will have a conversation with Simon, Chuck, and Tristan."

"Thank you." I won't point out that he didn't actually promise not to go to their homes.

"I'm going downstairs to the gym for a little while." He kisses me. "Get some sleep. We're starting our weekend first thing in the morning." His finger brushes my cheek and chin. "I love you."

"I love you too."

I sit on the bed with crossed legs and watch him go into the closet. A few minutes later he comes out wearing basketball shorts, a black wifebeater and running shoes. I wait for him to leave the room, then grab my cell phone. I'm calling Uncle Tony, Uncle Vinny, and Uncle Iggy to make them promise not to knock on doors either. They didn't come by tonight, but I have a feeling they know what happened.

It's midnight and I can't sleep. Bryan still hasn't come to bed. I go looking for him.

He's not in the gym. All the vehicles are in the garage. I look for him in the kitchen, his home office, and the family room. I go back upstairs to get my cell phone to call him. A small triangle of light shines in the hallway of the girls' rooms. I go to check on them.

Kourtney's door is cracked open and the lamp near her bed is on. I peek in her room. Bryan sits in a chair with a book in his hand, reading to her sleeping mind.

I listen.

It's the book I've read to her lots of times about beautiful Black people in all shades and shapes.

I understand his need to confirm her importance, so I don't interrupt. I go back to bed, falling asleep before he comes in.

Bryan wakes us at two thirty in the morning and we leave for the airport at four.

We bypass security check.

Kourtney is quiet and clinging to Bryan. He's calm, but it's the calm that comes before a storm. I don't question him about the security check and let them sit together for the flight to Los Angeles. Emma and I fall asleep holding hands. She doesn't like flying.

Two hours and eighteen minutes after takeoff, we land.

Kourtney's and Bryan's moods take a turn for the better. We collect our luggage and walk to the airport parking structure instead of boarding a bus to a rental car lot.

Bryan loads our luggage into the back of a cream-colored Cadillac Escalade. Once again, I do not question it.

We get on the 405 freeway heading south.

"Bry, it's after seven. Check-in isn't until three. What are we doing for eight hours?" It's a safe question. Right?

"I've got this," he says switching lanes to get on the connecting freeway going east.

Los Angeles freeway traffic isn't heavy in the direction we're traveling, and Bryan seems to know his way around without the help of GPS. He syncs his cell phone to the car's audio system and blasts kid's music. They party in the truck as we head to our destination. I close my eyes and doze.

The girls' screams of excitement wake me. We're pulling into the valet at the hotel. The concierge opens my door and greets us by name. I don't question how he knows who we are and why we don't check in at the front desk. We're immediately shown to our suite.

The girls jump on the beds in their room. Bryan joins them.

"Which park do you guys want to visit first?" He jumps from one bed to the other.

"I don't care. I just want to get on all the rides," Emma shouts.

"Me too," Kourtney adds.

"I want to eat," I inform them.

They stop jumping and look at me like my identical twin popped out my body.

I defend my hunger. "We left before sunrise."

"Okay, let's call room service, then flip a coin to see which one we go to first," Bryan says and starts back jumping from bed to bed.

I am the official backpack and souvenir holder who stands at the exit waiting for the riders. To keep me occupied, I'm given an endless supply of snacks. *Healthy snacks.*

Bryan is so overprotective. He won't even let me sit on a bench on the carousel. According to the Pregnancy Expert Bryan Hawk IV, I'm only allowed to take pictures with my favorite characters and watch parades.

Yippee for me.

For lunch we explore the downtown area before settling on a restaurant with a spectacular tropical forest atmosphere. Bryan encourages the girls to order everything they want on the menu. We share the over-the-top dessert.

The incident at their school is no longer a cloud over our heads. Kourtney and Emma are having a good time.

I'm too tired to hang out with them after we finish lunch. They walk me to the hotel, then ride the shuttle back to the park.

Late in the afternoon, a knock on the door wakes me.

"Per Mr. Hawk's request, he's arranged for a babysitter for later tonight. And asked me to make appointments at a few boutiques on Rodeo Drive," the concierge says. "I have a car waiting for you, ma'am."

I run to the bedroom to change my clothes. Shopping on Rodeo Drive has always been a fantasy. God, I love that man.

Not only did he make appointments for me at several popular stores, Bryan had the concierge arrange an open line of credit too. One of my stops is at a maternity store. I'm not showing yet, but I buy things I can wear for spring and summer.

At another store, I buy some things for the girls. And at a men's store, I buy a surprise for Bryan.

I stop by my favorite bakery, since I'm in LA, and pick up a half-dozen cupcakes.

I make it back to the hotel before them and soak in the tub.

Bryan and the girls close down the park. He's carrying one sleeping girl in each arm when he comes back to the suite. I help him get them changed and into bed, then he goes to get ready.

"You don't have to take me out tonight. I know you're tired."

He didn't sleep much last night.

"I'm not tired." The water in the shower turns off.

"I'm not sure about leaving the girls with strangers." I watch him dry off with a fluffy hotel towel.

"I only leave my family in the hands of someone I trust." He moves around the room getting dressed.

Someone knocks on the door.

"Can you get that?" he asks.

I'm torn between spending quality time with him and leaving my girls with a stranger. I open the door.

"I heard you needed a babysitter." Mom hugs me.

"Where's Dad?"

"I'm right here," he says dragging two suitcases down the hall.

Bryan comes from the bedroom carrying an overnight bag. "Thanks, Mom, Dad." He takes my hand. "The girls are asleep. They should be out the whole night." He tows me out of the room before I can protest or say goodnight.

As promised, Bryan shows me Anaheim, California, from the tallest view in a different suite.

"How did you do this?" I turn around. He's standing in the doorway to the balcony, smiling at me.

"I asked for a room fit for my queen and this is what they gave me." He bows. "How may I serve you, Your Highness?"

"I want to see fireworks."

He pulls out his cell phone and within seconds, colorful lights dance against the dark sky. Then Bryan gives me five fulfilling orgasms on the balcony and I return the pleasure.

Saturday morning, we make it back to the suite before the girls wake up. Bryan arranges for us to get into the park a few hours before it officially opens. The girls are too excited to eat breakfast. They ride the majority of the rides on their list. I even get to ride on a few with them, the ones safe for pregnant women.

Last night, I orally persuaded him to rethink his moratorium on amusement park rides. I'm sure I could have gotten him to sign over his company if I wanted to. I settled for alpha male's temporary abdication of his throne.

Once the park opens to the public, Bryan and Dad take off with the girls while Mom and I explore. She and I eat all the unhealthy snacks we can find.

For lunch we go to a members-only restaurant inside the park. By now I'm just going with the flow and not questioning anything.

"Can we stay an extra day?" I ask. "I want to show the girls Los Angeles."

"We can stay as long as you want," he says.

We spend the rest of this day as a family. I don't even stop Dad from buying the girls a bunch of souvenirs.

Early Sunday morning we're up at dawn to take Mom and Dad to the airport, then go sightseeing.

Monday we park hop then head to the airport.

Bryan gives the girls permission to take their cell phones to school Tuesday morning. He instructs them to call *him* if anything happens. Thankfully none of the students broach the subject. Jennifer tells me that the entire student body, along with parents, sat through an assembly about tolerance. Dr. Stevens and other therapists from the hospital put on the presentation.

We have an uneventful week. I don't even see black trucks following me.

Max hosts a brunch to celebrate the exile of Madelyn Brooks. I'm shocked by the number of parents who show up. And even more shocked by the number of parents who agree with the expulsion of the three students who called my baby those ugly, hateful names.

Holly and Melissa move to Littleton but promise to come back for the wedding at the end of March.

Tom and Max cave in and take Penelope to the pound. She begged for a baby sister. Instead, she came home with a bouncing, energetic five-pound deer head Chihuahua.

By the end of the month word about our engagement and the baby is still the hottest topic on the parent gossip hotline. And Ms. Williamson's attitude toward me takes a turn for the worse.

I'm happy, pregnant, and about to marry the man I'm deeply in love with. Everything else is insignificant.

Chapter Thirty-Three

"GOOD MORNING, GIRLS." I KISS my daughters' cheeks. "Are you excited about today?" I pour a glass of milk.

"Where's Daddy?" Emma asks.

"It's bad luck for the groom to see the bride before the wedding." Even as the words leave my mouth, I hope the superstition isn't true.

Jessica snorts.

Bryan snuck out of the house two hours ago after a few hours of pre-wedding sex. He crept into the house because I kept sexting him during his bachelor party.

"You slept in this morning. How are you feeling?" Marie fails to hide her knowing smile.

"I feel good."

Jessica smirks. "I bet you do."

"Are you nervous?" Mom has a smirk on her face too.

Did everyone hear us?

"A little. I just want everything to be perfect."

"Mommy, how does a baby get in your tummy?" Emma asks.

We've been expecting this question, but now is not the time to answer it.

"If you two are finished eating, let's get you ready for the ceremonies," Mom says.

Thank you, I mouth.

"I'll help," Marie snickers.

They lead the girls out of the kitchen.

"It's a good thing Mom took them from the table. I was going to tell them the baby got in there because of the noises coming from your bedroom *every night*." Jessi's hand hits the table.

"I'm sorry, I can't help it. I crave him more than food. Is that normal?"

She nods.

"Will it stop?" I ask.

"My brother isn't complaining."

I giggle.

The doorbell rings. I bite into a muffin as I walk down the hallway to open the door.

Jailynne and her assistants are here to get us dressed.

She made a champagne-colored dress that accentuates my plump breasts and flows down just below my knees. She also made the girls' sage-colored classic dresses.

The hair stylist straightens, then curls my hair, pulling pieces off my face, but leaving the back long and flowing with loose curls. I decided against a veil.

He gives the girls bouncy barrel curls, adding a headband that matches their dresses. Kourtney sits still for him.

Jessica, my bridesmaid, is dressed in a simple sage-colored dress. Her shoulder-length brown hair is curled and fluffed to appear fuller. Bryan and I bought her a tennis bracelet to wear today.

Marie is standing in as the Mother of the Bride. She cried when I asked her to take on the role. With Jailynne's help, I designed her sage-colored dress with matching jacket and she looks beautiful. Her long more-salt-than-pepper hair is swept up off her face. Bryan and I bought her an antique brooch to wear today.

Jailynne also helped me design the Mother of the Groom dress. When Mom came for her first fitting I tried to keep a straight face. No matter how many times I altered the design, my mind kept replaying the morning I heard the tapping sound coming from the guest room. The dress is a little more youthful than she normally wears, but Mom looks hot. Her bob-cut brown hair is layered to look trendy. Bryan and I bought her an antique gold locket to wear today.

Pascual and Joshua keep our makeup natural and fresh. Since today is a special day, I allow the girls to wear a light tinted lip gloss.

Max, my Male of Honor, arrives wearing his tailored sage-colored three-piece suit and navy blue tie.

Before leaving the house, I'm given the traditional tokens for a bride on her wedding day.

Marie gives me something old. The lace handkerchief she carried on her wedding day. "I want you to keep it and give it to the girls." She wipes tears from her eyes.

Jessica gives me something new. A shiny piece of silver to wear in my left shoe, she calls it sixpence. It's engraved with my new initials.

Mom lets me borrow the small Fleming family's gold cross that for seven generations, each bride held in her right hand on her wedding day. "My mother let me borrow it the day I married Bryan. Her mother let her borrow it the day she married my dad. When it's their time the girls will borrow it on their wedding day too." She wipes tears from her eyes.

Max gives me something blue. Blue diamond earrings the same color as the navy blue garter I'm wearing.

The limo arrives at two. We get in for our journey to the courthouse. Kourtney and Emma look out the window, playing the out of state license plate game. Mom and Marie discuss the girls' visit to Colorado Springs next month. Jessica and Max are reminiscing about last weekend's bachelorette party. I stare out the window at nothing in particular, but I'm thinking about a lot.

I can't remember ever being this happy. James said all the right things, did all the right things, but sometimes, it was like I was seeing two different people. He struggled with an inner quest since he enlisted, but it in no way diminished the way I felt for him.

When we were in high school, he'd jokingly say, if I loved him, I would have sex with him. One night, it wasn't a joke. I calmly asked, why I had to give him my most valued gift just to prove my love? I didn't stick around to hear the answer. Instead, I kissed his cheek and told him to be safe at boot camp. I knew about the other girls and I let it go while I was in California.

Adult James held himself back and because of that, I was never in love *with him. The guilt of my actions after his death is why I grieved for so long. It took some time to come to the realization that James was my friend, whom I loved, but not the love of my life, the man I wanted to call husband for the rest of my days.*

The first time Bryan told me he loved me, I felt his words more than I heard them. Now I'm uplifted and wrapped in warmth. My load is light and my worries vanish every time he says those words. They give me the courage to travel this road with him today despite the past.

Bryan is the first and last to possess *my soul, my life, and my body.*

Closing my eyes, I bow my head.

I thank you, God, for the man I'm about to marry. I thank you for the daughter I'm about to gain, and for the father my daughter finally has in her life. Thank you for the child I'm carrying and for the family and friends who love us. I promise to cherish them and love them every day for the rest of my life. Amen.

That song by Leela James, "Fall For You," plays in my head. I heard it one time, over the holidays, but the lyrics sum up what I'm experiencing this moment of time. I fell fast and I fell hard for Bryan. And those feelings no longer frighten me. I'm ready to commit to him.

The limo turns onto the one-way street for the courthouse. My stomach flutters, or it could be the baby moving. Dad and Willis stand at the curb waiting for us. The girls are the first to climb out, followed by Mom, Jessica, and Max.

"Are you ready?" Marie holds my hand.

"I'm ready."

She climbs out and Willis offers his hand to me. He's standing in as the Father of the Bride. And looking distinguished in his navy blue suit.

"You are a vision," he says, kissing my cheek.

He presents his arm.

Max walks alongside me, wearing dark shades, his head moving left to right. He jokes about an escape plan if I want to leave Bryan standing at the altar.

Colorado weather is unpredictable and I'm happy it's a beautiful day. I look to my left. Two black SUVs are parked in metered stalls. Today I will not ponder the reason. I glance to my right. A woman who could be Ms. Williamson's twin sits on a bench near a flower bed of red striped, yellow tulips. The fountain is sparkling with water. The surrounding flower beds are filled with purple faces inside the pansies.

The statue of a hawk in the courtyard confirms I'm on the right journey.

We enter the building and are escorted to the judge's chambers. Max fusses with my hair and touches up my makeup. Jessica hands us our five-roses bouquet.

The doors open and Bryan's parents walk in first, followed by Marie and Jessi, then Max and the girls.

I take a calming breath, and the last verse of that song floats through my mind as I enter the room with Willis.

The chamber is surprisingly bright, with wood bookshelves filled with law books. The American flag and the Colorado State flag are displayed on stands in the corner. Lady Justice adorns the wall behind the desk of Judge Gilbert F. Humphrey. His framed degrees hang with other certificates on the wall too.

We're not in his courtroom, but Judge Humphrey wears his judicial robe for the ceremonies.

Bryan stands in front of the desk, looking male-model good in his flawlessly tailored navy blue suit, white dress shirt, sage-and-blue patterned silk tie and matching pocket hankie, and immaculately polished black dress shoes.

Tom moves around snapping photos while a videographer captures the moment, live.

I acknowledge Holly and Melissa with a smile.

I nod to the three men standing with Bryan, also dressed in navy blue suits. Tony, Ig, and Vin are like my big brothers. I'm happy they're in our lives.

Finally, I make it to Bryan, but Willis doesn't let me go. His face is serious. Stern. He and Bryan lock in silent communication.

Everyone in the room grows quiet as we watch the two men hold a conversation with their eyes.

Bryan stands tall, shoulders back, chest out, towering over Willis. He nods. Willis shakes his hand, kisses my cheek and places my hand in Bryan's, then takes his place beside Marie.

I throw Bryan a look. He turns us to face the judge. The first part of today's ceremonies begins.

Judge Humphrey welcomes everyone and goes over his duties as a Justice of the Peace.

I hand Max my bouquet and turn to Bryan. Holding his hands, I press the cross into our palms.

Bryan recites his vows first. "You and Kourt are a part of me. Of us. You taught me to cherish the moments given and I will *not* abuse them again. You and only you captured my heart in a way that makes me want the title of husband." He takes a breath. "You are my haven and I am your protector even when it seems that I'm not. This is real. *We* are real. Dani, we will face each day together and I need you to remember that what we have cannot be broken. It's going to be tested, but my love for you will not falter." Tears pool in his eyes. "You have always been my connection. My forever and always is you." His voice cracks. "I promise to love you, Dani, unconditionally through all of life's journeys, even after I take my last breath." His final words are filled with love and devotion.

He brushes the tears from my cheeks with his thumb.

We rejoin hands and I recite my vows.

"You came into my life and found a way around my defenses. It's the little things you do to comfort me, take care of me, and protect me that made me fall in love with you. You love me without taking away my strength and independence. I can take a step back because I know you won't let me fall. We are forever connected." I lay our hands on my stomach and turn to look at Kourtney and Emma. "Bryan, I won't stand behind you, but I promise to walk beside you. Every path our journey takes, I promise to travel it with you. Step for step. Fall for fall. Run for run. Fight for fight." My voice quivers from the conviction of my words. "You can lean on me, like I lean on you. I will love you more tomorrow than I do today, and the next. I promise to love you forever and always, Bryan, even after I take my last breath." I reach out brushing away the few tears that escape his eyes.

The unmistakable sound of sobs coming from the two people standing in as my parents make me take a stuttering breath and squeeze Bryan's hands.

Even Tony's rubbing his eyes.

After Bryan and I exchange rings and say "I do" we share a brief, promising kiss, then motion for the girls to come stand with us. The second phase of the ceremonies begins.

"Young lady," the judge addresses Kourtney, "Bryan Kendall Hawk the Fourth is your legal father, and your legal name is Kourtney Allison Hawk."

"I know, your Honor." She turns to her dad, wrapping her arms around his waist. Bryan slides a ring on the middle finger of her left hand.

"Danielle Lauren Hawk is my mommy now," Emma shouts loud and proud before Judge Humphrey can speak.

After calming his laughter, the judge confirms her decree, and Bryan signs his name on the paperwork.

I hug my new daughter and slide a ring on the middle finger of her left hand.

"I now pronounce you Bryan, Danielle, Emma, and Kourtney Hawk," the judge says. "Please let me be the first to congratulate you." He shakes our hands.

"Finally," Bryan sighs, looking down at his daughter. The importance of that single word isn't lost on me. March twenty-eighth, two thousand fourteen, will always be remembered.

Our family and friends surround us with hugs and kisses.

We exit the judge's chambers, walking outside. Three limousines are waiting. Bryan leads the girls and me to one while the rest of our family climbs into the others.

Our reception is at the exclusive Goldman Hotel and Resort, a hidden treasure in the community of Eldora here in Boulder County. Other friends and associates, along with Trevor, watched the ceremonies via satellite. Prince Jawad received a personal invitation from Bryan.

The wedding cake is from my favorite bakery, of course. And I surprise Bryan with a groom's cake shaped like a hawk, a special request that the bakery's owner was happy to oblige.

We'll wait until after the baby is born to go on a real honeymoon, but we close ourselves off, for the weekend, in a penthouse suite before the reception ends.

Chapter Thirty-Four

BRYAN AND I HAVE BEEN married for two happy weeks. After school, we drive the girls and Trevor to Colorado Springs to spend spring break with Mom and Dad. Kourtney assures me I will survive a week without seeing her. She didn't let me help her pack and says she'll be okay without Mr. Cuddles.

With the girls gone, Bryan gives Marie and Willis the week off.

Jessica is presenting at a conference in Boston and will be back Monday afternoon.

Bryan and I take advantage of having the house to ourselves for the weekend. We get creative with a pair of Couple's Dice that name different areas of a house for location.

We stop long enough to eat.

Monday is a light day at work. Mr. Brumfield is my only patient today. He's rebuilding his relationship with his children.

"I'm selling the house and moving in to a seniors' condo."

"Can you tell me how you came to that decision, Mr. Brumfield?"

"With Agnes gone, I can no longer live there. I worked up the courage to tell my daughter the secret I've been carrying around for a long time." He pulls a handkerchief out his pocket and wipes his eyes.

"Would you like to talk about the secret today?"

He nods his head, but doesn't speak. I give him a minute to compose himself. This secret is what's holding him back from moving on with his life.

"I loved my wife and I always came home to her. I gave Agnes her heart's desire. Our children wanted for nothing. But I cheated. The person I met was special to me and I couldn't just walk away. Before Agnes died, she told me she knew about the affair. She said she forgave me a long time ago." He cries into his handkerchief.

I wait for him to let go of his pain. It's the only way. I place a cup of water next to him.

"How long did you have this affair, Mr. Brumfield?" I ask once he's able to resume.

"Forty-five years. I've been with George for forty-five years."

Needing to get out of the house, Bryan takes me to dinner and to see an action movie. After the movie, we walk across the courtyard of the plaza heading to the parking lot. Bryan is walking behind me with his hand on my small baby bump.

"Danielle."

I stop breathing.

He steps out of the shadows, pointing a gun at us.

Everything happens in *one heartbeat.*

The first shot whizzes past my ear. Yanked to the left. My husband grunts. Second shot flies past my shoulder.

He's holding on to me and we're falling. A third shot rings in my ear. Husband grunts. I land on him. Fourth shot zooms past my ear.

Unfazed, husband rolls me off, firing consecutive shots while shielding me. Tires gripping asphalt. Blood splatters onto my face.

My hands frantically search him. He falls on me. Gun drops from his hand.

Pressure. I have to apply pressure. I roll him off me, get on my knees to shield my husband. And press on his neck.

I call out to the two men dressed in black suits running toward us and look for the gunman.

He's gone.

One man drops to his knees next to me; the other talks into his jacket sleeve and runs past us.

"Please don't leave me, Bryan. I love you. Please don't leave us."

I hear sirens in the distance.

"Keep breathing. Just concentrate on breathing," I chant.

"Mrs. Hawk, have you been shot? Are you hurt?" the stranger asks.

I shake my head.

"She's uninjured," he says into his sleeve.

He checks my husband's neck for a pulse. "Colonel. Can you hear me? Your emergency team is almost here. Hang in there, sir."

"Secure her. Now," my husband commands.

The sirens get closer.

I'm lifted off the ground, my hands replaced by the man who called my husband "Colonel." I fight against the hands of the person whisking me away.

"Mrs. Hawk, please stop hitting me. I'm following orders." He opens the back door of a black SUV, closing the door once I'm on the seat.

He runs back to my husband holding something in his hand, waving off other people coming near the scene.

Another black SUV pulls up. Four men in gray suits jump out rushing toward the crowd.

The ambulance screeches to a stop, and the paramedics rush to the scene.

I hit and kick the window. It won't break. I try all the doors. They're locked.

Helplessly, I look out at the activity surrounding my husband. The paramedics lift him on to a stretcher. They rush him to the waiting ambulance. The two men in black suits run alongside him. Guns in their hands.

The truck doors unlock. They jump in the front seat.

"Ma'am, please put on your seatbelt." He hands me my purse.

I remember him from the first time I went to Bryan's office. Porter is his name.

Two more black SUVs pull up, one in front of the ambulance, the other behind us. The ambulance pulls away from the curb. We fall in line, flying through the streets of Boulder. Red emergency lights flashing on all four vehicles. Sirens wailing. I look back at the men in gray suits, still holding back the crowd.

I pull out my cell phone and scroll through the contacts to call Tony.

"Don't worry, Dani. We're already on our way," he answers on the first ring.

"How do you know what happened?"

"Porter called us. We'll meet you at the hospital. Listen, do not talk to anyone and stay with Porter or Mills. They will protect you with their lives." He hangs up before I can ask another question.

The movie theater is not far from the hospital, but we're driving in the opposite direction.

"Where are they taking him?" I ask. We're turning on to the highway.

"We're going to a military hospital, ma'am," the driver answers.

Through the back windows of the ambulance, I see two men working on Bryan. That isn't an ordinary emergency vehicle. It's bigger.

Porter rapidly types on a cell phone and talks in military terms in his sleeve. He's also doing his best to keep me calm.

We finally exit. Twenty tires gripping asphalt, making a sharp left turn. We caravan for a few miles, then turn into an underground entrance.

Porter and the driver jump out to talk to the men from the other trucks. He must be in charge even though he's definitely younger than the other men.

Bryan's stretcher is pulled from the back of the ambulance. He isn't moving, his jacket and shirt removed. There's an IV line in his arm, gauze bandages and ice packs covering his neck. Three men armed with rifles enter the hospital with him.

I make a run for the emergency room doors. My path is blocked by the driver.

"Mrs. Hawk, my name is Mills. We're escorting you into the hospital and taking you to a secured floor. Lieutenant Colonel Paul and Major Ricci will be here shortly."

"I need to be with my husband." I try to get around him, but he blocks me from getting by.

"Major Acosta is five minutes out. He'll brief you once he evaluates the Colonel."

Mills, Porter and two other men, also dressed in black suits and carrying rifles, whisk me down the corridors. Mills and Porter have guns in their hands.

Heads turn our way and people step to the side. The four men have me surrounded as we make our way to the elevators.

On the fifth floor, I'm led to a room. It's larger than the normal hospital room.

"Mrs. Hawk, do you remember me? My name is Porter." He doesn't wait for me to reply. "Is there anything you need right now?"

"I need to call my sister-in-law and Bryan's parents." I look at my husband's blood on my clothes and hands.

"Instructor Hawk is en route. Unless you require immediate medical attention, she'll check you when she arrives. Retired Colonel and Mrs. Langford have also been notified, ma'am. If I get a status update on Colonel Hawk, I will let you know." His smile almost reaches his eyes. "Mrs. Hawk, please don't leave this room without Mills or myself. There are other armed guards standing outside, but he and I are responsible for your safety until the Lieutenant Colonel arrives."

I nod.

Porter leaves me alone in the room.

Colonel? Lieutenant Colonel? Majors? Retired Colonel? Secured floors? Armed guards? Who in the hell are these people?

My fingers twist my wedding and engagement rings. I pace back and forth.

Time creeps by.

I wait for news.

I try hard to block the memory, but my mind flashes back to that day when two men in Army uniforms knocked on my apartment door. I'd just gotten home from a class. They told me James had been killed in action.

I remember immediately feeling lost and picking up the phone to call the only person I could think of in the moment. That same feeling threatens to consume me now and I can't pick up the phone to call that person.

My knees weaken and I sit on the couch. Curl up and cry.

The comfort of loving arms surrounds me.

My eyes flutter open. Marie is the source. I wrap my arms around her and squeeze tight.

"How's Bryan?" I ask.

"I don't know, dear. We just got here."

Willis is talking to Mills and Porter. The three shake hands. Willis walks over to the couch. The men leave the room.

I make room for Willis. He rubs my arm.

"What did they tell you about Bryan?"

"There's no news yet, but Ignacio is with him."

"Where are Anthony and Vincenzo?"

"They're with him too."

"Why can't I be with him?"

Willis sighs. "We'll explain everything in due time."

Tears drip on to my bloodstained fingers. "I can't lose him. I won't survive."

Willis rubs my shoulder. "You're a fighter. You will get through this."

I want to believe him. I do. But my heart won't survive burying the man I love.

"Marie brought you a change of clothes. Go get cleaned up." He points to the travel bag sitting in the chair.

I get up, taking the bag into the attached restroom. No wonder Mills thought I was injured. Dried blood is smeared across my cheek, hands, and clothes. My eyes are puffy and red, and my lips are chapped.

I turn on the water in the basin and wash off my husband's blood.

My hands shake, making it difficult to change clothes. I manage to button my blouse and change my pants.

When I step out of the restroom, I feel a little better knowing Marie and Willis are here. I rejoin them on the couch, resting my head on Willis's shoulder. Silent tears run down my cheeks.

Porter brings in a sandwich and fruit.

"You should eat something," Marie says.

"We ate at the restaurant," I reply.

A cot is brought in.

"You should try to go to sleep. I'll wake you if there's any news," she encourages.

"I don't want to eat. I don't want to rest. I want Bryan!"

"Leave her alone. She knows what's best for her and the baby." Willis rubs my shoulders.

Marie pulls out her knitting needles and yarn. Her lips form a thin tight line.

I feel bad. She's looking out for us. I lean over and I kiss her cheek. "I'm sorry for shouting."

She sets her needles down, patting my hands. "I know you're worried about him. So am I. He's like a son to me." The tears she's been holding back begin to roll down her cheeks and her lips tremble.

In my tunnel vision, I've only thought about how this affects me. I become her source of comfort as we sit and wait for news.

In the middle of the second hour of Willis and Marie being with me, Ignacio, Vincenzo, and Anthony finally walk through the door, wearing surgical scrubs.

I jump off the couch and go to them. Vin pulls me into a tight hug rubbing my back.

"He's alive, Dani. He's going to be okay," Ignacio says, pulling me into his arms, I sob on his chest. "The bullet didn't do any real damage. He's in recovery. They'll bring him in, in a little while."

"What about the other bullets? He was shot more than once."

Vin rubs my arm. "He was wearing a bulletproof vest."

I step back. Away from them.

"Why would Bryan need to wear one?"

"Dani, we need to ask you some questions. Please have a seat." Vin gestures toward the couch.

I cross my arms over my chest.

"Tony will answer as much as he can, but please have a seat," he requests. I sit on the edge of the couch in between Marie and Willis.

Anthony kisses my forehead and squats in front of me, holding my hands. His thumbs draw reassuring circles around my knuckles. "Dani, we need to know if Bryan's ever told you what he does."

"He owns Hawkeye Personal Protection."

"Is that all he's told you?"

"Does this have anything to do with the urgent business trips? Or the person hiding in my apartment? How about the fireworks on New Year's Eve? Or the black trucks following me?" I snatch my hands from Anthony's grasp. "Those men called him Colonel. And you, Lieutenant Colonel." I look at Vin. "And you, Major Ricci." I look at Ignacio. "And you, Major Acosta." My gaze lands on Willis. "And you, retired Colonel Langford." My voice grows louder with each accusation. "Who are you guys?"

"Bryan said he'll tell you everything once he's out of recovery," Anthony says.

"Are my children safe?"

"The girls are fine and the Hawk's home is secured," Ignacio says, stepping closer.

"Gentlemen, you need to wait for Colonel Hawk before you proceed," stoned-faced Willis speaks.

"Your opinion is duly noted, but we have orders to secure Danielle, and to do that we have to know who we're up against." Anthony's attention is back to me. "Did you see who shot Bryan?"

This is the first time I've thought about what happened.

"We were walking across the courtyard. Out of nowhere he says my name. After that it's a blur."

"But did you see his face?" Anthony asks.

I cry, nodding my head. "James is dead. It couldn't have been him."

"That's enough. Wait for Colonel Hawk." Willis exerts his authority.

Anthony stands. Back straight. Chest out. "You are not my leader, Langford. And while Colonel Hawk is unconscious I'm in charge."

"Since you're not the one authorized to disclose information, your line of questioning is jeopardizing your position, Paul." Willis rises from the couch.

"Things have changed since the good old days." Anthony steps toward him. "We're stronger. Bigger. Global." His head twists with each word until they're nose to nose. "Bryan didn't reinvent the wheel, he made it roll better." Anthony looks like he's about to beat the crap out of Willis. "I've been given the authority."

"Tony." Ignacio gestures in my direction when his friend's head snaps his way.

I'm in the same room as them, but I'm the only one who can't follow the conversation.

Chapter Thirty-Five

THE ROOM DOOR SWINGS OPEN. Bryan is wheeled in on a hospital bed. He is conscious. Before the door closes, I glimpse two armed men standing in front of the doorway.

Ignacio and the medical team hook him up to the monitors.

"Are you and the baby okay?"

Bryan reaches out to me.

I stare at his hand, then back at him.

"Now, will you tell me what's going on, Colonel?"

"Clear the room," he says to the medical team.

They leave without question, closing the door behind them.

Bryan looks at his three best friends. "Have you told her anything?"

"We had orders to confirm his identity," Anthony informs him.

Bryan closes his eyes, inhales deeply, and exhales slowly.

"Dani, come here." He opens his eyes, reaching for me again.

I don't budge.

"Get over here." A little more firmness is added to his authoritative tone. This is his alpha male voice and now I understand why he is one.

I stand, taking *my* time to get to his bedside. He wraps his arm around my waist pulling me closer, making me stumble over my feet. My hands land on his chest. He sucks in air, but pain does not show on his face. I try to pull back. His hold on my waist tightens.

Bryan's hand inches up my back, bringing me closer to him until our lips brush.

"I love you, Dani. Please remember that." His kiss screams of desperation and begs for understanding. "Can someone bring my wife a chair?"

Ignacio places one behind me and I sit. Bryan holds my hand.

"What I'm about to tell you is highly classified and you can't tell anyone, not even the girls. You'll become part of our infrastructure like Marie. It's time you know the truth."

I glance at the others in the room.

Bryan reaches under the pillow and pulls out an official-looking letter, signed by the President. "I had to get written permission to tell you this." He stares into my eyes. "I am Colonel Bryan Kendall Hawk the Fourth. Second Command of the United States Phantom Military. Ignacio, Vincenzo, and Anthony are not just my best friends; we are the Elite Special Operations Team. I report directly to the President."

What?!

"We've been investigating a homeland anti-government organization called Rebels Against Government Suppression, or RAGS for short. Somehow, they found out about the secret military branch. We are Phantom for a reason, and in the wrong hands, that information puts our government relations in jeopardy. To put it in layman's terms, if we're exposed, it could start World War III on American soil."

This is crazy.

"RAGS recruits orphaned youths. They train them in the mastery of espionage. The youths infiltrate military branches and branches of government. They steal top-secret information and sell it to communist or terrorist leaders for financial and political gain."

From the corner of my eye, I see Willis fidgeting on the couch.

"This member of RAGS stored Phantom information on a homemade laptop and was using his identical twin brother to help him attract buyers. That person was Sergeant James Andrew Edwards. His brother, a civilian, was Jamal Adam Edwards. During the raid we thought James Edwards was killed in the gunfight. And Jamal Edwards was arrested and sent to federal prison where he died a few years ago. I put a protection plan in place for you in case anyone came looking for back-up information. Once Kourtney was born, she became part of that plan too. On the thirtieth of June last year, a man fitting Sergeant Edwards's description was spotted crossing the Syrian border. I had you and Kourtney moved here. When you left Arizona, we exhumed the body buried in the military cemetery and positively identified it as Jamal. We exhumed the body of the man who died in federal prison. His face had been surgically altered. He had full denture implants and his fingerprints were chemically burned off. We don't know his true identity." Bryan coughs.

Ignacio hands him a cup with a straw.

This sounds like it's out of a Hollywood movie plot.

"Dr. Barrett watches over Kourtney at school. While you're at work, Vanessa Larson keeps you safe. In our home, retired Colonel Langford and his wife watch over both of you. Porter follows you; he's your Security Lead. He has orders to not make contact unless necessary. Lately you've noticed him only because of possible threats against you."

"This is a joke, right? This is too well contrived to be real. You're lying?"

"I realize this sounds farfetched, but no, Dani, I'm not lying."

I snatch my hand out of his. The phone calls. The familiar voice. The lilies. *That was James.* I gasp.

Bryan reaches for me. I scoot the chair back. "Don't. Touch. Me!" I say as I jump out of the chair, out of reach. "James was not a recruit! He did not have an identical twin brother! He was not selling military secrets!"

"Dani, calm down. Think of the baby," he says.

My hands go to my stomach as I realize...

"Don't," he pleads, pushing the button so he's sitting up higher in the hospital bed. "Don't you dare think that."

I step back. My mind replaying the first time we met. I keep stepping back. Looking into the faces of the people in the room. All of them are in on this.

My stomach rolls and I run to the restroom. I drop to my knees. My stomach contracts and I vomit. Everything I ate for dinner comes up, the acid burning my throat.

When I wake up from this nightmare, Bryan and I will be at home, in bed. *Wake up, Danielle!* I shout in my head.

Realization settles in. I'm not dreaming.

Images flash in my mind's eye. My stomach rolls again. I heave, gag, and cough until I count to ten to clear my mind.

My stomach starts to settle.

I flush the toilet and sit on the floor with my back against the wall. I rest my head on my knees.

"Here's some water," Marie says.

I lift my head, taking the bottle, but do not open it.

"Danielle..."

I halt her speech by holding up my hand. "Please, leave me alone." I cough, my throat is raw and it makes my voice sound raspy.

"Get Jessica in here to check her," Bryan commands.

What now? I ask myself.

My baby moves, the flutters making the situation that much more painful. Mental anguish pours out of me in the form of tears. Confusion. Anger. Curiosity. Heartache. I sit here, on the cold tile floor and let the feelings free.

My tears are plenty.

My legs start to cramp and my butt is numb from sitting on this hard floor for so long. Slowly, I climb to my feet. Wash my face. Rinse my mouth and take a few sips of water. I pull myself together and exit the bathroom, confusion and curiosity co-piloting my actions—anger loitering in the background ready to step up when one falters.

"I have questions and I want answers." Shoulders set. With my eyes, I dare him to tell me another lie. I fold my arms over my chest to keep from giving in to the urge to resolve this by throwing a punch.

He nods.

"The way we met, was that part of the plan?"

"It may have started off like that, Dani..."

I raise my hand to stop his unwanted explanation.

"Yes or no," I tell him and repeat the question.

"Yes."

"Did you use sex as a way to get me to open up to you?"

"Yes."

So Kimberly was telling the truth.

"That story about the escort business and Kimberly and how you met Emma's..."

"Necessary lies," he cuts me off. For a quick second, his eyes beg me not to finish that question.

If he so convincingly lied about that... I take a deep stuttering breath, preparing myself for the next answer out of his mouth.

"Is Emma legally my daughter? Are we married?"

His conflicted hazel eyes answer the question. I need to hear him say it though.

"My vows were re..."

"Yes or no Bryan!"

"No."

Marie gasps.

Never have I felt such overpowering, all-consuming energy of rage take over my body. It's frightening. I want to annihilate his existence.

"But, Dani..."

In the background of my reality an animal, in soul-wrenching pain, howls, interrupting his words. The wounded creature's unbearable pain affects everyone in the room. It shows on their faces.

The look in Bryan's eyes is pure and utter shock mixed with fear. I realize the sound came from me.

I make a run for the door.

Anthony steps in front of it. At once I drop into stance and aim a kick at his ribs.

He blocks it.

"You may not engage, Lieutenant Colonel," his commander barks.

I follow through with another kick to his ribs, Anthony doesn't fight back nor does he block me. He stands there like the good dog he is, taking every kick and punch.

I throw combinations to his abdomen, followed by kicks to his sides.

"Danielle. Stop," the Colonel barks.

"Please stop." Marie's plea rolls off my back.

They are the pack of dogs in my dream.

"Get. The. Fuck. Out. Of. My. Way!"

His arms move. I get deeper in my stance to prepare for a real fight. I throw a kidney shot followed by a good solid punch to the ribs to show him I will not go down easily.

He grunts and raises his hands.

"Stand down, Paul!" the Colonel commands.

"Bryan. What are you doing? Get back in bed," Ignacio says.

"Dani. Please. Calm down before you hurt yourself." He sounds close to me.

His voice fuels my anger and my punches get harder.

"Danielle Lauren! Stop this, now!" Willis's baritone voice fills the room, breaking through the tunnel of fire I've enclosed myself in.

I freeze, fists still in fighter's position. Anthony stumbles back against the door, holding his ribcage.

My lungs are about to explode. I'd been holding my breath. Panting, I try to get air in. Something tightens around my neck. I pull at it, hearing the pings of buttons hitting the tile floor.

"Breathe, Dani," Bryan chants, but his words are muffled.

Clawing at my neck. My knees cave in. I'm falling. The fuzzy sight of Ignacio and Vin rushing toward me. My eyes roll back. Everything goes black.

Chapter Thirty-Six

THE STEADY BEEP OF A heart monitor and the sound of a muffled rapid heartbeat awaken me. I feel the tickle of air from the nasal cannula giving me oxygen. An IV line is giving me fluids. I'm in a hospital bed.

My hands move over my stomach.

"The baby is fine," she says.

My eyes flutter open searching the dimly lit room. Marie sits by the bed, knitting.

"You were hyperventilating and fainted."

I turn my head, finding a spot on the ceiling to stare at.

The room door swishes open.

"Is she awake?"

I refuse to acknowledge Instructor Jessica Hawk.

"She just woke up," Marie says.

Jessica comes closer to the bed. "How are you feeling?"

I have nothing to say.

"Danielle, can you hear me?" Jessica asks.

As soon as I get out of here, I'm getting my daughter and leaving Colorado.

"Has she said anything?"

"No, but she turned her head to me when I spoke to her," Marie says.

Jessica leans over me with a penlight. I knock it out of her hand, turning on my side. Both monitors beep faster.

"I know you're upset, but you have to stay calm for the baby's sake." Marie pats my arm. "Jessica, I'll call you if she needs anything. You being in here upsets her."

I take deep calming breaths until both monitors beep at a steady pace.

"I'll have one of the guys bring her some food," Jessica says.

"Willis is already getting her something."

Once Jessica leaves, the room is quiet except for the sounds coming from the machines and the consistent clicking of Marie's knitting needles.

I concentrate on my baby's heartbeat and let it sooth me until I feel myself falling asleep.

Fingers softly glide down my cheek. I open my eyes.

Bryan sits in the chair by the bed.

"I want my daughter," I tell him. My voice is hoarse.

He picks up a cup, guiding the straw to my lips. I suck down the water until the straw slurps air. He sets the cup on the bedside table.

"She's mine."

"Dani, I promise she's safe."

"You promised me a lot of things." I turn away from him.

"It started as an assignment, but once I got to know you, it became more."

I would believe him; however, he's been lying to me since the day he walked into my life.

"I've been telling necessary lies," he says.

The sobs rack through my body. The monitors beep faster. He touches my shoulder.

"Please give me back my daughter." I cry myself to sleep.

I wake with a start. Someone called my name.

He hovers over me, covering my mouth to quiet the scream from my lips.

"Shhh." He looks over his shoulder. "Those people aren't who they say they are. Nod if you want to leave with me."

I nod.

James uncovers my mouth and reaches for the IV line. He slowly pulls it out and wraps gauze around my arm. He frees me from the monitors.

"Get dressed," he says, tossing black sweatpants, a black hooded sweatshirt, and a pair of black running shoes on the bed.

He's wearing an EMT uniform and some type of glasses pushed back on his forehead. James moves to the door, watching through the small window, a big backpack strapped on his back.

I ease out of bed, quickly getting dressed.

Sitting in the chair, I double tie the laces, then join him at the door.

I too peek out the window. The floor is empty. What happened to the armed guards?

James turns off the lights in the room. The screen from a cell phone comes on. I watch him dial a number.

The lights on the floor go out. James takes hold of my hand. "Don't let go."

We exit the room into the darkened corridor, sticking to the wall. I hear voices shouting and rapid footsteps coming from both sides. James tows me through a door and up three flights of stairs, exiting onto a deserted floor that is being remodeled.

We jog across the bridge heading to the east wing of the hospital, according to the signage.

He slows our pace down to a fast walk, getting on the elevator. I lean against the wall in the cab and catch my breath. We ride down to the lobby. James takes my hand when the elevator doors open.

He exits first. I freeze. Vin stands inside the lobby entrance doors watching as people come and go.

"Don't worry, we're not going out the front," James says, tugging me out of the elevator.

He leads me through the lobby, down a long corridor with arrows giving directions to the various departments in this section. We're following the signs for urgent care and the emergency room.

James opens the door to a unisex bathroom. He pulls me inside and locks the door. Several footsteps run past. Voices are muffled behind the thickness of the door.

"Here, put these on." James hands me a short-cut honey blond wig and an EMT uniform from the backpack.

I hesitate. I don't want him to see my baby bump. The room upstairs was dim when I got dressed. I turn my back to him and change as fast as I can. The pants are a little snug.

I pull off my engagement and wedding rings, putting them in the pants' pocket.

Without a wig cap, it will be a challenge to fit all of my hair under the wig. I quickly braid my hair in one ponytail and cover it with the wig, tucking loose strands under the band.

James has his ear against the door.

I go to him. He dials a number on the cell phone and waits a few seconds. He grabs my hand. "Don't let go, no matter what." James opens the bathroom door.

Black smoke fills the corridor.

We join the masses running toward the emergency room. Instead of entering the waiting room, James swipes a card, giving us access to the patient care area. We quickly walk through the ward and out the EMT's entrance and exit.

Climbing into an ambulance, he starts the engine. I barely have time to buckle my seat belt before we zoom up the ramp onto the streets, tires screeching on the asphalt. He turns on the sirens, plowing through red lights.

"Where have you been for nine years?" I ask.

"Syria."

"I was told you were killed in Iraq. Your body was shipped back to Arizona. Whose body is buried in that cemetery?"

"I will explain everything when we get to a safe place."

Gripping my seat, I stop talking so he can concentrate on driving. In high school, James received the lowest possible passing score on the driver's road test at the DMV. His behind-the-wheel skills have not improved.

Once we're several miles from the hospital, he turns off the sirens and emergency lights, and eases off the gas.

I know I should question him now that we're out of harm's way, but I'm too relieved to be away from Bryan to get to the bottom of James's nine-year disappearance right now.

He pulls into the parking lot of a closed park. It's dark, but the outline of a playground can be seen in the moonlight.

"Come on." He jumps out, leaving the engine running.

I follow him.

We fast walk back to the street. He pulls out the cell phone and dials a number.

Two blocks away, he unlocks the doors to a late model Ford Escort parked in the lot at a bar. I settle in the passenger seat and secure my seat belt. He puts the key in the ignition and backs out of the stall, barely missing sideswiping the car next to us.

He drives by the park. Black smoke billows out the windows of the ambulance. Red and orange flames flicker underneath it. The ambulance is rolling toward the playground in the park.

James takes the highway entrance heading to Boulder.

We ride in silence.

For the first five miles I keep my eyes on the side-view mirror, watching for SUVs. The headlights of a big-wheeler are the only things I see.

At this time of night, there are very few cars on the road. Dark-colored SUVs would be easy to spot.

Once I'm convinced we're not being followed, I stare at James. He looks the same, just older.

My baby flips around and I stop myself from placing a hand on my stomach. I need to get to the house and get my truck and then I can pick up my daughter and disappear.

Exiting the highway, James pulls into a four-story, economically priced hotel next to a twenty-four-hour diner.

"Are you hungry?" he asks.

"No."

We get out of the car and I follow him through the lobby of the hotel. He pushes the button for the elevator.

We exit on the second floor. As we walk down the quiet hallway, James unzips the front compartment of the black backpack he's been carrying to retrieve a keycard. He stops at the door in the middle of the hall. A "do not disturb" sign hangs on the door handle. He opens the door.

The musty smell in the room smacks me in the face, making my stomach churn. I look around the room and decide it's best for me to sit at the small table cluttered with electronic equipment parts and a laptop.

The drapes block off the view from the window. They match the bedspread on the unmade bed. There's a pile of takeout containers stacked by the overflowing trash can. Black duffle bags haphazardly sit around the room. Unfortunately, I can't tell if the carpet is dirt brown or brown because it's dirty.

Reaching under the uniform shirt, I unfasten the buttons on the pants.

"Do you want something to drink?" James asks, pointing to the mini refrigerator.

"Why were you in Syria?"

"I'll talk while you patch me up." He opens a duffle bag and pulls out first aid supplies.

James walks over, dropping the bandages, surgical tape, ice packs, and sanitizer on top of the cluttered table.

He stands in front of me, kicking off his combat boots, pulls his shirt over his head and drops his pants. When we lived together, him undressing in front of me made me uncomfortable. I was young and inexperienced back then. Now, the sight of a half dressed, hot male doesn't make me blush.

James poses in front of me in black boxer briefs. I roll my eyes.

A nasty black-and-blue bruise mars the skin over his heart. Surgical tape holds melted ice packs to his upper right arm, his left side, and the groin area of his left thigh.

"How are you able to move around with those injuries?" I ask.

"Morphine and ice packs." He chuckles. "Your husband is an excellent shot. He hit the uncovered areas once the first shot didn't penetrate the Kevlar vest."

"Bryan is not my husband." I stand, pointing to the chair. "Sit."

He plops down.

"Talk," I command as I clean my hands with sanitizer first then pull on surgical gloves.

I start with the ice packs covering the wound on his arm.

"I'm a member of a secret branch of the military. I was recruited because of my technological skills," he begins.

Where have I heard this horror story? Oh yeah, from my fake husband.

"Hawk and I were trained together, but he turned out to be a double-agent and is stealing top secret information…" James winces when I begin to clean the wound. "Since technology is my specialty, I'm the one who came across the breach. A female member of my team, Amelia Goodman, infiltrated his operation and started sleeping with him." He touches my left hand.

I tune him out.

Chatper Thirty-Seven

"HAWK HASN'T BEEN ABLE TO get the information off my laptop," James says.

I stare into his eyes. I watch his lips moving. Good, he didn't notice I'd zoned out. At times, he would get really angry when he didn't have my undivided attention.

"That information is worth billions and it exposes those close to Hawk. I can't trust the person who helped me escape that prison. They have their own agenda."

I finish cleaning and dressing the wounds on his arm. I break icepacks and tape them over the bandages, then wrap a self-adhesive elastic bandage around to hold them in place.

He looks up at me. "I tried getting in touch with you on the number in Arizona. When did you move?"

I gasp when I remove the tape and icepack on his side.

"There's no real damage. My body will eventually expel the bullet on its own. The wound will need to be stitched though. Just clean it and use the butterfly bandages to close it. Then cover it with the gauze and tape an icepack over it."

When did he become so knowledgeable about gunshot wound care?

"Before the holidays, I called Kimberly Baryshnikova…"

My hands falter at the mention of her name.

"She's a for-hire-operative who does deep-black-market jobs. I gave her the code to track my laptop. She got a hit on it in Denver. We met in Canada and I got the laptop back. I haven't heard from her in a while. I started a state-by-state search of licensed therapists named Danielle Tatum or Danielle Edwards. Your last place of residence is listed in Durham, North Carolina. That was you on the phone when I called in January?"

I nod.

Covering the wound with a gauze bandage, I break an icepack, tape it down and wrap a self-adhesive elastic bandage around his midsection to hold it in place. Nine years in Syria didn't change his toned abs.

Picking up his shirt off the floor, I throw it over his crotch and squat between his legs. I cut the leg of his boxer briefs to get to the wound in his upper thigh. When I peel away the tape and icepack, blood drips onto the carpet.

"It's slowing down, just clean the area and add a couple of ice packs, then tie a tourniquet around it."

I raise both eyebrows.

"I said Hawk's a good shot. He nicked the artery knowing I'd have to get it stitched or slowly bleed to death." He chuckles with admiration. "Once I realized you were in Boulder, it took me a while to get here. I didn't want to alert Hawk to my whereabouts. I've been watching you for two weeks."

My head snaps up. I look at him.

"When this is over, you and I will relax on the beach of a private island."

I wonder if he knows about Kourtney. He has to if he's been following me for two weeks.

I clean the wound and pack it with gauze. I break two icepacks, placing them side-by-side on top of the gauze. He holds them in place while I wrap the elastic bandage around his thigh.

I open another pack of the elastic bandage and unroll it, then twist it until it looks like rope. I wrap it around his thigh, a few inches above the wound and tie it as tight as I can.

He hisses.

I pick up the permanent marker off the table and check the time on the clock, writing it on his skin. I tie the makeshift rope again and push the marker through the knot. Enjoying this next part, I twist the marker, tightening the tourniquet.

James cries out.

Once I'm sure the bandage won't unravel, I stand and pull off the gloves.

"I need your help, Danielle."

"What do you need?"

He takes my left hand, kissing my fingers. Anger flashes across his eyes. "Where's the ring I gave you?"

"In my jewelry box."

"You were told never to take it off. But I guess you had to when you married that traitor."

"I didn't marry him."

"Then why did you take it off?"

He's angrier about the ring than he is about me being with Bryan.

"It's been nine years, James."

He stands, running his fingers down my cheek and leans in to kiss me. I turn away.

"You denied me your body for years. Why did you so easily give yourself to him?"

I step around him and pick up the bloody gauze and melted icepacks. He doesn't deserve an answer.

"Bryan has my laptop. Can you get it for me?"

"You said Kimberly gave it to you."

"She gave me a dummy."

"How do you know it's a dummy?"

"This one didn't make a sound when you sat at the table." He points to the dinosaur laptop sitting amongst the clutter on the table. "And the CD drive didn't open." It looks just like the one Bryan left on his nightstand the first time he left on an urgent business trip.

"Why would that happen just because I'm near?"

"I don't have time for a Q & A," he snaps.

"How do I find the laptop?"

"I'll give you the tracking code." He tears a piece of paper from a notepad, scribbling two sets of numbers on it. "I'm giving you the number to where I can be reached too." He hands me the torn paper.

James pulls me into his arms. I lean away from his lips.

"I'm hungry."

He shakes his head. "What do you want?"

"A turkey sandwich."

"The bathroom is over there." He gestures behind him and opens a duffle bag, pulling out clothes. "There's another pair of sweats and stuff you might need in that bag over there." He points to a black backpack near the bathroom door.

I turn my back on him when he steps out of his briefs.

"Still can't look at me in the buff?" he taunts.

"I've seen you naked, James, and I'm still not impressed." I smirk even though he can't see my face.

"Ouch." He laughs and bumps my shoulder as he walks past me, giving me a view of his toned backside. He still has thick, muscular, runner's thighs. James ran track in high school.

He takes a bottled water out of the mini fridge and turns to face me.

My gaze drops to his feet as he walks past me again. Bumping my shoulder, *again*.

I finish cleaning up the makeshift triage area while he gets dressed.

"I'll be back," he says. The room door closes behind him.

I pick up the backpack and go into the bathroom. Before turning on the shower, I inspect the cleanliness of the tub.

I strip off my clothes and glimpse my stomach in the mirror over the sink. My hand slides over the bump. I take off the wig and open the complimentary packaged shower cap, putting it over my hair.

Rummaging through the backpack, I find a bar of soap and body lotion. *James remembered.* I step under the hot water, thinking about Bryan's and James's versions of events.

Who is telling lies to hurt me? Who is telling lies to protect me?

I step behind the camera. Fast forwarding through parts, and slowing down others, I view my life with both men.

Distracted by my thoughts, I don't notice when the shower water transitions from hot to warm. Warm to cold.

I turn the knob and step out of the tub. The scratchy hotel towel dries my body and I use the body lotion to moisturize my skin. I put extra lotion on my stomach, sides, and hips.

I get dressed.

"James forgot to buy socks." I tiptoe out of the bathroom and go over to one of the duffle bags to get a pair of his.

Bending over, I unzip the top and peek inside.

I zip it and back away.

It's full of devices with timers.

My fingers shake when I unzip the next duffle bag and find more devices. Curiosity has me going around the room unzipping duffle bags and backpacks to see what's inside. A plan formulates in my mind.

Both men are dangerous. I need to get my girls and get out of Boulder. Technically, I know it's kidnapping, but I've loved Emma from the moment she came into my life. It's not her fault her father used her.

I get my engagement and wedding rings out of the pocket of the uniform pants. The scrap of paper James gave me falls to the bathroom floor.

"I swear those people kept getting the order wrong on purpose." James clears his equipment off the table. We sit down to eat.

He tells me about being held by the Directorate in Syria. I yawn out of boredom and wait for him to make the first move.

"Remember senior year? We broke up for two months because Ashley Hudson told you she was pregnant by me?"

I nod. *Where is he going with this story?*

"You guys were on the football field. She was describing my body to prove we were screwing?"

"I remember."

"She got stumped when I asked her about my birthmark. You didn't even know I had one until I pulled you behind the bleachers and dropped my pants. Once you saw it you charged that field like a soldier going to battle and beat her lying ass from one end to the other." He laughs. "Ashley looked like she'd been attacked by a mob. You"—he kisses my knuckles—"didn't have a scratch on you."

She was so convincing, and I was ready to leave him for good. His birthmark saved him.

"You went to battle for me once I proved my innocence. I'm sure Hawk told you a convincing story, but he's lying. I need you to trust me. I need you to go to battle for me again. Once I have the laptop I can prove everything."

"I remember seeing an old laptop in his office," I tell him.

"You think it's mine?"

I give him the 'are you kidding me' frown.

"Bryan has a new age, high-tech building. That outdated laptop looked out of place sitting on his desk. I remember hearing a bell like at a boxing match."

James's face lights up. "How will you get into Hawk's building? It's more secure than a military base." He jumps up from the table, packing his backpack.

This is too easy. "I have access."

"How did you get it?"

I throw his words back at him. "We don't have time for a Q & A."

James picks up a tablet, zigzagging his finger across the screen. He taps it a few times and turns the tablet for a landscape view. He waits.

His finger taps the screen again. And he waits.

"Fuck! The Wi-Fi is down." He tosses the tablet onto the bed.

I get nervous when he pulls a gun from under the mattress.

"Come on, Danielle. We have to go."

I stand and follow him to the door; he's dialing a number on a cell phone.

"What the fuck is going on? Something's blocking my signal!"

James pulls a small device out of his pocket, tossing it on the bed along with the cell phone. He cracks the door open, poking his head out. He looks back at me. "Let's go," he whispers.

We step into the dimly lit hall. Dawn's light shines through the window at the end of the hall.

"We're going down the stairs," he whispers.

I nod and step ahead of him walking toward the stairwell exit. I reach to open the door…

"So, we're at an impasse, Hawk?"

"I guess we are, Edwards."

Both men have guns on each other. And a gun on me. Correction, one is pointing a gun at me, the other's is aimed over my shoulder.

Bryan's covered in black from head to toe, including the bandana over his nose and mouth.

"You enjoy fucking my wife?" James asks.

Bryan chuckles. "Every. *Fucking*. Minute. Of. It."

James sneers at him. "My brother didn't deserve to die."

I gasp. What brother?

"You shouldn't have played this game with him," Bryan responds.

"I knew you followed Kimberly in Canada."

"You knew because I wanted you to know. Just like you found Danielle because I wanted you to find her."

"Bullshit!" James spits at him.

"You got what I wanted you to have, when I wanted you to have it."

How long has Bryan known James is alive?

"I'm good at what I do."

"I'm better."

Gee. Cocky much, Colonel?

"She's leaving with me."

Pushing the cross bar on the door, cracking it open, I hope and pray I chose the right one.

Bryan shifts to the side.

"I'm leaving by myself!" I tell them.

"No, bitch. You're leaving in a body bag."

The first bullet hits my shoulder. Pain spreads down my arm to my fingertips. The second bullet hits me in the chest, and I'm forced through the cracked door.

The last thing I see is him aiming both guns at me.

Chapter Thirty-Eight

Tumbling.

Rolling.

I fall down the stairs, curled as tight as I can to protect my baby.

Multiple gunshots ring out.

Everything happens simultaneously. I land at the bottom just as the gunfire stops.

There's a moment of complete silence. An eerie stillness in the air. My brain does a mental status check. I'm lying on the cold cement. My shoulder throbs. My chest aches. My hipbone hurts. I dare not move or take a deep breath.

The door I fell through hits the wall. Clunky rapid footsteps descend the stairs.

"Dani!" He sounds terrified. "Dani, can you hear me?" He asks. "Baby, please answer me!" His voice cracks.

I open my eyes as he drops to the floor in front of me.

The door hits the wall again. "Don't move her, Bryan!" Ignacio commands. Clunky footsteps come down the stairs.

Pain spreads through my body. I take a long blink.

"Keep those pretty brown eyes open," Bryan pleads.

Pounding footsteps charge up the stairs.

"Aw fuck!" Vin cries out, something or someone drops near my head. "He fired so I fired."

Bryan smiles. "She's wearing a vest."

"How do you know?" Vin sounds worried; I judge his emotional state from the quiver in his voice.

"Her chest is flat and bulky."

"Good girl," Vin whispers in my ear.

A brace is eased around my neck causing me to moan at the slight movement of my body.

"Where's that fucking backboard?" Ignacio's question is enhanced by his Spanish accent.

I need a moment to breathe. I close my eyes and inhale. Pain shoots through my chest and I groan out loud.

"Keep those beautiful brown eyes on me." Bryan kisses my cheek and my eyes fly open.

"Is Dani okay?" Anthony asks. The sound of his boot-covered feet being pushed faster than they're used to moving floats up the flight of stairs.

"We need to get her off the ground and to the hospital." Ignacio is the calm one, but he sounds anxious.

"This is the smallest I could find," Anthony pants.

"It'll do," Ignacio says.

Something flat is placed against my back.

"On three," Ignacio instructs. He's at the top of my head.

Bryan shifts, his hands on my thigh and hip. Someone grips my feet.

"One. Two. Three," Ignacio counts.

I'm rolled onto my back with Ignacio guiding my head and neck.

I cry out. Tears of pain roll down my temples.

Right away, they begin to strap me down.

"You're okay. You will be okay." Bryan kisses my lips and wipes away the tears. "Who's got Edwards?" he asks.

"Porter and Mills with Miller and Brown doing sweeps," Anthony says. The straps across my feet tighten.

"I need you in charge, Paul," Bryan says. The straps across my hips tighten, followed by the straps across my chest, pinning my arms to my sides.

"Negative, Hawk. We stick together." The tone of his response shocks me. It's the vow of devotion to their brotherhood.

Ignacio places a strap across my forehead, ensuring my head and neck do not move.

"Negative." Vin speaks before Bryan's mouth forms the first word. His devotion to his friend is evident in the tone of his voice too.

"We're sticking together, Bry," Ignacio confirms.

In this moment of crisis, I finally understand the dynamics of their relationship. These four men have a bond stronger than a typical friendship. Their job brought them together. Their brotherhood can only be broken by death.

"Leave Porter in charge, call in Anderson and Ricks for sweeps. Put Brown on inside watch, Mills on outside watch, and Miller on security," the Colonel orders. "Instruct Porter not to disclose information to any-one but you."

"Roger that," Anthony says and repeats the instructions into his sleeve.

Vin and Anthony slip the straps of their rifles across their chests so that the weapons rest on their backs. They bend to take a handhold on the backboard.

"Wait, Bry. Switch with Tony. Your left arm isn't strong enough right now," Ignacio says.

The two men change sides and they lift the board off the ground.

They carry me down the next flight of stairs. Each man in sync with the other. The board isn't jostled or off kilter. If I closed my eyes, I'd swear I was being carried by one man.

They exit through the emergency door to an ambulance parked near. I'm placed on a stretcher.

The act of inhaling and exhaling brings unimaginable pain to the spot in my chest where the bullet hit the vest.

Vin kisses my forehead, and then I'm loaded into the back of an ambulance. Bryan and Ignacio climb in too. Anthony smiles at me. Too bad he can't hide his real thoughts from showing in his eyes. He closes the doors.

Ignacio immediately starts an IV line. I concentrate on the wail of the sirens. We're moving fast.

"Can you hear me?" Ignacio asks.

"Yes," I answer.

"What's your name?"

"Danielle Ha— Danielle Tatum." I'm not an Edwards either.

"When's your birthday?"

"February fourteenth."

"Are you in pain?"

"Chest, shoulder, and left hip."

"What about your back?"

"No."

My shoes are removed.

"Can you feel this?" he asks as something pricks my toes.

I wiggle them. "Yes."

"Is the baby moving?" he asks.

"No." My voice shudders. More tears seep from the corners of my eyes, sliding down my temples.

Oh God, please let my baby be okay!

Ignacio picks up a cell phone. "Have Dr. Jessica Hawk meet us in the

ER. How long, Barrett?"

"Twenty minutes," the person up front says.

"ETA twenty minutes," Ignacio says into the phone.

He pulls on surgical gloves, taking scissors from a compartment behind him, and cuts the sweatpants. "I'm checking to see if you're bleeding."

My eyes go to Bryan.

Fear clouds his eyes as his friend cuts and peels away the material of my pants.

"How did you find us?" I ask Bryan. I really don't care how. I'm trying to distract myself from the possibility my baby didn't survive the fall.

"Tracking device in your engagement ring." Bryan sounds grateful for thinking of that little detail.

"No signs of bleeding," Ignacio relays to the person on the phone.

"Is the vest too tight?" Bryan asks.

"Yes."

He uses the scissors to cut the sides of the sweatshirt, and unsnaps the chest armor.

I exhale and pain shoots through my chest. "Ow," I moan.

Uncertainty flashes across Bryan's face.

Ignacio continues to evaluate me, relaying my vitals to the person on the other end of the call. I concentrate on the sirens and not the medical terms he's using to report my status.

Bryan and Ignacio are still wearing black bandanas tied around their heads. If I wasn't so emotionally hurt, I'd appreciate how good Bryan looks in that uniform.

The ambulance tilts downward, then comes to a halt. There is a flurry of activity. Bryan throws a sheet over me. Vin and Anthony help pull my stretcher from the ambulance. Ignacio shout instructions in Spanglish.

The four men run, pushing the stretcher down the corridor of the hospital. They move like four parts of the same machine as they bulldoze their way toward the emergency room with Vin leading the way.

Anthony yells at people to get the fuck out the way or he'll bust-a-cap in their ass.

Bryan focuses on me.

Somewhere in between, Ignacio is speaking a language I don't recognize. But whatever he's saying makes three nurses fall in line.

The men maneuver the stretcher around a corner and into a room without sending me flying off.

"You're okay, little sis," Vin whispers.

Anthony hugs Bryan first, then turns to me. "We're right outside," he whispers and kisses my forehead. He places his hand on the sheet covering my stomach and clasps hands with Bryan, who clasps hands with Ignacio, who clasps hands with Vin, who places his hand on Anthony's shoulder. They've formed a circle around me.

Anthony closes his eyes. All four men bow their heads.

I watch and listen to Anthony pray. It's obvious he has a strong religious background. And at the end of the prayer, all four men say in agreement, "Amen."

Anthony and Vin leave the room.

The sheet is pulled away and the cut sweatshirt removed. Someone places a different sheet over my top half and another covers my bottom half, leaving my midsection exposed. I'm being attached to wires, and those wires attached to machines.

Jessica storms in.

I hear the sound of water running in a basin, then the snap of medical gloves against skin.

"I'll check and see if imaging is crowded," Ignacio says.

Warm gel oozes onto my pelvic area. Jessica uses the transducer to search for the baby's heartbeat. I hold my breath as she moves and presses the device into my pelvic area.

"Hush," she commands and everyone in the room quiets.

Bryan's eyes water. His lips tremble. Those long eyelashes glisten as tears spill over.

I watch Jessica as she watches her little brother. She continues to search for…

A fast rhythmic beat is amplified in the quiet emergency room. My baby moves. I let go of the breath I was holding as I laugh with relief and cry with joy and pain.

Bryan looks up mumbling his thanks. He bends over, pressing his lips against my stomach.

I'm in mental and physical pain; defiance will not allow me to share in his joy. We keep ours separate.

His hand reaches for my face, caressing my cheek. I can't trust the sight of the love beaming from his eyes. I focus on a spot on the wall instead.

Sadness fills my heart. Our life together has been one big stinking lie.

Jessica continues to move the transducer around my pelvic area, pausing and tapping the keyboard several times.

"He looks good," she says.

My eyes shoot to the monitor now turned toward us. Jessica points to the image.

"You heard me correctly," she laughs. "Your son looks to be doing well. The placenta is still attached and there's no signs of bleeding." She freezes the image.

His legs are wide open.

Thank you, God, for saving my baby boy.

"Once you're unstrapped from the spine-board I'll hook you up to a fetal monitor. I'm keeping you here on bed rest as a precaution."

I drown out everything and everyone except for the image of my son.

"How are they?" Ignacio walks back into the room wearing scrubs and a lab coat. He places a hand on his friend's shoulder.

"He's fine," Bryan whispers. "Our son is fine."

Ignacio's shoulders relax. "Congratulations." The men hug, slapping each other's backs. "I need to get Dani upstairs."

Bryan nods, moving to the side, letting the medical team detach the many cords from the machines.

Another sheet is placed over me. Ignacio leads the way.

Vin and Anthony fall in line, asking questions.

"My son is fine," Bryan tells them, pride resonating in his voice.

This time the medical staff pushes the stretcher down the corridor, but six of us get on the elevator.

My eyes zero in on the gold rings each man wears on the ring finger of his right hand. I never picked up on that.

I block out their chatter until the elevator stops. Vin and Anthony pull their guns. The side of Ignacio's lab coat is pushed back to reveal his holstered weapon.

Why are they carrying weapons? We're in a hospital.

The elevator doors open. Two men holding rifles nod. "Sir," they say.

Bryan nods. They step to the side and my stretcher is pulled off by another set of medical staff while the two men walk alongside Bryan.

I'm wheeled into an imaging room.

Surprisingly, I have no fractures or broken bones. But I have bumps and I'll have bruises by tomorrow. And I will be stiff and sore for the next few days.

Once I'm settled in a room and hooked up to a fetal monitor, I'm given pain medication.

I fall asleep with my hands on my bump. *My son.*

"I don't have long to talk. Simon will be home shortly."

"Is Bryan dead?"

"No, you shot him in the neck or near his neck. I couldn't really tell."

"Shit! I was aiming for Danielle. Nothing happened to her?"

"I overheard the on-call doctor on the phone with someone in the ambulance. She fell down a flight of stairs."

"Did she at least lose the baby?"

"I don't know."

"Any chance you can get to her?"

"Hell no! Secret Service has that floor locked down tight. Bryan has a lot of government pull," I say.

"That's why High Commander wants him."

"Why does owning a bodyguard company make Bryan a hot commodity?"

Even after all these years, High Commander Toussaint still wants him on our side. The bonus is up to twenty-five million.

"I've been trying to figure that out for years."

Bryan could care less about her. She's too stupid to see that. James never cared about her either. I had a threesome with him and his brother. That was the biggest fight she and I ever had. But at least she got to see James for who he really was. A user.

She failed her assignment. I tried to warn her when the order came down from Toussaint. A million dollars to the person who eliminated her.

Everyone thinks she's dead.

To avenge her, I plotted and slept my way through the ranks of RAGS to get close to our leader. Their identity within reach.

Three weeks ago, the woman I loved revealed herself to me, and only because she's angry with her baby-daddy.

"How did you get that close in the hospital?" she asks.

"I dressed like hospital personnel. Bryan doesn't recognize me as a blonde."

"Be careful. He's a dangerous man. Those guys got overzealous on New Year's Eve. I told them to send him a warning, not take out his family. He can't prove it was me who hired them, but he suspects it and is messing with my parents. Bryan doesn't know you're the true love of my life; otherwise he'd come after you too."

I've waited a long time to hear her admit how important I am to her.

But it's too late. My loyalty's been swayed by the lure of twenty-five million dollars. My son and I can disappear with that kind of money.

"Have you made progress with that new guy? Ross is his name, right?" I ask.

"He's just like any other male dog. Dangle a little pussy and he'll chase it." She laughs.

"I'm close to discovering who High Commander Toussaint is. Tristan promised to let me search the national registry once he gets back from vacation with his wife and kid."

"Madelyn, don't put Jacob's life at risk. Toussaint's reach is far."

She's just saying that to mess with my head. Three of us signed up for the challenge to bring Bryan to RAGS. She failed. I will not.

A car's headlights flash across the window in the living room momentarily casting my shadow against the wall.

"Gotta go, Amelia. Simon's home. He's still mad about that video. The IP address is blocked. I can't figure out who posted it."

BRYAN AND DANIELLE'S STORY CONTINUES
IN THE SECOND NOVEL IN THE
MEN OF PHANTOM SERIES

LIES YOU TELL

Chapter One

"WHERE'S MY WIFE?" I SPEAK into my vest mic. "Mama Hawk's running through the East Wing with Edwards," Porter reports.

"I've got the lobby doors covered." Ricci's voice comes through the earpiece in my ear.

"Since they're in the east side of the hospital, I'm heading to Mobile Command." Paul's voice crackles.

I take out the earpiece, make an adjustment, and put it back in.

"MC's sitting at the loading dock," Barrett says.

"Porter, did you get that tracker on the ambulance still parked in the emergency room lot?"

"Affirmative, sir," he replies.

"We're ready for anything he throws at us." Acosta secures his weapon in the thigh holster.

They know I'm uncomfortable with Dani being with Edwards.

"Chen, you set?" I speak into my mic.

"Phantom Secret Service have freeway exits blocked. And I've got eyes on the Baby Hawks," he replies.

The elevator doors open.

Acosta and I jog to the midnight-black, semi idling at the loading dock in the back of the hospital. The eighteen-wheeler Phantom Bullet is our Mobile Command. Paul's already activated the hidden fold-down steps. He's climbing inside the trailer.

We follow. I push the button to retract the steps and bring down the door. Porter's sitting at a station viewing multiple screens at one time.

Paul's boots pound the metal floor as he jogs to the front of the trailer. A hidden door slides open, he walks onto the customized step attached to the tractor unit and through the passage of the sleeper to take his seat in the cab next to Barrett.

Paul designed and helped build this rig. It's bigger and better than the Milk Man truck Langford had when he was Second Command. I hated riding in that thing.

"We're picking up Ricci at the exit," I say as I plop down in the chair in front of my station, buckle the seat belt, and let the scanner read my palm. My computer comes online.

"Smoke bomb detonated in the lobby. I'm right behind Mama Hawk," Ricci reports. His mic rustles from the movement of his body.

I quickly access Riley to dispatch a backup team to retrieve the remains of the bomb and the device that caused the blackout.

On the monitor, I watch as Edwards presses a keycard on a sensor. Porter allows the emergency room doors to open and holds them until Ricci clears them.

Porter pulls up the satellite tracking as the ambulance flees from the hospital.

Our rig slowly rolls out of the loading zone.

The gears on the roll-up door hum. Ricci climbs into the trailer. He pats my shoulder and takes his seat.

Acosta turns up the volume on the speakers at his station. Since we're not on a seek-and-destroy mission, he's playing hip hop from one of his favorite artists, Lil' Wil.

On the outside, our Mobile Command looks like a regular semi. But the detachable trailer is armored, and inside the cargo haul is a state of the art military setup.

The ambulance is heading north toward Old Towne Arvada. We're traveling the parallel streets so we don't spook Edwards.

Paul does a city search and comes up with five possible locations where Edwards might ditch the ambulance. In all the years I've known him, Paul's always been on the money when predicting hiding spots.

Porter types in the locations and watches the map on the screen, directing Barrett on the parallel streets.

Dani knows about the black Suburbans. At this point, I don't know if she'd warn Edwards to be on the lookout or distract him from noticing.

The orange dot disappears. Porter is still learning, so I verbally tell him how to relocate the signal while I do it on my computer. He's too green for me to wait and see if it works. Hopefully his memory is as good as his file says it is.

On the central monitor, the image of the ambulance's last location comes up. The unit is engulfed in flames yet still in motion. It's on a collision course with the playground equipment.

I dispatch the closest fire station and send a message to Riley to transfer ten grand from my business account to the City of Arvada's Parks and Recreations funds along with an email to the mayor from Hawkeye Personal Protection.

I give Porter the code to activate the tracking chip in Dani's engagement ring. The green dot is heading south. Barrett makes the block; we change direction. The satellite view shows Dani and Edwards jogging up a dark street. I hope all this running doesn't harm the baby. Especially since I blocked her from strenuous workouts.

The car they dive into takes the highway entrance heading toward Boulder.

Having modified tandem axles makes it possible for Barrett to pick up speed once we're on the highway. Paul went to great lengths to ensure the frame and axles could withstand the weight of the trailer and still move at maximum speed with ease.

Edwards has been bouncing from hotel to hotel since he got to Boulder three weeks ago. With certain highway exits blocked, he has no choice but to go to the one off Baseline Road. It seems to be his favorite anyway. I breathe a little easier knowing he's heading to a location I can control.

Earlier, Marine Guards evacuated the hotel, planted remote-controlled toy cars in every room, and are posing as hotel staff.

Ricci starts cussing in Italian, then throws his phone across the cab. He *was* on a conference call with his division leaders. They must not have given him the answers he wanted. He's been barking at them since he sat at his station. This is Porter's first ride-along with the Elite team. The magnitude of Ricci's anger can be nerve-racking. He'll get used to it.

The Bullet exits the highway seven minutes after Edwards, and Barrett parks a block away from the hotel. Paul is using the remote-controlled cars to do a visual search of the rooms. The first thing we notice are the black duffle bags on the floor of Edwards's room and the room above his. Paul tries an infrared scan of the closest bag, but can't get a reading.

The rest of us get ready to set up a secondary command center in the hotel and bring in Edwards in—alive.

After a back and forth debate, I pull rank. Acosta helps me into the full torso armor vest. No one is stopping me from getting my wife out of here safely.

I disengage the magazine in my weapon and check the ammunition. "Vin, give me a live mag." No emotion in my voice. I toss the one filled with blanks back to him. "If I were going to kill him, I would have done it in the courtyard."

He tosses me a new mag. And four more.

Engaging the clip, I take the safety off and rack the slide, then put the safety back on and holster my weapon.

This time Edwards didn't search the room for electronic bugs. Paul's had to get creative with surveillance.

"Someone's trying to tap into our surveillance," Porter shouts.

The camera feed goes in and out. Wavy lines and static.

The monitors go black.

I rush to my station and start typing in a series of codes while watching the screens.

Nothing.

Don't panic, Hawk. Stay focused or Dani and the baby could get hurt.

Inhale.

Exhale.

"Riley?"

"Yes, sir."

"On my mark, shut down all IP addresses worldwide for sixty seconds," I command.

"Roger that."

"Porter, you have forty-five seconds to get the U.S. military back online before some serious shit happens. Chen, find the bastard trying to access our feed, block his ass, and send a team to the address."

"Roger that," both men respond.

I type a quick message to POTUS while watching the clock on the monitor. "And"—it hits the hour—"mark."

Porter's fingers punch the keyboard at his station. In the earpiece, I hear the keys of Chen's keyboard. Right away the gear of the roll-up door hums. One by one the Elite Team jumps out of the trailer. I'm always the last to exit.

Like the ghosts we are, we keep to the shadows and silently make our way to the back parking lot. I deactivate the fire alarm on the emergency exit and we infiltrate the building, going up the stairs to the second floor.

Even though Porter's already told me the camera is back online and Danielle is okay, the minute we get into a hotel room a few doors down from Edwards's, I log on to my laptop to see for myself.

I check the military's systems as an afterthought. If Langford were here, he'd ride my ass for putting my country second.

Ricci pulls up an area map and we plot our next move based on Edwards's only exit routes.

Acosta assembles a makeshift lab.

Paul is keeping an eye on Danielle. "Hey. Check this out." Using the controller, he gives us a close-up of her. She's blushing.

If I were an insecure man, I'd kick in the door and beat that traitor's ass for dropping his drawz in front of my wife.

While Edwards is walking around ass naked, I tell the Marine Guards posing as diner workers, to stall him when he comes in and places an order. We need time to search the room.

Barrett informs us our backup driver is here with an ambulance. I like that he anticipates our transportation needs and makes decisions without me telling him to. He's the best in his field and an asset to the team.

The guys and I wait until Danielle's in the shower to sneak into the room.

Paul scans the duffle bags, finding explosives. Using sign language, he assures me the explosives can't detonate and he'll examine them once we have Edwards in custody.

Ricci searches the room for weapons, finding several stored in the box spring. Porter's taking notes for whoever I assign to sweep the room once we leave.

Acosta collects samples of Edwards's DNA from the bloody gauze pads.

After I check out the equipment on the table and in the backpack, I have Riley block all Wi-Fi signals and cell phone towers within a hundred-mile radius. It's excessive but necessary.

The water in the shower stops. We quietly leave, going back to our secondary command center.

Acosta tests Edwards's blood samples so he'll know how much of the tranquilizing solution to fill in each plastic bullet. We want Edwards to appear dead, not actually be dead. At least not today.

We double-check each other's gear, then form a circle.

Heads bowed, we stretch our arms around each other's shoulders. Paul recites our team prayer.

Ricci starts the fight chant.

The ritual started as a way to relax us before our first official mission as the Phantom Elite Special Operations Team. Since none of us was killed or injured that day, we continued to do it before every operation, big or small. It's been our thing for nine years.

"I'll take him out if it comes down to it," Acosta tells me before he follows the others out the door.

Alone in the hotel room, Edwards and Danielle eat from take-out containers. I watch. Her nostrils are flared. Something's bothering her. I didn't peg her as a good liar, but she's convinced Edwards she's seen his laptop. Actually, she has. She used it back in December to research home spa stuff. I'd purposely left it out.

"Edwards knows the Wi-Fi is down. He has a gun in his right hand and one tucked in his back waistband," I say into my mic.

"Copy that," Acosta confirms.

Edwards's hotel room door opens and they creep into the corridor.

"Stairs," I tell my team, then shut down my laptop.

Ricci's on the rooftop of the adjacent building. He's the sniper. Paul will cover the exit.

I pull my weapon, take the safety off, and open the door, quietly stepping into the hallway. My steps are light as I come up behind Edwards.

We get to the door at the stairwell. I tap him on the shoulder. Edwards spins around, switches the gun from his right hand to his left and pulls the weapon from behind him aiming it at my chest.

"So, we're at an impasse, Hawk?"

"I guess we are, Edwards."

"You enjoy fucking my wife?"

Which wife are you referring to? The one you actually married or the one you got all dressed up for and pretended to marry? If you're talking about the real Mrs. Edwards, I wasn't the one who fucked her. But I was told she's a boring lay.

"Every *fucking* minute of it." I laugh to get a reaction out of him.

Yeah, I know you want to kill me, but you don't have the balls to do it.

"My brother didn't deserve to die."

Danielle gasps. Guess he still hasn't told her he had a twin.

"You shouldn't have played this game with him."

"I knew you followed Kimberly to Canada."

I didn't hide the fact that I controlled your every move. I wanted you to come after me.

"You knew because I wanted you to know. Just like you found Danielle because I wanted you to find her."

"Bullshit!" he sneers.

"You got what I wanted you to have, when I wanted you to have it."

"I'm good at what I do."

"I'm better."

Oops, maybe I need to take it from a ten to a two on the confidence level. I don't like the look Dani just gave me.

Playtime is over. It's late. Mama Hawk needs to be in the nest, resting.

"She's leaving with me," I tell him.

Shit! Shit! Shit! What the fuck is she doing? Danielle just cracked the door open. Edwards is too focused on me to notice and I don't have time to signal Ricci.

I slightly shift my position so Acosta will have to shift his; hopefully he can see why and warn Ricci.

"I'm leaving by myself!"

Paul, I hope you've got her covered.

"No, bitch. You're leaving in a body bag," Edwards barks.

Bang!

Her shoulder. Dani cries out.

Crackle. The sound of a sniper's bullet penetrating the glass window at the same time a second shot is fired from Edwards's gun. I reach back and punch him in the face as three aimed bullets whiz past me.

The stairwell door slams shut after Danielle flies through it. Edwards falls to the floor still squeezing the trigger. I kick the gun out of his hand and run for the door.

Reviews are encouraged and greatly appreciated.

For information about giveaways, upcoming books, and appearances follow me on:

twitter @iamjackirenee
facebook /iamjackirenee
instagram /iamjackirenee
goodreads /goodreadscomJacki_Renee

Other Books in Series

www.ingramcontent.com/pod-product-compliance
Lightning Source LLC
Chambersburg PA
CBHW060947120726
47910CB00002B/531